A Journey Must Be Taken – Playlist

A Journey Must Be Taken – Playlist

H. L. Howard

ISBN: 979-8-9870976-3-2

Dedicated To

Me.
That little kid locked himself in to read every book in a small remote country school library room.
That youth who wrote the first poem in front of Qutang Gorge, China.
That young man who chased every moving life goal.
That middle-aged gentleman who sat on his own throne.
That person who answered the inner child's call.
Good job!
I'm proud of you!

and

Cocreators,
including the Tarot Readers, the spirits and divinity via tarot readings.
You all inspired me to take the leap of faith.
You guide me to be where I am.
Love always.

Contents

H. L. Howard

Prologue

"The wish does come true! You'd better pay attention to what you wish for," Tauri told his preteen daughter Lara.

A simple wish from Tauri had turned his quiet life upside down. He had gone through heartbreak twice in two weeks. In search of his life's purpose, he embarked on a long, lonely spiritual journey...

CHAPTER I

A Surprise Visit

TAURI WAS IN a good mood on the way to give Libi a surprise visit. He connected with Libi via social media and an online music-sharing site. There were no direct phone or text message exchanges between them. He felt that it was the right time to break the ice and start a new chapter of his life after he had gone through a painful divorce battle and finally become a lawful single.

"Hey, I am going to be in town for a business dinner; I will drop by your place tonight. Let me know if you are not available," Tauri texted Libi. He had gotten her address from her business proposal they had worked on last week.

He checked Libi's page on an online music site. There, she had posted a playlist to express her feelings to him.

He could understand her concerns. She wouldn't want to see him if he were not a lawful single.

"I am ready. I am a bachelor now," Tauri told himself. He knew that Libi had been waiting for this moment since last May.

Tauri arrived at Libi's address around 9:00 p.m. on a chilly late evening in the fall. It was two levels, a small single-family house on Staten Island, one of the southernmost of five boroughs in New York City, a half-hour ferry ride from the famous Wall Street in Manhattan, which runs across New York Harbor. Faint lights were on inside the house. He knocked on the door. An old guy came out with a little Chihuahua.

"Is Libi living here?" Tauri asked.

"No, no such person is living here," the gentleman answered. He seemed to be in his sixties, with a bald head and a beard on his face.

"Libi told me that she lives here, along with two more tenants on the second floor." Tauri raised his voice.

"Let me check." The gentleman went inside. Tauri could hear him walking upstairs.

"The girl moved out two weeks ago." The gentleman came back after five minutes and talked in an impatient tone. Tauri didn't believe what he heard. He had been in conversation with Libi three days ago. She specifically mentioned that she had two other roommates. Tauri had a hard time consolidating this information.

"Are you sure that she moved out two weeks ago? Do you know where she moved to?" Tauri insisted.

"No, I can't tell you." The gentleman showed his displeasure.

"I am her friend. I drove three hours to surprise her. Can you please let me know about her new place?" Tauri talked in a begging voice.

"Let me ask my wife. She is handling the rental things." The gentleman went inside again.

"She moved to 298 New Town Road two weeks ago. I can't tell you anything else." The gentleman hesitated.

"How far away from here?" Tauri looked at this empty street.

"Only two blocks away." The gentleman went away with his dog without explaining any more.

Tauri had a few questions running through his mind. Did she use this old address on her professional proposal? Did she forget to tell me that she moved? Did she try to avoid me?

Tauri texted Libi this afternoon that he was coming. He trusted in her; he had known her for more than three years. Most recently, they'd had a phone conversation three days ago. Tauri decided to find out the truth about this.

⋄⊷⊙⊶⋄

Tauri parked his car along a narrow car-filled street. By the dim street lights, he could see a small single house in front of him. Yellow emergency lights flashed from a big van on the other side of the road leading to the hill. He got a weird feeling.

He closed his Mercedes door immediately once he came out and double-checked to make sure that he had secured his car. He strolled on the stone steps toward the house. A few small strings of Christmas lights decorated the windows. He knocked on the door a few times. No one answered. He fumbled on the door and finally found the two tiny buttons on the right upper corner of the panel. He rang, rang, rang, and waited. After a few minutes, he rang again.

A young man in a T-shirt rambled out from upstairs. He was in his thirties, short and built, with muscles on his chest.

"Is Libi here?" Tauri asked politely.

"No, she is not." The young man hesitated. It looked like he had seen this situation before.

"Are you delivering something?" The young man looked at Tauri for a few seconds.

"Yes, I am here to deliver some food." Tauri showed his gift bag in his hand.

"Let me see." The young man turned back and closed the door. Tauri thought that the young man had opened the door for him. He stepped forward to push the door.

"Stay out! Stay out!" The young man shouted as he immediately turned back and pushed Tauri out.

"I know Libi is here. Can you let me talk to her? If you don't want me to see her, I believe you held her against her will," Tauri demanded.

"Stay away from the house! Stay away from the door!" An old woman came out and yelled. "I will call the police." The woman raised her phone.

"I am OK. It is fine. OK, OK, OK." Tauri showed that he had empty hands. He walked back slowly and stayed ten feet away. The woman came out to stand between Tauri and the door. The young man entered inside and knocked on the left room on the first floor.

Here came a young girl standing right in front of the door. She wore black trousers and a black sweater. She looked elegant with filled-in eyebrows, as if she were ready to go out for a date. Her black hair was curling down naturally.

Tauri saw a pretty city girl he had known in his dream days and nights. He couldn't get a clear look at her facial expression in the dark. He expected a hug from her, as she had always done since they had met one year ago.

"Can you leave?" Libi shouted out with no emotion. "Here I am. I am free. Nobody controls me." Libi raised her angry voice. "I don't want to see you. Don't come to this place again. If you come, I am going to report you to the police," Libi said, as if she were issuing an order. She then went back into the house behind her and closed the door.

The young man looked at Tauri, a middle-aged Asian guy with a gray business suit on. Tauri sensed his suspicion; he started to talk to the young man about his story.

"Can you go? I don't want to see you anymore." Libi came out again after ten minutes and demanded in Chinese. Tauri and Libi had come from the same town in China.

"Why? I drove two hours to say hello to you. I thought that we were friends. We worked on your project two days ago. Does that mean anything to you?" Tauri reminded her.

"I am thankful for that. Well, I don't want to talk about it." She agreed with him. "I don't want to say anything about it. I don't want to see you! Don't come to this place! You don't contact me anymore!" She was emotional. "Don't talk to my friend!" "Go away!" She continued to issue the short orders.

Tauri felt insulted. This moment was the first time in his life that someone had booed him out. He wouldn't have come all the way to see her if he didn't believe that Libi was his genuine connection.

"I brought a box of chocolate from Manhattan. Want to keep it?" He softened his attitude.

"No. I don't need anything from you. Go away!" she cried out.

Tauri felt so confused. This was a disaster! What's the change? What's the rationale? Those questions flashed in his mind like a cyclone.

"I'll not come back if you tell me your story." He raised his voice.

"I'll find out your story. I'll need to talk to your friends and neighbors," Tauri said firmly.

Libi went inside without saying goodbye. He was in shock about what had just happened. She had expressed her love to me with her playlist; I can confirm what's in her mind via tarot readings. Has anything changed?

Tauri rushed to listen to tarot readings on YouTube for his zodiac sign, Taurus, and Libi's sign, Libra, as he drove home along the dark I-95 northbound toward a dense, narrow forest-covered parkway. One tarot video from the YouTube channel "BE.ByHER," published on October 7, 2019, caught his attention. It was titled "Taurus: The Guilt Is Killing Them Because They Are Still in Love with You, October 7–14."

"Oh! Did she record this video with her heart? Sting? She did feel my energy, the pain. She seems to be talking about what happened tonight," he uttered.

Another tarot channel, "Saturn Secrets," had published a video on September 26, 2019, titled "Taurus, October 2019: It Is Not Falling to Pieces; It Is Falling into Place."

"How so? Release my control?" Tauri murmured.

Tarot readings were very positive. Had Libi changed her heart in her playlist?

He rushed to check her playlist on this Chinese music online sharing site as soon as he got home after a three-hour drive. He kept this bookmark only on one of his personal laptops to prevent himself from constantly checking.

1. "Who Knows the Wandering Heart?"
2. "The Moon Tonight"
3. "Crying in the Party"
4. "Heartbroken at Midnight Club"
5. "Cheat Myself"
6. "Say Goodbye"
7. "Worrisome of the Youth Writer"
8. "Far Away at the End of the Sky"
9. "Spring, Summer, Fall, Winter, Who Accompany Me on This Life Journey"
10. "For Your Landscape in Your Lifetime"
11. "My Name"
12. "Good Night"
13. "Lake: I Will Commit to You and Find You"

Tauri translated her playlist as the message.

Who understands me with a wandering heart? Tonight, under the moon, I cried and was heartbroken at midnight after I said goodbye to you. I cheated myself to hide my feelings from you. For you, a worrisome youth writer, you are far away from me. Who would go with you on this life journey in spring, summer, fall, and winter? That'd be me! Good night! I am committed to you and will come to find you whenever I am ready.

Tauri couldn't reconcile what he felt via the playlist with what he experienced tonight. His mind was blank. He wouldn't believe what had happened if he hadn't seen it with his naked eye.

"Was this Libi I had cherished dearly? Was this Libi I talked to via phone for eight hours only two days ago? Was this Libi? I thought we were in love?"

He was shocked to see that someone would treat a friend, even a stranger, like this. Libi had little love, even little friendship, for him. She was cold and angry. She was totally out of character for some reason.

"What were the reasons?" Tauri's heart was sad. He'd had high hopes Libi would be the one he wanted to commit to love with.

"Libi, you have to make up for me," Tauri had said to her late at night after a long hour working together on the phone two days ago.

"I...I...I will." She paused. A warming feeling came up in his mind. He could feel her heart bumping up, as if he had sat next to her and reached out to kiss her cheek. A fire was burning in his throat. After a moment of silence, they calmed down and continued the normal conversation.

"Where was that Libi I talked to?" he questioned himself. A second heartbreak came in two weeks. Was it yesterday he had ended his long-term marriage and become a lawful single?

"Is she involved with some illegal activities?" the young man asked. Tauri had more questions than answers. From the young man's point of view, Libi was a pretty girl dressed well at his rental house with people coming and going. That was a red flag to him.

"A van parked on the side road with an emergency light on? A pretty young girl with makeup at the rental house?" he uttered and quickly related this scene to the movie *Pretty Woman*.

"Was she that same girl I met three years ago? Was she that same girl dreaming of pursuing her new life? Was she that same honest, soft-spoken, enthusiastic girl looking for her entrepreneurial career in this promising land?" His questions echoed louder, louder, and louder...

CHAPTER 2

A Simple Wish

Three Years Ago
Chongqing, China

"WELCOME TO OUR lab." A young girl with a soft voice came to greet him. Tauri was invited to tour the regional innovation center in the city, Mega-Concrete Forest, in southwest China, with thirty million people, the most popular metropolitan area in the world. He was on his yearly visit to his hometown to look for any investment opportunities as the Chinese economy was booming.

"What are you working on?" Tauri asked.

"See, this is our photo studio. There will be tens of thousands of mini studios across the country because of this project." This girl raised her voice as she showed a few major pieces of equipment.

"OK. That was an old concept. Anything else?" he asked.

"Thanks for asking. Our magic would be a strong online backend. We'd build a platform to provide the functions of photo and video editing. Here, those finished products could be one place for cross-social-platform marketing." Her voice was a little vibrating. He raised his eyebrows. He took another look at this girl.

"Did you sell or rent your studio equipment?" he asked straightforwardly.

"A few," she replied.

"Do you promote your service on social media? Do you make some money?" He came up with a set of questions naturally.

"We are doing it manually," she replied.

"How much did you make last year? Did it cover your expenses?" he asked further.

"Yes, we had a little profit." She confirmed this without providing additional detail.

"What do you want?" He felt the potential.

"We don't need...funds at this point. We do need advice from people like you to guide us," she said slowly.

"All right. Do you have a business plan?" he asked.

"What is that?" She showed her puzzled face.

"A business plan is a road map to make your business scalable." Tauri got a good impression with her can-do attitude. Tauri left his phone number and WeChat social media info with her and moved on to the next project.

After he had gone over ten projects, that girl's project stood out and attracted him to know more about it.

"Hey, do you want to talk about your project more?" Tauri sent her a text message.

"Sure, I will come tomorrow," she replied.

A doorbell rang. She came in along with a young man.

"Hello, I am Libi. He is Leo, from my team." She introduced the guy to him.

"It took me two hours to find here," Libi said in an apologizing tone.

Tauri's hotel was ten miles away from this innovation center. He always took a taxi to go anywhere in this city. He felt her sincerity.

"Welcome!" Tauri extended his hand to shake Libi's; her hand was soft. He recalled the experience of touching cotton. She looked like a regular college girl, in a white T-shirt and blue jeans. With lightly filled eyebrows, her face looked pale, like those of most Chinese girls. She stood a little higher than he, with a pair of white sneakers on.

Tauri felt a stream of fresh air flowing into his room.

"Hi, Leo." Tauri shook Leo's hand forcefully. Leo looked handsome. His black eyeglass frames gave Tauri a unique impression.

"How long has your team worked on this project?" Tauri asked Libi.

"In and out on this idea since I graduated from my college a few years ago." Libi smiled. Tauri noticed that her smile was gentle, reserved, and even shy, not like a girl with business acumen and with an acute, keen attitude.

"Leo joined my team on a part-time basis. He is good at the equipment," she explained.

"How did you come up with this idea?" Tauri asked.

"Well, I wanted to be a fashion model. I took the training at my college. I was featured in a few stage shows." She stood up, walked a few steps, and took a turn. A few tiny drops of sweat dotted her nose. "Then, I learned photo and video editing. One led to another. Here I am," Libi continued.

"Sit down! Let's talk more." He arranged the furniture to form a discussion setting centered around a small glass stand. He had Libi and Leo sit on a loveseat sofa. Then he pulled a chair to sit next to the bed.

"Leo, what's your role in this project?" Tauri turned his question to Leo.

"I am handling the equipment technical support and image editing," he replied as he adjusted his black-frame eyeglasses.

"I researched the term 'business plan.' It is defined as the business objectives and how to achieve them. It talked about products, marketing, finance, operations," Leo read from his phone.

"So what're your objectives?" Tauri looked at Libi.

"See, our chain studio would have a cost of a few hundred dollars and be adopted across the country, like going viral. Our client would take the product photo and upload it to our online platform to edit. There, they can promote their product and service across traditional media and social media in just one click," Libi explained.

"What is the number?" Tauri asked.

The meeting went well. Tauri, Libi, and Leo discussed the product strategy, team structure, and shareholder structure in this company. Libi sat there to write notes as she talked.

"Let me make the cash flow projection." Tauri turned on his computer to put her number into Excel, a data processing software. After a while, he came up with a few variable-driven calculations.

"Let me play around. I can do it. I can learn as I use it," Libi called out.

"That is great; I also want to take a break." Tauri nodded.

Leo got up and let Tauri sit on the sofa next to her. Tauri showed her his touchable laptop screen and explained what this Excel worksheet was about. To his surprise, Libi knew more than Tauri had expected.

"Look, the assumption is in the upper left corner of the worksheet." Tauri took the computer mouse from Libi, the vibrating waves pushing her fingers away when his hands accidentally touched hers. Ugh, a pinch! What is that? A static electric pulse? He sensed that she had also noticed the same. As Tauri went through a few scenarios, their hands bumped here and there.

Leo stared at her for a moment and pulled up a chair to sit next to her. Libi sensed his discomfort and shifted her body to the corner of the sofa, away from Tauri.

"Let's have dinner to celebrate our new business adventure," Leo suggested after a few hours of discussion.

"Yep, I can eat a horse now!" Tauri exclaimed.

"Need to find a vegan place since Leo is a vegetarian." Libi dumped cold water. No meat!

It took a half hour for a taxi ride to reach that restaurant. They were seated at a small table.

"I liked to eat vegan food when I was in Beijing years ago." Tauri made Leo fit in.

"A dish called 'the noodle strips with tofu' was my favorite. The chef made the noodle strips from dough, boiled them, then stir-fried them with tomato sauce, red peppers, and fried tofu. Hmm…mouthwatering…Is there a similar dish here?" Tauri asked.

"Let's have beer to celebrate." Leo smiled.

"Yes, we will make a lot of money by listing companies on the stock market one day," Libi added.

"Three beers?" Tauri asked.

"No, I don't drink any alcohol," Libi cried.

"Let's have two beers and one mineral water, please." Leo took over.

"Wow, a giant bottle of beer. This must be three times more volume than what's in the United States!" Tauri yelled out after the waiter brought the drinks.

"Drink big, dream big, win big!" Leo yelled as if he sang.

"Cheers for our success. Bottle up!" They bumped their bottles. Tauri took a sip and looked at his business partner, emptied the bottle, and felt optimistic about this adventure.

"Can I connect to you via WeChat, Libi?" Tauri asked her after a few sips.

"You can pass information to Leo." Libi politely rejected him. She showed her special relationship with Leo.

Tauri suggested working on the investment agreement after dinner. As they realized, it was around midnight.

"Gosh, the rail service stopped already. We will have to take a taxi home," Leo bubbled.

"Hmm…how about you guys stay in this room? See, there are two beds and a sofa," Tauri suggested. Tauri didn't know how deep their relationship was. He wouldn't mind them staying in his room for the night, like a slumber party in the United States.

Libi moved her head slightly from left and then right for one second and then nodded to Leo. Her face turned pink.

⋆═◉ ═⋆

Tauri was on his fourth day in China and still felt jet lag, as if he were still in the New York time zone. He told Libi and Leo that he'd step out for a moment to let them settle in. When he came back, Tauri noticed that a sofa was pushed, aligning with the window-side bed where Libi stayed; Leo rested on the sofa. They had covered themselves with one white bedsheet.

Tauri turned off the lights. The room was quiet and calm. "I can hear a needle drop on the ground. A girl is staying overnight here!" He felt the peaceful air in the room. He fell into sleep right away.

He woke up in the early morning. It was the best night of sleep since he had landed in his hometown in China. He had barely gotten any sleep on the first three days and had woken up at 3:00 a.m. and hadn't been able to fall asleep since then. But this night was different; something remarkable happened, as if he were at home with a family, a soul tribe.

"Do you guys want to get breakfast at the hotel? I can get a free meal for you," Tauri said.

"Leo can't eat here. He can take the leftovers from last night," Libi said in a soft tone without hesitation.

"How about you? Come with me? It is a buffet; you would like it," Tauri said.

"Thanks. I will stay with Leo." Libi looked at Leo to see if he'd encourage her to go.

Tauri got the impression that Libi and Leo were in an extraordinary relationship. He admired Libi's caring for Leo. He was also surprised Leo didn't bother to consider her breakfast.

Tauri went to the dining hall. This was his favorite moment each day. Mm-hmm… fresh vegetables, all sorts of fruits, oh! Dark coffee, how can I miss that? Hmm…that poor girl would get hungry. Tauri thought about Libi at the end of his meal. He got a carry-away cup and adjusted the espresso machine to make a lighter coffee. He added one bag of sugar and one shot of cream, as he always had done for himself at the coffee shop in the United States.

"Hey, Libi. I brought a cup of coffee for you." Tauri handed it over to her as Libi opened the door for him.

"Wow! Thanks." She took a sip with a deep breath and gave Tauri a thankful glimpse.

⋅⊷═◉ ◉═⊶⋅

Leo, Libi, and Tauri decided to have dinner to celebrate after another intense day of work.

"It's your turn to choose a restaurant," Libi announced.

"Let's walk down the nightlife street. I saw a lot of street vendors there." Tauri pointed to one light-filled street.

The air was filled with the sweet, spicy smoke from the charbroil grill mixed with laughter, shouting from the vendor promotion, and the liquor-drinking game.

How vivid nightlife is here! Tauri lived in quite a suburb, a one-hour drive away from Manhattan, New York.

"Let's do grilled fish," Tauri told Libi and Leo. They were seated at the table on the pedestrian pass.

"Two beers and one water, please," Tauri said. After twenty minutes, a cooking pan was brought to the table. The grilled fish was submerged in red spice oil; various green vegetables, white mushrooms, and spices decorated the surface.

"Cheers! How do you guys know each other?" Tauri toasted to them.

"I used to work at the registrar's office in college. One day, he came over to hand over some documents. That was when I met him." Her eyes were sparks. Her face turned red with a girl's shyness.

"I took the photos for her stage show. I joined with her team after that." Leo had a big smile on his face.

Leo had a unique look the regular ethnic Han didn't have: a high nose, high forehead, and narrow face. He looked more like a Westerner than a Chinese. Libi looked pretty, not gorgeous but pure, like a breeze when she was there. Tauri saw the attraction in their eyes when they looked at each other.

"Leo, you and Libi seem to be a good pair." They had drunk a few bottles of beer. Tauri felt a little drunk.

"What is your plan?" Tauri knew that they had this new business adventure now.

"I work with my dad for the family business. We bring the fresh agriculture products here from my hometown," Leo said as he looked at the sky far away. "Libi...I...I...I can't marry you!" Leo shouted out suddenly without looking at her. He stood up and drank his beer.

"Leo, what did you say?" Tauri was in shock.

"Libi, I can't marry you!" Leo stared at Libi and spoke slowly but firmly. She lowered her head and wiped something from her face. Tauri didn't hear her cry out.

"Why? If you and Libi are in love, why can't you guys get married?" Tauri asked. If I love a girl in my lifetime as pure and innocent as she, I would give up everything to marry her.

"I am engaged to a girl arranged by my family. We plan to get married in two years." Leo uttered as he avoided eye contact with Tauri. "My grandfather followed the rule. My dad followed the same rule. I will have to follow this rule." Leo showed his deep-rooted belief.

"Would love overcome all obstacles?" Tauri questioned.

Libi's face was pale. She wiped her tears momently with her voiceless cry.

A love tragedy was happening right now, at this moment. My first time ever to watch the heartbroken unfolding in front of me. A hurricane was running through Tauri's mind. In his fifties, he felt as if he were in his late thirties or early forties. He had a stable family, with a wife and two daughters. He had had a sense of accomplishment in his life so far.

He was in shock, disbelief, confusion. He felt sorry for her. But I can't find any words to comfort her. Can I give her a hug? No, in Chinese tradition, people don't hug, especially a man and woman. It might be best for her to leave this place so she is able to begin a new life! That must be the better way for Libi to free herself from Leo.

Tauri had lost his appetite. He paid the bill and walked back to his hotel. They kept silent all along the way, speechless about what had just happened.

"You are welcome to stay, like last night," Tauri suggested.

"No, we will find another hotel to stay in," Leo replied.

"Are you sure?" Tauri asked.

"Yep!" Leo had made up his mind. Tauri waved his hands and looked as the two lovebirds disappeared into the dense, foggy night.

Would it be a big fight or a last love affair? He felt his heavy heart, and his thoughts went out to this girl he had known only a few days.

⊷⊨◉◉⊨⊷

The next morning, Leo and Libi came earlier than Tauri expected.

"Did you guys have breakfast yet?" Tauri asked. In Chinese tradition, the most important greeting was to ask if they had eaten anything.

"No, I don't need it," Leo replied. Tauri noticed that they both had red eyes. "Tauri, I want to tell you something." Leo's voice was hoarse.

"What is this about?" Tauri said.

"I am sorry. I can't join with this new company." Leo talked with his eyes on the ground. "My dad and my whole family don't agree with me," he explained.

"I need to go home now." Libi got it up and talked it out. Tired of this drama and a true roller-coaster ride, especially for her. The air was filled with sadness.

"Libi, why don't you come to the United States to work? I will help you." Tauri turned to Libi without looking at Leo as he spoke word for word. "I will give my email to you. When you are ready, don't hesitate to get in touch with me," he said slowly. This would be the only way to offer this beautiful soul hope. "Contact me if you need me." Tauri wrote his email on a paper and handed it over to her. "I hope that you can make it. Leave this place to have a new life. You can do it," Tauri told Libi. She shook hands with him and left with Leo.

This business adventure was broken down at the last moment.

Knowing Libi and Leo would be the outcome for this visit.

There would be a considerable life change for her if she could make it abroad.

I would do anything to help her succeed in the United States. Tauri watched Libi and Leo leaving. He put his wish into the universe.

CHAPTER 3

The Touch

TAURI STARTED HIS busy routine as the new year kicked in. The changes were constant and everywhere in his life. His job was changing, with a new leadership team in the place. He started to work to organize a nonprofit organization national convention. The biggest change was that the girl he had met two years ago made it into his life.

"What would you recommend to me?" Libi had asked in a WeChat call, a Chinese social media app, with him one year ago.

"I can't tell you. But I can tell you the ways to decide this." Tauri didn't want her to regret her choice later on.

"What is that?" she demanded with curiosity.

"Find a coin. Make the face as the job in New York and the tail as in DC. Then throw the coin into the air. When it lands on the ground, you choose what result showed on the coin," Tauri joked. She laughed like a lark. It was a random choice, like giving her a choice in the hands of God.

"Another way to determine it is with the game of paper fortune teller." He brought out a counting-out game Lara used to play. "You make a paper square and fold it together. Write the job location on each side of the paper. Then, talk with the magic like 'Eeny-meeny-miney-moe, catch a tiger by his toe. If he hollers, let him go. My mother chooses the very best you. One and two.' You continue to read this until you feel good enough to make the decision. The name on the paper opening is the job place you want to choose." He described this slowly. She giggled.

"OK, I will think about this," she told him with a smiling voice.

⊷━◉ ◉━⊷

As the summer was approaching, Tauri felt it was the time to introduce Libi to a few of his friends who could potentially help her career. They met a few times, as if they were good friends who had known each other for ages.

"Hey, do you have time to have lunch together? I have not seen you for a while." He texted her as usual.

"Sure, I am available," she replied.

"What is the time that works for you best?" he asked.

"Tuesday evening," she replied back. Tuesday? Evening? He was totally surprised to know that she wanted to have dinner with him instead of lunch. That was something new! He thought she wouldn't want to see him again since their goodbye hug had electrified them last time. Will those electrifying feelings stroke me again? Why am I continuing to do this? Oh! It is calling, calling for connection, calling for something more. He argued with himself.

He sent her the info about this restaurant. She seemed to like it. Yes, she and I are planning the dinner. A *date*?

Tauri stepped out from his office one hour ahead of the regular time. He dressed in office-casual clothes: a blue dotted T-shirt and gray pants. With pure joy, he was about to meet with his thirty-year-younger friend, a girl, to have dinner.

"Can you pick me up at the shopping mall?" she texted. Did she go shopping in working hours or avoid her guy friend last time? He flashed his thought.

It was a bright, early spring afternoon with a perfect temperature, like sixty-five degrees Fahrenheit. She stood on the sidewalk with a white dress shirt and tight black trousers. With a gentle smile on her face, she climbed into his car.

"Good to see you again!" He smiled as he hugged her as usual.

He glanced at her: a small oval tender face and rounded cheekbones with a pointy chin just like a bigger scale of a swan egg. He could feel her smooth pale, ivory skin and small nose fit perfectly on her frame. With double eyelids, her round black eyes look sparkly. With a slim body and legs, she seems like an under-matured girl compared to local curly teenagers. Something made him take another look. It is her hair which is dark, thick, and shiny. She looked graceful as she slewed those on her face covered to the side of her shoulder.

Tauri looked in the mirror for himself: a middle-aged Chinese man with a round face and a narrowed eyelid. His short hair was dense, slewed toward his right side to expose his wide forehead, and his flattering Fringes showed him a youthful appearance. His eyebrow looked dense but almost wore it out at the corner; his face was reddish, giving people a healthy, strong expression. He looks decades younger than his actual age. He is in a sky blue shirt and dark blue tight trousers, and he is happy with the casual business dress with self-confidence.

It was only a short drive to the restaurant, a pavilion in a wealthy town with red brick buildings scattered across a few major streets. A small courtyard was outside of the main entry. Every black lamppost pole had an American flag and was dressed with a pot with hanging petunias bearing hundreds of small bell-shaped plants cascading down like flower falls. A gas-burning torch with a yellow flame was at the top of the center tower, and streams poured out at each corner of the fountain located in center of the plaza. This made him feel warm. Why do I have such a pleasant feeling? He smiled.

"How many persons came with your party? Two?" A waitress greeted them.

They were seated at one end of a cube in opposite couch chairs. With a double-size dinner table and a teenager laughing pretty loudly at another group, he barely caught what Libi had said and needed to raise his voice to make himself heard.

"Mind if I sit on your side?" he asked. "We can hear each other easily." He grinned.

"Sure, come over." She nodded. He moved to sit next to her and felt at ease.

"Do you want to anything to drink? Maybe red wine?" he asked. She didn't drink any alcohol a few years ago. Had she changed? "See, there is white wine or red wine." Tauri pointed to the menu. For red wine, you can choose pinot noir or cabernet sauvignon." He found a few familiar names.

"What is cabernet sauvignon?" She seemed to have had little exposure to this.

"A dry red wine made from this grape especially from the Bordeaux region of France and in Northern California. You will like it," he explained. He knew that red wine went well with seafood. He liked dry red wine.

"I don't drink any alcohol," she reminded him.

"Oh, yeah! I forgot. I thought you didn't drink beer," he recalled. Tauri recommended a three-course meal to Libi. A moment later, the waiter brought a melted cheddar cheese pot and a veggie platter filled with cucumbers, carrots, other vegetables, and assorted cheese cubes.

"Hmm. The veggie tastes different when it is dipped in melted cheese." She nodded.

"The cheese is forever milk, a kind of healthy food," he suggested.

"I like aged cheddar, but there are different flavors from the goat, and parmesan, gorgonzola." He knew only a few. He felt he should have learned more before he came to this dinner. "I saw your photo taken when you traveled in Japan. Tell me something about your trip." Tauri sensed her fond feelings toward Japanese culture.

"Yep, I loved it. I spent ten days in Japan alone last year. It was a wonderful experience," she uttered. "Japan was a clean country. I loved everything there: the food, the scenery, the people." She moved her eyes away and seemed to be going back to her memory lane. "What I liked most was the Japanese culture. It is based on the chrysanthemum and the sword." Libi talked softly with sparkling eyes.

"What was that? How so?" He had heard this before and never talked to a person admiring it so much.

"See, the chrysanthemum is pretty, with bright red, shining yellow, dazzling white, deep bronze, and a variety of other colors. Some of them are full, dark-green leaves. Some of them presented layers of the petals with each tiny individual floret. It blossoms in fall and is a symbol of loyalty and devoted love. It also represents happiness, love, longevity, and joy. You can see this spirit in Japanese girls' beauty, the city's cleanliness-next-to-godliness, and people's politeness." Libi spoke nonstop. Tauri stopped eating. He turned his head right to stare at her and focus on what she was saying.

"There are two sides of the sword. It is used either to defend their land by killing the enemy in the war or to defend their own honor by cutting their stomachs. It is crude. Is it? It is the spirit of Japanese society." She continued to express her own understanding. "You see, it represents the two extreme sides: extreme beauty with extreme crudeness." Libi said this as if she were talking to herself. He gazed at her as if he saw a different side of her. She was as pretty as a regular girl—not sexy, not gorgeous by pop-culture standards. She was just as charming as a classic, beautiful chrysanthemum. Is her crude side as sharp as the sword? Could she grow the sensation due to her heartbroken experience with Leo? Whom will she use this sword on? Tauri never brought out the topic of her ex, Leo, with her and noticed her post to breakup with someone forever by a song.

A waitress brought the second pot with boiling soup. Tauri boiled a prawn and put it on her plate. He did a scallop cube for himself.

"Hmm, this tastes tender. Really good." Libi praised it.

"There is a photo you published on a WeChat Moment titled 'Hey, come to date me since I can't see you in this misty morning.' Where was it? Can I date you?" He showed her the photo with a joking smile. Her face flushed.

"That was a dense, foggy morning in New York. I wondered if I could grab a passerby to date." Libi laughed.

"Ha ha. Want to find a date? I raised my hand!" He stood up. "Next time you are in a foggy city in China, let's have an encounter every morning." Tauri continued to chide her. They both knew well that world-famous foggy city. She giggled, and her face turned rosy. He didn't know if it was because of the hot pot's heat or her natural beauty.

After they finished the meat, the waiter brought a melted chocolate pot and fruit platter with slices of strawberry, pineapple, apple, and pear.

"Look at this photo: you and a boy with a skateboard. Is he your boyfriend?" Tauri joked.

"My friend in the Great Lakes area. One time I went there to visit him." She hesitated a little bit. "We walked along the lake as he played on his skateboard. Do you know what happened?" She stopped with a smile. "He dropped it into the lake." She raised her voice. "The water was about ten…feet…deep." She spoke word by word. "He didn't know how to swim." She held a breath and stopped talking.

"What happened?" he asked. "What happened next?" He stared at her face.

"I…I…I jumped into the lake to grab the board from the bottom of lake!" she exclaimed.

"How funny! A girl rescues a boy." They laughed aloud. "Was that true? Do you know how to swim?" he asked curiously.

"I still can't believe what happened. I did it." She talked as she raised her head.

"Did you feel cold in that weather? Did you take your clothes off before jumping in?" He smiled, as he felt it would be hilarious if she came up onshore only in her shorts over a shivering body with both hands covering her front.

"I wouldn't do that," she chided. "I went back to the hotel to change clothes right away," she clarified. He guessed that there must have been a wet romantic moment with this boy at the hotel. But she had already told him that they were only friends.

"There will be a pride parade in New York City. Are you going to join the party?" Tauri didn't know why he popped out this question.

"I may not have time to go, but that is normal for people to express themselves," she replied.

"Are you heterosexual or homosexual?" He felt rude when he talked it out. She smiled toward him. Just smiled! This conversation turned to a little flirtation.

Tauri opened Libi's WeChat Moment to look at what she had posted. He noticed her passport photo with the formal business suit. She looked professional, with her hair falling over her shoulder like a black waterfall.

"Do you always have long hair?" he asked curiously.

"Yes. I love it." She raised her right hand to finger brush her hair from top to bottom. Her hair was silky black.

"Have you tried to cut it short?" he asked, since the notion of business women with short hair made them look sharp and entrepreneurial.

"No, I never think about that." She continued to play with her hair, moving her long curtain bangs from the left shoulder to the right shoulder.

"Have you tried to tie your hair up?" Tauri looked at his phone to search for the hairstyle; he showed her what braided hair looked like in long hair. "Look. You'd look like a Greek goddess with your braided hair." He pointed to his phone.

She then tried to caress her hair to move it up and release it to let it down.

Tauri found his hands reached out and grabbed Libi's hair. It happened so that even he didn't realize what he was doing.

His heart was pumping harder and harder; his body was frozen up. His blood flew up into his head; his hand took one stroke of her hair to wrap it around and caressed her hair up and down.

Libi leaned her head toward him to make it easier for him to play. He realized that he was touching the surface of the silk. It gave him a smooth feeling. He found that he measured the length of her hair from the top of her head to the end at her waist; he fondled her hair into two parts to try a french braid and a half-up-half-down fishtail. He built a bun with a braid, turned it into a waterfall braid, then released its natural, silky fall. He felt the sensation of a soft, glossy, fine, smooth surface from the wool at one moment.

"Did you have a special treatment for your hair? It felt so silky and smooth." Tauri heard his vibrating voice.

"I didn't have any special treatment. I wash it regularly. It grew naturally." Libi spoke softly with her hair still in his hands. Her body seemed frozen.

Tauri felt that they were in another world. There, he and Libi enjoyed each other as if they had known each other for a lifetime. It was so peaceful. Time didn't exist there. Only the background music was playing there.

It was a forever moment.

Music was playing at the restaurant! Tauri woke up to the real world; he felt awkward as he quickly realized that she was a young girl, and he was still in a marriage.

"Are you done with the food? Should we go?" he asked.

"Sure," she replied in short.

They knew that their minds were somewhere else. They didn't talk about what they wanted to talk about.

It was getting dark outside. The yellow flame burned brighter and cast golden sparkles over the pond. The projected lights shone on the spring fountain from the corners.

Tauri and Libi could only hear the "drip and drop" sounds and their heartbeats as he walked her out from the restaurant. He extended his hand to her waist to guard her. She is almost the same height as I am, even a little taller with low-heeled shoes on. Is she cold? He felt a little chilly at this late evening hour.

Should I hold her shoulder to warm her up? Should I give her a kiss? When? Where? How? What if she doesn't like it? What if she yells out? What if? Tauri's mind flashed out a few scenarios as they walked slowly and quietly toward his car.

The sunset poured white into the pink-striped clouds radiating across the sky. He saw the pink radiance all over her face.

"Thanks for coming up to have dinner." Tauri stopped and looked at her in front of his car. He heard that his voice was vibrating. She was glowing and shining.

I need to give her a kiss. This is it. This is the moment. He turned to face her and leaned forward to approach her face.

Libi pulled back and put her hand in front of herself to shield herself from him. A surprise showed up on her face.

"I want to kiss you goodbye," he uttered with a hoarse voice.

"Let's have a hug." Her face turned pinker.

Tauri and Libi opened their arms to hug each other. He leaned his head to touch her and kiss her hair gently. He felt the electrical current flowing through him.

"Do you want to sit in the back seat to stay a little longer?" He still desired to hang out.

"No, let's go home." She hesitated a moment.

Tauri seated her in and turned on the GPS navigation to find the direction in which to go. Libi picked out gum from her bag and handed one piece to him.

"Did you listen to any new songs?" he asked. He noticed that she posted a song called "Life," by Japanese singer Ikeda Ayako.

"Let me search to play!" She picked up a long list of Japanese singers and put it on speaker. In about two songs' playing time, they were in front of her apartment.

"That was so quick," Libi murmured.

"Yes, that was still in twenty minutes." He didn't give a thought about what she meant.

Libi leaned to give him a hug as usual. She opened the door to step out, then closed his car door and waved. He watched her disappear behind the closed door.

The time flew only when they enjoyed it! Tauri wanted to see her again.

After one day, Tauri sent a thank-you note to her.

"Last night was great. Can we do it again?" He sent her a message via WeChat.

"The message is successfully sent. The receiver rejected it!" A message showed up with a red exclamation mark. He didn't believe his eyes. He restarted his phone to make sure there was not a system issue. The same message showed up. After a few more tries, he realized that Libi had blocked his WeChat connection.

Chrysanthemum and the sword. A sword from Libi?

What Tauri didn't know was that this was the beginning of a long twin flame journey between the zodiac sign Taurus and a Libra. The latter was labeled as "queen of the sword" by Tarot Worlds.

"This relationship begins in severe imbalance," one tarot reader from the YouTube channel "The Gypsy Psychic" called out, since there had been thirty-five years in the cycle of Saturn and Pluto retrograde.

Libi and I are on two different life paths. Will I ever see Libi again?

CHAPTER 4

The Love Like a Light

WAS LIBI MAD at my hair touching or good-night kiss?

It's definitely not the hair touching. She leaned toward me to let me touch and play, but not a kiss attempt. She even suggested a hug.

Why would she want to cut our connection? Does it make sense? Tauri replayed the scenes again and again to make sense out of it. Why would she be mad? Would she feel the same attraction as I felt?

A few weeks passed. He felt she might cool down from her decision. He sent her a text message, which was still open to him.

"Hey, Libi. How are you? Something's wrong with my WeChat. I'm not able to send you messages anymore." He was very careful to avoid the blaming game. Instead, he found an innocent excuse.

"Hey, Libi. So many things we can help each other with? Emergencies? Activities? We'd always be friends. Would we?" He texted her to plead again.

After a few days, he noticed that her WeChat post feed showed up. She enabled my access! That is so…great! Tauri felt a stone drop off his chest.

By observing her WeChat posts, he learned how to use it. Send a message directly to the person or publish a post to either a group or an individual contact. The recipient of the post was not sure the message was explicitly sent to one person or a group. The message could be retracted or deleted.

A few days later, Libi posted a song, "White Tiger Field," by Japanese singer Hirasawa Susumu.

He scanned the lyrics. A silent girl was awakened with a strange dream; she stepped into the unknown by following the flame lighting her unknown path. Did she want to tell me she had feelings for me?

One week later, a post from her stroke his heart.

"Love like a light. It is so wonderful," she wrote. This post came with a few pictures: a blue sky with the stripes of the pinky clouds, like a classic, beautiful painting.

Look, that was the same pink sky as that fated dinner! Did she take the picture of that dinner, or did she go to that restaurant again?

Did she feel the love on that day, the same way as I did? Tauri had a warm feeling about this.

Would it look like the sparks after the big bang in the universe, which started something beautiful? He imagined further.

On the same day, she published a post titled "Listen at Least Once for a Lifetime." It was a wedding speech by a twenty-five-year-old writer in Taiwan, China, Lin Jihan. In this speech, she described her experience as a complex of Stockholm syndrome. Tauri sensed the contradiction in Libi's heart. She felt "the love like light. It was so wonderful!" But she used Ms. Lin's speech to hint that she had a similar experience. She might have the "hair-touching" event in her mind when she posted this message.

July 4 came and went. She showed some photos taken with her friend of the fireworks along with another Japanese song, "Planetariumプラネタリウム," by Ai Otsuka. Did she make a wish on July 4? What was her wish upon the shooting stars? Tauri felt excited about the idea that she had feelings for him. Should I post a message to respond? What if she sent the message to someone else?

⊷━◉ ◉━⊷

Tauri had checked Libi's WeChat message every day. Some posts expressed her random thoughts; some posts recorded her gatherings with her friends.

"OMG, she posted her fortune teller readings, a marriage Bazi—eight characters of birth!" Tauri exclaimed.

"My dear bear friend, you thought about my other half in an exhausted way. You went to order me a marriage fortune teller reading. Thanks! Love!" she wrote.

The Fortune Star:
Always calm, logical. Don't be swayed away from romance.

Romance:
High Age Window: 23 years, 28 to 31 years.
Romance Empty Age Window: Before 20 years old, 25 to 26 years old.
Your Fortune Star in your destiny represents a stable life. In your love life, you usually look far. You typically think about issues beyond romance. It rarely happens to you by sweeping away the love. Even when you love each other very much, you can still judge it rationally and logically. You'd consider the possibility for further deep connection at the early stage. You'd check the partner's

information; you'd decide to continue based on the factors like health, money, and career potential.

Fated Lover:

There is possible matchmaking. You'd need more or less impulsiveness in your love life. Perhaps you're too wise, too overthinking in your inner world. You'd pull back into reality from the butterfly moment at any time. You'd rather limit yourself than be open to intimacy. If you're not sure, you may only be able to find your future partner via your family or friend's match-making. Although this isn't that bad, you're advised to lower your standards; build the relationship with a normal attitude. You'll find many love interest potentials.

Fated Love Characteristics:

At 23 years old, you'd have the opportunity to encounter a partner. He'd have a similar value system and view of life. You'd need a little courage to make it a stable connection. At 28 years old, it's going to be your highest probability to get married. Your friends surrounding you may affect you. So does family pressure. You'd have an impulsive idea to get married. It'll depend on your judgment as to whether your partner is the best fit.

"Yes, she was at her romance window with Leo when I met her," Tauri yelled out. *Wow*, she and I have a similar value system. Would I be fated to love her if her Bazi is believable? Tauri felt the lighting flash through his mind.

After a week, she posted another song, "Night Changes," by One Direction. From this beautiful song, a few words caught Tauri's attention.

No regrets? Breaking through her hair? Was that what Libi wanted? Tauri exclaimed. She seemed to be referring to the "hair-touch" event. Nothing to be afraid of about it? She changed her Facebook profile photo to one with a red dress and bright-red lips. She became a very sexy, lovely lady with firing energy. Tauri was not sure whether she had posted her song to him exclusively. He liked to see her attractive lips. This made him excited. He sometimes even got aroused.

The next day, she posted a Chinese song called "Don't Break My Heart!" Tauri's face turned red once he listened. OMG, she is using this song to express something. Does she have feelings for me? This would be the first time she expressed it indirectly.

Tauri sang along with the music.

Tauri, I am in love with you at that moment you touched my hair. Love me, please. Don't break my heart! My hear-r-r-t!

He translated her song as her message. He was so very excited to feel her emotion. But he wanted to talk to her directly to confirm his understanding.

A few days later, Libi posted a story about the movies *The English Patient* and *The Piano Lesson*.

Tauri read her comments on extramarital relationships and society's reactions.

"The love can break the wall of an unhappy marriage! The love won at the end. I agreed with those conclusions!" Libi wrote as the title of her message.

Did she want to say this to me? He reinforced to himself the notion that she had feelings for him. A young girl is in love with me! His mind filled with joy. Tauri had not been in this love-filling heart for any time he could remember. His marriage was in trouble. The personality growth from both sides started a tiny hole and grew into cracks. He found himself spending more time with his younger daughter, Lara.

The summer had come. He asked Libi to meet and got no response from her. At the beginning of August, Libi shared a song called "Summer of '69," by Bryan Adams.

"Oh, when you touch my hair…" Tauri sang along with his variation.

Now or forever? The best days of her life? He tried to figure what she had implied. He had his suspicion that every song or comment on her WeChat post feed was sent to him exclusively. The meanings of those songs and posts became more specific and direct. Tauri felt confident about what he found.

A few days later, Libi posted a few photos of her mom. This convinced him that her posts were sent to him personally. He wouldn't post his family pictures on social media.

Libi wants me to know her, her feelings, her family. Tauri still didn't know how to reply to her hints for her love. He kept silent.

After two weeks, she posted a message titled "My Wake," a pretty-girl photo with pink cheeks and bright-red lips, with the lyrics from the song "I Thought You Said Summer Is Going to Take the Pain Away," by Hello Saferide.

Did she miss me?

Was she in pain for missing me?

He felt her gentle heart. It made him want to give her a hug or even kiss her. He knew that she was in a summer program and was busy with her training. She was lonely. She needs me. Tauri decided to express his love to her.

"Maybe it was meant to be," Tauri uttered when he reserved the cruise trip with Lara. This was the only one with a schedule that fit into her school plan. The cruise ship was called *Breakaway*.

After Tauri and Lara went on board, he started to write busily. He was so excited when he finally clicked the Send button to express his feelings for Libi.

Travel Post One: *Breakaway*
Can you believe destiny? Something you are set to be! I don't. I always think that people can control and change their lives. Time and time again, I am convinced that there has got to be a destiny for a relationship.

Three years was a long time when you lived with someone under the same roof as a brother and sister. One of my relative couples did that for thirty years. I vowed to myself that I would never repeat the same lifestyle. Instead, I would live life with full potential. It grew outward to separate gradually, like North America separated from the South America and the African continent. It was driven by internal magma's force from the initial one piece of land—Pangaea. There was nothing wrong with the couple. They grew separately.

It's a breakaway. It was a little scary, a little unfamiliar, like life starting from the ground up, learning everything again.

I would be fine.

Copenhagen, Denmark, Berlin. Next stop where?

Taurus also posted a cruise ship photo titled "Breakaway." He included the lyrics from the song "Breakaway," by Kelly Clarkson.

"Breakaway. Breakaway!" He sang and figured Libi would understand his decision to break away from his marriage. Once he started his travel posts, he found himself having so many things to share with her.

Travel Post Two: *Breakaway*, Woodstock, Germany
I failed to catch the train to Berlin. But the city of Woodstock presented Germany's best part of the treasure, the country of Einstein, Karl Max, and Friedrich Wilhelm Nietzsche.

Friedrich Wilhelm Nietzsche believed life has no meaning. In other words, when I think that I am existing, I am living; when I don't feel that I am existing, I am not existing.

He really let me think about the meaning of this life.

But I liked another philosopher Epicurus better. According to the teachings of Epicurus, the human body is made up of substance and soul particles. Without these particles, the body is dead; without a living body, the soul particles are incapable of feeling anything. Because of this dual existence, no part of the human can survive after death. There is no eternal rest or torment, no great reward to work toward, and no great punishment to avoid. That means that all I have is what I have on earth; while I am here, I need to make the best out of it. Since the soul particles are what allow us to feel pain and pleasure, the Epicurean's meaning of life is to maximize happiness and reduce pain.

Sometimes, the lovebug can really let you feel the pain. Love is a sort of germ you can catch. It can make you feel light-headed, giddy, and weak with lots of sentimental emotions. You are not sick. You feel the difference between when you are in love and not in love.

I thought about the meaning of life a lot. With the endless blue sea, I have had a lot of time to do deep thinking on this cruise ship, to read some good articles. I like the idea that there'd be nothing after death. I have not been a religious person up to this moment. In just a short year, I am in the process of being transformed. I prayed to a higher power to make this wish come true, to let me manifest to have a happy life with this girl in my dream. I feel the love in the air but can't touch it.

After a day, Libi posted a WeChat message to respond to his philosophic letter.

"To live with missing each other in this lifetime, then to live eternally by resting beside your grave. The sadness and happiness are the finest hesitations in the Asian culture," she wrote. "Even if they are in love, they may not live together in this lifetime."

Tauri continued his travel.

⭢⭢▬◯ ◖▬⭠⭠

Travel Post Three: *Breakaway*, Saint Petersburg, Russia

I'm so looking forward to visiting this city. Finally, I was here to feel, touch, be part of this great city, land of the birthplace of Tchaikovsky, writer of *Swan Lake*, Leo Tolstoy, the writer of the novel *Anna Karenina*. I was in zero distance to enjoy the entire premiere show of *Swan Lake*. It was performed by Hokkaido's international ballet dance company at the State Hermitage Museum. In the show, Prince Siegfried and Princess Odette fell in love. They were in defiance of the evil magician's spell on a white swan, Princess Odette. The love had won and had broken the devil's spell; the radiant light of the rising sun fell upon the lovers.

Lara and Tauri went to see the palace where Anastasia's story happened. He reminded Libi that "life is too short."

⊷━◉◉━⊷

Travel Post Four: *Breakaway*, Saint Petersburg, Russia
I visited the empire's grand palace as if I walked over the time capsule of the Russian heyday. I visited the summer palace for the first emperor, Peter I, and later empress Catherine, a grand palace like the forbidden city in China.

Is life too short?

The Broadway show *Anastasia* was based on this place. This brave young woman embarked on an epic adventure to find a home, love, and family. The song "Once upon a December" is remembered for the good old days.

⊷━◉◉━⊷

Tauri continued with his cruise trip. Almost every day, he got to visit one new country or city. Every day was a new day.

Travel Post Five: *Breakaway*, Helsinki, the Capital of Finland
It is the seventh day since this ship has been at sea. I felt a little tired.

"Are we getting into Finland or tired land?" one traveler complained.

"How do you spell Helsinki? Is it called hell-sinki? Or heaven-sinki?" another one said.

This city didn't disappoint me. With clean streets, crisp air, endless blue lakes, stylish beaches, small dot islands, amiable English-speaking people, and incredible Finnish food, there are the reasons why this country is referenced as the "number one happiest place on earth."

"How do you spell Stockholm? Stock-holm?" Tauri made a joke about what happened during his trip to this city.

Travel Post Six: *Breakaway*, Stockholm, the Capital of Sweden
I bought a shuttle bus ticket at 7:00 a.m. to go to Stockholm. Instead, I woke up at 7:00 a.m. and realized that the shuttle was gone. See, I was at "stuck at home." Later I found out that I had forgotten to adjust my time zone. I got one hour back in time to catch up on the shuttle, which let me take a train ride to the city. I brought fond memories about the city: the Nobel Academy,

the royal palace, the wooden paintings of the horse, the smoking fish food, the Swedish meatball, and the noisy speakers for political campaigns on the street corners.

Tauri thought about Libi when he was in front of *The Little Mermaid* statue.

Travel Post Seven: *Breakaway*, Copenhagen, the Capital of Denmark
I checked the luggage in at the airport. There were four hours to kill before my flight. I jumped onto a train to see *The Little Mermaid* statue from Antusheng's story. There, he wrote many children's books: *The Emperor's New Clothes*, *The Ugly Duckling Turns into a White Swan*.

I am looking forward to coming back to the States and having pleasant ice cream with you.

Tauri shared a final message about his trip with Lara.

Travel Post Eight: *Breakaway*, Retrospective for Helsinki, Finland
Love "heaven-land"!

The steps from the city center plaza to the dome of Helsinki cathedral are forty-six. I rarely pray, but this time was an exception. I prayed there for you and myself, for more happiness and less pain for this relationship.

I will come back to this "Heaven-sinki" soon.

⊹━◉ ◉━⊹

This summer came and went. Libi posted a few photos to show her celebration of finishing her summer training.

One summer morning, he woke up to see her comment on a "An Old Man with a Girl's Heart," by Japanese singer Kan.

"The love will win! The love will win!" she wrote.

Tauri felt Libi's joy after he broke his silence about his feelings.

CHAPTER 5

The Power of Absence

"IT WOULD BE fortunate to have the three lifetimes where I can eat Husky Track ice cream at the grassland called Three Miles, Three Worlds, and Three Lives."

Tauri saw Libi's messages and her selfie when she enjoyed an ice cream. Two forks on that cup. Was another fork for me? Was this another metaphor of her expression?

In that evening, he made a smoothie called Watermelon Sunshine. He shared the recipe on WeChat with her.

Watermelon Sunset from Grassland of Three Miles, Three Worlds, and Three Lives
Can't find it in three-generation times.

1. ½ watermelon
2. 6 tsp. grape juice
3. 6 tsp. orange juice
4. A dash of lime juice
5. A blender, 5 minutes

October was approaching. Tauri was daring to desire to talk to Libi. He hadn't heard from her since he broke his silence to express himself. I need a miracle to talk to me.

"Smoking mirrors…a miracle…" Tauri sang the song "Let Me Love You," by Justin Bieber, in his morning shower. It came into his mind with a beautiful vibe. Tauri shared this song in a post on WeChat to Libi.

Hit the wall, need miracle.
Never let me down. Please!

I chose a sunny and positive side. Hope my project can sail through the last three weeks of the most critical time.

Love this heartbeat music pulse!

⊷═◉═◉═⊷

The next morning, as usual, Tauri found a message from Libi.

Wow, she took a photo in front of the mirror.

What? She must have climbed on the top of the sink counter to take that photo. His heart was pumping hard.

That was her response! It was a "mirror-to-mirror," "heart-to-heart" emotion exchange. Whenever he looked at her mirror photo repeatedly, his heart melted.

⊷═◉═◉═⊷

Tauri got Libi's birthday info from her WeChat post in her Chinese fortune-telling readings about herself. It would be wonderful if I sent her a flower bundle. How would she react? Is she excited because there is a mystery person who sends her a flower? Is she going to throw it away to avoid her friend finding out?

He didn't think too much. He went to a florist store in his town to see if they could deliver to the city twenty miles away.

"I want this flower basket to send to a friend's birthday. Would you guys be able to deliver there by 8:00 a.m. this Saturday?" Tauri asked.

"We don't deliver out of this town unless you pay an extra delivery fee," the flower lady explained.

"Yes, tell me the total price." He asked no details.

"Do you need all red roses for your girlfriend?" the flower lady suggested.

Hmm. Libi and I are starting to flirt with each other. We have love on our minds. She would not accept it if I sent all the red roses.

"How about that flower bundle in a warmer theme? Please add a few red roses and this teddy bear to it?" He asked for advice.

"How many do you want to add?"

"Five, please." Tauri thought about it. It was her twenty-fifth birthday. Tauri went back to this florist shop and reviewed the final makeup of this bundle the day before the delivery. He couldn't wait to see the response she'd have in her WeChat message.

As Tauri expected, she received the flower on the eve of her birthday and posted a message to inform him.

"Since there is an extraordinary day on the twenty-eighth day, here is what I want to talk to my baby bear. A song, 'Just You and I,' by Japanese singer Jun Hanaue." She wrote along her birthday gathering photo with her friend.

Common twenty-eighth day? She must refer to July 28 two years ago, when she and I met on the first day. I almost forgot that special day. "Just you and I?" His heart filled with love for her.

Had she fallen in love with me at first sight? Tauri couldn't get to sleep to think about her, that first night, their story.

On the following day of her birthday, a short WeChat message showed up from Libi.

"A gift to my twenty-fifth autumn: lend me a twilight year, lend me some pieces by Chun Mu," she wrote.

Tauri quickly went to Baidu, a Chinese search engine, to get what it means.

A poem from Chun Mu, a famous Chinese poet? He read the story behind the poem. Mr. Mu, in his senior year, wrote this poem after a young girl fell in love with him. Tauri studied this poem for a few hours and tried to get a sense of what Libi wanted to express. Did she hint that our love wouldn't bear fruit? His heart became heavy.

She took a deep think about this love. Tauri sent a post to make the remark in a positive tone:

I am surprised to zoom in on the fact that you are at such a young age. All I wish is nothing but the best for you. You have a great life both in friendship and love ahead of you.

There are a series of contradictory things that appeared in Mr. Mu Chun's poem. For example: a twilight life versus teenage life, looking forward versus looking backward, being grown up versus childhood, plain versus understandable fool, soft rudeness versus playful solemnness. In the poet's mind, those can't be coexisting other than in the imagination world for those who borrow. By choosing the word "borrow," he made himself clear that it was not possible to change it. In his mind, he wanted to go back and keep to his original aspiration.

In the last two sentences, he had a deep desire to demand the life to hold it on and not being torn apart. He expressed the beautiful feeling and passion would be remembered and not be given up, including family, friendship, and what he loved.

In the sentence "Lend me a fall, but you said it's winter already," it expresses helplessness, powerless. It was as if it is missed already.

Let it go, this feeling.

The time flows forward, life moves forward. It can't go back, no matter how beautiful the feeling and people were. It was in the past. Let it be in the past.

There's a future waiting for you.

Sorry to make comments!

To me, it's cynical to conclude in this way. Maybe that is the reason why this poem is poplar in Chinese culture. In fact, it is one step away for people to go back to their original aspirations. When you do that, you gain one hell of the whole world; your road becomes wider.

Yours,

Tauri

I hope she doesn't stick with Leo, the old way of life. He prayed.

"It's too happy to dance with my friends whom I wanted to see most. They traveled from far away to celebrate with me." Libi shared a message and her group photos with her birthday party at the bar. Tauri felt happy for her and posted a message to her:

Happy birthday! Heh.

Everything is the best arrangement.

Be grateful for what happens in life—no need to refuse. Just smile and face it.

I like this song, "Just You and I."

A toast to you by the song "A Cup of Toast to Pretty Girl."

Tauri reaffirmed his feelings to her. How did she feel? Would she like it? He acted like a boy with blank love with another sleepless night.

As a reply to his message, Libi shared a song, "Addicted to You," by Avicii, back to him.

Tauri read the lyrics. His heart was flying. *Wow*, the lovebug infested us. Libi, I am also addicted to you! He can't get her from his head at any moment. A beautiful young girl was in love with me! He went to bed with this idea in his mind.

The following morning, the "Addicted to You" post was gone when he checked her WeChat message. Did she set it as private or remove that song? She must feel that it was too much for a girl to show her vulnerability! Tauri wrote a message to remind her that silent treatment would hurt people.

How I want to hear that magic song again. A song can make people sick or heal their heart. Can you post it again?

Is it possible to heal the people caused by silent treatment?

Tauri was so immersed with her showering in love. His curiosity led him to thirst more. He saw a back-naked young pretty-girl photo showed up in her WeChat message.

I watched Sasaki Nozomi's movie *My Rainy Days* I finally understood why my straight guy friends like her.
Yes, I'm her follower in the picture.

Tauri found the original Japanese movie and watched frame by frame to see when the photo was taken and what was before and after.

What? This's another hidden message from her. His heart lit on fire. The movie told the love story between Rio Ozawa, an independent and cute seventeen-year-old high school student, and Kouki Ozawa, a thirty-five-year-old university lecturer. Rio was beautiful and attractive. She never cared about anyone due to her traumatic past; she was only interested in money from cash for dating, even from extortion. She fell in love for the first time with this professor, Kouki. To her, he was different. She felt pain and confusion for her emotions. She had a huge crush on him. Rio quit her cash-to-date scheme to be with him.

Yes, she was Rio's admirer. Rio's naked back was deadly seductive to me. Was that her trying to make me itch at my heart? I want to touch hers. Tauri reconfirmed to himself that Libi was longing for this love, even with the vast age difference.

⤙═◑ ◐═⤚

Tauri posted a song, "I Am Sailing," to tell Libi that he would start to pursue a single status. He did some searching to figure out the "do-it-yourself" divorce process and downloaded all the court-required forms and process guidelines.

It looks more complicated than I thought. Do I need an attorney to handle it?

"Would you feel hurt? Are you going to be jealous if I walked with another man home?" She posted a photo to explain to him she went to a concert with a guy friend. She sensed his doubt and came out to defuse the mine at his suspension. He trusted her.

His desire to see her was growing day by day. He found that she posted a photo of a toy called "My Beast." He didn't understand; what did it mean? He went to the Baidu app to do an image search. A picture with a poem showed up.

If you are in love, I'll wait for you to break up.
If you are in marriage, I'd wait for you out from the relationship.
If you do not want a divorce, I'll wait for you to be widowed.
If you die ahead of your spouse, I'll rush to buy the grave beside you.

If you are all right, I will be third party until I'm getting old!

Tauri was astonished to read this poem. Even though it sounded like a joke, he would never expect Libi to express her strong feelings like this. He posted a message to her on this topic and shared the song "As Long as You Love Me," by the Backstreet Boys.

Drove at dark night with a mind empty. Thanks to a magic animal that guided me. A promise is *a promise*!
Don't care who you are!

Tauri was really in love with Libi. They both expressed love for each other. He couldn't wait to see her for a date.

The next day, he found that the toy image had been removed from her WeChat history. She posted a message with her girlfriend's group photo.

If it's not from you, I can't believe this. The dear friend is more loyal than the lover.
Happy birthday! My Scorpio girlfriend. Wish you happiness every day!

Had she talked to her confident Scorpio about them and gotten reminded of something?

Two days later, she posted a message titled "You can't escape the love, even if you are cool," along with a photo of a printed page from a book.

He typed the keywords from this page to do a search. Oh! From the book *The Girl with the Dragon Tattoo* by the Swedish author Stieg Larsson. OK, I got it. Mikael Blomkvist launched an investigation to uncover what happened to a woman from a wealthy family who disappeared forty years ago. He recruited help from a young girl, Lisbeth Salander. The fifty-six-year-old boss, Mikael, had an innocent hug with Lisbeth. She refused to talk to Mikael since then. This acted like a punishment to Mikael. At the end of the story, they reunited together with a thirty-year age difference. Tauri went in deep thought as he read this.

The power of absence? What is this about?

He knew he'd want to marry her, to build up a traditional family with her. He was in love dearly. He would not treat her as a mistress.

At the beginning of November, Libi posted the lyrics of the song "With Me, Only One Person."

It has been one year past since I watched the sunset at the Xiannan coast. Now
I am witnessing autumn leaves falling. A song of "wondering" is in my mind
at this sunset moment.

She looked stunningly pretty with the golden foliage background. Tauri couldn't help but click the "Like" button on her post. A moment later, another "Like" was prompted from a girl who used to work as a coworker at his company.

My thumbs-up got everyone's attention! Tauri found her WeChat post history was gone.

She turned off her WeChat message feed. This is it. This is it.

Tauri was blocked from her WeChat, as the song "With Myself, Only One Person" described.

"The power of absence is a kind of punishment strategized by her Scorpio girl-friend," he uttered.

I will wait my whole life for this love.

He felt her strong desire. He knew he wouldn't have any chance to meet her again until he was single.

CHAPTER 6

Conquer and Conquered

TAURI LOOKED AT where he was at this moment for his connection with Libi. He could see through her mind by the WeChat message history; he could still send direct WeChat messages and had her phone number to text her. But with either, he got no reply.

"Deep autumn, deep love. Where are you now?" He sent her a short message and shared a URL for a song, "Faded," by Alan Walker. No response from her.

A few days had passed. Tauri got anxious about her. Am I losing her? He decided to express his love. He remembered "I just want to call" from the song "Hello," by Lionel Richie. What I really wanted to say was the next phrase: "I love you!" It'd be a sacred moment for me to say *that* to her. I didn't even have the chance at this point.

He went on a beach walk to gain some thoughts about this. One day, he was stunned by what he saw and started to daydream about the scene.

Tauri and Libi were walking on the sandy beach with their bare feet. She wore a short white skirt just up to the knee. The soft powder made their footprints trail them. The sunset with pink-and-white cloud strips cast its aura over the Long Island Sound; it splashed ink over the shallow water on a tiny sandy surface with blue, pink, and golden colors. The warm, gentle waves flew onshore with their rhythm. The round moon was rising on the edge of the far sea. The stars looked spotty on the blue dome. The breeze blew her long, silky black hair.

He slowed down and stood still with her left hand. Then he looked at her sparkling round eyes and opened his mouth slightly without any words coming out. He reached out his right hand to pick up a seagull's feather from her flying curly hair.

"Libi, I have something to tell you." He had a solemn expression on his face. She had expected this moment was coming. Instead of meeting Tauri's eyes, she looked toward the moon on the edge of the sea.

"Libi, you are beautiful, I...I..." He seemed to have trouble finding the right word. "I...I...bought you a golden retriever puppy." Tauri finally said the word. He was surprised to hear what he said. She showed slight disappointment in what she heard and burst a laugh.

"Libi." He raised his voice. "Libi, what I want to say is I…love…you!" He spoke slowly and felt relief after he said it out.

"I knew it. I knew it. I was looking forward to hearing from you for three years." She talked back slowly with her signature soft voice.

Hmm, that was my beautiful daydream! I want to say that like this way. At this point, *yes*, this is the best song I can use to show my love. He clicked the Send button. A message titled "I just want to call" with the URL for the song "Hello," by Lionel Richie, was sent. He knew that she'd have a blushing face when she heard the subsequent phrase: "I love you."

⊶═◉═⊷

Valentine's Day came. This was the most important day for people in love. A strange image showed up on her WeChat profile background. A black screen with the letters "n55!W!" What is that? Some kind of secret code? Tauri's curiosity grew as he tried to figure it out. He uploaded the photo to do a search.

Oh! It is "I miss you!" Yep! When I look at it upside down and read it backward. He laughed as he lowered his head to read it.

"I miss u! It was a net word originating from the movie." He read. He was happy to decode this. Again and again, he was drawn into her flirtation—the hints and clues to incite his curiosity, light his fire burning inside of him. Sometimes she used a photo to show her pretty face. Sometimes she mentioned her hair to remind him of their love commitment. Sometimes she brought out a movie as a love message. Sometimes she used a photo to lead to the entire paragraph of the mottos. She was like a magician girl with unlimited stories within stories. This had been putting him in a hyperexcited mental space.

As Tauri clicked through the search result, the URL led to a music-sharing site, a Chinese version of Spotify, with a user name as "Anonymous." Under this user's playlist, there was a saved folder named "I missed u." The folder had been created one week ago.

As he read through the songs in the playlist, his face turned red; his blood was filling up his brain.

"This is a layer-in-layer flirtation! This is her love confession. It's an announcement for her love. Is it her playlist?" Tauri yelled out.

1. "Lover Boy 88"
2. "My Age"
3. "Lover Boy 88"
4. "Anonymous, I Just Like You; I Love You Deeply"

5. "I Felt Sick Since I Miss You"
6. "Innocent Year"
7. "Focus on Me"
8. "Former Boyfriend"
9. "East and West"
10. "Can We?"
11. "I Am Not Your Song Dongye"
12. "Lovesick"
13. "Conquered"

Tauri scanned the names of those songs. He came up with the message from her.

You are my lover boy.
I am twenty-five years old now.
I want you as my lover boy. Yes, I love you deeply.
I felt sick since I miss you.
I am still in the innocent year. Yes, I am still a virgin.
Please focus on me and don't shift your love away.
I don't have any relationship with my former boyfriend anymore.
I am willing to go with you for a life journey, no matter where you go in the East or West.
Can we?
You are not with your true love yet. I am your true one.
I fell in love with you. I felt lovesick.
I am conquered by your love.

He was overwhelmed to get the meaning of this playlist and shocked to see her last song, "Conquered."

Was she conquered by my love, or had her love conquered me? He felt exuberant, even intoxicated. Do I have that kind of charisma to conquer the heart from a girl as pretty, innocent, and young as her?

Tauri listened to this playlist repeatedly. He tried to figure out what it meant exactly. He downloaded the lyrics from the song and read through them thoroughly. He was in a more shocking mindset once he got the insight.

The first song, "Lover Boy 88," seemed to link back to her message of "I missed you." Did Libi especially talk to me or send a message to another guy, like her ex-boyfriend?

One phrase even mentioned the announcement for marriage. He felt jealous that other people also could see her playlist.

The second song, "My Age," expressed her honesty that she felt a little too old to play around. She wanted to settle down. That was true in Asian culture. To him, age was just a number; he didn't pay much attention to it, though he was thirty years older than she.

The third song was the same name as the first song but a different version. Tauri got more meaning from the rap lyrics. It made him move.

The fourth song was named "Anonymous, I Just Like You." Tauri confirmed his guess that Libi owned this playlist. Look, this song mentioned a "story that happened in June," "three years again." Yelp! We met at that time. Our relationship was innocent, as if we were childhood friends.

The fifth song, "I Felt Sick Since I Miss You," was what Libi reconfirmed in her background image. This song described the situation Tauri and Libi were in. It has been half a year since we hugged at the dinner and came away with a forever memory of a hair-touching moment. But I was in a marriage relationship; she was alone in waiting. Oh! She believed the magic as far as I pushed forward with my true desire.

"Is she still a virgin?" Tauri exclaimed when he read the sixth song, "Innocent Year." He knew what "innocent" meant for a girl in Chinese culture. When the girl claims to be still innocent, she implies she is still a virgin. There had been folklore for the girl to die to defend her innocence. The emperor would build up a memorial stone plate to engrave the names of women who defended their value. That was where the ethnic code of conduct was promoted by the Confucian culture.

Did she give her first night to Leo, her ex-boyfriend? She is such a pure, sweet, honest angel. She guarded her first night and will only give to her true love. Tauri felt the sense of responsibility to love her with his whole heart.

He got Libi's yearning for their love by the seventh song, "Focus on Me." He felt the strong pulling force from her. He heard her call. This song also referred to when they were studying abroad, which linked their experience together.

Did Libi trash her ex? He was thrilled to know their relationship was over from the eighth song, "I Am Your Former Boyfriend." He learned that Libi and her boyfriend had broken up already. This song put some bad words on her boyfriend. Tauri had been jealous of their perfect match with their youthful looks. That was the most formative obstacle we had to overcome for our relationship to blossom.

From the ninth song, "East and West," Tauri was exuberant to know that she wanted to build a life with him—travel with him, have a school of kids and pets with him. He got a bright picture of their life together. He had the same wish to bring her to Paris and London for a cruise trip and take a lot of photos of her; most of all, he wished to build a family and enjoy his time with her.

From the tenth song, "Can We?" Tauri got Libi's willingness to get back together. Yes, it had been three years since that magic night. She did talk into my heart directly.

Regarding the eleventh song, "I Am Not Your Song Dongye," Tauri was puzzled for at least one hour about what it meant. He read the comment with this song and finally figured out that she wanted to tell him his current relationship was not in true love. His true love was not showing up yet.

"Libi, yes, you are my true love." This song was like a bomb set off in his heart.

The twelfth song, "Lovesick," mentioned two things: teddy bears and a letter, which he sent to her for her twenty-fifth birthday. Was my gift teddy bear still with her? He had a fire coming up in his chest.

From the last song, "Conquered," he felt a shocking confession from her. There was no doubt in Tauri's mind Libi was the owner of this playlist. She used the "n55!W!" image to lead him to this online music-sharing site. He truly felt her determination to be in love with him.

Tauri was shocked with the playlist. Even more, he found that the folders under this user were organized for the different love situations, which was from an album published by Luto, a Chinese singer.

1. This love can't be achieved because of an imbalance of the heart—created in November three years ago.
2. A boat could be used to cross a sea—created in April two years ago.
3. This love is apart between mountain and sea—created in November two years ago.
4. This love can't be achieved due to the distance of mountain and sea—created in December two years ago.
5. A road taken to cross mountains—created in August one year ago.
6. This love can be achieved, even though there is a distance apart at mountain and sea—created in February this year.
7. This love can overcome the distance of mountain and sea—February this year.
8. This love can be achieved, no matter that there is a distance apart at mountain and sea—February this year.
9. Accompany you for this life journey—created in February this year.

The "mountain" is referring to the emotional distance; the "sea" is to describe the "geographic distance." OMG, Libi might have started to have feelings toward me three years ago. Tauri was so happy to realize this. She had been prepared for this love confession for a while. *Wow*, this is her own version of "shock and awe"!

Tauri listened to this playlist and felt Libi's strong determination to be in love with him. Libi is such a beautiful girl at heart. What did I offer to make her have such strong expressions? She belonged to me; I belonged to her. Tauri felt such a soul-level connection. He seemed to hear her soft voice calling him to take action.

He decided to pull the trigger to start a legal separation in his family life. This'd be the first step required by law, which he had held off on for a few years. He moved his stuff to another bedroom with his wife's approval.

Tauri posted the message to Libi via WeChat along with a URL of the song "Accompany You for This Life Journey":

I've been experiencing life changes since I posted my trip log "Breakaway." I'm in my legal separation now and will be a bachelor pending logistics arrangement and legal papers. I'm looking forward to having my new life unfolding and spending some time with my princess, you. Perhaps there's a telepathic link between us. I'm willing to be the white horse to go with you to follow that dragonfly and lead us to perfect lives.

This started Tauri's leap of faith to seek his freedom and pursue Libi's love.
It was a journey that must be taken by him.

CHAPTER 7

Born to Be Noble

LIBI WAS HAPPY. She seemed to like the letter Tauri sent to her along with a basket of flowers. She posted a pretty, sunny selfie on WeChat to show her joy. But he still felt that her face looked less cheerful than before. She looked tired.

What happened to prompt her to show the photo from the revenge scene from the Netflix show *Love, Death & Robots*?

Did Leo take advantage of her against her will during this spring break?

Did something happen with her guy friend? She shared a few party photos. One boy definitely had a crush on her.

Was a crime committed in her town, where she was the victim?

He went to search the criminal history in her town. He found nothing.

Did she want to vent her pain while she waits for me? He finally came back to himself. He went to get clues from her updated playlist.

1. "Curry, Curry"
2. "As If the Old Friend Come"
3. "Malaysia Chabor"
4. "Love Old, Like New"
5. "The Garbage"
6. "Lovable or Not"
7. "I Just Like You"
8. "Felt Guilty"
9. "As If the Old Friend Come"
10. "Sweet Girl"
11. "I Just Like the Look When You Don't Like Me"
12. "Winter Sleep"
13. "She Lived"

14. "Wait, Wait Longer"
15. "Longing"
16. "My Heart Will Go On"
17. "The Silence Is Golden"
18. "Love Song 2018"
19. "Butterfly Effect"
20. "I Am Not Your Sun Dong Ye"
21. "Falling"

Tauri translated her playlist as a message.

Dear Tauri,

Curry! Curry! Hurry! Hurry! Please marry me quickly. I felt impatient to wait for you. You were like my old friend, though we met only a few times. I knew you were following my playlist every day. That was lovely. You are my old lover and the new love. Even though I was with that "garbage guy," I just liked you. I can't control myself. I felt guilty about the idea that you would leave your marriage behind. But we connected as if we had known each other for a long time. I am a sweet girl. I liked your look when you don't like me. After that heartbroken summer with Leo, I almost felt that my love life was gone forever. I told myself to hold on, hold on longer, with the feeling of longing for you. My heart is moving on forever with you. The silence is golden at this point since we fell into love three years ago. It'd have a butterfly impact on my reputation. So does it on my career and my family. At the same time, your true love has not been with you yet. It is me who your loved one is. I fell in love with you.

Please catch me with your angel's hands if I am falling.

OMG, she had a suicidal mind that winter three years ago. I should have reached out to her for more support! He felt sadness in his heart.

Tauri went to the gym for his twice-a-week exercise. He did a virtual bicycle tour around Paris, where he had visited three years ago. He thought about her during his ride. I will definitely travel with her in Paris again. He came up with a poem for imagining their tour in Paris and sent it to her as a WeChat post.

Tour Paris with You

Want to ride the bicycle to have a tour around the Eiffel Tower,
then do the climbing Arc de Triomphe as the competition to chase your hair;
on the eighty-first top floor to taste your sweat,
carry you on my back to show my bravery.

Want to watch your beauty along the avenue of the Champs-Élysées,
enjoy your look comparing side by side with Mona Lisa at the Louvre;
have nightlife at the Moulin Rouge show,
find no way to attract your interests to go.

Want to have an encounter with you at Ladurée Paris,
didn't know that macarons could also be served like this;
having desserts can cost hundreds of dollars,
as if a villager went to work as a royal gardener.

Let me be the bell ringer at church Notre-Dame,
caregiver of my bae on the Left Bank of the Seine;
jump into the river to rescue your hat from thee,
just to hear your scream to be sure you are the one.

Tauri was pretty happy about his poem. It came with lighthearted energy. He wrote more to her on WeChat.

Dear Libi,
When I saw the dozens of sentences you wrote, my heart was warm. Although I didn't fully understand your situation, my heart was always with you. If something bad had happened and can't be changed, you just had to accept it.
　　Without regular communication, we were all in a sad and painful state. The good love teaches us to grow and promote our mental maturity. The perfect love was that you would get better without exhausting each other. Let's be a little easier for us.

Tauri didn't see any updates on her playlist or background image. He felt that his daily message would make her happy. He knew that he was about to kick off his legal process to be single in order to pursue her.

Wow, she doesn't want to continue to go on with this relationship anymore! Tauri exclaimed to read the playlist. Not a home-wrecker! She is a noble person! He was at a loss for words. Libi seemed to make a stern statement to tell him about her decision.

1. "Mountain and Sea"
2. "Don't Want to Go to Li River"
3. "Surrounded on All Sides"
4. "Last Party"
5. "Laugh and Fun"
6. "I Am Still Young, I Am Still Young"
7. "Almost Home"
8. "Embarrassment"
9. "She Lived"
10. "Born to Be Noble"

Tauri translated this playlist into a message.

I know that you can't afford to leave your marriage. We'd never meet again. This relationship put me in a dangerous situation. Our last dinner together was fun. I felt really embarrassed to be a third-party person. I am still young. I want to go home back to China. That person you knew was gone. I was born to be a noble person. I will live up to my moral standard.

He was not surprised by her announcement. So many hurdles in front of us. She didn't need this relationship—she is young, pretty, talented, and intelligent. She has every reason to step out at an early stage. I'd respect her decision. He sent her the message at WeChat to make sure that was what she truly wanted.

Bae,
I missed you. Those songs pulled my heartstrings when I heard them.

Sometimes, I feel that I'm not smart. I'm trying to make sense out from the context of those ten songs you posted. I'm so looking forward to the date we meet and understand you more when I see you, and then I'll move things quickly. At 6:00 p.m. on this Sunday, let's have the mood like the song "Nineteen Years Old." I'll come to pick you up. I'll wait at the place for a half hour until you come. We can go to the "one if by land, two if by sea" place in the city. I'll stay at the hot pot place if you don't come. Let me know if you can't make it, or you can imagine that I'll be running crazy on that day when I'd love to spend time alone to think about you and our three years of memories, life, and love...

Tauri was so worried about Libi's mental status. The song "She Lived" described a girl who jumped from a building to tell her story. He wrote the message to her via WeChat.

Hey, Bae,
It's sad to hear the song "She Lived."
    I'm worried about you. In any case, if you take one step back, you will find a whole new world. You can't have both spring flowers and autumn moons; there're no perfect options. If so, please make peace on it. We'll keep a beautiful memory in life when we take a deep breath and enjoy the heart singing.
    You can see the mountains and the sea. I'm different. My eyesight is relatively short. I only see you and your song.
    Hey, if you're not busy, can we meet like the song "Nineteen Years Old"? I haven't seen you for such a long time. I don't know if we still know each other.
    I'll wait for you.

After a day, she responded to his message with a playlist of thirty-four songs.

1. "Mountain and Sea"
2. "Almost Home"
3. "Never Go to Li River"
4. "King of Karaoke"
5. "Surrounded on All Sides"
6. "Man in the Moon"
7. "Last Party"
8. "Laugh"
9. "I Am Still Young"
10. "She Lived"
11. "Thought to Die"
12. "Unsent Letter to the Sister"
13. "I Don't Know How to Love"
14. "Born to Live by Moral Standard"
15. "My Man"
16. "Too Much"
17. "Back to Original"
18. "1874"

19. "Guilty in the Heart"
20. "Stranger under My Skin"
21. "Story about Clearwater River"
22. "Nineteen Years Old"
23. "Never Grown Up"
24. "Mountain"
25. "Walking Horse"
26. "My Dream"
27. "Embarrassment"
28. "Love Triangle"
29. "Ivy"
30. "Colorful Days"
31. "Only Loverhood on the Eyesight"
32. "Memory for Those Sleepless Nights and Unforgettable Things"
33. "Twenty-Eight Years Old"
34. "Thinking about You Suddenly"

Tauri spent a few days going through the playlist. It was so confusing to him. He sent the message to Libi at WeChat about the playlist.

Dear Libi,

I spent hours staring at the screen to make sense of it. Not sure those songs were talking to me. Let me use one sentence to see if I catch the meaning.

Section 1: Headline

1. "Mountain and Sea": There are too many hurdles between us, like a mountain and sea.
2. "Almost Home": I want to go home to China, away from you.
3. "Never Go to Li River": I don't want to take you away from your marriage.
4. "King of Karaoke": Even we committed at that moment.
5. "Surrounded on All Sides": It was totally against the social norm.
6. "Man in the Moon": You are a man in the moon with social status.
7. "Last Party": Last time we meet.
8. "Laugh": It was fun.
9. "I Am Still Young": I have a promising future.
10. "She Lived": That person was gone. I am a totally new person now.

Section 2: Content

11. "Thought to Die": I was torn by this love. Sometimes I just want to die.
12. "Unsent Letter to the Sister": I have unspoken words to the other party in your marriage.
13. "I Don't Know How to Love": I am a newbie in the love department.
14. "Born to Live by Moral Standard": I am a noble person with a high moral standard. I never think I am in this situation.
15. "My Man": I have love interests pursuing me.
16. "Too Much": Many young boys want me.
17. "Back to the Original": For our connection, I thought about why it happened. I came up with an important reason.
18. "1874": It is like a past-life connection.
19. "Guilty in the Heart": I have guilt in my heart to get into your marriage life.
20. "Stranger under My Skin": You are the stranger under my skin, with me all the time.
21. "Story about Clearwater River": This is forbidden love. The family tragic event would happen.
22. "Nineteen Years Old": I am still young and immature.
23. "Never Grown Up": I am still growing up.
24. "Mountain": There is a great future ahead of me.
25. "Walking Horse": I will carry my life like a walking horse slowly.
26. "My Dream": I will pursue my dream career.
27. "Embarrassment": I felt embarrassment about this connection with you.
28. "Love Triangle": In your marriage triage as the third party, which was never in my moral code.

Section 3: Last Words

29. "Ivy": That game was over.
30. "Colorful Days": With those beautiful days.
31. "The Only Livelihood on the Eyesight": I will focus on my career.
32. "Memory for Those Sleepless Nights and Unforgettable Things": For those memorable things.
33. "Twenty-Eight Years Old": When I am twenty-eight years old.
34. "Thinking about You Suddenly": I will think about you suddenly.

The question in my mind is to look each other in the eye and ask if we do what we said, assuming we are equal today. Tauri felt an urgent need to meet with Libi to know what precisely was in her mind. He wanted to confirm with her as their anniversary was approaching.

Bae,
Will we talk? We'd be healed by the heart-to-heart conversation.
We need to talk. At six o'clock tomorrow, I'll wait at the place we first met in the United States for a half hour. I know you are busy…far away…want to disappear for a new beginning. Don't know how to love. Can we have a talk, a drink, a short conversation? It hurts you and me when we are not talking.
   I'll stay at the restaurant where we met the last time if I miss picking you up.
   By listening to the song "She Lived," it worried me. I won't assume that everything will be all right for you.
   You're going to be OK. I have a pinky promise to you.
   Tauri

⤖➤◉◉➤⤖

It was a Thursday, a regular working day. Tauri ended his office work earlier than usual. He reminded Libi he wanted to see her on the anniversary day. He believed that he'd have the best chance to talk to her.

He arrived at her apartment at 5:30 p.m. He parked near the entry hall. She'd notice his car immediately when she came out. There were few people going in or out from that building.

When the clock turned to 5:50 p.m., he started to get nervous. What if she doesn't want to come? What if she gets sick? What if she ignores me? What if? What if?

When the clock turned to 5:55 p.m., a young girl with short hair walked out. She is not Libi; Libi has long black hair.

When the clock turned to 6:00 p.m., the time when he had asked her to meet, no one came out. He looked at the third floor, where her room was. There was no sign someone even looked down from those windows. The street was tranquil.

Could Libi have gone to the restaurant already? He knew she tried to avoid her friend by catching up his car from the place next to the mall last time. Let me wait until 6:30 p.m. so I can check out at the restaurant. Tauri started the engine of his Mercedes.

As he drove away from her apartment, he felt that she might not want to come tonight. There's little chance that she'll show up. He drove to that restaurant where they had departed one year ago.

"How many people are in your party?" A waitress led him inside.

"Can I sit at that table?" He walked quickly to pass the waitress to the table where Libi and he had sat one year ago.

"Sure. How many guests do you have?" The waitress talked to him with a professional smile.

"Two. Another one will come later," he told the waitress.

"Would you like to drink something?" the waitress asked.

"Sure. Can I have a cup of IPA?" He wanted something bitter now.

"What kind of dish do you want? A melting pot or grill? Do you need your guest to come before you order?" the waitress continued to ask.

"No. I would like to try the grill. Can I order it now?" he asked. He felt that the smoke came out from his chest as his heart was on the grill.

In his mind, there was little chance that she'd show up. He was ready to try something different, something new.

"Would you like some red wine, Libi?" he had asked her last year.

"No, thanks. I don't drink wine or liquor," Libi had replied politely. It had been one year since he had met with her on this day and at this table. One year had passed. What a dramatic change happened in my life. I'd better watch out about what I am wishing for. The wish might come true.

The grill was easy to operate. Tauri ordered his favorite seafood with jumbo shrimp, scallops, and salmon. When the barbecue sauce was poured over the food, the sweet smell came out and filled the air. His mood was extremely low, even with a cup of fresh IPA beer.

"Is your friend going to come?" the waitress asked after half an hour.

"Probably not," Tauri replied.

As Tauri paid the bill and walked out of the restaurant, the strips of pink clouds were still magically there. Though it was similar to what it looked like one year ago, she was not here now. Why didn't she send a message if she decided not to come? She doesn't want this relationship anymore—the conflict with her moral standard?

There might be a possibility that I will never see her again.

I was led into this playlist. This is killing me.

How can I be free from this? Any other way to understand her behavior?

Tauri didn't have the answer. This was the first time in his life he didn't understand what had happened to Libi, to him, to his life.

He didn't have closure.

He was totally lost.

CHAPTER 8

The Individual Journey

TAURI LEFT THE restaurant and drove on the highway aimlessly. He missed his exit and spent another half hour getting back to his house. After one wide-awake night, he sent a message to her on WeChat: "A sleepless night under your spell."

He had the whole night to go through what had been going on between Libi and him. He also thought about Aquri, his wife, and him and even his daughter, Lara.

The idea to be a hero to rescue someone was unsound. I need to make changes to be happier and more peaceful than I am now. Maybe Libi was right. She is not a home-wrecker; I am not someone who pursues a shining new girl. I need to actively work on my marriage to see if it can be rescued.

In the past three months, he and Aquri had been under the marriage counseling process. This was the second time in four years she had requested that he go to the appointment. The first time, he was so fearful their personal differences would be exposed publicly. This time, he was prepared.

"Welcome to this session. I want to emphasize that my role is not a judge to tell you who is right and who is wrong. My role is here to listen, to have this conversation be organized in a civil way. I will let you guys talk." The counselor started to set up the ground rules.

"The sessions are weekly, one hour each. It'll last at least five sessions. You can request extra, which are not going to be covered by your insurance," the lady said. "Each of you can raise one topic and talk about it for five minutes without interrupting; the other person can have five minutes to respond. You guys can have an interactive conversation about this topic after that," the middle-aged lady then added.

It's like a debate. But this is real life. He ran through it in his mind.

"Let me talk first." Aquri brought out a paper prepared with the list of topics.

The one-hour time passed quickly. He felt he didn't have enough time to talk through his point of view. He was surprised to know that they had totally opposite views about those topics. It seems to me I don't even know her anymore! he uttered in his mind.

⊷▰◖▰⊶

"Well, we've spent five sessions about a variety of topics related to your marriage. As I told you guys initially, I am not here to judge people or give you a conclusion. I am here to be a facilitator for this discussion. Since your guys' opinions are at opposite point-to-point views, I don't see any further sessions needed," the lady said at the end of the fifth session.

"This documentation of this session will be private. But I will provide it to the court if any legal proceedings are needed. You are greatly appreciated for your calm and peaceful way of discussing things." The lady finally gave their manner a thumbs-up.

Tauri knew all the issues had been openly discussed. He and Aquri held their own positions with no consolidation. He walked out the door with the understanding that their marriage was heading to the court proceedings, as the lady had mentioned. He could tell that Aquri felt the same way.

She is a new Aquri, standing in front of me. Tauri had moved into a different room in February of this year. They seemed to continue carrying on their daily lives in their own ways. They had dinner at the different sides of the dinner table, sometimes with different dishes.

Tauri started to prepare the documents required by the court. As he looked at his property distribution plan, he figured it would be nice to know Libi's plan. He knew she had decided to end their connection to focus on her career; she also wanted to go back home to China to avoid him.

The following day, he was in the kitchen preparing his breakfast. He had a cup of black coffee in his hand to plan his day.

"You'll be wrong for those things I mentioned in the sessions." Aquri talked as she walked to pass him from upstairs to get ready to go to work.

"I want you to take a video to admit your mistakes. You'd slap your face by both hands many times with a loud sound and send it back to me." She talked fluently as if she had rehearsed it many times and unloaded peacefully. His face turned hot. He did feel someone slapping his face with a loud sound already.

"Wait, what?" Tauri didn't believe what he heard.

"I want to divorce you!" Aquri shouted out without explaining.

Tauri looked at her in a prolonged silence to make sure what she said was what she wanted. He felt that she was not acting impulsively. Those words may have been in her mind so long that it was natural for them to come out.

"Sure, I'll prepare the agreement. We can have the marriage mitigator review before we file at the court." Tauri replied calmly after a long moment of silence.

Aquri opened the door to the garage and stormed out and slammed the door.

As he drove to his office, he realized that his happiness was not dependent on someone else like Libi. This was his own journey to be joyful and at peace within himself.

"This is my own journey!" He shouted out as he raised his right fist as he drove along the familiar highway. He felt so different, with much excitement and unknown anxiety.

"Welcome to my marriage mediation service. I require you to have a minimum of five hours' service. You can come to have a one-hour session every week until you two reach an agreement." An old lady in a business suit talked as he and Aquri sat in front of her desk. "This agreement will be filed with the court to save time for the trial process. I'll prepare a formal court filing for you if you want." The lady hired by Aquri talked. "You'll pay for every session. My colleague charges over a thousand dollars per hour. I'll give you a discount." The lady talked about her money requirement first.

"I prepared all the documents and agreement. Can it save some time and money?" Tauri asked.

"That's for sure. I need time to go through it. Oh, you have thirty pages of documents." The lady flipped through them. "Now let's talk about your questions." The lady started to take questions after a half hour of her business discussion. The first session didn't result in the exact direction that he had expected.

Tauri had asked Libi to meet with him to have a conversation. Sometimes he felt that he was begging her for this.

At his birthday, Libi had sizzling love expressions. It made him very happy. Then the thing took a 180-degree turn. At first, she asked him to be only a friend, and then she flirted with Leo for her ten-year bigger plan. This blew Tauri's mind. At this point, he knew it was his own journey to pursue his happiness and carry out the divorce process. He'd not have Libi in his decision-making process.

Why did she expose her plan at her playlist? She knew that I would look at it every day. Tauri was really in a puzzle.

Why did she still go back to Leo? There is a bright future here. He didn't understand

Libi. He didn't understand Aquri. He didn't understand himself. He didn't understand this world anymore.

⊷═◉═⊶

Tauri was on a video-sharing online site to search for love songs. Tarot reading topics showed up at his phone screen.

What is the tarot? Why is it related to zodiac signs? He had little knowledge about this. He recalled that one of Libi's songs mentioned a zodiac sign.

From "Fall in Love," by the singer ICE, he started to know the zodiac sign Taurus, which Libi used to refer to him.

This's a wonderful world. What is Libi's zodiac sign? He googled Libi's birthdate to find out that she was a Libra.

"There is going to be a 35 percent compatibility in sexual intimacy," Tauri read at one website.

"Libra is like a stylish city girl; Taurus is like a country boy with casual style. They are totally opposite of each other. But they are ruled by common Venus, the goddess of love." He was totally pulled into it.

"The only way to make their relationship successful is to embrace their own fear." Tauri seemed to find a critical understanding of their relationship.

He clicked a few tarot readings about Libra. It was resolute with his situation by "303 High Priestess" published on July 10, 2019, titled "Libra, July 2019. Prepare Yourself for This. Someone Wants You, but Can They Have You Yet?"

This changed Tauri's whole world.

"My energy as Taurus showed up at Libi's Libra reading. How could this happen?" he exclaimed.

But his heart was heavy. So glad to find this magical place to read my and Libi's energy. Our love story was not in my imagination or illusions only. This reading was accurate.

Another reading gave him a little comfort with what Libi might do next by "Channel 143 by Antonia," on July 11, 2019. It was titled "Libra, July 15–31: Someone Comes Back! Two People? Love Horoscope."

Oh! The first person must be Leo, who had deceived her in the past and didn't honor their relationship. I am surprised that Libi is still in her past. The second person must be me! Yeah! I have 100 percent pure intentions. This is like a live broadcast for me to have a glimpse into her mind.

Tauri was excited, not only to know his situation with Libi, but he also had an entirely new way of looking at this world. How could people's thoughts or ideas be read out via a few paper cards?

Here is what going to happen from now on. Libi broadcasts her message via the playlist to her love interests, led by her WeChat profile photo "n55!W!" I'll read through her mind via tarot readings and take corresponding action. I definitely have the upper hand in the competition.

⊶━◉ ◉━⊷

Tauri was happy to have this competition in motion. A thunderstorm came one day when he was on the way home from his office. A double rainbow hung over the skyline. A sense of emotion came into his mind. Too many things happening in my life: Libi's safety, my divorce, my unknown future. Tauri's mind came with a poem.

A Thunderstorm: To My Lady

Even though a storm is coming,
Even though the flood is alarming,
Even though the lightning is flashing,
Even though the thunder is trembling.
May my love shield the pouring rain from you,
May my heart provide a safe harbor form the whirlwind for you,
May my passion light the path as the lightning to lead your way,
May my poem cheer you up as rumbling beats as the thunder.
May my soul be there to wait for you,
May we enjoy a quiet evening after the storm,
One bed, two persons,
Become one, happily ever after.

It was almost the end of July; Tauri liked to walk on the beach alone in the evening. It was so peaceful there. He thought about Libi and their future life. He wrote a poem and sent it to her.

The Boat of Our Hearts

Floating quietly in the middle of Long Island Sound,
along with a slight calm wind around.
Shake gently.
The golden sprinkles cover it friendly.

I see the smile on your face,
I see the bright light in your eyes dance,
I see the colors over your long black-silk hair,
I see you cuddle up at my armchair.

The time is frozen,
The space is nonexistent with no motion,
No grudges,
No right or wrong for judge.

Just watch the setting sun with the afterglow,
Just observe the jade rabbit to cover over with silver light slow,
This is how we count the blessings from our Venus goddess,
This is how we imprint our sun's reflection on us.

That is our vision of the mind,
That is our source of our life to make us blind,
That is our tomorrow's chart,
That is the boat of our hearts.

Tauri had so many unanswered questions for his future. When he listened to tarot readings, he didn't understand what those tarot readers talked about. I heard applause from those cheerleaders. What's a project? Is it my kitchen remodel? How could this inspire people and ease my pain?

The tarot channel "Dane Hart Tarot" offered her advice in August 2019 in her reading titled "Taurus August 16–31, 2019. It's Your Time after So Much Struggle // Tarot Reading." She described the formation of a diamond.

Did she indicate that I, as a Taurus, have unique creativity? Yes, I was drawn to the thing because of shared connection, because of the love, he told himself.

The tarot channel "Holistic Fashionista" offered a reading titled "Taurus August 2019: Your Higher Calling Is Getting Its Wings!" on July 12, 2019. She described that Taurus has been invited to do a project. She gave some examples as calculated risks.

⊷═◉ ◉═⊶

"Welcome to this show. Here is your brochure." He was handed a small book with the lyrics of the songs and introductions. He and Lara went to watch *Hairspray*. The laughter and applause started to fill this small theater with about three hundred attendees.

"Dad, Tracey had a dream to audit in this national show. Do you think she can do it?" Lara wanted to know the result.

"Wait, let's watch to see how the story unfolds." Tauri lowered his voice.

"Yes, this was my story. This was my struggle." Tauri's mood brightened up from this song on the stage. He looked back at how far he and Libi had come from three years ago. How much transformation had been in their lives? How much understanding did they have of each other? He wrote a message to Libi on WeChat.

Even lonely, a journey must be taken.
I wanted to share the song "I Know Where I've Been," by Queen Latifah in *Hairspray*.

Tauri knew that this'd be a journey he must take alone for his future, happier life. A journey has to be taken! A journey is being taken! A journey must be taken! His mind echoed only with those thoughts.

CHAPTER 9

The Twin Flames Awaken

"I AM GOING to move to a new place this Saturday." Tauri talked to Aquri when he saw her pass him to go to the car garage. They had barely had a chance to talk after she asked to divorce him. She stopped and looked at him for a moment and continued to walk without saying a word. It was one of the court's requirements in his state for a divorced couple to be separated for half a year.

It was a simple task for him to pack his own stuff. All his clothes went into a few plastic boxes from Office Depot. A computer backpack, a few kitchen things, all the bar stuff goes with me, including the wine and liquor. He smiled to himself. He was happy to make a cocktail to entertain his friends at the house party.

"Dad, where are you moving to? Can I help?" Lara came to ask.

"Lara, Dad is moving to that new place. You are going to visit me, right?" He looked at Lara dearly.

"Sure, Daddy." She came over to hug him.

Tauri hopped into his car. He clicked his garage key to make the door pull up and drove out slowly. Something is itching on my face. He saw Lara was standing in front of the colossal bay window waving to him. His eyes turned red. He looked at this huge house, the biggest house on his street. He knew there would be no return after this moment. He turned on his smartphone and took a few pictures as memories.

As he parked outside his new apartment where he had planned to move for a few months, no one was waiting for him. It was quiet, and he was standing there, lonely. But he felt warm. I finally have a place of my own, maybe with Libi.

"Wish all the lovers to have beautiful Double Seven Lover Day: 7/7." A few posts showed up in his WeChat friend circle. His heart was soft with Libi in his mind. He had a lot of emotion flowing out from his thoughts at this moment. He put it into a poem and sent it to her.

H. L. Howard

7/7 To My Lady

July seventh every year,
每年的七夕,
Magpies built a bridge at Milky Way galaxy pier,
喜鹊在银河搭上鹊桥,
The deep love between the Cowboy and the Weaver Girl,
牛郎和织女的恋情,
It moves God to grant them to embrace into a curl.
上天也让他们相逢.

Even a moment of eye touches,
即是双目相视,
expresses the love from the thirsty
传递爱的渴望,
Or ten fingers twisted on each other,
或是双手紧扣,
shows the affection for a year further.
道不尽一年的思念。

I travel to the one end of the invisible bridge,
我也拔涉到隐形桥边,
look over the endless space between heart's wedges.
望着那无尽的心河,
A Honey Bunny is waiting at another end,
那边有我的小娇妻在等待,
Who would build a rainbow for Tauri to mend?
谁来为金牛搭桥相见?
Wish we build this bridge by our soul,
愿你我的魂建周桥,
Wish we build a palace by our love as our home,
愿你我的爱建殿房,
Wish my lady long life at my heart,
愿我的真爱长住在我的心上,
Wish our reunion as if we were at first sight to start.
愿我们相逢如初漾。

"No response, no contact. What person is this?" Tauri was so looking forward to hearing from her.

The tarot channel "Your Soul's Journey Tarot" offered a reading titled "Libra, My Beloved! (Deep/Spiritual Read! Chance Encounter = Activation/Anchoring 5D union into 3D)" on August 23, 2019. It caught him by surprise.

"She cried out as a joyful moment!" Tauri exclaimed. "Did she mention that Libi and I were in the contract written at the beginning of the time?" he uttered.

OMG, that could explain why Libi was so attractive to me, not only for her youth, beauty, innocence, anything more attractive than a soul connection? Yeah! When I met with her at her heartbroken moment, that was a fated event.

Wow! Her "conquered" playlist captured my heart.

Funny she posted the song "Living in Your Ears," similar to the concept of clinching this person's soul into my heart.

Do I have the key to unlock her heart? What key?

Tauri had a deep thought about this. The tarot card seems to fall out randomly from their shuffling. Then the readers interpret the meaning of the card, the layout of the card, and their life experience to explain and provide advice. It was really magic.

He wrote what he found at the tarot readings to her on WeChat. The following day, her playlist was empty.

Removed!

Did Libi close two channels connected to me?

Could she totally disappear from my life?

What would happen if she were not there for me once I am out of my marriage?

Would it be my personal journey for divorce no matter if Libi were there or not? Is it? Tauri could see that possibility now.

⊷═◉ ◉═⊷

A few days later, Tauri found her updated playlist.

OMG, something terrible happened in the deep, dark night at the end of March. What was that? She thought she died for that! His mind ran crazy.

Men who eat whales. How bloody that was! Was that so sad? His heart sank.

1. "Deep Dark Night at the End of March"
2. "She Lived"
3. "Terminal Illness"

4. "So Transparent"
5. "Thought to Die for This"
6. "Men Who Eat the Whale"

Tauri translated her playlist into a letter.

Tauri,
In that deep, dark night at the end of March, she had died for her new life. She lived. It was a terminal illness. Her story was obviously transparent to the world now. She thought to die. You are the one of men to eat the whale with everything I have—my beauty, my youth, and my wealth.

"What happened at the end of March? Someone died?" Tauri yelled it out.
Who are the men eating the whale? The lyric was bloody.
He sent her a text message directly, even though she told him that she'd report to the police if he contacted her again.

Dear my lady,
How is everything going? I really missed you!

I saw your playlist. That was so heavy, sad. My heart tanked. It made my tears come out, which I don't usually do until recently. Sorry for hearing about your loss. You shouldn't carry this heavy burden on yourself.

I'd care less if you reported me to the police because I sent a text message directly to you. It's worth it for me to take the risk to simply tell you my thoughts. You can ask me to stop if you don't want to receive a further text message.

I wanted to say that there was someone in love with you deeply in the heart at this world if you open your heart to allow this.

When you first posted the song "Deep Dark Night at the End of March" back in February, I thought you were self-blaming for my move-out action. When it showed up again, I realized that there must be a terrible loss for you. I felt the same pain as you did. My uncle passed away in May this year. He was the guidance of my life. I followed his footsteps to go to Beijing and beyond and to the place where I am now.

I truly apologize for your pain if it was caused by what I did. If it wasn't for that dinner, we would still be good friends; you would have talked to me all along.

Let's figure out something to reduce your burden. You don't have to carry this alone.

To help you is to help me. Remember, we are kind of mirroring each other—you feel the pain, I feel the pain.

I want you to know my marriage situation happened a few years before I knew you. I told you before and stood by my statement. Every step I made for my divorce was independent of what role you played. You bear no responsibility. Don't feel guilty about this. It is totally out of your influence, even mine.

I've shown my love to you, and you also show affection and fondness to me. I knew deep in your heart that my love will never compare to the depth and breadth of your ex-lover Leo, who broke your heart. I'd never do that. I just can't, no stone heart. That's something I never understood. If I commit to this love, I'd have a relationship with you as if we are Guo Jing and Huang Rong in the book *The Legend of the Condor Heroes* or Yang Guo and Little Dragon Lady in the book *The Smiling, Proud Wanderer* for the rest of our lives. Perhaps you and I have a little more forthright chivalry spirit since we came from the same culture.

I even thought that you can disappear from my life at any time, any moment, since I can't talk to you, contact you now. I don't know where you are. You were totally free from me in that sense. All I could do was to lower my expectations to the level that I didn't expect anything from you at all. It's OK for me to not receive any reply from you, not be treated equally, not to have an open and honest conversation, not to acknowledge my message as what regular people do like "I hear you" or "Hey, or that is hush" or "Please stop." But I care about you deeply.

The silence of treatment was the best medicine to kill the relationship. We didn't have to go with my plan or our relationship plan if you or I don't feel comfortable about it. I'd be a friend with whom you talk. There's no reason why we shouldn't do that. It's not as bad as you thought to be. There's no reason why we can't build a beautiful, fun life together if we feel clicks and sparks. You're definitely not that whale; I'm not that hunter; I'd treat you like an angel in my life. Everything will work out. Everything will be OK. I promise you!

Let's talk to figure out something that would definitely give you solid ground, a way to help you. We can untangle it later if it's needed. Don't worry about me; I am pretty sure that I can take care of myself. People sometimes do make honest mistakes. Open and honest conversations are essential for relationships. It's also crucial for any friendship to survive and grow. It's OK to text me or call me. I just switched into my own phone carrier two hours ago. Love!

Wow, Libi replied to my text at last! Tauri's phone showed a text promptly from her after a half hour.

> All you said is too much. Actually, I don't treat our relationship like you imagined; I treated you simply as an elder, not even a best friend. I'm sorry you misunderstood the relationship and the way I think. You've your own life. I'm not any part of your life. You don't need to care about me either. Likewise, I gotta go my own way. I care about what I love but not you. Please stop texting me. I wish you the best.
> —Libi

"What! Why? Is this the response I am waiting one year for?" Tauri cried out. His mind went blank.

It was early morning as he scanned through recent tarot readings. He went to bed, turned the light off, closed his eyes. But his heart raced quickly.

What's going on today? Another sleepless night? He'd had many sleepless nights recently.

⊷═◉═◖═⊷

He found himself in a movie theater. There was a screen displayed in front of his eyes. A dense forest showed up with many trees with green leaves up and down. The wind blew strongly. The leaves flew and scattered everywhere. It lasted awhile, like a hurricane ran over.

Tauri opened his eyes and realized that he was dreaming all along; the dream related to the text message from her. She denied true feelings for him.

Was she playing some game? Was she shy?

Why was she doing this?

Would she apply some tricks to push me away?

Tauri didn't feel rejected; he just felt a sense of loss. He never thought that she'd write something like that.

What could I do to win her love? Would it be possible? How?

Some tarot readers talked about the "push and pull" technique like two partners performing the tango dance. When one partner pushes, another partner pulls. When one partner pulls, another partner pushes.

If Libi was angry, I need to show love. If she shows love, I need to show anger. Tauri realized they'd have a love-hate relationship.

Some tarot readers advised Taurus to pick up a battle once at a time to fight egos.

Some tarot readers talked about dying down on this connection.

Tauri realized their action might create the strong energy flow picked up by the tarot reader community.

One reader explained what Libra's expectation was for commitment and marriage and suggested to take action to upgrade this commitment.

He wondered if he proposed marriage, she would be happier. He sent a long text message to her.

Hey, Libi,

It's me who misunderstood your song expression.

Can we talk? I may write too much. I can't hide my feelings when I have a chance to express myself. I get used to English writing and thinking. Maybe when my skill becomes good enough, I will write a book or something.

My manager always thinks that I need to improve my communication skills like written English. Every quarter, he'd set up a goal for me to improve it. Guess what? The next quarter, he'd bring up again.

"Stop texting or talking everything." Libi replied after five minutes.

"I'll do it if you explain why?" Tauri texted back.

"You make me feel sick," she shouted back.

After a few hours of thinking, he texted her a well-thought text message.

I'm sorry for causing you that feeling.

How so? Example?

Is it because of my marital status? Does a married man have freedom to express love? My court case is at the final stage. After that time, I'll be single. I've been working on this filing since last October. I don't feel shame in seeking happiness. My love is beautiful and unconditional. In fact, I want to tell you right now that I'm in love with you. I want to marry you.

Was it because of age? It is ordinary in this society for there to be a big age gap. There's French president Emmanuel with First Lady Brigitte, twenty years older. There're age gaps in married couples such as George Clooney and Amal, Madonna and Brahim Zaibat, Celine Dion and René Angélil, Harrison Ford and Calista, Leonard and Camila, Michael Douglas and Catherine, Alec and Hilaria Baldwin, Richard Gere and Alejandra, David Foster and Katharine McPhee. We'll build a most beautiful life together when we invest our energy fully.

Tauri can imagine she might be under her friend's influence for this change of heart. The song "Speechless," from the movie *Aladdin,* came into his mind. He sent the message to her at WeChat.

Libi, no one should keep you speechless.

My lady, everything will be all right.

Can I see you tonight? I can't focus on my job or anything else. Just wanted to have a huge for closure and leave.

Please give me your GPS location via Tauri@mymail.com. Or you can send me a WeChat message.

That evening, Tauri felt compelled to send her another text to explain himself.

Dear Libi,

How are you? Send peace and love. I am here for you.

I can't get into sleep. I want to see you.

What happened? Did it make you so sad ten days ago? We are so patiently looking forward to reconnecting with each other.

When you're unhappy, I also feel sad. No matter what your burden is, I am here for you.

Talk to me. Let's us face this reality. I just want you to smile instead of being sad.

No response! Tauri texted her next morning to follow up.

Hey, morning, sunshine! Hope you have a good mood today. Trust me, everything will be all right! I'll give you a call around 12:00 p.m. Are you OK?

"Just go away! F—— off." Libi replied quickly.

Ouch! Ouch! Ouch! His heart got pitched.

"Are you OK? If you tell me your story about sadness, I will be at peace," he replied.

"If you text me again, I will publish all your messages you posted. I want to see if you still care about losing face." Libi issued her warning.

Wait, what? Did she just tell me she will ruin my reputation? Tauri shouted out with both hands in the air. He took a deep breath. He thought they were in love. He felt lost.

His low energy was picked by the tarot channel "Crystal Healing Vibrations" on September 8, 2019. She spent over two hours offering advice in a reading titled "Taurus: Twin Flames Reignited. It Is Soon to Be Reunited."

Oh! She cried for this reading. Did she call me to be the bridge to *God*?

This really resonates with Libi and me. I'm stunned, speechless.

Aquarius, who is my wife, on my side, Leo, her ex-boyfriend, and Scorpio, her girl-friend, on her side. That was such an accurate dynamic in this love connection, Tauri reasoned.

Libi was my twin flame come from the same coil. She is the one. There'll be many soulmates in a lifetime, only one twin flame. A coil was cut in half that belongs to the same body.

Tauri felt the lighting striking. He could see the faint light on the far side of the tunnel.

CHAPTER 10

Written on the Stars

"Do you want to save your grace or lost face?" Libi texted Tauri after he sent her a text message about her recent sad playlist. At this point, he already knew she didn't tell the truth, her true feelings.

Something went terribly wrong! Am I crazy in my mind?

His first reaction was to fight back. No one should block me from expressing my love, seeking the truth, having this closure.

He drafted the pushback message and reviewed it once more time before he sent it out. Libi might want to carry out what she said she would do! Though I am OK with it; I have nothing to hide, not for this love. Calm down! Can't get distracted from what is coming in: the divorce proceeding, board meeting, honorable dinner event.

"Take one step back; you'll have a world." He talked aloud.

"Go away! F—— off!" How could a friend have turned into such a rude monster? Tauri developed a theory: Libi might be in an uncontrollable situation to send those text messages.

Was she held against her will? Maybe she was involved with a religious cult? He made sense out of her situation now.

There had been no change since she published the last one.

Those songs described a catastrophic event: so transparent, that moment changed everything, "She Lived," "Thought to Die for This," "Terminal Illnesses." He was convinced that she was calling for help.

In the evening, Tauri flipped through tarot readings at an online video-sharing site about Taurus. One video mentioned that Taurus would experience a difficult time during the harvest moon.

"If you need a cry, please cry it out to cleanse it," the tarot reader suggested.

Libi was sad and needed help. But she denied her feelings of love to me. Don't you underestimate me? I know that I am honest and have personal integrity; I am powerful.

I won't go speechless. He suddenly sang a phrase from a song Lara liked to sing at the breakfast table: "Speechless," by Naomi Scott.

Tauri found that song. As it played out, his tears started to pour out. You can drive me away, but you can't keep me quiet. I wouldn't be silenced by your bullying behavior. As he repeatedly heard this section of the lyrics, he cried silently. After a song ended, he clicked a replay button to hear it again.

"I won't go speechless! I need to figure something to fight back." The tears came out like a tide when he heard the phrase every time. This was the cleanse that was supposed to happen in my life at this moment. This was what that tarot reader predicted a few days ago.

He typed the keywords "Speechless one-hour loop" on an online search site to find a nonstop video of "Speechless." He felt hopeless to cry.

Deeply in my mind, I was just sad that something was lost, something was taken away. The sense of loss in the innocence he had held in his highest moral place, perhaps in the traits or characteristics of a person who was sinless, pure, trustful, and uncorrupted by ego, perhaps an inner child who, as compared to the adult, was inexperienced, with no knowledge of evil things.

"Could anyone in my friend circle be as crude as that? Would someone act like that to put a sword into your heart? Did I do any damage enough to cause this?" Tauri talked aloud and started to reflect on what he had experienced in his life.

The morning went by. Tauri kept hearing this song; his tears kept coming out.

After lunch, he decided to go for a walk on the trail in the state park.

"You'll need to find a special place where you can have your thoughts and mind clear it out," the tarot reader had suggested.

During the three-hour hike, Tauri came to the reality that Libi meant what she said.

Libi would act to destroy me. She would, she will. What do I do? I can't be speechless. This is my life, my love. She can't destroy this greatest love story in mankind.

Tauri's defiance energy was picked up by "San Tarot" at September 10, 2019. She gave out advice by telling the story in her reading titled "Taurus: Destined to Be a Way-Shower."

Yes, I always wanted to write a book about my journey from China into the United States. It'd be like Chinese immigration version of the Forrest Gump story.

OMG, that's something I can do, I want to do. I want to write what happened at that "hair-touching" event; I want to write how I have put myself into legal risk to pursue Libi like a moth flying into a flame. I want to write down my pain. I want to show the world how the spirit via tarot gave me the confidence to move life forward. Tauri's mind had a light bulb bursting out.

"Taurus, you're cocreating the life reality with your twin flame. It's a gift from the divine! It's a blessing in disguise!" Tauri was in deep thought to understand those messages from the tarot readers.

Tauri did have an *aha!* moment. He felt as if he were in a war zone. The information he gained from tarot readings was single-sided and transparent to him and really enabled him to fight this war with a complete understanding of what was in Libi's mind.

Libi was committed to me. She was planning to marry me via many songs like "You and I," "Grow Up Old with Me," "I Want to Go with You in Normal Life." But something huge happened. Someone took her girl's first night. It was not her true love, me. Tauri reasoned it out when this idea came into his mind. He felt sorry for her. Not only sad but also a pain for the experience she'd had to go through.

⊶⊷⊜ ⊜⊶⊷

Tauri kept himself away from looking at her playlist for a few days. On the fifth day, he couldn't help but click that saved-bookmark URL.

"Wow, it's empty now. It automatically redirects to a historical playlist, one hundred songs in the ranking!" Tauri exclaimed. "Nothing she wants to say? Not even 'I hate you' or 'bye-bye'?" He shouted toward the wall. "Would she want to echo my 'speechless' response in this way?" he uttered. "Why is she speechless? Didn't she worry about my misunderstanding? Did I misread her songs?" Tauri murmured.

He read the lyrics many times and found himself stuck on the phrase "tolling bell."

A bell striking slowly at a funeral service in the church. OMG, did she want to be separate at a funeral service in church? This described an end-of-life scene. Would it be a reverse way to describe staying together till the end? He translated these lyrics into a message in understandable English.

Dear Tauri,
It's been seven days since I expressed my commitment to you by the end of August. I was too egotistical and arrogant to come to have a face-to-face talk. I pretended not to care about your feelings. But you brought me happiness, which made me vulnerable to you. This filled my days with sighs, exposed to my family and friends.

But our destiny was linked with the "red wire." This truth I refused to acknowledge for so long and ultimately realized now.

If you have the same feeling as me at this moment, what do you do? Do you treat this as a regular sleepy day, or something more like "I love you"? So, I finally decided to walk away far from you. When that moment finally came,

I'd carry all my feelings into my daily life. I'd release myself from holding on to you, to wrap up those days dreaming about you.

Am I wanting to fade away to avoid you? No, that's not true. Do I want to walk out to let the moment pass by me? I always ask myself this. Why can't I move far away from you so you can't reach for me? Would I keep you as my secret in my heart and make peace within myself?

Instead, I chose to stay near you. I want to be in this life journey with you till the end, like in this no-exit room filling with the lights. When the "tolling bell" is hitting, that's when our destination of this journey reaches the end. Even we don't say goodbye to ourselves; we separated. From there, I'll let my hand go to wind up all those days. I'd move on.
—Libi

"How sweet Libi is to use this song to express in a reverse way! How sad she is to look at the end game! That's the commitment on her mind." He bubbled as he took a deep breath to think through. He felt compelled to tell her that he misunderstood her expression. He posted her a message on WeChat.

To my lady,
Your "Speechless" reminded me to reflect where our disconnect would be. I finally realized it expressed, "You and I stay in a room without exit until the tolling bell rings."

I got the impression that you were in a "situation" without an exit. This finding keeps my heart really warm. It's the expression of "life together till the end." Everyone has their own pride, arrogance, weakness. It'd be safe to expose these to your loved one.

I wanted to let you know as soon as I understood your true expression.

I felt really sad about the dark time you went through. You expressed your emotion via songs from "That Moment," "Terminal Illness," and "She Lived" to "Whale Eating." I felt helpless and powerless. I wish I was with you so you didn't need to go through those sufferings alone. There's a bright future ahead of you and us. Trust yourself.

I don't know your true situation; it's the best way to make me go crazy by letting me manufacture scenarios.

Waiting for you to talk to me whenever you're ready.
Love,
Tauri

No response from her. The tarot channel "NomadSoulWarrior" offered advice at September 27, 2019, in a reading titled "TAURUS: Someone Will Offer You What You've Been Waiting For: WLC Oct 2019."

⊶═◑ ◐═⊷

Libi's birthday was coming soon. Tauri decided to utilize this opportunity to restart this connection.

"Hey, I ordered flowers from your store before. You'd have my friend's address and phone information," Tauri told the flower girl. "Can you do a bouquet with four sunflowers in the center and twenty-six red roses surrounding it? Please add filler like gypsophila, statice, and poms to decorate it. Oh, also add some green leaves, like bells of Ireland and honey bracelet." Tauri described his idea. He was surprised he had learned so much about flowers because of Libi.

"Does this look positive, sunny?" Tauri asked her. "I also need this to be delivered."

"Sure!" the flower girl said.

"One more thing. My girlfriend and I are on a break. Can you call to confirm the address?" he asked.

"Can you stay here for one minute so I can call her to confirm?" The flower girl grinned.

"No problem. I will wait at the Subway restaurant for my lunch." He went next door.

"Sir, sir, I called!" the flower girl shouted aloud as he came back.

"And…" He waited.

"She accepted the call." The flower girl hesitated.

"And…" He stared at her with the result in his mind.

"She already moved out of the old address." The flower girl stuttered.

"And…" He became impatient.

"She said she doesn't want to anything from you. Nothing." The flower girl talked with a motionless face. Everyone at the shop looked at him and went silent.

"I really appreciate it. Thanks!" He raised his head high with a smile and walked out.

Tauri didn't show his emotion. He didn't feel sad.

Something was off between his understanding and what was genuinely in Libi's mind. Libi showed her love and affection via this playlist. But she constantly put him down in this real world.

I acted like a real fool. I'll not make further contact with her for the sanity of my self-esteem. Maybe I will track her down to ask for the closure and then move on? Maybe the magic will happen to bring her back into my life?

Tauri turned to the tarot world to find some answers. His energy was picked up by "San Tarot" on September 20, 2019. She gave him an astonishing reveal: "Where you are and what you are up to" in a reading titled "Taurus: To Make It Sacred."

Oh, the middle world is actually another term of China: "the Middle Kingdom." Am I destined to take this role? Yeah! My relationship with Libi is a gigantic myth. I am fully embedded in the situation and also outside the situation. Tarot readings let me watch my personal life unfold in real time from a higher perspective. Our love story would show the interaction between human life and the divine world. Any event that happens in our relationship, the spirits via tarot readers will describe and offer help. This relation would be a light beacon in human history and show love from the divine and God. As our love overcomes the obstacles of the age gap with blessings and financial abundance in our future life.

Wow, all those tarot readers would be part of this collective earth and cocreating process.

"My wish will come true if all those tarot readers, spirits, universe, divine, are right!" Tauri sighed after he heard this reading. "I will see what will happen next. I did my best to get the relationship to move forward."

The tarot channel "Star Seed 11:11" picked up this energy and offered her prediction. "The good news is coming in for Taurus" at September 26, 2019, titled "Taurus Next 48 Hrs.: Big Decisions."

Oh! Anything changed on her playlist? Yeah! She updated her playlist with only one song: "Big Brother Welcomes You!"

"What? Libi called me a big brother instead of a boyfriend?" This idea immediately came up. As he read through the lyrics, the number drew his attention.

"So '520' is pronounced as 'I love you' in Chinese; '66' means 'Liu, flow smoothly'; '1314' was pronounced as 'one life forever.' Libi is expressing her commitment again. Very positive," Tauri shouted out.

Libi asked for a "new beginning," the reset button. This is what I am looking for. But...but no matter how great song is, the action speaks more loudly than any words.

"The truth, the closure was what I needed to move my life forward," Tauri uttered. "I wouldn't be surprised if she didn't want to directly connect with me at all." Tauri was a little afraid to face his own ultimate truth.

Why? Why? Why?

This energy was picked up by the tarot channel "Heavenly Star" on September 21, 2019. She went to extraordinary lengths to explain the "what" and "why" questions for the Taurus community, including Tauri, in the reading titled "Taurus: Definitely Written in the Stars to Reunite and Start Your Life Together September Midmonth 2019."

OMG, she basically read my story via the cards. Is my destiny really written in the stars? Tauri was amazed about the extraordinary power of the tarot card and divine world.

If Libi can understand his love, there was no need for gifts from him, no flowers! No powerful gifts can compare to true love from the truth, the honesty, the integrity, Tauri reasoned.

A light was at the end of the tunnel?

He raised his head and looked far beyond what his court battle was about to unfold.

CHAPTER 11

A Lawful Single

TAURI WAS CONVINCED that it was in his and Aquri's best interests to be on different life paths. The attorney fees could rip off our checking accounts. Self-service divorce might be the most cost-effective way to navigate this process.

He had spent his spare time collecting their financial documents, filling out all the forms required by the court. He went through several iterations to finalize those forms during the summertime.

It's normal to be in the divorce category, since there is around a 50 percent divorce rate in the United States. The least impacting divorce is a collaborated process. Yes, I can follow this guidance to find a mediator to help with the negotiation. I can resolve any unexpected issues before the court proceedings. Tauri gained his confidence in this unknown.

"Thanks for your help to guide us through this process. I'd want to proceed with court filing by myself. This will be the last session with you. Can you give me back all the documents we paid for?" Tauri talked out after the mediator opened up the conversation at the fifth session.

"Are you OK with this, Ms. Aquri?" the lady asked.

"I'm fine with that," Aquri replied.

"Well, you may ask an assistant from the court to review your agreement. You can make sure your concerns are addressed to meet with local laws to protect women's and children's rights," she reminded Aquri.

"I really appreciate the advice," Tauri concluded.

"Yes, me too." Aquri was thankful that the lady mentioned women's protection. Tauri drove to the court and filed the case to start the ninety-day waiting requirement, since they were in a collaborative process. After two weeks, the letter from the court informed him the date was scheduled for his case.

The tarot channel "Ray of Light Tarot" picked up his energy at September 8, 2019, and offered advice with titled "Taurus | Taurus: Finding a Way to Honor the Connection, September 15–30, 2019."

⤙━◉ ◉━⤚

A parental education class was required by the court. He and Aquri went to attend.

"Is there an item we need to modify in the agreement before the court date?" Tauri asked Aquri.

"Yes," she said without hesitation. "I want to add one more sentence. You wouldn't be able to prevent me from pursuing Lara's medical treatment. You'd also not prevent me from sending her to private high school for four years!" she exclaimed. Tauri felt her forcefulness.

"Are you not going to sign the agreement?" Tauri asked.

"No," she replied in a firm tone.

"Do you not agree to divorce?" Tauri asked indifferently.

"No, I want to renegotiate all agreements before court day," she replied without hesitating.

This would drag out the divorce for months, even years. His heart sank. He was busy working on finalizing the last-minute changes for the court appearance. He had never been to one before. But he had little hesitation to give up his ground.

The tarot channel "San Tarot" picked up his energy on October 1, 2019, and offered her advice from the spirit in the reading titled "Taurus: It's Bigger Than You Think."

Yes, I'm working tirelessly to prepare all the documents. Those were all my life experiences so far: financial records, family history, photos of friends, and my career path. Too much at stake.

Tauri was aware he was on his journey to align with the divine. That is my fate; I am destined to be there. He thought about writing his book and spreading the divine's love over the world.

⤙━◉ ◉━⤚

On the eve of the court day, Aquri texted him to discuss the marital agreement.

"What's changed?" Tauri asked when he got to his old house.

"Look, there're four cashable asset items on your side; I have none." Aquri pointed at a section on a printed page.

"If you want it, let's split it up. Those are sellable assets—handy for an emergency," Tauri suggested.

"No, I need all of them," she insisted. Aquri sensed his weakness and took her bold action.

He stared at her stone face, heard her calm and firm voice. No options for me to stand my ground. I don't want to dispute in front of the judge tomorrow. This would cause lengthy court proceedings.

"Meet in the middle. Meet in the middle." One of the tarot reader's readings echoed in his mind.

"OK, those belong to you," Tauri said reluctantly.

"Do you want to defer the marriage dissolution certificate date to next year? This could keep joint tax filing status to get the tax benefit. I consulted with a law assistant and got his advice," she said.

"I want to finish this as soon as possible." He spoke firmly. "You can take the kid as a dependent this year. I don't want to stay codependent any longer." Tauri felt bullish. He found his strength to demand, with a notion that Aquri would make an excuse to delay this.

It looks like Aquri and I both want this! Tauri came up with this idea as he walked out of her house—his old house.

He had no idea what the result could be. The court proceedings would be in favor of me. His confidence came from the tarot readings; some tarot readings called a victory for Taurus. In addition to this, Aquri made a last-minute modification as the addendum to the existing agreement.

⊹⟞⟐⟐⟞⊹

Tauri met with Aquri in front of the elevator inside the court building. She walked too clumsily, as if she had gotten hurt.

"Are you OK? Do you need to see a doctor?" Tauri had lost track of her situation since he moved out of his old house two months ago. She didn't reply. They took the elevator to the fifth floor.

"Sit on that bench. Let me figure out which courtroom we are in," Tauri told Aquri.

After a while, the secretary in this court came over to him.

"I reviewed your document. It looks like you have an addendum. You'll need to go to the second floor to get approval from Family Services." She wrote a note and handed it over to him.

"Hi, I'm Susan, a legal assistant for Family Services." She looked very sharp but friendly. She flipped his documents on her desk like reshuffling poker cards.

"You missed one number here," she pointed out. "Let me quickly make a new worksheet." She turned on her computer and started to type numbers.

Wait, it took me months to come up with that worksheet. Susan wants to do it on the fly. He heard the sound of the keyboard without interval.

"Do you have another child to support?" she asked.

"Why?" Tauri was curious about this.

"If you don't have another child to support, you would remove this line. The number came up..." She carefully compared it with his number.

"This number per month is less than yours," she said as she showed them. Tauri immediately recalled the tarot reading's "turning out in your favor" comment.

"OK, let me make the new document for you." The lady started to work on it as she spoke. "Here is the number change. The percentage of the payment for child medical turned the other way around. It was made up of 60 percent of Tauri's responsible, 40 percent of Aquri's responsible. At my new calculation, it was 60 percent of Aquri's responsible, 40 percent of Tauri's responsible," Susan explained. "Do you guys agree?"

"Why is that?" Aquri demanded.

"Well, since the child support is counted as your income, you have more monthly income than your husband." She pointed at her number after she printed out the new document. "Do you guys want to make this change?" Susan asked.

"No...not really. I'd like to keep my number." Tauri looked at Aquri for a moment and told the assistant firmly. He hoped this would make Aquri feel better and remove any blockage she might raise in the front of the judge. He also wanted to do more on his part, even if he didn't know how his future would unfold.

"Look at the alimony section. You guys could adopt the custom that each party pays another party one dollar on the modifiable amount in an unmodifiable term of 7.5 years. This would keep the alimony open with the time limit." The lady pointed it out. "I'll modify those words. This would make sure those documents fit into court requirements," the assistant concluded.

Tauri walked out from Family Services with new respect toward the law professional. Wow. Susan resolved my six-month effort in front of my eyes. My court case will be smooth sailing!

"Only one more case ahead of you." The court clerk came to get them ready.

This was the first time he had witnessed a true-to-life court proceeding.

"Much simpler than what I expected," Tauri uttered as the judge read through her questionnaire. The attorneys from both parties provided either documents or verbal answers, one by one. The judge approved the request to dissolve the marriage in the proceedings.

"Do you need a Chinese language translator?" the court clerk came over to ask him and Aquri again. Hmm, Lara always called out my broken English. I felt confident to present myself in court.

"No, I don't need one," Tauri replied.

Tauri handed the signed and notarized document over to the court assistant. Then, the court guard led him to one table, Aquri to another table.

"Can Aquri sit at the same table with me since I have all the documents?" Tauri asked the guard.

"No, you stay there." The guard pointed to the table. "You, stay there!" the guard said again.

"All rise! This court is in session," the guard announced. The people in the court stood up and watched the judge walking in and being seated. In front of her table, a secretary was on her left front; her assistant was on her right side. One court guard was standing on the left side of the courtroom.

"This case is Tauri versus Aquri, a request for dissolution of the marriage." The assistant announced the case and presented the judge with a folder of the documents. The judge turned her computer on to find the case in system. The judge, a female with a soft voice, like Judge Judy on TV, stood up and asked Tauri to raise his right hand.

"I swear that the evidence I provided shall be the truth, the whole truth, and nothing but the truth. So help me, God!" the judge read.

"I do." Tauri answered.

"Have you lived in this state for over one year?" The judge started her questions.

"Yes," Tauri replied. The judge continued to go through her questionnaire. He answered most of the questions with "Yes."

"Do you feel that your marriage is repairable?" she continued to ask.

"No." Tauri was hesitant a little bit but said it with a firm voice. This is the moment that this marriage is over.

"Do you agree that you signed those agreements voluntarily? You did it under no influence against your will?" the judge asked.

"Yes, I do," he replied. This is really shocking me. This judge was like in a regular team discussion. His confidence had doubled.

"Do you agree that this agreement is fair, justifiable?" the judge asked.

"Yes, Your Honor," Tauri answered.

"I saw that you filed the initial case in August. You then filed the motion to waive the statutory period. You have an agreement of a legal separation at the end of August. The agreement was filed early in September, and you also filed an agreement addendum today. There're some conflicting paragraphs between those agreements. Do you agree that a later document will overwrite the previous document?" the judge asked.

"Yes, I agree," Tauri replied as he nodded. "We went to a child education class last weekend and found out some areas in the agreement were not covered. That's why an addendum is needed," Tauri explained.

"That is fine," the judge said. "By the way, I didn't see the education document on the system. Can you guys please go file it at the clerk's office after this? I need those documents as part of this verdict."

"Sure, I'll do it," Tauri replied.

"No more questions for you," the judge said.

"Do you agree with your husband's answers to all the questions?" The judge turned toward Aquri.

"Yes, I do," Aquri replied.

"Do you agree that you signed those agreements voluntarily? You did under no influence against your will?" the judge asked.

"Yes, I do," Aquri said.

In a short time, the judge started to wrap it up. Wow. The judge skipped over twenty questions she asked me. That is a good sign. Tauri ran this idea at light speed.

"Upon the vested power from the state, I hereby declare this case resolved. This court granted the resolution of marriage dissolution between Tauri and Aquri. You're granted as single," the judge declared as she hit the gavel on her table.

Tauri heard what the judge announced. He felt calm, not as joyful as he imagined before. Can't believe that this is over!

"Is there anything else I or we need to do after this?" Tauri asked the judge.

"No, you come back after ten days to pay twenty dollars to get the certificate." The judge looked at him and wondered why he represented himself.

"Do you guys work at lunchtime? Now it is 12:30 p.m." he said. Everyone in the courtroom laughed out.

Tauri carefully compiled the documents into the folder.

"Have lunch together? There's a noodle restaurant down the street?" Tauri asked his now ex-wife Aquri after they walked out from the elevator to head to the exit.

"How far away? My car is parked on another side of the street," she replied with a worried face. "Maybe next time." She politely declined.

He watched her walking out of the front building slowly. Oh my gosh! She seems like she is hurting physically. I wish I could help! he thought.

Like the marriage direction, Tauri walked out in the opposite exit door.

The sun was shining in this October day, a blue sky with no clouds, like a rain wash. He strolled to pass the green lawn surrounding this courthouse. He sat at the noodle restaurant with a blank mind. When the dish came, he realized he ordered the same food as what Libi had ordered one year ago. He texted his manager to take a half day off.

"One door closed! Another window open?" He posted a WeChat message to Libi with a few court-building pictures.

As he drove back to his apartment, his mind gradually came back to what he had done for his life.

Yeah! Aquri got what she wanted as much as possible.

What is left for me? Still have a job, maybe the playlist? Tauri thought suddenly about Libi, who had rejected him a few weeks ago because he was still in the marriage.

I'm legally single again.

Now what? Tauri asked himself.

CHAPTER 12

A Cocreation

NOW WHAT? TAURI asked himself after his court proceedings.

"Now there is no obstacle for me in pursuing Libi," he uttered. "Now I can find out if she's the person painted on her playlist or projected out via her text message."

"Now it's the time for Libi and me to have a real conversation." Tauri had had high hopes for this talk for over one year.

During his lunch break, he wrote a message and sent it to her on WeChat.

To my lady/bae,
I'm single now.
We've been in love. I don't see any obstacle to separate from us. I've everything we need to get together. We don't need anyone's approval, including friends and parents. I can't imagine anything else prevents you from talking to me.
—Tauri

After a few days, Libi updated her playlist with a new song, "The Love Letter."

Libi wrote me a love letter! Is there an action item in her letter? He anxiously read through.

1. "The Love Letter"
2. "The Stranger under My Skin"
3. "I Believe Our Love"
4. "She Lived"
5. "Heartbeat and Breathe Normally"
6. "The Love Story: First Episode"
7. "Only Livelihood Left at My Sight"
8. "Wild Wolf"
9. "You"

10. "Journey to Steal for the General"
11. "Focus"
12. "Beyond the Memory: July"
13. "How Do You Feel?"
14. "City Center"
15. "The Boy Walt's Worrisome"
16. "The Foundation, Ground Beyond"
17. "The Dark Night at the End of March"
18. "Seasons Die One after Another"
19. "Sorry, No One Wants Codependence"
20. "To Heartful Person"
21. "Your Commitment Will Never Be Forgotten"
22. "Seasons in the Sun"
23. "A Maze"
24. "Youthful Life"
25. "When You Are Gone, My Dear"
26. "I Am Not Your Song Dongye—Your True Love Yet to Come"
27. "Falling"

Tauri took a deep breath. He didn't see any immediate action for her to get together.

Libi still posted the "true love" question, even though I told her that I am single now. Does she suspect my legal proceedings? In his mind, this didn't make sense from her playlist; she expressed her warm love to him. But on the other hand, she broadcast the playlist to the listeners that she's not in love with. There was no logical explanation for him. He also wanted to open a door for this consolidation. He didn't know how to approach her anymore.

Tauri turned to tarot readings to find any clue in her mind. One reader mentioned that the main thing for this week was to "release your burden for Taurus."

This energy was picked up by the tarot channel "Katie McLaughlin" and published a video on October 6, 2019, in a reading titled "Taurus, Important Decisions Guiding You toward Happiness and Victory."

"Did she describe what is happening as being already planned before I was born and throughout my life has brought me to this moment?" he uttered. "She shared five techniques to ground myself at this critical moment in my life to avoid panic. I love it," he murmured.

Another tarot channel, "Mocha Love," also offered advice on this energy and released a video on October 7, 2019, titled "Taurus Pulling the Plug on Sum BullSh**, October 2019."

After long consideration, Tauri drafted a message with strong warning. I want direct contact or to be ready to walk away.

To my dear lady,

After reading your message again and again, I concluded that I can't get true meaning out of it. Sometimes I felt you were talking to me. It expressed precisely the meaning you texted me last time. Sometimes I thought you spoke to another or two persons in the same playlist.

I've almost broken my head to start direct communication with you. I even "traveled thousands of miles" to be ready to reach you. But I realized that it may be my wishful thinking. I may never have the chance to see your face or have a call or do whatever other lovers or even friends do; I may never have closure with your story or mystery, which I'm losing my curiosity quickly with.

Maybe I don't deserve your love, or you don't deserve my love.

As a result of that, I'll unfollow your "mermaid voice" to withdraw from your pool of lover competition.

But you know we're like mirrors that reflect ourselves in each other's minds. I'll always be in love with you, who's in that bittersweet, that innocent, that curiosity mind, that beauty, and grace, that true you.

I'm happy to have an open conversation with you. We can do direct calls, text in a straightforward, honest way. We can do the things you do with your friends, like hiking, having some fun together.

I'll be there for you to start a new chapter of the book.

If it's not, I wish you the very best with my whole heart.

Love and peace,

Tauri

After he pressed the Send button, he felt relieved and good about himself. I really spoke my truth without offending her. I stood up for myself. Tauri realized that this may be the way they depart each other. He felt lucky that he didn't consider her connection as the primary reason to get divorced. He didn't go with what this playlist demanded.

"Was this the reason I got divorced? No or yes." He spoke it aloud. It made sense that she cut off direct communication with me since I was in a marriage before. Now I am legally single. Yet she still didn't want to talk to me. Something was extremely fishy.

⋅⊷⊫◉⊨⊶⋅

The following day, Tauri checked the tarot reading related to Taurus zodiac sign. There're lots of videos talking about "incoming communication." He found that Libi had posted an updated playlist.

This playlist expressed mixed signals. Some songs in the context seemed to be talking to as many as three suitors watching this playlist. His heart hurt. I am the one following through to make a life change for her. He sighed.

1. "Who Knows Heart from Wondering Man?"
2. "Love Letter"
3. "Stranger under My Skin"
4. "Sleepless Night, Lil Chaos"
5. "Beyond the Memory: July"
6. "Focus on the Livelihood"
7. "Love and Honesty"
8. "Moon Tonight"
9. "Crying in the Party"
10. "Midnight Heartbroken Club"
11. "Talk about Memory Again"
12. "Cheat Myself"
13. "She Lived"
14. "Goodbye"
15. "Young Walt's Worrisome"
16. "When the Cherry Blossoms Dance"
17. "I Am Sorry, No One Wants to Be Codependent"
18. "The Thirty-Year-Old Woman"
19. "The Loneliness Lover"
20. "Easy Come, Easy Go"
21. "The Worrisome of the Amateur Writer Boy"
22. "The End of the Tunnel"
23. "The Spring, Summer, Autumn, Winter"
24. "The Love Story: The First Episode"
25. "The Life Landscape about You"
26. "The Attractive Danger"
27. "My Name"
28. "Those Sleepless Nights and Unforgettable Things"
29. "I Am Not Your Song Dongye—Your True Love Is Not Here Yet"
30. "Falling"

31. "Like New, Love Old"
32. "Good Night"
33. "The Lake: I Will Find You"

She cried for my breakup letter. Is she really in love with me? She will find me! Will she come forward? Tauri questioned.

Tauri was busy with his plan to fix the house and sell it as part of his divorce agreement. One thing he always wanted to do was to remove the small tree in front of the yard.

This tree blocked the view from the street. As time went by since he moved in, there were a few branches that had dried out and fallen down. He felt a rotten tree was not a lucky sign at all. He even contacted feng shui—literally, "wind-water"—an ancient Chinese geomancy that uses the energy to harmonize the people with their surroundings, change the luck and fortune. It was very popular in upper society in New York City. It evaluated his house. His idea for tree removal had been blocked by his family member.

Now he felt free to take action and make the house marketable.

It was a sunny Sunday afternoon. He drove to Home Depot to get a tool he needed. In just a half hour, he cut down the main trunk, then chopped the breaches and trunk into pieces and piled them up in his backyard to make his lawn clean.

Yes, this's what I wanted. Tauri looked at the neat lawn of his old house.

He returned to his apartment and noticed a sedan parked opposite his street.

"Two Chinese sitting in the car: a boy in the driver's seat, a girl with big pink reflecting sunglass sitting on passenger side. Look, they lowered their heads to play cell phones to avoid my eye contact! Oh! The girl seems young and pretty, a similar age to Libi." Tauri bubbled and was alerted.

There're only local people living in his white-majority neighborhood. It'd be rare to see people with yellow skin, dark hair, and black eyes showing up here.

He got into the house and went upstairs to take a shower and put on his clothes in just a short time to get ready to go out. As he locked the door and walked toward his car, he heard a tire squeak sound. A vehicle sped it up and zoomed it away.

It's that sedan with two Chinese. Oh my gosh, do they watch me? he questioned.

The tarot channel "Dane Hart" picked up this event and published a video on October 7, 2019 in a reading titled "Taurus, A Piece of Paradise Is Handed to You // Psychic Tarot Reading October 11–20, 2019."

Another tarot channel, "Jennifer Walker Zen," picked up this energy and published a video on October 10, 2019, in a reading titled "Libra Weekly Love OMG! Unexpected outcome! Oct. 11–18 weekly."

"Oh! Did she mention 'Libi,' 'a Libra,' and 'tree'?" he uttered.

Tauri immediately realized Libi and her friend watched him that day. They might also drive by his old home to witness the tree branches all over the front lawn.

"Libi did come to visit me!" Tauri yelled.

"This is a failed attempt. It wouldn't work since there's another guy with her," Tauri uttered. Some tarot readers suggested Taurus try new approaches for the situation.

What're the new approaches? If I call her, she wouldn't take my call; I can't text her since she already warned she'd destroy my reputation.

"She didn't say what she'd do if she receives an email." Tauri talked it out aloud.

The tarot channel "Ace of Pentacles Tarot" picked up this energy and published a video on October 5, 2019 in a reading titled "Taurus Oct. 7–Oct. 13, 2019: Their Mind's on You, but You Are a Million Miles Away! Turning Point Ahead!"

"Is one chapter finished and the other one, a new and fresh one, opening up? How?" he asked himself.

Another tarot channel, "NicLoves," even suggested that Taurus could engage the love interest in a creative work.

Ah! That's a great idea, to have her be involved in writing a book. Tauri was exuberant about this idea. He had been head-down on the book, writing for a few weeks already.

He sent her an email to propose to coauthor this book.

Dear Libi,

I have been working on a book since September of this year. The book is about two regular friends falling in love; they connected via songs and social media on a soul level against all the odds. The twists were the huge age gap with no common background. They were not in each other's daily lives, with totally opposite personalities. Their relationship is guided by the tarot readings on the twin flame of the spiritual journey.

You're in Generation X. You can offer your valuable insights for this book and invaluable ideas on story plots and endings.

I'm very confident that this book will be a huge success. It'd not only be our personal achievement but also business success. Think about the potential value of the book—it'd be marketed by your song singer's tours. It'd be published in many languages, specifically both in Chinese and English. It'd also be a movie deal for ultimate success.

I'm willing to have you as my business partner as well as coauthor. In addition, we can share 50 percent of any royalties associated with this book.

Looking forward to hearing from you.

Yours,

Tauri

After Tauri sent out this email, he went to set up a file share online account and uploaded the first a few chapters of the book. He sent the invitation to Libi's email address for editing permission. Once he was done with all those steps, he felt free for himself. I had done every communication way to reach out from me. I'd be at peace if she didn't reply back. But I knew that she would read what I wrote at this file sharing online site. How? Well, I write my story and express my feeling at this book. She will read it and respond via her playlist. Yeah! I can see the reaction. We have a direct communication in the virtual realm.

Still, why am I in pain in quiet time?

"I can't beg her to talk, since it's my problem, not her problem, right?" He talked aloud. What is the worst-case scenario? I still went through a great love story in my lifetime! During one of his daydreams, he wrote down a poem from his mind.

The Journey Must Be Taken, by Tauri

Your love gave me the inspiration,
your love gave me the pain,
your love gave me the strength,
your love gave me the intuition.

This is a journey destined to be,
travel a thousand miles to reach there,
you're the light that guided me,
enjoy the landscape along the way.

No matter what the outcome would be,
life is a journey with a legacy lasting forever,
if Cupid and Psyche made to the sacred marriage,
this love written on the stars will be in fruition.

The tarot channel "Eat Read Love Inc" published a video on October 21, 2019, to offer the reading titled "Taurus: You Will Receive Something Very Important October 22–31."

Tauri was calm to find an empty playlist at her page. No matter how I tried, what effort I made, I'm hitting the no-response stonewall.

Tauri went to search her name to see what she was up to. The result led him to LinkedIn, a professional job site. He clicked and found her page.

Let me say hello to her!

Am I totally fooled?

I'll learn my lesson if she doesn't want to connect. Or do I make a breakthrough? Tauri's mind ran crazy.

⊷══◉ ◉══⊶

The following day, Tauri got up to make his breakfast.

Whoa! It is 11:11 p.m. Is that a divine number? He saw the digital clock on his new coffeemaker showing as 11:11 p.m. as he glanced toward it unintentionally.

This's the first time I've noticed for three months since I moved in.

What were the odds that a power outage had happened at 11:11 p.m. last night? He gasped. Tauri immediately realized that it was spiritual power in action. He took a photo to prove that he was not crazy.

"No one would believe this. I swear that this's what I see," Tauri uttered.

The number didn't change. He pulled the power plug out and replunged it to reset the clock. Then it turned to 11:41 p.m.

The solid evidence of 11:11 p.m. for a soulmate connection? But what it does for my situation?

After his breakfast, he began his busy office work. When he had a chance to glance at his computer clock, it showed 11:33 a.m.

Something must be happening! Is this related to Libi?

He found a message alert from Libi at this professional website timestamped at 11:33 a.m.

OMG, it's happening. The magic is happening! Tauri muttered.

Hi,

I'm looking for a new job.

Please feel free to contact me if you have a good match with some positions open.

Thanks!

"Will do. Do you have time to have a talk tonight, like 9:00 p.m.?" Tauri quickly replied.

From her replied message and attachment, he found her home address, email.

Oh! My gosh! I thought I'd already lost her.

→═◉ ◉═←

"Tauri, you are happy today. Are you?" one of his coworkers asked. His overflowing joy made him walk outside of the office building to cool himself down.

It was a cloudy and chilly day. He spent ten minutes circling the building with only a thin T-shirt on this autumn day. He felt cool outside but warm in his heart.

"Sure, I'm available between 8:00–9:00 p.m.," she replied later that afternoon.

"Great, thanks!" He firmed the appointment.

Was this a new beginning with Libi?

What would this new approach bring to me?

Tauri couldn't hide his joy. However, some tarot readers predicted that Taurus would experience an emotional roller-coaster ride.

"I can handle this roller-coaster ride," Tauri yelled.

This seems like the uplift on a roller coaster. Is there downward? he wondered.

CHAPTER 13

The Partnership Forged

"Long time, no see." Libi greeted him in the phone.

Libi's voice was soft. Tauri had not talked to her for over a year. He felt he'd just spoken to her yesterday.

"Where is your business proposal? Can you put it on the screen so we can modify it together?" he suggested.

"Sure, let me do it right now." She responded promptly.

"What service are you going to present?" he asked. "Hmm, it's the payment processing company. Your expertise and service are what they need," he said as he looked at the proposal in detail. "Let's understand the business model of this company first," he continued. "This company provides services for transaction settlement. It takes a percentage of proceeding as a commission fee. So the merchant or store can provide a convenient way for the customer to pay; the customer is also willing to spend more since it's easy to pay." Tauri felt dry for all his talking.

"Hmm...the merchant is like the song 'Little Carelessness Seller' you posted." Tauri found the example for both of them to understand. He could feel her grin. The conversation naturally turned into his favorite topic: her playlist. Tauri pointed out a few things he used to do at his office; Libi seemed to be happy to listen to his views.

They both avoid talking about the topic important to them. They knew it.

The time passed quickly.

"Well, I am sorry for treating you badly." Libi lowered her voice to break the ice.

Boom. His mind was spinning. He knew she referred to "the text message."

"I also felt hurt the last time," she said with a trembling sound. He knew she referred to the "hair-touching event," which she'd texted him back with "I felt sick about what you did."

The silence crept in for a few seconds.

"Let me talk about that from three perspectives." Tauri broke the silence. He had thought about this question before.

"First, I am sorry if that caused any emotional harm for you. Truly sorry." Tauri offered a genuine apology. Even though Libi can't see him, she can hear his quivering voice. He doesn't usually apologize to anyone; he felt that he can say, "I apologize for this." It was a polite way to show empathy. But not "I am sorry." This one was coming from his heart.

"It's always in my mind if we'd ever see each other again, I'd let you touch my hair so we can be even." He offered his silly idea to settle the score. He heard silence from another end.

"Well, I felt our bond there, true bonding. I didn't feel offended or take any advantage from you; you didn't resist." He offered his true defense.

"Your family issue should be resolved by yourself." She lowered her voice to turn to his recent event. She apparently thought about offering her empathy for what he went through.

"Libi, yes, I mentioned it to you in my message on the *Breakaway* trip. She and I mutually agreed to depart in this way," Tauri said sincerely. It truly reflected what happened during his divorce drama.

"I prepared all my documents. It's complicated. I filed my case, went through the lengthy process, and even represented myself in the court to face the judge. It's a friendly, self-represented divorce. My ex-wife didn't bring any disagreement." He described the process as if someone else had done it. He still didn't believe he did it. He paused for a moment.

"I'm sorry I sent those texts last time. I didn't mean it." Libi brought back this topic again.

"Did you send them by yourself?" Tauri had a chance to ask her directly.

"Yes," she replied.

"When you sent the text to make me go away, were you with someone?" He always imagined that someone whom the tarot world called Scorpio drafted those messages.

"No, I was alone," she mumbled.

"I'm in love with you; I made all the effort to try to reach you." Finally, he couldn't control himself to say what he always wanted to say if he had chance to talk to her again. He chose the words carefully by saying, "I am in love with you" instead of "I love you." He finally made his breakthrough to let her know his commitment.

"The love is caring. You are my soulmate, who is the last person in my mind before I go to my bed and the first person on my mind when I wake up in the morning." He talked at the phone, but he faced toward the computer screen. He felt he was bold enough to talk about what was in his mind since she couldn't see his face.

"Am I that person to you? If that's not the love, what's the love?" he cried out. Tauri could fight through all the obstacles without fear, but he felt misunderstood by the one in his dream.

"Well, I already told you I treated you as my elder friend. But of course, a friend might instantly mirror the other. But to you, I treated you as more than a friend; I don't have feelings to have a love relationship with you." She spoke softly and slowly.

Tauri stared at his phone screen and tried to see through her face.

"What about the playlist? All the interactions and love expression from you?" Tauri yelled it out.

"What's the playlist?" she asked.

"The playlist you posted at the Chinese online music-sharing site?" He was puzzled. "See, I sent the WeChat message to you a few days again. You updated your playlist with thirty-three songs to explain your life." He described the details of each song. She was quiet.

"The song 'Midnight Heartbroken' may be involved with a bar incident. There's a song talking about your guy friend hiking at the highest mountain at my state." Tauri listed those songs one by one in his memory at her playlist.

"He's my colleague at my last company." Libi broke her silence to explain it.

"The next three songs were referring to your girlfriend who was thirty years old, a lonely lover?" Tauri posted his question. "There's a song, 'Lake,' at the end of the playlist who committed to this relationship with no regret. The person will come to find her or his lover." Tauri felt that he didn't describe the full power of her playlist.

"I don't know what you refer to!" Libi exclaimed.

Tauri quickly went to that music site, made a screenshot, and sent it to her via text message.

"That's not my playlist. I swear," she shouted out. "See, the gender is male." Libi pointed it out.

Tauri looked at the owner, a male sign with the image of a blue circle and pointer right upward. He went to check the other female user with the image of pink circle with pointer left downward.

"See, the owner's name is 'Anonymous.' Not me!" She maintained her calm manner to bring up a few more things to support her.

His mind went blank.

Libi seems sincere, Tauri told himself in his mind.

"I followed your photo of 'n55!W!' last February and found this online music site with the same folder name and come to this playlist." He still wanted to argue. "See, I posted my feelings to you at WeChat; someone updated this playlist to respond to me. Do you see the interaction?" Tauri wanted to get to the bottom of it.

"That's not my playlist." Libi stood firm.

"How could that be possible? That image 'n55!W!' came from your WeChat profile, which linked to your phone number." Tauri wanted to stare at her eyes to see if she'd evade.

"My number may be used by some other people." She argued as a possibility.

"Is your roommate accessing your phone?" Tauri didn't want to rest this topic.

"That's possible." She talked at the usual speed.

"Is your girlfriend your roommate?" Tauri suspected.

"No." She shouted it back right way.

Tauri felt shocked to hear what Libi said.

"Are you saying that someone got the WeChat message I sent to you, then came up with the playlist to respond to me? Who has your WeChat account access? Was it your roommate?" Tauri repeated himself again. He came up with an impression that someone else may have updated this playlist to flirt with him, even mind-control him.

Was there another person other than Libi in this game? His mind came up with the word "game."

"Are you saying there has been someone else using this playlist to express her love with me? You don't know who that person was?" He didn't understand this. He didn't understand himself.

"If I can't find this person to get the closure, this'd leave a hole in my heart. Do you know that?" He made a plea for her to help him.

This was the first time in his life when he'd pulled into the unknown lover and followed her to make life changes to pursue her. This made him feel stupid. He'd been mind-tricked for so long. He felt lucky that he didn't commit suicide, even. Sometimes he felt helpless, powerless, and trapped.

"Libi, I think that you've a personal character disorder. You need to see a doctor. You posted a song, 'Me and Myself,' which talked about two characters within one person. Are you like that?" Tauri was shocked to hear himself bring out this honest question. He still didn't give up the notion that it was Libi who owned the playlist.

She didn't reply at first, then said, "Can we not talk about that?" She softened her voice.

The conversation went through a moment of silence.

"Hmm...did you try to get revenge?" Tauri said it again.

"No, I didn't," Libi replied.

He thought through a few the scenarios. If she'd treat the "hair-touching" event as being taken advantage of, she might be determined to take revenge to make him pay the price. Tauri had been considering this scenario. The evidence had been mounting as she'd continued to block her communication with him.

He wasn't totally convinced. He'd known her for over three years already. He'd trusted her on this.

At this point, he didn't know whom he could trust. He felt cheated by this situation.

"I broke up with Leo two years ago. I didn't contact him after that. I had a relationship with a Singapore guy who liked to play guitar last February. We had a lot of arguments and broke up. Because of this, I decided to move to New York," she explained.

"Are you still in that company?" he asked.

"I left that company this May," she replied.

The conversation turned into a lighter mood.

"I noticed that you always wear pants. The girl loved to wear a skirt. Do you wear a skirt?" Tauri asked. He felt strange she also had pants on from the photo he collected about her.

"No, I always wear pants," Libi confirmed.

"What about this?" He asked a few questions in her personal life.

"I don't want to talk about that." She firmly spoke after a while. "Can we return to our work and forget those questions?" She protested one more time.

"We need to go through your business proposal to modify it. Work on the rest of it tomorrow?" Tauri suggested. As far as we keep talking, I am happy at this moment.

"Sure, I will do it. Good night!" Libi politely closed up the conversation.

Tauri noticed his phone showed four hours of calling time. He had been waiting to have this conversation with her for one year, four months, twenty-four days, two hours, five minutes, and ten seconds.

⊷═◉ ◉═⊶

It was a new day when Tauri woke up the next morning. He was in a good mood. He flipped through the tarot readings to check the Taurus energy readings. Some tarot readers talked about Taurus's reunion with the soulmate.

"I guess the phone conversation was kind of a reunion, a remote reunion." He smiled toward the mirror. At lunchtime, Tauri sent Libi a direct text message about one of the tarot readings.

> Libi,
> I can't help to share this tarot reading video with you.
> Remember this video is just another viewpoint. So just try to understand it. Don't need to take it personally.
> It's this phrase that struck me. "If people repay good with evil, the evil will never leave from people's house. The people will stay in the cycle of one tower with another one."
> You've not acknowledged our real connection yet. This letter is written to the person who created the playlist to express love to me.

Tauri felt she was back to a normal friend now. However, he almost forgot that she'd not responded to his direct messages for more than one year.

"Call?" he asked when the next scheduled time came.

"Okay," she replied. Libi wrote formal English, like "Okay" instead of "OK" or in short as "K."

"Libi, you need to mention what your experience is." He brought up personal integrity as one of the good traits in the corporate world.

"See, there's a new VP at my group. He gave us a half hour, talking about the most important personal traits in the corporate world. He condensed it into only three sentences." Tauri hesitated to continue.

"What are the three sentences?" She was curious.

"Say what you do! Do what you said! Say what you did!" Tauri talked slowly to make sure that she listened clearly.

"What does it mean?" she asked.

"'Say what you do' means to talk about what you plan for action. Once you have the plan, you need to perform 'Do what you said,' to do what you plan to do. Once you carry out your task, you need to do 'Say what you did,' to report what you worked on. You can stand by your planning, carrying out your plan, and honestly reporting about the result." Tauri talked to his team at every possible occasion.

"This'd be the same to your personal life. You always need to be true to yourself, especially to your love life." He felt he was onto something. By referring to this personal integrity, he still wanted to know the owner of the playlist. She kept silent as she muted the phone and talked to another person.

"Can we start to go through the rest of the work?" Libi asked. Tauri suggested a different approach to phrase it when they went through the proposal. She modified it on the fly on the screen. They really worked like a team.

"Did you throw the chocolate away with my flower basket on that Thanksgiving Day?" Tauri asked. He randomly threw out the question to her.

"I ate with my coworkers. We ate it all." She grinned.

"Are you married?" he asked suddenly.

"No, I'm not." She answered right away without thinking.

"I still have a chance, do I?" Tauri joked. He could hear her smiling face. She was in a relaxing mood for this moment.

"The tarot reader said the true lover would change in the DNA level. So they'd grow to mirror each other." Tauri brought out his favorite topic.

"Uh!" She continued to type.

"Look at my photo at this professional website. My face is round; your face is long like a swan egg." He flattered her as this kind of face is a standard of beauty in Chinese culture.

"I found my face is becoming long," he told her as she kept busy typing.

"I found my face is becoming round," she replied in a strange tone.

"Yes, was that unusual? You look different compared to last year," Tauri told her. Tauri couldn't see her face.

"Do you know the funny thing about a long face?" Tauri asked.

"No, tell me?" she replied.

"Having a teardrop last year, it still didn't reach down to your cheek this year." Tauri talked slowly and read it.

"How so?" She stopped typing.

"It describes how long does it takes for a teardrop to travel down the face." Tauri repeated himself again. Libi giggled. She finally got it.

"Do you know the Chinese ancient poet Mr. Su Shi, who lived between 1037 and 1101?" He showed off his knowledge.

"Not really. I heard his name. What's he good at?" she asked.

"One day, Mr. Su Shi and his little sister joked to spat. His little sister looked pretty. But her forehead was large and slanted backward with deep eyes. Mr. Su Shi came with a poem to mock her: though you're two or five steps away from the door, your forehead is already outside. His little sister giggled. She found Mr. Su Shi had a long horse like face as long as over one foot. She ridiculed back: a teardrop came out in last year; it didn't reach to your cheek this year. Mr. Su Shi stroke her head and laughed tears out." Tauri finished his story. He heard her contagious laughter.

"This one is what I like most."

"It is called 'Intimacy Night,' by Mr. Su Shi, and translated by Lily." Tauri read it word by word from his phone.

A moment of intimacy at night worth of tons of gold,
Scented flowers sweet while dim moonlight cold,
On the tower singing and wind music fade quiet,
In the courtyard a swing is lonely at a deep night.

"How beautiful it is!" Libi sighed. She knew this poem had been used to describe the lovemaking moment among lovers. He heard her voice quivering.

"Li...bi...we are changing to mirror each other on physical appearance. Do you know what it means?" he uttered. "Libi, life is a journey. Go with your true love. Go with what your heart wants, no matter who that person was." Tauri tried to let Libi admit her love to him.

"I will wait awhile. I will do later," Libi muttered.

"Did you still have the bear I delivered to you?" Tauri thought about another question.

"What bear? I didn't receive any bear." She's sincere.

"I built a 'happy hugs teddy' at the Build-A-Bear shop. It's a bright brown and white teddy bear. When you press the paw, there's a Barney song, 'I love you, you love me,' that comes out." Tauri searched the lyrics of the song and texted her.

Tauri sang this to her via phone. There's a romantic feeling in the air transmitted into the airwaves. Tauri can't hear anything from Libi, but he can feel her flushing face.

"You posted a song, 'Pathological Change,' which referred to the bear?" he continued.

"I didn't receive any bear." She listened and kept silent. Tauri felt that she knew this song in her heart.

As the clock was pointing to 2:00 a.m., the last section was still being worked on. He read it out to make sense of it and have her come up another way to express it.

"Well, I am such a smart guy. I did great work." Tauri found the reason to congratulate himself. She burst out in giggles.

"I stayed so late with you. I read poems to you. You need to com...pen...sate me. I de...served it." Tauri talked silly. They both stopped talking. The air seemed frozen.

He could only hear her gasping gently with a deep breath. Tauri's mind ran into an image that he and Libi would hold each other in the late evening beside the computer table. His blood started to pump up into his face. His breath was short. He could hear his pulse zooming in.

Tauri felt to reach out to touch her hair. He slowly put his lips on her. An intimate feeling came out throughout his body. He was aroused.

After a few seconds, Libi calmed down from gasping breath.

"It's too late." She laughed nervously. They kept a moment of silence.

Tauri felt she and he were on the same page in the love zone. In his mind, this was the first time he felt they were connected on a mind, soul, and physical level.

This "clicked" moment was so strong that only the loved one could feel it. He reconfirmed his belief that Libi was the *one*, his true love.

They finally finished the last section of her work in the early morning.

"Do we want to continue to work on this? There's still something to be tuned," he suggested.

"I may not have time this Thursday evening. So let's get together this Friday to get this done." She checked her schedule.

"Can you please wake me up tomorrow at 8:00 a.m.? I need to go to work," Tauri whined.

"Sure, I'll do." Libi talked in a smiling tone.

For that night, Tauri had a sound sleep he had not enjoyed for months.

CHAPTER 14

Ms. Runner, the Pusher

TAURI WOKE UP next in a wonderful mood. I can conquer the whole world with Libi back in my life. He smiled and smiled whenever he thought about this.

He sent a set of direct text messages to her.

Libi, good morning, sunshine!
You forgot to wake me up. I am missing my work.
Just kidding. Having such a good mood.
Remember to continue to work to finalize your proposal.

"OK, will do," Libi replied in the late morning.

"I slept only three hours this morning," the whiner texted back. "Felt sick. It must be lovebug, lovebugs, love buggy!" The lover texted again.

In the evening, Libi sent a text message to Tauri: "I'm so sorry I can't meet with you tomorrow because I'll have to prepare a series of client meetings."

The next day, Tauri thought out what she had been doing. He felt that he could help her on other perspectives. "Are you sure that you don't want to meet again? I feel that I can help," he texted her. "It may save you from doing research for a few hours if we talk fifteen minutes." He pitched his idea. In Tauri's mind, he had what he called million-dollar book project he wanted to talk to Libi about.

"Hey, is there anything I said that made you uncomfortable? Please let me know. Otherwise, I don't know what's in your mind," Tauri said.

There's no response from her. She seems to be in another world.

Tauri felt strange. He left a note for her at the professional site since she was actively on it.

"Hey, just want to confirm that you'll still be available for our talk? I am available after 9:30 p.m. Let me know ahead of time," he reminded her.

There was no response from her.

This evening was slow for Tauri. He replayed every conversation and moment for the last two marathon phone conversations to figure out if what she said was true.

In the late evening, Tauri began to suspect that her client meetings might not be true to life. She might be consumed by more important things than the task she desperately needed.

What's that kind of situation would she be in? This question kept coming up in his mind.

The tarot channel "Deep Thoughts with Dana" picked up this energy and published a video on October, 25, 2019, in a reading titled "Taurus. Warning! Run Now!"

Oh! She woke up at 3:00 a.m. to deliver this reading. The tarot reader was really a professional.

With his suspicion, Tauri went to search online to see if there was any court case related to Libi. He found her job training certificate public available to confirm what she said.

Why is she totally unavailable during the weekend? He wondered and recalled their conversation again.

"Do you need any help from me?" Tauri had asked Libi about financial help at the last phone conversation. "Do you need money or anything like that?" He repeated his question with sincere concern.

"No, I don't need it," Libi confirmed.

Tauri was told that she went to many network events in Manhattan and had a few client meetings without much success.

Oh! She did mention her part-time bookkeeper job in the Bronx, New York.

What kind of job takes precedent over her client prep? Don't go negative! The negative thought could manifest the negative result. The tarot reader's advice echoed in his mind.

It was a Sunday morning in the autumn. Tauri was invited to a dinner party in New York City.

How about paying her a surprise visit since I am at her neighborhood? Maybe a breakthrough? Tauri was excited about this idea.

He sent her a text message right before he left his home.

Hey,
Today is supposed to be sunny. Instead, it has been raining since your mood was not cheerful. Do you see how powerful and lovely you were?

Hmm! The sun just broke out.

I'm attending a going-away dinner party tonight and will be done around 7:00 p.m.

Since I'm already at your neighborhood, do you mind if I come over to say a quick hello? I'll ring your doorbell so we can continue to work on your proposal. I could be at your place around 8:30 p.m.

I'll give you a magic wand telling me to change the plan. For example, I'll not come if you text me three times like "I'm not available."

That's a fun idea. Otherwise, I'll use my free will to do a good thing for you and me.

Libi would have time to cancel my plan to visit her! Tauri checked his phone periodically.

The tarot channel "Jodi Stadeli Mahoney" picked up this energy and published a video titled "Taurus! Congratulations! The time has come!" on October 25, 2019.

Yeah! Even the tarot reader felt it happening for me.

Continued from the End of Chapter 1

Tauri's hands were still uncontrollably shaking, though he drove away a few street blocks. He stopped his car to set a GPS location.

A stranger could have treated me politely. Why was Libi so rude to me? She was totally out of character!

For some reason.

What were the reasons?

Is she involved with some illegal activities? Tauri recalled Robert, a young owner's question. A single pretty girl dressed well in a rental hotel with people coming and going. That was a warning sign to Robert.

Is this a *Pretty Woman* movie, the Libi version? Tauri asked himself.

It looked like Libi was doing some underhanded work. Tauri can't wipe his thought off his mind.

His heart was heavy. If Tauri didn't see it in front of his own eyes, he wouldn't believe that this was a girl he knew and trusted. He felt a hole in his heart.

"Libi needs help!" Tauri yelled.

She definitely didn't expect me to show up at her door. Did she use another phone? Why did she move in here to live in a hotel room from an apartment? His mind wandered all the places as he was on the way home.

"Did I look like a psycho or mentally crazy person to her?" he asked himself.

The tarot channel "Lee Sur Pisces Moon" picked up this energy and published a video titled "Taurus Love. Someone Worried to Death about You and Your Next Move!" on October 29, 2019.

"Why did a friendly visit turn into a crime scene?" He cried it out. He felt lucky that the owner didn't call the cops.

A few scenarios flashed through his mind.

Something happened in that room that made Libi so mad about his visit. What was a single girl doing at a hotel room in the late evening, with her makeup on, in the professional, casual attire? Could I accidentally bump into her appointment with her client? Tauri recalled her playlist. A song called "Who Understands the Heart of Prodigal?" gave him a hint on what Libi was up to. Owner Robert's comments also made his stomach sick.

Tauri felt strongly that Libi needed help.

"Who can help her? Her parents are not here. Should I contact her friend?" Tauri blurred.

He finally got back to his apartment around midnight. I am happy to be home, a place to rest a piece of my mind.

He went to the kitchen to make himself a bowl of fruit salad when it was usually his most relaxing time. He was still shaking with what happened at Libi's place.

"Do you need any help?" Tauri recalled asking Libi over the phone a few days ago.

Maybe she's enjoying this kind of lifestyle, dating different people. Tauri came up with a worst-case scenario in a negative view.

He went through a few tarot readings. Some tarot readers suggested that Taurus can't change someone; they can only change themselves.

"Yeah! God can help only those who help themselves," Tauri muttered.

If Libi's that kind of person, she's not worth my love. His mind became clear and straight.

Tauri turned on his phone and began to delete all the text messages sent to her. He went over the WeChat message he wrote explicitly for Libi to delete those posts.

I want to remove her from my memory, my life at all. Tauri flipped through one by one to see how they got to this point.

Those interactions were so beautiful. It's a great love story. I was in love with her. This girl made my life change forever. I knew her in a past life, even though we only met in person a few times. Tauri went into his memory lane.

Let me set the permission for the WeChat message as private. It took him a half hour to turn off all his love messages to her. He felt his heart was protected.

The following morning, he drafted a message and sent it to her before he left his home to go to his office.

Libi,

Thanks for coming out to show me that you're not held against your will, a free person.

By moving from where you stayed into temp. rental, are you try to avoid facing me? Do I look like a psycho to seek revenge? You felt guilty about something you did to me. Is that because you used the playlist to express love, which caused my marriage breakdown? But as I told you, that's not my reason. Your playlist just inspired me to pursue the wonderful life. Even if you're behind the curtain to pull me into the love mirage, in reality, you're not the person you said to be.

I forgave you on that.

I don't feel angry.

I just felt sorry for you.

I believed that we have a soulmate or twin flame connection.

At this point, our trust and personal integrity were broken.

I'm so glad yesterday I got the sense of who you are by my own eyes.

You need to seek professional help for your mental issue. This may relate to personality disorder or borderline issue.

Please always remember: you say what you do; you do what you said; you say what you did.

Without personal integrity, you'd always be living from one drama to another, moving from one place to another one to hide from some psycho hunting you down.

I'm not psycho; at least you don't need to be afraid of me.

You'd be better than that.

Best wishes for your future luck!

After he sent the message, he felt that he needed to warn her about her owner's concerns. One of the tarot readers advised the way to win the true love back is to completely release it.

Tauri decided to break up with Libi. He sent her a text message.

Libi,

By the way, Robert, the landlord guy, asked me if you're a prostitute. I told him you're my friend. You're not that kind of person. Please be careful. You need to understand the regular people's attitude toward the suspected activities.

Since my love for you is unconditional, I want to help you out from the situation.

I am in love with you, since we have a soulmate and twin flame connection. I want to marry you to build a wonderful life together. Fate will win. The only question is how long and how much suffering before we can get together.

Our connection is destined.

Since you didn't acknowledge your love to me, I'd start my dating life now.

Hope you have a good life.

Tauri heard the alerts from Libi's returned message within minutes.

Tauri,

I don't know what you said to the landlord that caused his misunderstanding. I just have two calls with you without doing anything. I said I don't want to talk to you.

I've already claimed I don't love you.

You're the one who needs the therapy of mental health.

You always have the fantasy and imagination, which doesn't exist between us.

What you did makes me sick!

Don't talk to me.

Thank you!

"Will do," Tauri replied in short.

Tauri totally lost the direction where he was going. He didn't feel defeated. He started to question the accuracy of the tarot readings.

He checked her playlist again to see if she had any new messages. She did.

1. "Who Knows the Wondering Heart?"
2. "The Moon Tonight"
3. "Crying in the Party"
4. "Heartbroken at Midnight Club"
5. "Cheat Myself"
6. "Say Goodbye"
7. "Worrisome of the Youth Writer"
8. "Far Away at the End of the Sky"
9. "Spring, Summer, Fall, Winter: Who Accompanies Me on This Life Journey?"
10. "For Your Landscape in Your Lifetime"

11. "My Name"
12. "Good Night"
13. "Lake: I Will Commit to You and Come to Find You"

Tauri translated her playlist into the message.

Who understands my wandering heart?

Tonight, under the moon, I cried and was heartbroken at midnight after saying goodbye to you. I am cheating myself and hiding my true feeling from you.

For you, a worrisome amateur writer, you're far away from me in physical distance, age, etc.

Who'd go with me on this life journey in spring, summer, fall, winter?

Along the landscape in your lifetime, it'd be on my name forever till you rest in peace like "Good Night."

I'll commit to you and come to find you!

"Was Libi still committed to me? I can't consolidate what I felt and what I saw," he uttered.

The tarot is a stack of cards made by the designers who wrote the messages on the card. When the reading happened, the cards were presented randomly. The tarot reader's understanding or channeled message tell a story.

Would it be true to life for the divine power to exist, even if it's proven to not be realistic in my situation? But there must be reasons why tarot had existed for a few centuries.

If tarot reading prediction is true...

If Libi' expression via playlist is true...

If Libi is doing some underhanded work...

If I had a misunderstanding on Libi...

If...

If...

If...

Tauri's mind was in a free loop.

CHAPTER 15

Mr. Puller, the Chaser

TAURI LOST THE direction where this relationship was going.

"I'm done with Libi. I don't want to bring all the drama to my life," he uttered.

"Your love interest is famous in a public place, very charming, intelligent, an authority figure," tarot readers mentioned at multiple readings.

Tauri took a beach walk to think through this.

Libi shared a song, "Kiss Everywhere," which described an escort girl's experience. Could she be involved with that kind of role? Tauri flashed this idea. She'd make herself visible at an online dating site.

He went to search "online dating service." A screenful of websites showed up. One of sites, called "The Moonstar Online Dating," caught his eye.

Bingo! Tauri gasped. This is the magic of the tarot readings. He was thrilled. He registered an anonymous email account alias name as his childhood name and signed in to this dating site. The site showed the attractive, pretty girls and handsome guys.

Look! This girl Monicana looks familiar, but her side face is in shadow!

It's a profile photo with a girl sitting on a wooden groin on the sandy beach. Her right face rested on her palm, the pose as *The Thinker*, a bronze sculpture by Auguste Rodin, which darkened her left face as her eyes looked down at the sandy ground. With her round left shoulder naked, her long black-bluish flowers on a white skirt made her a unique eye-catcher. Her left hand held a sun hat resting on her crossed legs, which emitted an artistic aurora. The background was filled with a blue sky with white clouds, and a deep blue sea reached a far sky as the white waves were pounding the sandy shore.

She looked as pretty as in a classic painting.

Tauri immediately recognized her signature long silky black hair, her half oblong typeface with dense eyebrows. It was a typical classic Chinese pretty girl.

Libi told me that she doesn't wear skirts last time. But this Monicana wore a long skirt. Tauri noticed this. She was not happy. Was she? He felt her worrisome face expression.

Whoa! That makes sense. She posted a seductive girl's photo from the Japanese movie *My Raining Day* on WeChat one time. It's a story about an escort girl falling in love with an elder teacher. Was she inspired by that movie? Tauri couldn't hide his hyper fever about this finding.

Any other roles she was playing? Tauri felt sorry for her. It was he who had encouraged her to come to the United States to pursue a new life four years ago. He felt a sense of responsibility to help her out of her trouble.

"Dance through the night!" Tauri recalled Libi's WeChat announcement; he could imagine she and her friends shaking their twisting bodies with loud music under the faint light.

Monicana, nice name!

Tauri noticed her profile photo at WeChat changed when he checked it: the cherry blossom trees on the bank of a small river.

Libi used this photo to give him a hint about time.

Why is it in spring, not in Christmas?

Would she be under some contractual obligation that needed seven months to be free?

Would she? Tauri's mind was running wild.

—⬥—

It was a Halloween day.

"Right now, she must be in a nightclub to dance with her friends or clients," Tauri muttered.

I'd let her go, or should I? He was in huge agony.

Since he found this girl Monicana with a picture like Libi, his intuition convinced him that Monicana was actually Libi.

"Monicana, can we schedule a time to have a chat?" He sent a request. But Monicana never replied to his message.

His energy was picked up by the tarot channel "Tattoo Tarot" on October 30, 2019, and offered a reading on this topic titled "Weekly Taurus: Opportunity of a Lifetime; It Will Be So Worth It."

Did she call me to express myself to make the magic happen at the last hour of Halloween night? How about talking to Monicana as if she were Libi? The divine is on my side! Tauri came up with an idea sending out the message at 11:11 p.m., the synchronized divine number.

At 11:11 p.m. on this spooky night, Tauri kicked off the messages line by line to Monicana in her private chat room.

Hi,

Knock! Knock! Who is there?

Hey, Monicana, can we connect?

I saw you have a good heart. I want to know if you can coach me on how to talk to my girlfriend.

I'm already in your VIP status. I would appreciate your time. When do you have time available?

There're stars twining in your profile. That was lovely. I like it. You look pretty.

Monicana, how is your Halloween going? Someone told me that tonight is going to be a magic night. The good thing happens at the last hour. I guess that I try to get some dating advice from you.

I hope good things happen for you. When the magic happens, your dream will come true.

Are you there?

I asked for a date, a chat with you.

It looks like you are not available. I can pay whatever amount you charge with other clients. I just want to tell you my story as part of the dating advice fee.

I have a girlfriend, Libi.

You're a nice girl, a good listener. You never replied back to me on what I wrote to you so far, not even to say hello. Sometimes you made me wonder if there's a real person there.

Sorry I mentioned the money. I shouldn't do that since you didn't even reply to me yet; you and I could build up a friendship if we ever connect.

I know you'd like my personality. I'll make you laugh since my zodiac star matches you at 70 percent compatible if you are Libra.

My girlfriend always talked to me with harsh words like "I don't like you!" but her voice was soft. Her laugh was soft; her heart was soft...I mean, tender...while I chatted with her some other time. So I made jokes to make her laugh; I even sang Barney's song "I love you; you love me" to make her giggle.

We've two channels to communicate with each other. With direct phone or text, Libi is very tough. She pushed me away a few times; she wrote back I was an imaginative and fanciful person. However, in an indirect space, she always uses a playlist or pictures as a metaphor to express her love to me, share her life experiences, show our future plans.

I really wish she could express her true feelings to me as an equal give-and-take in direct communication. I hope this magic happens. Magic does happen.

I'm in love with her. However, she seems to be in doubt about this relationship.

She hinted our love would blossom next spring at yesterday's indirect message. Why spring? That's still seven months away.

Can the love be put on hold? If she doesn't love me, why would she use the playlist to express her commitment to me?

I told her she painted a mirage love relationship with me last year. She responded directly as "I claimed I don't love you." But later, she deployed a playlist to express this love is genuine, not fabricated.

I got so confused.

I guess she must be under the control of someone whom she lived with. How'd this happen in this free society?

I've a stable job with a high salary. I also have the funds to buy a house. However, I can't make any plans, since she's not on the same page with me.

I'm working on an excellent book project with great financial promise with 100 percent success. Libi disagreed with my idea, even though I am willing to split 50 percent of royalty to have her to participate in this book.

I understood she worries about our future. But I'd say let's enjoy this moment first. Though couples get married with the mindset to live forever. Unfortunately, there is a 50 percent divorce rate in the United States. So they're tied to the forever-ever together knot instead of enjoying every moment as if today is the last day of marriage. That mentality would make her and me cherish every moment we're together, appreciate every little detail of our life. How wonderful is that?

I also want her to know her worry is not warranted. It's only in her mind. It's not a hurdle between us.

We can enjoy what we have now and worry about life ten or twenty years later. We'll leave each other when we feel in our heart.

I am in love with her and want to marry her.

I may invite you to our wedding if this magic happens. She mentioned to me in a song that my dream would come true. That means she'd marry me.

I checked every tarot reading with my zodiac sign. I was convinced that this connection is divinely guided and destined.

I'm not sure this will definitely happen since there'll be also free will.

I like a song she posted for me, "If I Can." The lyric said, "Can we stay together?" to celebrate our third anniversary.

I guess that I'm telling my story as if I am Forrest Gump sitting in a chair to tell his story to passersby. I hope that my story didn't bore you.

Thanks for reading my story!

Have a good night!

⊶▬◉▬⊷

Once Tauri sent those messages line by line, the time had just passed midnight.

Where was the magic? Tauri didn't see any response from "Monicana" Libi. He wondered about the effeteness of what the tarot reader talked about. This energy was picked up by the tarot channel "BE. ByHER" on October 31, 2019, and published in a video titled "Taurus: It Is in the Cards You Are a Part of Their Future Nov. 1–7."

"This reading is so resolute with what the situation Libi might in," he mumbled. He made his mind to do something about this.

If she is under some physical controls, how do I help and rescue her? What kind of evidence do I need to collect to tip the police? Tauri ran through a few ideas from the crime movies and decided to book a room at the same hotel to observe her for their operations.

"I'd be safe since I'm guided by the divine," he reconfirmed for himself.

⊶▬◉▬⊷

Tauri decided to go his own way to express his feelings, heartbreak, and love to Monicana/Libi.

Be positive, don't shame her. Tauri signed in to the MoonStar.com and posted the next batches of the message her.

Hey Monicana,

Thanks for not blocking me. You must be interested in my story.

I'd appreciate if you can reply to at least one word to show that you are reading. I have hoped someday I can have a walk with you for the conclusion of my story.

Tauri found out that Libi had updated her playlist to respond to his chat message to Monicana.

1. "The Lake: I Will Find You"
2. "Sleepless Nights: Lil Chaos"
3. "5:10 a.m.: Fool and Idiot"
4. "Refresh"

5. "Meet with a Similar Soul"
6. "Fire: The Queen Bee"
7. "Aloha Heja He: The Stars"
8. "The Fawn Jumping"
9. "The Bluebird: No Return Point"
10. "The Person Like Me: Not Easy"
11. "Sleepless Night: Lil Chaos"
12. "Wish: To You at That Time"
13. "Unravel"
14. "The Slave"
15. "Beyond the Memory: July"
16. "Those Folk Rhyme: Enough to Hear Once"
17. "Puma: Nine One"
18. "ZzHhOoUuZzHhAaNnGgYu: Shut Up"
19. "Irony"
20. "USA"
21. "The Lost Lamb"
22. "The Flower Fallen"
23. "I Really Can't Drink Wine"
24. "The Youth Rebellion Manual"
25. "Deep in Neon Lights"
26. "This Age"
27. "No Hesitate"
28. "Who Goes with Me on This Life Journey?"
29. "Ghost"
30. "Mr. Busy Man"
31. "Kiss Everywhere"
32. "Go Back to Childhood"
33. "Encounter"
34. "Time Thief"
35. "The Message to Ten Years Future Me"
36. "Allure"
37. "Golden Word: That's Why You Go Away. Because You Don't Want to Anything + No Delay, Owe Nothing + Disheartened + Who Love Me + He Is Extra + I Will Always Love You"
38. "The First Love"
39. "You Hide, I Deceive"
40. "The Spring, Summer, Fall, Winter"

41. "Porcupine"
42. "The Boys and Girls at the Big Field Club"
43. "Aggressive"
44. "Dreamland"
45. "Is There Still Anything You Can Love?"
46. "Maze"
47. "Why We Here"
48. "Meet with You at Deepest Emotional World"
49. "Those Sleepless Nights and Unforgettable Things"
50. "The Love Song 2018"
51. "Describe: Honest"
52. "Like New, Love Old"
53. "Glad to Know You"
54. "Katharsis: Cleansing Katharsis"
55. "You Heard This Song Which Didn't Sing Yet"
56. "Airflow: Mob"
57. "History: 88 Rising/Rich Brian"
58. "Promising Youth"

Tauri didn't fully understand her message. Though she reconfirmed her love and commitment, it'd be only in a mirage world. She didn't provide any action items for this connection to move forward. After a few hours of consideration, Tauri sent a direct text message to her.

Hey, Libi,
We need a face-to-face talk.
Only honest conversations can be true to ourselves. Understand your perspective to see if our life paths can cross with each other again.

Libi didn't reply his message as usual. He knew she was playing the same trick. He decided to continue to talk to "Monicana," Libi.

Monicana,
Hope you've a wonderful weekend.
As I told you yesterday, I posted the WeChat message to Libi, my girlfriend; she updated her playlist in responding to me. We loved each other like this. But she never acknowledged her love in direct communication such as phone, text, email, or face-to-face talk. We knew in our soul we synced with

each other in the 5-D world. This's the trickiest part. It makes me excited, makes me sad, makes me wait, makes me stuck.

Our relationship made a breakthrough when Libi deployed a playlist on this Chinese music site in a folder called "Go with you" while I was attracted by an image of "n55!W!" to find her folder.

She started with the song "Lover Boy 88." My favorite part was the expression. She called me "Lover Boy"! Hmm, who doesn't want to hear this whisper of love?

She arranged the second song, "My Age." This reminded her audience that at her twenty-five years of age, it's time for her, a regular Chinese girl who is about to pass golden marriage age, to commit her future.

The third song was the first song with additional variant, "Lover Boy 88," to emphasize her desire. It described the scene where she and I met at the first time. Again, pay attention to the rap section. It pointed to the time "three years ago at summertime" with a story of "innocence year," that sleepover. You know what it means, right?

The fifth song showed her emotion, "I Felt Sick Since I Miss You." This also reminded me every day. So, I really felt the urgency to get her hand.

The sixth song, "Innocent Year," has a special meaning. Do you know what the word "innocence" means for a girl? I was so admiring that she didn't give her first night to Leo, her ex-friend. I guess she kept it to give it to whoever her true love is. She's such a pure, honest angel. After that time, she didn't talk about it anymore. But she did share a song to question "Why True Love Can Also Get What They Want?" I got what she meant. If her true love happens to be me, I want to let her know I am here not to take things from her; it's to love her, no matter what happens. The person would be cursed if he took her treasure away from her without her consent.

Her seventh song is called "Focus on Me." She used this song to remind me to claim it.

Her eighth song, "Former Boyfriend," really put bad words on her ex-boyfriend Leo. This song tells me she was not in a relationship with her ex-boyfriend when we met the first time. I actually worried about this, how to win her heart. I continually reminded her not to bring this drama into my world. Finally, she did address my concerns.

She arranged the ninth song, "East and West," to paint her future plan with me. She wanted to plan the Paris trip where my poem referred to that place; she agreed to have a school of babies with me. My dream is to have at least two kids with her, one boy and one girl.

The tenth song expressed her determination to move this relationship forward: "Can We?" The three years in the lyrics referred to the time when she and I met. If there's a girl to express herself like this, I'd be willing to do anything to make her happy. A journey must be taken. This is a yearlong crusade for me to change my life upside down, downside up in order for me to be eligible to marry her. She inspired me to move life forward to reach the end point.

The eleventh song moved this love feeling even further, hotter. "I Am Not Your Song Dongye." I was puzzled for at least one day. I finally realized she wanted to tell me that my relationship was not with my true love. My true love is yet showing up.

The twelfth song is "Pathological Changes." This song mentioned two things I sent to her: a baby bear and a love letter. She reminded me my gifts to her had been with her. I had the fire coming up in my chest when I heard that.

The last song, the thirteenth song, pushed this love expression into the highest point. "Conquered." She told me she was conquered by my love.

Look, your dream girl shared a playlist like this. If this's not a soul contract, what'd it be for the highest commitment? We're looking upon for the good deed by all the angels, spirits, God.

Monicana, here is my question to you: How do you recommend I convince my girlfriend to acknowledge her love to me? To open the heart-to-heart communication with me?

Do you think she is playing my heart?

My intuition told me she was in love with me. There is more evidence to support that. But she never admitted it. This makes me look like a fool. It put a hole in my heart. There won't be progressive relationships if there's no open communication.

This relationship really made me question all the social norms. I doubt the meaning of trust, personal integrity, loyalty, honesty, love. All those things are moral blocks built by this society.

If I move away from this mirage relationship, my intuition at least would be all right again; I'd trust myself, have the confidence I'm the person who controls my will and destiny.

How much the conscience worth? Is there a Libra scale for this since it's the will from the above. When you don't hold your deed/conscience high, there'll be karmic lessons to be learned. That's what those tarot readers interpreted to me. Then, bad things would happen, like those crimes reported every day.

You may not believe that; I believed it.

Everything happens to me is written on the stars, interpreted by the tarot cards, blessed from spirits, the divine, God.

You can deviate from your fated path to learn more lessons. Some lessons would be simple, but some lessons would make you pay a heavy price. You know what I meant.

That sounded like a battle my girlfriend is fighting.

Ultimately, fate will find you, or you will find your destiny. That sounded like a quote from Forrest Gump's conversation with his mom before she died.

Sorry for writing to you so late. This might take your valuable time away to accept your date's appointment.

Have a nice night!

Tauri was fully aware of the possibility that Libi would end this relationship. To him, it's an allusion to continue with this waiting path. This is the right way to make my effort to wake Libi up.

His energy was picked up by the tarot channel "II 3Loka II," which published a video on October 31, 2019 titled "Taurus, the Name of the Game Isn't Love!" She described the status of this showdown. Naturally, she wanted Taurus to stop. But, on the other hand, she felt Taurus wanted to show their power of judgment.

Another tarot channel, "The Illest Illuminator" published a video on November 1, 2019, titled "Taurus—It All Works Out in the End, What Progress! November 19 Tarot Reading." She called Libra to have a meaningful way to speak to Taurus. Be honest. Don't jump or judge a situation based on insecurity.

Tauri felt those tarot readings were resolute with his situation. He heard the call of stopping this conversation from the spirit team.

He came up with the idea to conclude this chat with Monicana/Libi and set up a stage for the next phase of the work: the book.

CHAPTER 16

Breakup

TAURI NOTICED LIBI updated her playlist at noon. He didn't have time to look in detail till the end of the day. He rushed to read it.

Hmm! Is this Libi's rebuttal for Monicana's conversation? Did she call me a wicked monologue? Shut up? Why? OMG, was she envisioning life after ten years with me? Tauri yelled out.

1. "The Lake: I Will Find You"
2. "Sleepless Nights: Lil Chaos"
3. "Why We Here"
4. "Meet with a Similar Soul"
5. "Mr. Busy Man"
6. "The Message to Future Self in Ten Years"
7. "The Fire Queen Bee"
8. "Aloha Heja He: Trouble Time"
9. "The Fawn Jumping"
10. "The Bluebird: No Return Point"
11. "Time Fly"
12. "Stranger under My Skin"
13. "The Person Like Me: Not Easy"
14. "Sleepless Nights: Lil Chaos"
15. "Want to Keep You at Here"
16. "Slave"
17. "You at the Yesterday"
18. "Beyond the Memory: July"
19. "Refresh"
20. "Innocent Year"

21. "Your Look"
22. "Shut Up"
23. "Rain King"
24. "Mr. Wicked"
25. "I Don't Have Any Control"
26. "Twelve: Monologue"
27. "The Youth Rebellion Manual"
28. "Deep in Neon Lights"
29. "The Song Sing at Sunset"
30. "This Is Called a Life Journey"
31. "This Age"
32. "No Hesitation"
33. "Ghost: A Drop"
34. "Waste Time"
35. "Old Newspaper Before Bed"
36. "Faith"
37. "Rejuvenation"
38. "We Had a No Spring Daydream at the End of April"
39. "Ideal"
40. "Time Thief"
41. "To Me after Ten Years"
42. "Allure Over the Town"
43. "Very Difficult"
44. "Early Autumn and You"
45. "Lost Happiness"
46. "The Sky for Bad Children"
47. "Porcupine"
48. "The Boys and Girls at the Big Field Club"
49. "Dreamland"
50. "Is There Still Anything You Can Love?"
51. "Maze"
52. "Love the Career, Love Beauty More"
53. "Meet with You at Deepest Emotional World"
54. "Those Sleepless Nights and Unforgettable Things"
55. "Describe"
56. "Shout It Out"
57. "Faith"
58. "Like New, Love Old"

59. "Good Night"
60. "Very Glad to Know You"
61. "Katharsis: Cleansing"
62. "3:00 a.m.: Gold Washed from the Sand"
63. "Promising Youth"

Tauri spent some time translating the playlist into the message.

I'll find you like a drop of water in a lake evaporating myself to embrace the cloud. I've had many sleepless nights since my life had been in chaos. Why're we here to have this conversation? You're the similar soul I met, Mr. Busy Man.

This is a message to future me in ten years, the fire queen with a bad temper: "Hello, you two are like fawns jumping around to kick each other." There's no returning point like a bluebird promise.

You're the stranger under my skin, not physically attached to me but with me any-where, anytime. It's not an easy life for a person like me, a young person starting new life in this unfamiliar land. My life is in chaos. I've been having sleepless nights. I wanted to keep you with me as if you're yesterday. But unfortunately, those times are beyond our memory.

Let's repeat myself: I'm still in my innocent year. I knew what I meant. I'm still committed to you.

Look at you, an old face. Just shut up, and go to cry, Mr. Wicked! I don't have any control over your monologue. Are you a youth rebellion?

You'd been in many years of the marriage as if you're in a deep neon light district. You're already at your old like sun-setting age. You had your life. At your age, you shouldn't have any hesitation to be with me; otherwise, you'll be a dead like a ghost soon. Don't waste your time looking at anyone new. You're at the age of someone who reads old newspapers with granny glasses before bed.

Just have faith to rejuvenate our relationship. We can dream to have the family life without dating as if it goes to the end of April directly without spring. It'd be an ideal situation for me to spend only ten years with you—a challenge for me to go all in, spent the rest of my life with you. You're in your early senior year as seasons like early autumn already. I'd lose my happiness with a nasty kid day in and day out, irate as a porcupine in those boys' and girls' clubs. Is that your dream? Is there love still left for me?

This's like a maze that makes me doubt my choice. I love my career but love my beauty and happiness more. But we met in my deepest emotional moment; you're my wish fulfillment. This is the reason why I have sleepless nights and unforgettable mem-ory. So, I revealed my true intention to you here. But I also want to shout out to you I've faith in you. I like you now but loved you before.

Have a good night. I'm happy to know you. You made me stand out as if you picked the gold by washing off the sand like the Chinese ancient legendary BoLe, a talent scout. You made me become a promising youth.

Tauri felt Libi's anger. His heart was sunken. This would be the first time in a long time that someone pointed the finger to his nose and tell him who he thinks he is! He found himself falling from heaven down to earth, fantasy to reality, self-confidence to uncertainty. His fairytale story was breaking into pieces by her playlist.

OK, I took a shot at her; she is scoring now. We are even. He felt calm and avoided taking another glance at her playlist.

One thought constantly came into his mind as he went to bed that night. Libi never had once used a song like "Goodbye" to break up. She always used songs like "Faith," "Like New, Loved Old" to express her feelings. Would this be her way to hook me up as a person in a song "Slave"? What about the songs "Want to Keep You at Here," or "Meet with the Similar Souls"? Is it destiny she can't and doesn't want to escape?

Tauri couldn't get a sure answer. He decided to continue his conversation with Monicana/ Libi.

Monicana, are you still there?

Sorry for talking to you so late. I promise that this will be the last time I talk to you here. I'll give you a surprise announcement at the end of this conversation.

Monicana, I may give you too much information. You can see how powerful the writing or song could be if it's aligned with the power of love and affections.

My girlfriend updated a playlist with a total of sixty-three songs today. It's just too much information for me to consume.

OMG, Monicana, this's actually the first time I understood her true intention via her playlist. It made me happy; at least I knew I'm not a fool.

I truly felt my girlfriend's golden heart. She's a pretty girl with a big temper described in the song "Fire: Queen Bee."

She and I need to cool down a little bit.

She proposed a ten-year marriage term in the song "To Me after Ten Years," which I generally agreed with. However, I need to talk through it with her.

Since she and I are life partners, we should treat each other in even give-and-take. This is related to my life and her life.

I like her honesty expressed via her playlist. But actions speak louder than words. Libi and I need to have a face-to-face conversation to clear the air.

I told her I want to take a week to sleep on her ten-year arrangement during my business trip to China. At the same time, I'll unfollow her playlist and not accept any more incoming messages. This will give me a clear mind.

I want to invite her to go to Las Vegas since I planned to attend a training the third week of this month after my business trip. She and I could have a good retreat there.

Monicana, I guess that is the answer I initially came to you for. In the end, I suppose we figured it out together.

Tauri posted the long messages to unload the heavy stone from his chest since Libi's new playlist came out.

Tarot readers talked about the actions to be taken for Taurus to release this energy. I can have a plan to break up with her by comparing our character differences—everything is different except our unexplainable bond. He questioned it.

Tauri continued to send a chat message to Monicana/Libi via this online dating site.

Monicana,

My girlfriend and I both knew we're soulmates and twin flames. Our bond would never break. It's divinely guided.

One tarot reader mentioned there's a third party surrounding my girlfriend. They (his or her birthday between Oct. 23 to Nov. 21) now hired a psycho to launch an attack to break this bond. They'd not only get backfired; they'd also be losing money or go broke potentially.

It's serious business to mess with the divine power. The tarot reader talked of the demon, who would be on his or her doorstep with this third party. My girlfriend is protected by the divine.

In talking about the divine, it sounds scary. I don't think of it as a supernatural phenomenon. It's some energy form that Libi and I created.

For the last three years, our minds emitted the energy into the universe for this connection. It's the thoughts of each other constantly, the mind yearning for each other, the desire to hold each other, the care of where each other is. It's ultimately retreated into the ground or hide out in open heart space, every daydream longing for each other.

Our energy in the 5-D universe interacts with each other and other energy surrounding us. This energy "light beam" carries the feeling she and I have, missing each other in our hearts. It's an attraction. It's like the family was together at our childhood. It's the father or fathering kind of feeling she's missing and longing for a piece of mango fed into her mouth when she was tired.

129

It's the mother or mothering like love with the soft, soothing voice to calm me down on the same bed with my mom to warm each other up on a cold winter night in my childhood.

Those are the missing pieces we found in each other. In that sense, the bond will never break, couldn't break. It's built in our bloodline or DNA, part of life. It has been growing since our childhood.

Once I thought about this, my mind was crystal clear. What I want to do and am willing to do is to make my girlfriend happy.

There might be a past-life theory. I would highly doubt it, since I was a trained mind at university to use science to explain everything. If we're past-life loves, I'd have found her when she was in her childhood; I'd follow her steps, nurture her growth, protect her from the bully boys, fight the love against the ex-friend who broke her heart. That's not our story.

When I met her on that memorable summer day, only one glance, two individual energies found their life. They touched, hugged, twisted each other and ascended toward the light of Esther. When her tears came out from her innocent mind, it transcended as the flame exploded into the mushroom cloud and formed the fusion being into a glowing crystal in pure light.

Those evils who took advantage of my girlfriend in any form would never experience this kind of love, would regret his or her life for what they have done to her. The Libra scale would rebalance when the time came. The judgment would be served.

Monicana, my girlfriend and I both felt stuck, for better or worse. I initially wanted to break up with her to give us space since she chose to push me away. Think about it. She and I are magicians; some tarot readers called us a power couple. So we can turn this negative experience into fruition. Instead of setting the terms and goals like a marriage transaction, how about Libi and I go with the flow to see how far we'd carry this love forward? All I wish is to give her happiness. I want to have a relationship with an equal give-and-take, take care of each other, be honest with each other, be loyal to each other, commit to each other. We'd pursue the highest moral standard, carry on the mission which the divine set us to do.

This book project would bring us abundance, happiness, joy. I truly believe that there's a higher power controlling this universe—energy from the spirits, divine, ultimate power of Jesus Christ, and God.

She and I are such different people. I can't change her past life and personality; she also can't change my past life and marriage experience. But we'll have each other in the future. All we can do is to respect each other's lives and improve our relationship; we both cocreate a world belonging to only two of us.

I'm happy to start the first step to have a face-to-face, nonjudgmental, open conversation to understand each other's points. Yes, there might be the heartbroken moments for us; we shall overcome any obstacle in front of us.

I need her help to speed up this book project. Maybe she can start her own. Perhaps she and I can do a project together like we did before. In this way, she and I would have the opportunity to know each other along the way. The song "Love the Dynasty, Love Beauty More" sounds like a cocreation with the divine. This would enable us to pursue an abundance of life, unimaginable love, and wealth.

Monicana, that was the update from my girlfriend and me. I may not post any more for a few days.

Hope I didn't bore you with your time.

Tauri checked the public chat room at the dating site. A young guy posted his photo to show his handsome face. A few hours later, a middle-aged businessman posted a picture on a yacht with a cigar.

Is that Libi's new boyfriend? Or dates? Showing force? Tauri asked himself.

This didn't bother him.

"The Libra would feel completely happy when her mind, body, and soul loves one person. She wouldn't fall into any person if one of those three things was missing from that connection." One of the tarot readers made comments on the Libra reading.

"Libi, you sang the song 'Your Life is a Drama, My Life is a Battle.' Now the table has turned. 'Your life is a drama; my life is a battle!'" Tauri yelled as he was ready for any trouble coming from this dating company.

Tauri wasn't sure Libi was at the dating website to look for a boyfriend only.

Maybe she is.

Was she the mastermind behind the head of the girl crew for the dating service? The bookkeeper role sounds like counting cash to me. Tauri smiled to himself.

He continued to chat with Monicana/Libi.

Monicana,

I thought I'd stop chatting with you for one week. But I realized I had some exciting findings about my girlfriend.

Why did my girlfriend constantly share the song "Like New and Loved Old"? Is she treating me as both old and new in "love interests"? I decided to check out her ex-Leo.

"When was the last time you contacted Libi?" I asked Leo.

"I haven't heard from her for over three years," he replied.

"I suspected she's under a wicked influence. She's supposed to find a job after her training. But she behaved totally differently while I talked to her," I explained.

"I really didn't contact her. I can take the screenshot on my WeChat message from her and send it to you," he responded promptly.

After a minute, he sent me the pictures of the last few days' information Libi posted. The latest message was a picture with a caption from a Hong Kong movie, *Han Zhi*: "When you take a break, you will conquer this world." Libi added her comment on this picture: "So please continue to live forever with dominated power just like before." That sounds like a sarcastic expression to me: "How can you get my hand if you don't take any action?" The second message was even more intruding: "You used your dominating power over me last time; please continue to treat me like that."

"Can you give me the screenshot of her message since April last year? This might help her," I demanded.

"No, I don't think that's a good idea," Leo replied after I waited for ten minutes.

"If you don't, you may not help her when she really needs it most," I further demanded. He went silent then.

Something happened between Libi and Leo, as my intuition always reminded me.

I told myself to meditate and fell into shallow sleep one night. I kept reasoning why Libi wanted to put out the song "Like New and Love Old." Is there something she wants to let someone know? Why did Leo change his attitude?

If nothing happened, nothing is to hide. Right? Leo proved himself by providing me the screenshot from her.

Could Libi not love me? She actually is in love with Leo, just as she told me at least twice in text messages. She might honestly tell me the truth.

It's like lighting striking in my mind at the moment.

Yes, that's *the truth of the mystery* I have been looking for. Libi actually has been in love with Leo. Even he doesn't know.

But based on Leo's reaction, he lost track of Libi. At least he didn't even look at WeChat messages from Libi.

Libi had been sending Leo love messages but never got a response from him. In this drama, I constantly sent love messages to Libi, as I believed that Libi was in love with me. Instead, I was being treated with her cold shoulder.

That can explain why Libi wanted me to go to a mental evaluation when

I told her that she has two different personalities and suggested for her to see a psychologist.

If that's true, Libi had been acting like a fool all the time when it came to her relationship with Leo; so did I. It's reflected in one of Libi's songs, "The Two Similar Souls Met."

What does this mean to me? What was left for me from this connection?

Once I came up with the conclusion, my head was spinning like a cyclone. I told myself that I was not heartbroken since I had so many heartbreaks from this connection. I should feel something.

I felt…

I felt…

I felt…

I felt relief.

I felt relief. I was released by her action.

I felt relief. I didn't have to pursue something or overcome an insurmountable mountain.

"When you feel the most difficult things to overcome, they are actually the easiest things to overcome," one tarot reader mentioned.

I felt relief because I'm free to open my brand-new love life. I'd pursue a more responsive woman who is open, transparent, polite, honest, loyal to me. Something I'm dreaming about.

If Libi could just simply tell me that she's in love with Leo, there'd not be any suffering, pain, or heartbreak for me; I'd simply walk away with my chin high. Even though I would still feel the agony since my soulmate was the creator of the playlist. Libi forcefully denied she was that person. If what she said was true, there's someone else in this picture.

Who is that person?

Those curiosities have brought me into this drama so far. It's like a soap opera, with every other day up and down.

At this moment, I totally lost my interest in pursuing the truth to follow her drama. I may never find out who's the creator of that playlist. Why should I? It doesn't bother me anymore. It made me stuck on this drama so long. It's time to unhook it. It no longer means anything to me anymore.

Now I think that I'll treat Libi as "my girl-friend" instead of "my girlfriend." It's just like referring to a guy as "my guy friend" or simply "my friend."

Monicana, I knew my story came with a few twists. So, this might be the last twist I'm going to post here.

If I'm boring you, I feel really sorry about it. I'll wrap up this chapter and look for the next fool's adventure.

Thanks.

Oh! I almost forgot to tell you. All these posts are part of my writing project.

I'm an amateur writer. I used this chat room to develop my storyline.

There are no direct relations with any real person's name and story as my disclaimer.

They are all fictional actors' or actresses' roles described in those posts. Please do not try to match them with any specific person or person's storyline.

Monicana, you can provide your story as my coauthor to further develop those plots.

I'm just kidding.

Hey, you never know what it'll bring you.

Monicana, since you help a lot, I hope that you'd accept my invitation to attend my book opening ceremony.

Have a wonderful life at this fantastic online dating site.

Tauri looked at what he had done so far. All those posts definitely affected someone's life.

The tarot reader also mentioned to be true to myself.

Did it meet my high moral standard? Yes.

Do what I say! Say what I do! Do what I said! Tauri felt confident about what he did.

Who is my soulmate? Where is my true love? Can you tell me, Spirit? Tauri was in a deep soul search.

Tauri went through every detail of the drama with Libi from the beginning to now.

Libi's playlist and her random WeChat messages were the shadow space she operated in. In that world, she used her beauty to attract the love volunteer. By deploying different types, ranks, and lyrics of the song, she painted magic imaginations to manipulate the mind. There was no accountability for her ideas, expressions, or thoughts to her audience. She can offer any love, any apology, in her fingertips. In the end, it doesn't mean anything! Tauri summarized.

When that space was merged with the real world, she'd vigilantly put up a defense to deny it.

This is the way to keep her safe from breaking down her wall, no matter who that person was. That digital space would never be materialized, Tauri concluded.

But Libi's playlist was not easy to create. It needs time and effort to develop an idea and implement it at the right time and occasion. Nevertheless, the feelings expressed did not sound like they were being fabricated. Tauri was cast in doubt for himself.

Her playlist expressed her ultimate desire to marry me. Tauri argued in his mind.

But…

But…

But I wanted something tangible, a fact-based relationship.

Yes, this is the time to pull the trigger to completely release this soulmate connection. Tauri affirmed this to himself.

His energy was picked up by the tarot channel "High Vibrations," which published a video on November 6, 2019, titled "Taurus Love November 2019: Y'all Are NOT Playing This Month! And It Pays Off Big Time!" She called Taurus to let it go, release this connection.

As Tauri finished his last posts in Monicana's chat room, he congratulated himself on accomplishing 60 percent of what the spirit told him to do. He expressed his love to Libi. Yet he deliberately skipped the steps to pulling the breakup trigger.

Maybe I still need to do a breakup step to wake her heart chakra up? He didn't have enough time to think it through.

⊷══◉ ◉══⊷

Tauri went to his business trip to China as he planned. He joked with airline ticket personnel and smiled at the flight attendant on the plane. He felt good about this trip, which the spirit called a "new beginning."

Walking away from her was the right thing to do. It'd benefit both her and me. Tauri sighed.

He sat in the plane on the way to his hometown in China across the earth. He was amazed at how many changes were in his life compared to his last trip one year ago.

I'm a normalized US citizen now.

My wife became an ex.

My committed playlist girlfriend never showed up.

What more shoes will drop?

I have a team of tarot readers guiding me now!

Tauri believed he was walking on his path toward true love and abundant life nudged by the spirits and the divine power.

He couldn't get one minute of sleep on a fourteen-hour flight. He looked at rays of sunlight coming into his airplane window above the crossing of the North Pole.

Here I come! The new world!

CHAPTER 17

The New Life

TAURI'S AIRPLANE TOUCHED down at the Chongqing Jian Bei International Airport in the early morning.

It was foggy and drizzling. It reminded him of the alias name of "Foggy Capital," the world's largest metropolitan city of over thirty million people where he had grown up.

His memory flashed the fresh spring wind, cooled summer watermelon, azaleas red in fall, and spicy air above a hot pot in winter. The feeling would never be fully understood by the people outside his hometown.

I'm not a Chinese citizen anymore. My life is like a sheet of blank paper here. Tauri returned to this place with a strange feeling. Everything was familiar, but everything was different now.

"What is the plan for today's luncheon, bro?" he joked in his family WeChat group. Hello! My dear family—dad, brothers, sister, nieces and nephews.

He flopped through the tarot readings for Taurus, his zodiac sign. A few soulmate tarot readers talked about a "tower moment" for Taurus, like a death transformation and coming out as a new.

One reader advised a baby step to learn something.

"A baby step?" he uttered. "The spirit's guidance to have me to be a beginner and learn how to love?" He had not been in a flirtation with another girl for such a long time. He almost forgot what it'd feel like.

He could feel the pain from his double heartbroken drama from the last two weeks when he was alone. But he felt calm when he listened to the tarot reading for Taurus, as if he were talking to someone like his dad, who understood him, gave him comfort, and supported his passion.

After his breakfast, the bus brought him and the conference participants to a convention center. They waited in line to get into the conference hall.

He turned on his phone and listened to some tarot readings while he was waiting for the formal opening ceremony. A tarot reader talked about how to end this chapter for Taurus. He noticed that "The Blue Bus" was the title of this reading.

"*A blue bus?*" Tauri exclaimed as he walked back to his bus, a light-blue shuttle, for his lunch place after the ceremony. He immediately realized that this shuttle would be part of his journey to end this chapter of his life.

"Can you go with me? The S5 group," one of the tour guide girls reminded everyone.

Two girls at my bus were amazingly pretty!

Look at Wendy! She is a Chinese version of Barbie doll alive.

Caiti, a girl with a wide forehead, big eyes, narrow-brushed willow leaf eyebrows, and a tight hair bun, looked elegant and graceful.

Tauri noticed Caiti always allowed herself to smile back with her gazing eye. Their eyesight would touch for a few seconds.

"Caiti might like me," Tauri uttered. He felt intimately connected with her.

He came back to his hotel with this bus after one full day of the conference. He went to bed and fell into sleep immediately, losing a sense of time. He woke up after a one-hour nap. He grabbed his phone and found this reading published on November 6, 2019, by the tarot channel "Love and Abundance Tarot" titled "Taurus Weekly Tarot Reading: The Blue Bus…Is Calling Us!"

Oh! A learning experience is required after the "spell is cast"? The dot line to the "blue bus"! Do I need to do something with those girl groups before that conference is over?

Achieve the victory from the study of knowledge, become the best of what I am going to, and close this chapter. Will Libi come in quickly?

Did she predict the results of Libi and me to go to the next chapter of the journey with abundance?

With all those questions, Tauri walked into his hotel dining room. It was a buffet-style restaurant at this five-star household hotel chain in the United States. But the menu was so authentic that he seemed returned to his childhood.

He filled the two full plates to meet his nutrition criteria: one-third protein, one-third vegetable and fruit, one-third carbs from rice or wheat products. He had been very proud to tell his friend about his preference. He kept a very nice body shape.

"Hey, did you pick up the dessert before you have a formal meal?" Tauri saw Caiti walking over with other girls.

"Hey…hi! Tauri." She was surprised to see him.

"I don't eat much. I just want to have some cakes and fruits." Caiti smiled. She kept eye contact with a charming gesture. The youthful, innocent energy made him really excited.

All the tour guide girls went to sit far at one corner of the dinner hall quietly. A blond girl faced in his direction.

Who is my teacher? I'll lose the opportunity to learn if I don't act now. Tauri roughly remembered a blond girl mentioned at the Taurus reading.

The blonde must be the one! How do I approach her?

Look, there're two empty seats at their table. Tauri came up with an idea.

"Do you mind if I sit here?" Tauri asked the group as he seated himself next to Caiti with his dessert plate. He didn't even pay attention to their approval or disapproval.

"Hey, what's the plan tomorrow?" Tauri asked Caiti.

"We'll have a morning tour. There's nothing arranged after that," she replied back with a gentle grin.

"I like your golden color style. I thought I was in the US." Tauri looked around and turned to the girl with the blond hair.

It'd be polite to praise a girl about her black-silk hair, a standard beauty style for thousands of years. Libi's black silky hair attracted him to touch; she even posted a photo with her hand pointing to her hair at her WeChat profile to flirt with him. Tauri, in return, texted her the song "Just the Way You Are," by Bruno Mars, in which the hair was mentioned in the lyrics.

"I don't have this blond hair. It's not what it seems to be." The girl, the blonde, had a pretty face, smaller than Libi's. She talked softly and seemed more mature than other girls. Tauri noticed her name tag as Cherry.

"Are you guys working overtime?" Tauri turned around to everyone at the table.

"We are the singles. We don't have anything planned in the evening." The Barbie girl took over to reply.

"I'm single too. I just got divorced." Tauri lowered his voice.

"Oh! I'm sorry for that," she replied. "I'm Wendy." She didn't offer her title and introduced the rest of the girls at the table to him.

"I like to sit with the team. Do you guys know any game to play?" he asked.

"How about Chenyun, the Chinese idiom game?" Wendy took over.

Tauri grew up in China. He learned Chenyun when he was at his primary school. However, he had forgotten most of them. Like an idiom in the United States, it usually came with four Chinese words to express a story based on a historical event.

"I knew the Chenyun like 'Kill two birds with one stone,' 'piece of cake,' 'it takes two to tango'?" Tauri rehearsed in his mind.

"Here's the rule: I'll start to say four words Chenyun. The next person has to find another one starting with the last word in the previous Chenyun." Wendy explained.

"Would it be like this? I start with 'It takes two to tango.' Then, the next person would have to start with an idiom with 'tango,' like 'tango to Evora piano.'" Tauri gave an example to understand the rule.

"Yes, that is the rule," Wendy confirmed. Everyone was excited to show off their knowledge of the Chenyun.

"If someone can't speak next Chenyun in thirty seconds..."

"What's the penalty?" he asked.

"She or he has to jump three times with hands wrapped on the head," Wendy announced.

"Sure, let's play." She smiled. Everyone clapped at the table.

Tauri found himself really getting into it since this was the funny thing to do.

Wendy asked Caiti to start the first round. He realized that Wendy wanted to fix him to be the first one to jump. He was OK with that since everyone would have a good laugh. The laughter was what he needed most at this moment.

"Let me start with this Chenyun. 'Broken lotus still linked with threads.'" Caiti started and turned her face toward Tauri. He didn't switch his thought process yet. Instead, he translated Chinese into English to come up with another Chenyun. Then, the thirty seconds had passed.

"You lost." Wendy didn't hear his words coming out and shouted out.

"OK, OK. I lost." He nodded. He held his head and jumped three times to do a 360-degree turn. Everyone laughed their heads off.

"Let's start again. Since you lost, you can start this round," Wendy told him.

"Broken lotus still linked with threads." Tauri started with the same Chinese idiom.

"Threads used to fish." Cherry took over and pointed to Wendy.

"Fish grew in a mountain," Wendy turned to Caiti.

"Mountain outside of the mountain." Caiti handed it over to Tauri.

"Mountain...mountain..." Tauri tried to find the next idiom with this word. "Mountain outside of a mountain!" He finally put it out.

"You lost again. Jump! Jump! Jump!" Wendy ordered with a burst of laughter.

"Look, what is the rule for this game?" Tauri stood up and raised his voice. "A person starts with four words, a Chinese idiom. The next person has to find another one starting with the last word in the previous Chinese idiom. Right?" He repeated the rule.

"Yes," all the girls said.

"What was the last word from the previous person?" He asked everyone at the table.

"Mountain!" they replied together.

"What did I say in the first word?" Tauri asked further.

"Mountain!" the group agreed.

"Did I follow the rule?" Tauri grinned.

"Yes!" The group laughed with his weird logic.

"That doesn't count. This would allow everyone to say the same idiom for a whole night," Wendy demanded. Everyone laughed throughout the dinner hour.

"Let's don't count this. I will start another one." Tauri dodged this turn.

"Broken lotus still linked with threads..." Tauri kicked off another round and pointed to Cherry to take over.

"Threads used to fishy..." She thought a moment and shout it out.

"No, no, no. It is 'Threads used to fish,' not 'Threads used to fishy.'"

"You spoke Chongqing-style Mandarin," someone pointed out. The laughers burst out.

"Are you try to say, 'Threads used to fishy'? You look fishy," someone added. Everyone laughed again.

"It was too hard for me. I can't think of another Chenyun in a short moment. Can we choose another game to play?" Cherry twisted her eye with the white part more in just a second.

Tauri knew it was called "rolling eye and lips out." This was the first time he noticed a girl with such a beautiful moment. She'd roll her eye upward, then close her mouth with her lips projected out to last one second. The little actions on her lips, in the eyes, made him feel loving and beautiful.

"How did you do the 'rolling eye and lips out'? Can you do it again?" Tauri asked the blond girl, Cherry. She turned her face toward her left and made a perfect turnover white eye.

Everyone laughed aloud.

"I loved it. How did you do that?" Tauri demanded.

"I just want to show my little disapproval like this. My mom usually punished me if I disagreed with her, so I closed my mouth and projected my lips." She told her story; she made another demo of turnover white eye.

"Can you do it again?" Tauri yelled.

"Can you do it again?" Tauri clapped.

Tauri continued to ask. Cherry did it three times. Everyone at the table just laughed. Tauri felt like being part of this team.

"Let's play some other game?" the blond girl, Cherry, proposed.

"Sure, what is the game to play? Let me learn." Tauri got excited.

He wanted to find an opportunity to develop a relationship with one of the girls. I only needed one of them to learn.

Would it be pretty-girl Caiti, the girl who sent me the WeChat message via the private channel? Or the Barbie girl Wendy, the group leader? Or the blond girl, Cherry, mentioned in the tarot reading? Tauri asked himself. This would make him archive the goal to close this chapter and move into a new one. There, he and Libi would have the opportunity to reconnect.

"This game is about talking words. Let's give you an example," the Barbie Wendy explained.

"What's in the fruit garden? I would start with apple. The next one needs to say another fruit name like pear, and so on and so forth," Wendy explained to everyone.

"What is the penalty if you fail?" Tauri looked around. Everyone seemed to know the rule except him.

"Well, we usually drink liquor. But we can't do it tonight. We have to work." Wendy felt sorry for herself.

"How about beer and red wine?" Tauri exclaimed.

"What is in the zoo? Monkey." Wendy started.

"Elephant."

"Chicken."

"Rabbit." It's Tauri's turn.

"Duck." He was happy to respond right away.

"Snake."

"Tiger."

"Lion."

"OMG, it's my turn again." Tauri searched English words first. Finally, Tauri decided to use "whale" as his answer. When he translated it into Chinese, it had passed five seconds already.

"You lost; you need to drink," everyone shouted out.

"OK, OK, OK. This is a warm-up run." Tauri claimed with a smile.

"We'll start the formal game, all right?" Tauri played his trick again.

"What's in the Chinese volleyball team? Coach." Tauri knew there were only two levels in the team: coach and team member. This game would automatically end in a third person.

"Team member," the girl next to Tauri shouted out.

"Ow, ah! I can't find any words," the blond-haired Cherry exclaimed. "This is not fair." She raised her voice.

"Aha. I just designed the game to make you drink." Tauri turned his head from low toward high to the blond girl with a turnover white eye. Everyone laughed out. Cherry drank a sip. She knew that Tauri had outmatched her.

"What's the plant in the garden? Jasmine flower." Cherry started the next round.

"Rose flower," the girl sitting next to her shouted out.

"Apple tree," Caiti answered.

"You lost. How can you use a tree as the plant?" Wendy cried it out.

"Is a tree a plant?" she argued.

"Yes, the tree is a plant. But this game required a different plant in the garden instead of an orchard or farm. So you would say apple tree, pear tree? On and on," Wendy countered.

"Drink! Drink! Drink!" everyone shouted.

The whole restaurant filled with their laughter.

Who would believe that I'd be sitting with the young pretty girls laughing? Tauri told himself. The laughter seemed to throw his heartbreak away.

"Do you still need anything else since it'll be closed in ten minutes?" A waitress came over to remind them.

"It's time to go. Let's toast and bottoms up," Cherry suggested.

"*Gan Bei!* Bottoms up!" All of them drank up.

⊷═◉ ◉═⊷

They squeezed into the small elevator.

"I'll go to your room. Are you in number 626, right?" The blond girl, Cherry, broke the silence and asked Caiti.

Tauri waved to say good night and walked out of the elevator alone.

Is that it? Why did the blond girl, Cherry, mention Caiti's room number? She seems to hint something? Do I need to knock the door to ask for a walk? Would something need to happen, as I was asked to do so? Tauri asked himself.

He returned to his room and checked the tarot readings to get more hints from the spirits.

The tarot channel "Dream Queen" picked up this energy and issue a warning in the reading published on November 7, 2019, titled "Taurus: Warning—Limit Reached (Twin Flame Journey)." She mentioned the goal is bigger and brighter. Therefore, Taurus needs to avoid little diversions or any argument down the road.

Tauri immediately realized that this was resolute with his situation.

It still made sense to go with my plan to develop the friendship, set up the stage for further action. He bubbled.

"I'm ready, I'm ready," Tauri uttered. He can capture the girl's heart by deploying Libi's magic weapon: the playlist to flirt with those girls. He was amazed by the power of the playlist Libi created, which indeed built up a connection on the soul level.

That must be the spirit's intention: stop developing a further relationship with the blond girl. OK. OK. I'll stop here, Tauri told himself.

Oh! Libi wants to hold onto me. Tauri started to think about Libi and went to check her playlist.

She just wants me to stay alone and have my ex to keep the kid.

Did she want me to keep a secret if I left this connection?

1. "Lake: I Will Find You"
2. "The Message to Future Self in Ten Years"
3. "Why We Here?"
4. "Why?"
5. "The Time Fly"
6. "Stranger under My Skin"
7. "Want to Keep You with Me"
8. "Yesterday You"
9. "Innocence Year"
10. "Your Look"
11. "Rain: Kriiq"
12. "Big Things Start Small"
13. "Lone Wolf"
14. "Wicked: Ex"
15. "Keep"
16. "Troubled Youth: Bones"
17. "Twelve (Monologue)"
18. "The Song at the Sunset"
19. "This Life Journey"
20. "Waste Time"
21. "Mr. Busy Man"
22. "Old Newspaper before Bed"
23. "Faith"
24. "We Had a No Spring Daydream at the End of April"
25. "Ideal"
26. "Very Difficult"
27. "Early Fall and You"
28. "Lost"
29. "Sky for a Bad Kid"
30. "Love Career, Love Beauty More"
31. "Shout It Out"
32. "Faith"
33. "Good Night"
34. "If You Want to Leave"
35. "Done in the Heart: Deep Blue"
36. "Nobleman"
37. "3:00 a.m.: Beach Sand"

Libi seems to be having a good plan. Don't know if she'd keep her words. Let me see if any tarot readings pick her up for this, Tauri told himself.

One tarot reader reminded Taurus that it was time to show the romantic gesture to the love interest.

Tauri decided to send Libi a direct text message as a friend about her ex, Leo.

Hey, I'm about to leave Chongqing airport.

I talked to Leo. I'm really happy for him.

Leo dated a girl for two years. He will marry her next year.

Well, my next stop will be Las Vegas for a conference. If you're there, maybe we can grab a drink together.

Our book is in excellent shape. I can show you the chapter I wrote in China.

Caiti would be the last person to think about him at this moment as he was seated on his airplane taxing on the runway. He wrote a message to her.

I like your statement at WeChat: there are more than eight or nine chances to get unfulfilled wishes and fewer than two or three opportunities to find your true friend to talk to. It is like Lin Daiyu's feeling in one of four famous Chinese novels, *The Dream in Red Mansions*. It presented a girl's feeling to remember the old good days in a scattered rosy life.

She'd be pinched at her heart since someone understands her feelings. I definitely can feel it, Tauri told himself.

"Bye. My plane is about to take off. Keep in contact!" Tauri sent a final message to Caiti and turned off his phone.

He came to this trip by following the spiritual guidance to close the previous chapter and start a new one.

Did I close the last chapter of my life?

What does the future hold for me?

One thing was for sure from all the tarot readings: his love life was destined. His twin flame would start the new chapter of his life with him, well…in the future.

CHAPTER 18

The Youthful Energy

"IT'S NOT MY business anymore," he told himself. In Tauri's heart, Libi was the one he was truly longing for. But he didn't know how to get there since she pushed him away.

It was noon on this magic day when his plane landed in Las Vegas. He checked in at his hotel and went to the convention hall to register his attendance.

"It's 11/11. Taurus's new moon is about to come in." One of the tarot readers predicted a breakthrough for Taurus's life in the coming week.

Is this November 11 going to be a magic day for me? How? Tauri asked himself.

A tarot channel, "Fire Intuition," offered the reading on November 11, 2019, from an astrology perspective titled "11:11 Messages + Full Moon in Taurus, True Love, Commitment, Abundance Is Yours!"

Another tarot channel, "Guided Intuition," offered a reading on November 12, 2019, for this divine event titled "Full Moon in Taurus November 2019—Nothing Can Stop You. You Are Grounded in Your Hearts and Desires."

Oh! The spiritual and divine energy is with me today! Tauri smiled to himself. He quickly walked into the hall to find his first meeting place. It was like a maze, with people flowing from all directions to look for their own session.

"How do I get to Oceanside C?" he asked one yellow T-shirt helper.

"Walk toward this hall. At the end, turn left, take the escalator up to one floor, then turn right and go past two doors. There, turn right at the third left door, then go directly through the wall. You'll find your room," the helper explained. His mind was spinning, with his session starting in ten minutes.

"Can you explain to me how to get to Oceanside C?" A soft girl's voice was on the far right. She repeated it a second time with a high pitch. The helper was not available for her.

"I'm going to the same place. Come with me." Tauri shouted to her. Tauri led the girl into the hallway.

"Going to this Agile info session?" Tauri turned his head back to ask as he rushed forward.

"Yes, I am," she replied.

Tauri started to notice whom he talked with. Oh! She looked to be in her midtwenties with a long, square face, pinky cheeks, densely filled eyelids, and a green skirt of a tight plastic strip. What a gorgeous body with every part that a woman dreamed of.

"Hi, I'm Tauri." Tauri finally remembered to ask her name.

"I'm Florenza." She smiled back.

"What? Florensa?" Tauri thought about his neighbor.

"No, it's Florenza," she repeated.

"Oh, is your name having anything to do with Florence in Italy?" Tauri had a cruise trip along Italy and heard about this city.

"Yes, but my name has little to do with the city. It's derived from a Latin word for 'flower.'" She explained patiently with a smile squinting her eyelids to a narrow line.

"OK, I got it; I got it." Tauri nodded.

"Yeah! We made it" she yelled out.

Tauri saw her full smile in a hair distance and was infested by her joy.

The session ran quickly. They stroked along with the flow to the lunch hall.

"Come to see our product!" a guy dressed in suit shouted to them.

"What do you want to do?" Tauri asked Florenza.

"Let's walk around." She didn't mention the lunch.

Tauri and Florenza were given a quick conversation about the vendor's product. After scanning their name badges, they were given a T-shirt.

"Which size do you want?" the salesperson asked Florenza.

"Small," she replied. A black T-shirt was given to her.

"What size of T-shirt do you need, sir?" the salesperson looked at Tauri.

"Small," Tauri replied. She smiled at him.

"How'd a small size fit you?" Tauri asked Florenza. She enjoyed his compliment on her gorgeous body. She just smiled without saying anything.

The next booth came with a name: "Narwhal."

"What does this word mean?" Tauri asked the salesperson.

"It's a whale with a unicorn on the head, a magic fish. This's the only animal with a real unicorn on it." Tauri immediately was drawn to this product.

"Tell me something your product can do." Tauri wanted to get the conversation down to the points.

"This product is for data people who like data wrangling." He started his sales pitch.

"A wrangling? That's a data science term." Florenza showed interest. Tauri realized he talked too much.

"I may use your product. Can you give me your brochure and information? I'll bring it back to my office." Florenza was finally done with the questions.

"Here's a toy narwhal for the gentleman and the lady." The salesperson handed over the toys.

"No, we need T-shirts!" Florenza tweaked to Tauri.

"What size T-shirt do you want?" The salesperson asked Tauri first since he started the conversation.

"Small," Tauri replied.

"What size T-shirt do you want? Lady, medium?" he asked Florenza.

"Small." Florenza smiled at Tauri.

"Another T-shirt, yeah!" Florenza was hyper. They raised their hands to do a high five.

"How about a T-shirt hunt?" Florenza exclaimed. He opened his mouth wide.

"We need to collect as many as six T-shirts," she announced. Her face flushed as if she were in high school or came from a cold winter walk.

"A T-shirt hunt? How exciting it is! I don't actually want to keep any vendor's gift. I always throw them into the garbage can," Tauri exclaimed

"Come on, Tauri. It'd be fun!" Florenza begged. He saw her big smile with eyes glowing.

"Sure, let's do it." Tauri nodded.

To their surprise, the next few booths didn't offer T-shirts.

"Let's take a photo." Florenza led him to walk into a photo booth, a wall with a convention logo as the background and a photographer standing by.

"What sign do you want to pick?" Tauri looked at Florenza.

"Women love data?" Florenza posed with the sign. She giggled. She seemed exuberated.

"Data is the new oil!" Tauri did his pose.

"Data and me!" Florenza tried another pose.

"I love data!" Tauri tried a different sign.

"Let's pick a sign of 'We're the data people!'" She pointed to a sign.

"Can you, lady, take your bag off? Gentleman, smile. One, two, three...cheese!" the photographer guided them to arrange the pose. The photos were printed immediately. Florenza picked up the picture and laughed at Tauri. He looked at his overexaggerated smile on the photo and burst out.

"Let me take this group photo in case your boyfriend has a misunderstanding," Tauri joked.

"Just send to the photo-sharing online site. I'll send the URL to you." She wanted to keep the memory.

"Come over to sit. There's another session beginning in two minutes. You can get a T-shirt if you listen through our full presentation," a loud voice announced.

"T-shirt again?" Florenza and Tauri leered. Only they'd understand. They found a place to sit next to each other.

Tauri got all the salesperson wanted to pitch in the first one minute. After that, he sat there to endure the onslaught from the demo. Oh! This pain! Seems it lasts forever! he thought.

"We'll do a raffle now. If your number is called, you'll get fifty-dollar credit on our company's next convention registration fee," the saleslady declared.

"The winning number is eight," she read loudly.

"Yeah! My first number," Tauri whispered to Florenza.

"The second winning number is two," she shouted aloud toward the left.

"Gosh, that's my second number!" Tauri waved his fist.

"The third winning number is zero," she shouted aloud toward the right.

"OMG, that was also my number." Tauri held his breath. This is my lucky day!

"The last winning and the final winning number is…" She stopped and looked around the audience.

"It's one!" she ended in a high-pitched voice.

"Yeah! I won! I won!" Tauri heard someone next to him jump up. She waved her ticket to declare a win. It was Florenza.

"Wait, I have an almost perfect winning number. Do you have a more perfect number?" Tauri questioned her.

"Yeah…I won. Yeah, I won…" She shook her shoulder as her body twisted with a rhythm. Florenza held a winning ticket in the air.

"Which size do you want?" the salesperson asked Florenza.

"Small," she replied. A blue T-shirt was given to her.

"What size T-shirt do you need, sir?" Tauri was asked.

"Small." When Tauri replied, Tauri and Florenza both laughed. Woo! Woo! Woo! The T-shirt hunt game was at full sway! Tauri kept a smile.

"Look, there's another T-shirt booth. It's your turn to do the talk." Tauri led the way toward that booth and then stepped back to let Florenza go first.

"Welcome to our booth." An old gentleman walked toward Florenza and stared at Florenza directly. Florenza smiled back at him and posted her question here and there. The gentleman's body was shaking. He seemed attracted by her incredible beauty and attitude. Great! "The fourth T-shirt is a done deal," he uttered.

"Well, I got what you say." Tauri interrupted their conversation as he ran out of patience to wait.

"What size T-shirt do you want?" The salesman turned to Florenza.

"Small." Florenza gazed toward the gentleman as he looked at her from top to bottom. He finally handed one to her.

Wow! The T-shirt hunting had achieved a critical milestone.

"Gosh! I have to go to the afternoon session. It'll start in ten minutes," Florenza yelled out.

"What about your lunch?" Tauri asked. Florenza totally forgot her time as they had fun with this treasure hunt.

"Let me walk you to your location. Where's your session?" Tauri led the way out from the dining hall.

"I don't know. My app is not working. I can't get the info from my phone." She talked in worried tone. Tauri knew that it was the spirit who created this opportunity for him.

"Let me find out for you." Tauri turned on his app and searched for her session. It was on the second floor at the Mandalay Bay E.

"What's your zodiac sign?" Tauri asked as he stepped onto the escalator to stand by Florenza.

"You mean the Chinese zodiac sign?" She was puzzled.

"No, the Western zodiac sign!" Tauri shouted.

"I'm a Cancer." She smiled.

Libi's moon sign, the emotion controller, was Cancer. His thought flashed in his mind. He quickly opened his zodiac Chi-Chi to look at the traits on Cancer.

"Your great strength is highly imaginative, loyal, emotional, sympathetic, persuasive." Tauri read it. "Your weakness is a little moody, pessimistic, suspicious, manipulative, a little insecure." He announced it. "Look at your compatible sign. Taurus is ranked number 1, which is my sign." Tauri was shocked. "Look at Taurus's compatible sign. Cancer is ranking number 1. We're a perfect match on the personality." Tauri was proud of his findings. "That can explain why she and I immediately felt a click, even for a few conversations," Tauri muttered. "I like to see your smile, Florenza. Let's get together after you finish your last sessions," he told her with a firm voice. "Can we meet at the gate of Data Village at 5:00 p.m. so we can do more T-shirt hunts?" Tauri asked. She nodded and disappeared in the traffic flow.

A few minutes past 5:00 p.m., Florenza emerged up from the human cloud. Tauri recognized her from far away.

"Hey, do you want to have dinner first?" Tauri greeted her as they walked shoulder to shoulder toward the booth.

"Let's go T-shirt hunt!" Florenza set her target.

They visited several booths only to find out that T-shirts had run out, and so had their patience. As they almost gave up, a small booth on the corner with only two staff members was in front of them.

"Can I have a T-shirt from you?" Tauri asked a straight question to a sharp lady.

"You'll get the T-shirt if you want to understand our product," the saleslady said firmly. She probably had a lot of people here only to get the free gifts. Tauri looked at Florenza with a smile.

"This one is going to be tough. Let me take it down," Tauri whispered to Florenza.

"OK, tell me something about your product compared to a start-up narwhal in Silicon Valley founded by a group of computer engineers from the famous company Hackbook." Tauri threw a hardball. He twinkled at Florenza and showed her that no matter how hard this might be, he'd find a way to get the T-shirt.

"Hmm, it's funny. Our founder's a chief engineer on Hackbook." The saleslady raised her eyebrow.

"How long has your company been set up?" Tauri continued.

"Over three years," she replied.

"Do you need some investment?" Tauri asked a different angle. He knew most startups needed funds.

"We got well-funded by two most prominent investors in the valley. No, we don't at this point. We do need users like you to use our product." The saleslady shut him down.

Let me change the strategy, he told himself.

"I'm indeed very interested in your platform. Let me see if I can hook you up with my boss." Tauri showed a sincere attitude and surrendered his company information.

"OK, that'd be great." The saleslady hailed and brought up the question they had been looking for.

"Let me give you the T-shirt," the saleslady announced.

"Do you have a small size?" Tauri asked first.

"No, there's only a large size available." The saleslady looked at her inventory.

"Do you still want it? Florenza?" Tauri turned to her.

"Yeah, we'll have it. I can use it as sleepwear," Florenza exclaimed.

They collected the fifth T-shirt and walked out in a happy mood.

"That's a tough one!" Tauri uttered as they did a high five to a laugh.

Tauri and Florenza strode around to find another booth to hunt. However, most booths were empty already.

"Let me take you back to your hotel." Tauri wanted to stay with her as long as possible.

They walked out from the convention center.

"Well, here we are. I have to go this way." She stopped in front of her hotel after they stepped out from the train. She waved to him and stood still there.

My gosh, is this time to go for a hug or a kiss? Tauri's mind was running wild. For some reason, his foot stuck to where he was. I just had a pure friendship feeling in my mind. He saw Florenza walk toward her hotel lobby and disappear.

Why didn't I go for a hug or kiss or one-night stand? Am I single? Yes! Am I attractive? Yes! Is there someone who loved me? No...yes...no. Tauri constantly questioned himself. He finally came up with the realization in his deepest heart that it was Libi who was with him all along.

How long would it take me to let Libi go from my life—most of all, from my mind, my heart, my soul? He wandered aimlessly in the Vegas streets with the neon lights flashing in the skyline.

Tauri's life had been totally changed for the last two weeks. So many young friends brought youthful energy into his life. He didn't feel alone anymore; he felt in love.

His energy was picked up by the tarot channel "True Love Tarot" on November 14, 2019. She published a video titled "Taurus Love 15–17 November Weekend. You Deserve This! Stop Questioning." She predicted that there would be a message from Taurus's soulmate to tell their true feelings.

Another tarot channel, "The Aussie Goddess," published a video titled "Taurus Weekly Reading for 17 to 23 November: An Opportunity for a Lifetime" on November 16, 2019, to offer advice. She talked about public recognition of their love. She mentioned a new message and a new job coming potentially.

What? Libi's WeChat profile statement changed from "Dance through the Night" into "Get Myself Back." That was a good sign. He was thrilled.

Oh! Libi's playlist was updated with only one song left.

1. "Lake: I Will Find You"

Tauri translated this song into her message.

Dear,
I lived in my world with everything I have. I ignored the young guys surrounding me.
    It's you whom I have a crush on. I've made all my effort to be near you.
I got warned by my friends and family for this connection. But I can't control

myself to be in love with you. I forwent the matchmaking by my family. I gave out everything to embrace your love.

Hey, I want to find you, who touched my heart at my worst life moment. We have been separated since then. I knew that I lost myself. I have everything like a perfect life now except you at my side.

After I gave my love to you, I pushed you away from me. Once I decided on this love connection, I vowed to continue to love you. Can you stay with me?

We fell in love with each other. How can we take it back? How can you retrieve water after it is dropped on the ground?

Dear, where had you gone with my heart? Would it be a failure for us to be away from each other? Wherever I go, whatever I do, whenever I am, you are always with me. I can't control myself to think about you.

I want to find you since we committed to each other. I'd be with you finally. With a fire of your love like sunshine, I would be like a drop of water in lake evaporating itself to embrace the cloud.

Libi's still in love with me! When does she come forward?

Actions speak louder than words. Does this translate into action?

Would that be a prelude for a new beginning for Libi and me? Tauri was daydreaming.

CHAPTER 19

The Soft Light

TAURI HAD A fantastic feeling along with the dark desire left at Las Vegas as he looked down from his window when his plane took off from Sin City.

What happens in Vegas stays in Vegas! Is Florenza going to do that? I may never see her again.

I can manifest anything. Right? I wish Florenza cherished this whirlwind two-day friendship. Those memories would last in her lifetime. Tauri uttered.

Tauri checked Libi's playlist periodically. An empty space showed up for a few weeks. It was like darkness, a deadly silence from her.

I'm flying blind.

Fortunately, the spirit guided me like a radar for the direction I am going. Tauri calmed himself.

On the eve of Christmas, the song "Lake" reappeared as Libi's playlist.

Did she reconfirm her commitment? She'll come to find me. Tauri felt overjoyed. His heart sang.

I heard her heart beat for me! He smiled and smiled.

Tauri utilized this holiday break to work on his book.

Now I understand what "cocreation with spirit" is.

Yes, it's a cocreation with my writing to Libi, her response via her playlist and tarot reading guidance as the writing block. He thought about this.

He shared every chapter with Libi for her to review.

"Libi posted a new playlist. Is she going to find me after four seasons?" Tauri gasped.

"Does she ask to let our hurt go or let her go?" Tauri uttered.

1. "Lake"
2. "The Four Seasons"
3. "Soft Light"
4. "Step Aside, Let It Go"

What does a soft light mean? Tauri puzzled.

At least she reconfirmed and has the timing for their reunion. Tauri muttered.

The new year was approaching. Tauri built up new confidence about the relationship.

By the last day of the year, he flipped through his WeChat message and noticed a video shared from Ms. Caiti.

I'm making a great effort to give you the best in this life since I don't know if I can meet you in the next lifetime.

Tauri's heart was pitched. That "blue bus" girl was a sweet girl in his hometown. They had a click. I can easily capture her heart if I deploy Libi's playlist magic. He smiled to himself.

"Taurus, you're powerful; you have to be careful about how to use your power. Focus on the big picture and divine mission." A few tarot readers repeatedly talked about this.

Yes, I'll have a breakthrough in my love life next year, Tauri told himself.

The holiday time was extremely lonely for him. However, with Libi in his mind and listening to Libra's tarot reading, he didn't feel alone at all.

Tauri noticed that a new song, "Seventeen Years Old," was added to her playlist. He went through the lyrics and came up with the message.

Dear Tauri,

Please express your true feelings to me.

Every song I posted was from the true feeling of my heart. Please express your love one more time.

He drafted the message and sent to Libi via WeChat.

Libi, my lady,

Will you be my girlfriend?

Here is my expression from the song "I Lay My Love on You," by Westlife.

Happy New Year 2020!

On New Year's Eve, Libi left him the message via her playlist.

1.   "The Four Seasons"

2. "The Soft Light"
3. "Let It Go, Let It Go"
4. "Lake"
5. "Seventeen Years Old"

"Please tell me you love me as if Cupid struck again!" Tauri was exuberant. The tarot channel "Awakening to Spirit" picked up this energy at December 31, 2019, and offered the reading titled "Taurus: The Maze of Love Brings You Closer Together."

Tauri laughed while listening to Cyndy's reading.

I'd be that elephant. I fought all the way to reconnect to Libi by bumping into her hideout. Finally, I raked through the maze of chat rooms at an online dating site to get her recommit again.

"The first hug, the first kiss. That'd be a miracle, my wish coming true!" Tauri uttered.

During the New Year's weekend, he looked back at how much he had accomplished so far in this writing project. He was happy with himself. It'd be the wildest dream for him to write a book. Now he could almost smell it.

On New Year's Eve, he sent an email to Libi about his progress on this book.

Libi,
Please review the draft of chapter 10.

It looks like I was able to get thirteen of the planned twenty chapters done up to now.

It's a huge milestone since I invited you as coauthor for this project on October 14 last year.

I hope that you can continue to find an opportunity to contribute to the idea.

It'd be fascinating to meet with you to discuss our project at your convenient time.

The song "Not Alone," by Zhang Li Yin, truly reflected my thoughts at this point.

Thanks.

As he worked on this long chapter at hand, he sent an email to her once he uploaded the first half of this chapter.

Libi,

Please review the draft of Chapter 4A.

These two chapters would have the story of two individuals to unfold their love journey.

The song "Love Me Like You Do," by Ellie Goulding, is my feeling for you.

Yours sincerely,

Tauri

After two days, Tauri finished the rest of the chapter. He sent another communication to her.

Libi,

Please review the draft of chapter 4B.

You can contribute by adding your side of the story. For example, what happened between Libi and Leo on that night after Leo told Libi that he can't marry her? What was the thought process Libi came up with to block Tauri on WeChat after that hair-touching event?

Those storylines would definitely add more flavor to this book.

The song "Don't Dream It's Over," by Miley Cyrus and Ariana Grande, is my wish for you to contribute it.

Sincerely yours.

Tauri was happy to figure out a way to consistently keep in touch with her, as the tarot reader guided. His energy was picked up by the tarot channel "Katy Parot" on January 5, 2020, in a reading titled "Taurus: A Big Push toward Success, January 6–12."

"Katy did pick up my energy to have a big push on this book project," Tauri yelled out. He felt real magic on the tarot's power.

⊷━◉ ◉━⊷

Monday morning was busy at the office. By the afternoon, Tauri took a glance at the clock randomly. It was 2:22 p.m.

Is there her message calling? Tauri got alarmed.

Here they are! A thirty-five-song playlist was showing up.

"Libi has a lot to say," Tauri murmured. "Did she want to see my WeChat message history again? I blocked her after she rejected my visit?" Tauri uttered.

1. "The Lake"
2. "Seventeen Years Old"

3. "Iron Arm Atomy"
4. "Regret That I Can't Drink Alcohol"
5. "Focus"
6. "Paper Is Limited, Love Is Limitless"
7. "I Am Still Young; I Am Still Young"
8. "Little Careless Seller"
9. "Sweet Grape, Red-Eye"
10. "I Don't Have It Anymore"
11. "My Dear Art"
12. "Shape of You"
13. "That's It"
14. "Journey of the Mercury"
15. "Psycho"
16. "Wait for Me, Wait Longer"
17. "Virtual World"
18. "Heart to Heart"
19. "Youth Rebellion"
20. "You Don't Even Know"
21. "This Age"
22. "Farmer, Fishermen"
23. "Let Me See You Secretly"
24. "My City"
25. "Queen at North"
26. "World at the Bottom of the Teapot"
27. "Nobody"
28. "Your Answer"
29. "Has to Love"
30. "Mago Seed"
31. "Those Sleepless Nights and Unforgettable Things"
32. "Star Failing"
33. "My Man"
34. "Tasteless and Grease"
35. "Can You Send Me the WeChat?"

Libi did explain why she doesn't come forward, and her plan for the future. Would it be materialized? Tauri asked himself.

He was afraid an accident had happened when he reset his permission on old WeChat messages. Instead, he took the screenshot of all the old posts and sent them to her.

Bae, my lady,

I just want to hear your voice, touch your hair, hold you tight. That feeling was described in the song "Power of Love," by Laura Branigan.

You're my lady, sweetheart, honey bunny!

Do you need any help? You can come to my place. I'm available on weekdays and Sunday if you want to see me.

Love…

By the end of his office hour, he found the song "Seventeen" was rearranged to the end of the playlist.

If you love me, don't hide it. Express again. Tauri got this from this song.

"Does she thirst for my whisper of love?" Tauri talked to himself.

He went to send her a direct WeChat message and got rejected.

"But how and what does she need?" Tauri uttered.

The tarot channel "Spirit Mail" picked up this energy and published a video on January 7, 2020, titled "Taurus: Spirit Says This Was No Fluke. This Is How You Can Live Your Life Every Day!"

"OMG, there's no secret in the eye of the tarot reading!" Tauri yelled out. He was shocked when he heard those readings.

"God is talking! Divine power is alive," he often told himself. He couldn't have enough admiration for the magic power of tarot reading, the high power, the spirits, the divine, God.

Tauri found Libi's updated playlist.

Wow, she used the opposite meaning to hide her true feelings to her listener. He waggled his eyebrows.

"Did she tell her story about her hotel night with Leo?" Tauri exclaimed.

1. "No Reason"
2. "Night, Ladybug, and You"
3. "Almost Home"
4. "Soho"
5. "Adjust Volume to Biggest; I Have Something to Talk to You"
6. "When I"
7. "Kill That ShiJiaZhuan Man: Youth Hotel"
8. "Liu Chuan Feng and Aoi Sola: Boyfriend and Girlfriend"
9. "My City"
10. "Rare"
11. "Want to See You"

12. "Aspirin"
13. "Sleepless Fly"
14. "The Only Livelihood Left on My Eyesight"
15. "Discord"

After spending a sleepless night, Tauri wrote a long WeChat message to her.

Dear Libi,

Another sleepless night for me.

The tarot reader always explains to wait for divine timing. When'd it be the divine timing for our reunion? Remember, we're cocreators of our reality: our life, our love, and no one else. God helps those who help themselves. So, God doesn't help anyone who doesn't help themselves. In this sense, we're part of our own divine. You're your own divine, I'm my own divine, we're cocreating our future.

If you mean what you said, what you sing as, what in your heart, how easy can you pick up the phone to say, "I love you"? How easy can you text me back to say, "Why do you feel like this"? How easy can you send an email to me to say, "Here is my situation; can you help me?"

I'm in love with you. As I repeat again, this love is unconditional. I want to have a breakthrough on the no-contact situation. This had led our lives to nowhere but in standstills and drama.

How long do you want to keep this secret to yourself, keep us in a power-less, hopeless, and emotionless life?

To open communication would give us the power to come up with a better decision. The truth will set you and me free; the honesty creates a predictable and expected solution. The transparency creates trust.

Sometimes I dream of doing little things with you to make up for the time we lost.

1. Dinner where we left
2. Dinner for my birthday you missed
3. Dinner at "One by Sea, Two by Land, and Three by Air" we planned
4. Study night at your favorite spot
5. Movie night at your apartment
6. Bar night to dance at your photo spot
7. Ice cream night at my town
8. Make out at Sunday Park

9.   Walk on the sandy beach at low tide
10. Hike trails at Sleepy Giant Mountain
11. Walk and run at Washington DC Cherry Blossom weekend
12. North European cruise ship
13. London/Paris week trip
14. Southern, Eastern Asian breaks

Pick up your phone to make a call; you'll find out how different our lives would be.
Let me see you! Let me hold your hands! Let me hug you! Let me...
Dear, I wrote a little poem for you.

Red Berry grows in the north,
It shines on snow and ice.
As my heart on the sleeve,
From my sacred love place.

Tauri was thrilled to find a way to show his love to her.
Is she starting to trust the Spirit?
If so, will she follow the guidance to start a new beginning with me?
Will she text me back? Tauri posted a set of questions into the universe.

CHAPTER 20

Reconciliation

TAURI MADE A demand to ask Libi to make a choice.

The tarot channel "Heart Passion Tarot" offered a reading on January 1, 2020, to predict the new cycle titled "Taurus: Surprise! Just the Two of You! January Monthly Love Reading." She mentioned that Taurus's love interest had just completed a cycle and came in to clarify. It is a wish fulfillment.

After a few days, Libi updated her playlist to respond.

"OMG, I never thought of the deep impact on her life on that trip," Tauri said. "Does Libi want me to text her my story?" Tauri uttered.

1. "Sleepless Fly"
2. "Sleepless Night"
3. "Asphyxia: Tell You a Story"
4. "Austin Mahone: Send It"
5. "Lemon"
6. "Summertime"
7. "No Party: Blue Sky and White Cloud"
8. "Conquering over Lakes and Rivers"
9. "LOSER"
10. "Sparkler"
11. "Game"
12. "Falling"
13. "Go Wild"
14. "There for You"
15. "Southern Bound"
16. "Brain"
17. "Farewell at the End of September"
18. "The Girl with Big Breasts"

19. "Loser"
20. "Single-Blind Love"
21. "Closer"
22. "Black Bird"
23. "Road Trip at Night"
24. "This Is It"
25. "Blue Sky and White Cloud"
26. "Crazy Sunshine"
27. "Irony"
28. "Old Newspaper before Bedtime"
29. "It Is Well"
30. "Five Hundred Miles"
31. "Irony"
32. "That Possible Night"
33. "Talking to the Moon"
34. "My Friend"
35. "The Right Path"
36. "Three O'clock in the Morning"
37. "Last Dance"
38. "Sleepless Night"
39. "Good Night"
40. "So I Quit the Music"
41. "I Am Willing to Accompany You in Normal Life"
42. "The Heart as Quiet as Calm Water"
43. "Girlfriend at House"
44. "The Stars"
45. "The Mountain and Sea"
46. "Out of Mountain"
47. "Don't Think about Him"
48. "Sunset/Sunrise"
49. "Leaning on the Everlasting Arms"

Oh! She painted our future life as "Sunset/Sunrise" for the age gap. That is so sweet! I totally agreed. At the end of day, we are leaning on God's arms. He gasped.

The song "Loser" might call all her potential lovers to express themselves.

"What? Is it return of the martial art contest for the princess's marriage?" Tauri yelled. In ancient China, the princess stood on a podium to invite the kung fu masters to compete. The winner would marry her.

Tauri wanted to make fun, as Libi asked him or other people to express love in a song, "Game." He drafted a message and texted her.

Libi,

The first round of the podium competition—make a statement.

Leo disqualified himself since he'd get married next year or so. He gave you up three years ago.

Your Aries boyfriend was not the contender; you broke up with him back in last September.

The Virgo might be a serious contender, a black horse. You didn't disclose this one yet. His energy showed up recently on Libra's tarot reading.

Your girlfriend Scorpio played a role in cutting our ties off. She might give you all those ideas from the book *The Girl with the Dragon Tattoo.*

This idea made me laugh now. I might wake up in the middle of the night with bursting laughter.

The tarot world called your disclosure only half true and my second half of this month a most creative time. I didn't understand a week ago until now. Don't kill the messenger.

Here are my tricks to win this game:

Show my ambition. I can take the journey to get your hand as if I can conquer any mountain or river.

Show my strength. I am strong to pursue you as if I can pull the willow tree upside down.

Show my stability. I can maintain balance as if I walk straight, though I am drunk.

Show my loyalty. I don't look at other attractions as if my heart is as quiet as the calm water; my body is as still as a mountain. Ripples in my heart do not happen.

In any scenario, I'd win. I have nothing to lose. There's no lower ground for me to go to anymore.

Besides this, all my writing and expression will be the content of this book project. I am speaking the truth I'll stand by.

This tarot reading inspired the idea, the cocreation with spirit. Whatever Taurus does would accumulate toward abundance. Nothing would be wasted. It turned out that is the best advice I ever got.

Yeah! The winner of the first day of the podium competition is Tauri, winner with highest score for this presentation.

The second round is the intelligence game.

There're fifteen multiple choice questions.

If Tauri gets a question right, Libi would remove that song from the playlist.

If Tauri gets a partial answer, Libi would move that song up one position.

If Tauri gets it wrong, Libi would move the song down one position.

If Tauri gets three questions right, Libi would give a virtual kiss.

If Tauri gets every question right except one, Libi would agree to give the winner title to Tauri.

The last question would be Libi's oath to marry Tauri.

Are you ready?

Question 1. The song "The Girl with Big Breasts"

A)   More disclosure on Tauri's Vegas friend
B)   Libi's proud bra size, cup B
C)   Libi's proud bra size, cup C
D)   Libi's proud bra size, cup D

Tauri's answer is C. Libi's proud bra size, cup C.

Question 2. The song "Southern Bound." Where is Libi now?

A)   Home at the southern side of the river, Shu Zhou, China
B)   Southern bound to Florida, USA
C)   At hometown to express love via wind, Hometown, China
D)   Staten Island, New York, USA

The answer is C. Libi is at her hometown in China.

Question 3. The song "Game." It could be expressed as:

A)   There'd be fewer spats if Libi speaks Japanese and Tauri speaks French.
B)   Express a whisper of love.
C)   Heal the sad and angry memory.
D)   Carry a divine mission to become the bridge between humanity and higher power.

The answers are B, C, D.

After Tauri clicked the Send button, he seemed to hear her laugh.

By the end of the day, Libi responded to Tauri's text message by removing half the songs.

What? "You have questions; I have answers!" he exclaimed.

Did she still call her lovers to express themselves to her on the phone?

1. "Asphyxia: Tell Your Story"
2. "Austin Mahone: Send It"
3. "The Game"
4. "Go Wild"
5. "Southern Bound"
6. "Farewell at the End of September"
7. "The Girl with Big Breasts"
8. "Blue Sky and White Cloud: No Party"
9. "Crazy Sunshine"
10. "Talking to the Moon"
11. "The Right Path"
12. "Last Dance"
13. "I Want to Go with You in Normal Life"
14. "The Stars"
15. "The Mountain and Sea"

"Did she call the 'game' as 'wild'?" He laughed aloud. He drafted another set of Q&A and texted it to her.

Libi, my honey,

I stared at your playlist and felt your worry, doubt, fear. Let me use one sentence to translate your questions one by one.

1. "Asphyxia": Please tell me your story.
2. "Send It": Send via phone. You don't tell anyone else.
3. "The Game"

Question: Can we have fewer spats with each other? Forget what happened?
Answer: I totally agree with you. We definitely can get over it. I don't feel hurt anymore. But sometimes I want to have the closure, understand your rationale and reasons for this separation. Sometimes I just want to give up this connection.

I had a hard time carrying on my life, maintaining my emotional sanity. That was the reason I kept writing and writing, for my pain relief and my feelings' release. This enabled me to focus on collecting the material, writing in the truth. At the same time, tarot readings really helped me to understand people's behavior and encouraged me to look forward to having a happier life.

I might be exaggerating for this. You treated me well beyond my imagination when I knocked on your door. I would not be mad anymore if I have the right expectation.

4. "Go Wild"
Question: Do you worry this love would be slipping away?
Answer: Yes, that is precisely what I felt. When I didn't care, I'd ignore you and pursue my future life. I question myself how long I'll continue to carry on in virtual space. No talk, no fun in the real world. Our life would be at a standstill. At some point, you and I will need to determine the direction to go.

I know you are thinking, thinking, and thinking with no action.

5. "Southern Bound"
6. "Farewell at the End of September"

Question: Was your aloneness a joke last September?
Answer: Let me explain. After the court ruling, my ex and I knew the marriage was over; the feeling was gone. I still treat her as a respected friend. We kept open communication on Lara's education and other business-related topics.

7. "Girl with Big Breasts"
Question: What about that girl with big breasts in the photo?
Answer: As I said again, there wasn't any love relationship between her and me. We're friends attending business training. Everything was written in this book. It's you who was in my mind most of the time. When I tried to start a relationship with another girl, I always believed our union would happen sometime soon. But if you can't get over it with my explanation, I have nothing else to add on.

8. "Blue Sky and White Cloud"
Question: Since our relationship is new, I felt curious, doubtful, fearful, mindful. What do you think?
Answer: You also have the opportunity to discover something new every day.

We need to have the beginner's mind like a wondering kid to this fresh, new experience to enjoy the new moments.

Question: A lot of guys are pursuing me. What do you think?
Answer: Yes, you can attract what you're looking for. That's your life. I believe in love, fate.

Question: You used to be the only one in my mind. Now I don't feel you're untouchable. How do you think?
Answer: Yes, we're equal. I'm a regular guy; you are also just like the girl at my company, my community, my neighborhood. So, let's have a new beginning.

9. "Crazy Sunshine"
Question: You wanted to expose this secret relationship by writing a tell-it-all story. Do you know it'd hurt me badly?
Answer: I got your concern. As I said again, once I have the first draft, I'd make the changes to make you happy. I'll not give up on this project. This is well beyond our experience, a story about the interaction between humanity and a higher power. I genuinely believe it and have evidence to prove it.

10. "Talking to the Moon"
Question: I'm on another side of the earth. I'm thinking about you. Are you?
Answer: I've the same feeling and have no one to talk with. The only thing keeping my emotional sanity is to write this book and listen to the tarot readings.

11. "The Right Path"
Question: Is this the right path to go?
Answer: I got your honest feeling. You might have your reason to question it.

12. "Last Dance"
Question: Is this our last chance to connect?
Answer: Yes, I'm in love with you. This is unconditional love without considering any return. But there's a boundary and time limit. Without direct communication, life for me is stuck. Well, our book project will definitely keep moving forward, no matter what happens.

13. I'm willing to go with you in ordinary life.

Question: Do you want it?

Answer: How I wish that we could start our life together soon. Though you just want a regular life, we are destined to bring the divine's love into this world by playing the role between humanity and higher power realms.

14. "The Stars"

Question: Do you realize how risky our connection would be?

Answer: I'm not aware of any risk. All I'm looking at is to make you happy. I want to live a life in full potential, including love life.

Question: Do you know that I don't want that supernatural talent?

Answer: The supernatural talent is not something that you want or not. It's a gift given naturally to enable you to make things happen. In doing that, you can enjoy your blessings and abundance and help other people at the same time.

Question: I'll not participate with your writing project. You'll have to work alone. What do you think?

Answer: OK, I got you. I totally respect you as far as you're happy.

15. "Mountain and Sea"

Question: Do you blame me for your marriage breakdown?

Answer: I'd never blame you for the drama in my life. My ex and I started to go to marriage counseling three years ago, even before I met you. But, as I said before, you inspired me to pursue my happier love life. It's a fate you and I'd ultimately get together.

All the messages I heard from tarot readings are that this connection is in the twin flame, a soulmate relationship. It is following a particular behavior pattern. In addition to this, Taurus was guided to have a financial abundance life. Those readings, as part of a writing block, led me to write the book as my experience. At last, if you hadn't said the "angry words," I wouldn't have pursued a series of actions that let me fill this book with colorful storylines. We're destined to be together.

Question: I want you to live a better life so I can take care of you. Are you OK to wait until I'm ready?

Answer: I'm absolutely confident in my choice. I'm in love with you and ready for this love. However, I don't understand what blocks you from coming forward. Tell me about it.

I want to marry you. I am excited to have you in my life. But I don't want my life to stand still.

Question: Do I understand it right that you can't afford this connection?
Answer: Absolutely not. There's no going back to my ex. I wanted to have a new life for myself. I wrote a poem for our new life.

How I wish to go on a cruise trip with you,
Buy a Gucci bag at Italy's street shop as brand new.
Drink whiskey in winter at Saint Petersburg's bar,
Hug you under the Eiffel Tower next to Champ de Mars.

Then I want to spend some time in Japan,
to reflect our journey, we have been.
I want to spend a long weekend,
to smoke a cigar on Cuba's street.

Enjoy famous sushi at the Plaza,
When we visit Hollywood Boulevard in California.
We need to wait until our baby can tag,
we can ride a camel through the Sahara.

We will skip snow-playing at Everest,
only take a ski trip to Killington to see your frozen, red face.
Want to watch your clumsy balance,
hear the scream from falling embarrassingly.

Pour the fresh snow on your neck,
kick off a laughing snowball fight trek.
Held your hands to make a slow move,
While I dance the groove.

The tarot channel "The Violet" picked up the energy and published a video on February 4, 2020, titled "Taurus: Unexpected Magic after a Release, Feb. 2020 Tarot Reading."

Is my energy, a Taurus, directly interacting with Libi's energy being read out as a soulmate and twin flame connection? he asked himself.

Tauri had been busy commenting on Libi's songs. He took a break to have a beach walk to switch his mind to describe her playlist in the story better.

When he came back to check her playlist update, he found that the song "Lake" in second place had been replaced by another song, "I Know," in the blink of his eye. He took glance at the clock randomly; it showed as 5:55 p.m.

Wow, 555 represents significant positive changes happening imminently. The divine being, the wholeness of creation in human form with five fingers, five toes, five senses (touch, taste, smell, hearing, and sight), the saint body (two arms, two legs, one head). He exclaimed. He noticed the synchronized number "11:11" in the evening.

Are Libi and I connected via the spiritual realm? He thought about it.

The energies for Libi calling Tauri the "Sparks at Her Life," and Tauri calling Libi a "Bridge between the Divine and Humanity" were picked up by the tarot channel "Spirit Mail." It offered a reading on February 8, 2020, titled "Taurus: Spirit Says Purveyor of the Light? Again? Yes! You Are Meant to Bring It!"

Tauri was content at this point. He and Libi broke up last October. Since then, Libi went to have a "dance through the night" life on the online dating site.

Libi is in love with me. I'm in love with her, even if I flirted with a few young girls. But she still didn't take my call, reply to my text message, or unblock my WeChat communication. Why, what, how long? Tauri constantly questioned this.

"You need to give time for a baby to grow," one tarot reader explained.

CHAPTER 21

The Valentine Wish

VALENTINE'S DAY WAS approaching.

"Opportunity is coming!" Tauri exclaimed as he looked at the calendar. He wanted to know if he and Libi could meet again.

What would Libi do this Valentine weekend?

How long does she need to grow to let me connect with her on an equal give-and-take? He thought about this.

"I definitely can gain some inspiration from a ski trip in the mountains in Vermont. But Libi is my real inspiration for this book. Where are you now?" he uttered.

Libi left him a playlist message.

1. "The Tree at Early Spring"
2. "Lake: I Will Find You"
3. "I Know"
4. "I Like the Feeling That You Are Better Than the Weekend Snacks of the Cut Fruit, the Center Part of the Iced Watermelon in Summer, the Unscrupulous Lazy Bed on Sunday, and the Quilt in the Air-Conditioned Room. But I Dare to Tell You."
5. "You Are Just a Passerby"
6. "The Beauty"
7. "We Are Different When We Depart and Meet Again: I Have a Job Now"
8. "The Girl, How Can I Be Willing to Let You Be Sad?"
9. "At Your Side"
10. "As If the Teenager Looks"
11. "Colin Wine's Mailbox"
12. "Zhi Ming and Chun Jiao"
13. "Girl"
14. "The Phantom of a Whale as An Island"

15. "Little Fool"
16. "That Possible Night"
17. "Aspirin"
18. "She Is Not"
19. "This City is Not Pleasant"
20. "Memory Loss"

My gosh! Is she still a virgin? "The Tree at Early Spring."

Oh! Libi called me a "passerby," and it worried her to be sad to stay at my side!

Did she use the song "She Is Not" to clarify she's not the lead girl at the online dating site?

Tauri texted her to respond to Libi's songs.

Libi,

The song "The Lake—I Will Find You":

It's Valentine's Day this Friday. Let me be the water on a lake to evaporate myself and find you as a cloud in the sky. Can we meet to have what the song "That Possible Night" described? I'm available on Wednesday, Thursday, and prearranged on Friday evening.

When can we meet to end with "blur words" and unveil the masked you? Why did it prevent us from seeing each other?

We can't control what others say; I don't care. You're the only person to know if the shoe can fit or hurt your feet. Are we treating each other heart to heart? Only we can feel it. Otherwise, the pain is still within us.

We're only admired by the same age people due to this fated love. We both wanted this love. We've been pursuing and overcoming so many obstacles in the past to reach this finishing line.

What we want is also what our spirits want: to align with the higher power and God's will. We pursue our happiness; we'll be happy in our spiritual and physical lives! Trust in spirits, the divine, higher power, and God.

We're carrying its mission to show the world love can transcend age, appearance, personality differences. We're the twin flames who bring our past life experience into this life. The road and solution for our happy life would present itself.

I realized your playlist is only talking about your mood in your mind. The beautiful things described can be repeated year after year, month after month. This year is the same as last year. And next year is the same as this year. In fact, the higher the expectations I had for you every time, the more disappointment I ended up with. There will be no disappointments if I don't have any expectations.

Do you know what makes me happy? Working on my book. I don't have any idea about the ending; I may need to find the inspiration from you. I also noticed the song "The Girl, How Can I Be Willing to Let You Be Sad?" As matter of fact, this book is a beautiful story, like a chronicled journal in which we find the happily-ever-after life under the guidance of spirits and the divine. I'm hoping you'd look at this book from a reader's perspective. For me, the truth set me free.

I had requested your participation in writing this book. However, this idea is a little bit unrealistic. The playlist is owned by an "anonymous" owner, and you didn't confirm your ownership yet. I basically created this story myself. Given such a situation, I once again suggest that you be the coauthor.

I spent a few days speculating on your intentions from the playlist. Unfortunately, the cost of such communication is too high. I'm barely able to concentrate on finishing this book.

Happy Valentine's Day!

Love,

Tauri

⋆⟞◉ ◉⟝⋆

It was Valentine's Day Eve. Tauri went to the office earlier than usual.

"Happy Valentine's Day!" one colleague greeted him as she placed a small clementine on everyone's desk. He immediately felt the air filling with friendship and romance.

Maybe I have overflowing emotion for Libi. He smiled to himself.

But Libi didn't respond his text message yet. He hoped a miracle for her to show up to meet him on this Valentine's Eve.

In recent days, he did notice the number synchronicity as tarot readers described.

In the afternoon, Tauri had a glance at the computer clock. It was 3:33 p.m. He searched online and found that meaning of this angel number:

"The angels were nearby, ready to help," he uttered.

"Libi is actually working on this playlist now." He watched the list change periodically. It started with twenty songs this morning. By the end of the day, the number of songs in the playlist reached over seventy.

"Libi has a lot to say today," Tauri told himself.

It took a while for him to go over this playlist. He jumped at the first screen of the ten songs to get the main idea and any action items.

1. "Lake"
2. "I Know"
3. "I Like the Feeling That You Are Better Than the Weekend Snacks of the Cut Fruit, the Center Part of the Iced Watermelon in Summer, the Unscrupulous Lazy Bed on Sunday, and the Quilt in The Air-Conditioned Room. But I Dare to Tell You."
4. "You Are a Passerby Only"
5. "Beauty"
6. "We Are Different When We Depart and Meet Again: I Have a Job Now"
7. "Right Here Waiting for You"
8. "Thinking about You"
9. "Pitch Black Night"
10. "Colin Wine's Mailbox"

"Does she have a plan to visit me tonight?" he uttered as his mind ran wild about this possibility. He decided to skip the regular gym and go to buy a rose bundle on his way home.

The grocery store was jammed with people.

I want to buy those prettiest long-stemmed roses. I can't wait to see her smile while she kisses on those roses. Tauri grinned. He chose deep red roses with a semitransparent glass tower vase package. It looked so charming.

He drove slowly along his neighborhood to see if Libi walked along the sidewalk. When he parked in front of his apartment, he found no one at his door.

"Would Libi come tonight?" he asked himself. During his dinner time, Tauri randomly took a glance at the timer at his coffee machine and noticed 11:11 p.m. show up.

"Something wrong with my coffee maker but the number 1111 signifies an energetic gateway opening up for me. This would rapidly manifest my thoughts into my reality." Tauri recalled what he had learned.

He imagined she'd come to knock on his door. They'd let this night unfold, like in the song "That Possible Night: Make 'No' into 'Yes.'" After he finished his fruit bowl dessert, he went upstairs to check Libi's playlist again.

As he reread through, he got a strong sense Libi wanted him to go to the mailbox to get instructions on how they'd meet.

Tauri remembered that one tarot reader mentioned this person would give Taurus some clue. The clue led to another clue to play the game.

Would Libi play the game like the movie *National Treasure*? At the end of the movie, Dr. Abigail gave Ben a clue that led him to find romance.

"Is there a clue in the mailbox she wants me to follow?" Tauri asked himself. He immediately rushed outdoors to get all the mail.

"There are the advertiser materials today. Am I wrong with her message?" he uttered.

Look again! Look again! Tauri walked a few steps in his room and reminded himself. One poster with an address caught his eye. It's an advertised postcard from a real estate agent.

"I sold for 1 percent total commission and saved $22,960 for the address 185 Brookie Avenue. Sold for: $547,000."

"Yes, that's the clue: the address she wanted me to go to meet her," Tauri yelled out to himself.

Tauri's mind dashed through his prep to meet with Libi. He went to have a quick shower to cool himself down.

Calm down! Tauri, calm down! You have to be careful. Tauri grinned to himself.

He grabbed a bundle of a dozen roses and hopped in his Mercedes. It was almost 10:00 p.m. when he left his apartment. The night was pitch black. He found the direction once he put the address in the GPS.

"Oh! It's only ten minutes away, not bad!" he uttered. He drove slowly to find the house shown on the postcard at the end of the street.

There were outdoor holiday lights from the houses along the street except the one he was looking for. The faint light showed one room on the second floor over the top of the garage. Tauri matched the postcard with this house in his car.

Yeah! This is it. But no one seems to live there. Should I go? Tauri debated with himself for a minute. He felt a little scared to leave his car.

He pulled back his car toward where he had come from and passed a few yards on this corner house. He was about to drive off.

"What if Libi is here and waiting for me? I would miss the opportunity of a lifetime," Tauri murmured.

He stopped the car and stepped out with a deep breath. He walked toward the dark porch in front of the house and felt lucky the light of doorbell button was on. He reached out to press the doorbell.

"Ding, ding, ding." After three times, Tauri stepped back and waited. There was silence inside there.

"Who would live in the house that was for sale?" Tauri asked himself.

"Ding, ding, ding." He rang it again after a few minutes.

The lights on the second floor turned on. Someone walked down from upstairs.

"Who are you?" An old lady with a nightgown opened the door. Another old gentleman held a flashlight, standing right behind her.

Tauri's face turned red; his mind was frozen. His pulse was bumping up and up. That was a huge mistake! After a brief blank out, he pulled himself back into this reality.

"I'm so sorry for bothering you." Tauri realized there was no Libi here. "I apologize. I thought that my friend was here," Tauri said.

"Whom are you looking for?" the old gentleman asked as he looked at the roses in his hand.

"I'm so terribly sorry. I thought my friend would be here. I must have the wrong address," Tauri explained politely. He turned around without explaining further. He quickly got into the car and sped away.

Let me drive as quick as possible. This guy might hold a gun and go after me. He looked in the mirror. He felt lucky that he dressed well and had a rose in his hand. Even though he knew this neighborhood well, he could get shot if the owner suspected his ill attempt to trespass.

Did Libi trick me? Is the address or instruction in another envelope? He questioned himself as he drove.

He came back home to check his mailbox inside out. There was no extra mail. He opened all the advertisement envelopes and scrutinized every piece of the ad paper and found no meaningful address where Libi might stay.

He rushed upstairs to look at her playlist again and found the total number of songs in this playlist was reduced from seventy to thirty-seven; it came with a different meaning as he clicked "View more" from the first screen of ten songs to see the entire playlist.

"Oops!" Tauri seemed to hear Libi's voice and saw her face with a loathsome grin or nefarious frown, her teeth biting down on her lower lip.

"What? Libi did trick me!" Tauri's mind ran crazy.

1. "Lake: I Want to Find You"
2. "I Know"
3. "I Like the Feeling That You Are Better Than the Weekend Snacks of the Cut Fruit, the Center Part of the Iced Watermelon in Summer, the Unscrupulous Lazy Bed on Sunday, and the Quilt in the Air-Conditioned Room. But I Dare to Tell You."
4. "You're a Passerby Only"
5. "Beauty"
6. "We're Different When We Depart and Meet Again"
7. "Right Here Waiting for You"
8. "Thinking about You"

9. "Pitch Black Night: Tonight"
10. "Colin Wine's Mailbox"
11. "Send Lover Away"
12. "Don't Send Me"
13. "Miss You Tonight"
14. "No Result"
15. "Going South"
16. "I Don't Want to Do This"
17. "Zhi Ming and Chun Jiao"
18. "Girl"
19. "Mr. Sun the Old Divorcé"
20. "Little Fool"
21. "Missing Person"
22. "Ship in the Sand"
23. "Gold and Silver Hotel"
24. "When You Are Old"
25. "Run Away Together"
26. "You Belong to Me"
27. "You're Not Alone"
28. "Blue Lotus Flower"
29. "Aspirin"
30. "Not Happy in This City"
31. "Memory Loss"
32. "ATM CYPHER 2019"
33. "One Day at a Time"
34. "You're Far Away"
35. "I Want You"
36. "Storyteller"
37. "Can't Stop Love"

"Oh! It's not her trick. It's my fault. I didn't read through her full playlist." Tauri laughed since her message was loud and clear.

"That's scary but fun. What happened to Libi?" Tauri read a few times and translated her playlist into a message.

Dear,
I want to find you like the water evaporating itself to embrace the cloud. I know. I just know I want to come forward to you. When I think about you, I

can't describe the exact feeling, but you're better than the weekend snacks of the cut fruit, the center part of the iced watermelon in summer, the unscrupulous lazy bed on Sunday, and the quilt in the air-conditioned room. But I dare to tell you.

I told myself that you're only a passerby to me, your beauty. Remember, we're different when we departed and meet again; I've a job now. But I am right here waiting for you. I'm thinking about you tonight.

I want to send you off since you're going north to a ski trip. Don't send me off. I'll miss you tonight. This is not the end of it. I'm going south; I don't want to go.

We're like the two characters in the Hong Kong movie *Zhi Ming and Chun Jiao*, two lovers who pursue their own independence. I'm that girl; you're the old man who had marriage experience and a little fool.

If you try to find your "missing person," I'm heading south and will go to a casino on the sea and stay in the Gold and Silver Hotel.

Hey, old man, I want to run off with you. You belong to me; you're not alone. I'm always with you.

We're like a blue lotus flower. Nothing is going to prevent us from pursuing our freedom. You're like aspirin, which heals me.

Though I don't like a big city, it's where you can make big money. Let's build our relationship one day at a time.

For that person who is far away from me, I want you, the storyteller. I can't stop loving you.

The tarot channel "Your Souls Journey" picked up their energy and published a video on February 13, 2020, titled "Taurus, Someone Has Your Heart! Doing What's Necessary to Move Forward in Their Direction!"

Yes, there's divine timing. Let it unfold naturally. Tauri nodded to himself.

"Libi, I miss you!" He left a voice memo via text to Libi before Tauri went to bed.

I spoke one sentence in Japanese I just learned. That was truly creative!

Tauri smiled to himself.

CHAPTER 22

That Possible Night

THE CORONAVIRUS NEWS from China was getting heavier and heavier every day. The CDC prepared for the possibility of the virus pandemic in the United States. There would be a lockdown where Tauri and Libi stayed.

Libi left him a long message at her playlist with seventy songs.

Oh! She seems to confirm she has no sexual experience in the grown-up world, like Alice in Wonderland.

She cried twice at night alone. Poor girl, why? Tauri sighed.

Does she regret pushing me away? Tauri admired her honesty.

Did she still want to be with me with a ten-year term described in "Reykjavik"? he opened his mouth wide.

Did she imagine to only play my "pigeon" when I get old? Yeah! The age gap is an obstacle.

Oh! Did she just want to do it?

1. "Alice"
2. "Alice"
3. "World Borderline"
4. "Alice"
5. "A Dark Night at the End of March: Commit Each Other"
6. "The Moonlight Restaurant: Old Man"
7. "A Young Girl Gregorio"
8. "IVY"
9. "No Situation"
10. "Star Sky: Two Steps from Hell"
11. "It's Raining in Beijing"
12. "It's Raining in Beijing"
13. "Alone"

14. "Mr. Northern Bound"
15. "It's Always the Little Things"
16. "Sorry"
17. "Last Party"
18. "Love You"
19. "We"
20. "Unravel"
21. "Love Too Late"
22. "To Be Good"
23. "Blue Sky and White Cloud: No Party"
24. "Arrogant"
25. "Unicorn"
26. "The Memoir"
27. "Wish You: Days and Nights"
28. "Simple Remember"
29. "Youth: Honest"
30. "As If a Youth Outlook"
31. "Heart Desire"
32. "Bittersweet"
33. "Mercury"
34. "Can't Let Me Go"
35. "Powerless"
36. "This's Why"
37. "Time Is on Our Side"
38. "Writing a Song to You"
39. "Intro: The Dawn—Dreamtale"
40. "Kill That Man: All Around Youth Hotel"
41. "Liu ChuanFu and Sola Aoi: One Couple Can't Be in Union"
42. "Reykjavik: Let's Commit Ten Years"
43. "Blue Sky and White Cloud"
44. "South Man"
45. "Canon in D Minor: Two Steps from Hell"
46. "Victory: Two Steps from Hell"
47. "Slow Before: Man"
48. "Emily: I Will Be There"
49. "Fly the Pigeon"
50. "I Hate I Love You"
51. "Talk the Talk"
52. "The Time Is for a Juvenile Offender"

53. "The Best Mistake I've Ever Made"
54. "Shattered: Trading Yesterday"
55. "I Don't Want to Be Remembered by You"
56. "Life Is a Dream"
57. "Broken Song"
58. "Whom Do You Want to See Most When This Is Over"
59. "Fox"
60. "Just Do It, Just Do It"
61. "Want to See You, Want to See You!"
62. "March Is Not the Right Time to Make a Decision"
63. "Your Answer"
64. "Only Six Centimeters Away from Your Teardrop"
65. "Overturned"
66. "As If a Boy: The Withered Tree in Spring"
67. "Want to Die but Dare to Do"
68. "Is There Still Anything You Can Love"
69. "In Fact, There Is Too Much I Want to Say"
70. "This's Not an Ideal Song"
71. "Final: 831 Chorus"
72. "I May Lose You"
73. "Chain Reaction"
74. "The Evening Stars"
75. "Wonderful Time Arrival"
76. "Three O'clock at Early Morning"

He translated the playlist into the message:

Dear Tauri,

I'm like Alice in the grown-up wonderland. I'm new, young, inexperienced, a little curious, a little scary. I want to dip my toes to test the water. I followed the butterfly in my stomach for my passion, pulled by the invisible hand toward you within the borderline of this new forest. I'd desire to get into a no-exit room with you to walk this life journey, echoing with the tolling bell for a happily-ever-after life. You'd be like that old man with white hair walking with a young girl, which would make this love lasting like the evergreen ivy.

There's no situation; everything is normal. Do you believe it? I cried under a night sky filled with stars! I cried for missing you for so many opportunities to connect like this Valentine's Day.

Mr. Northern-Bound Man, I want to make a confession. I'm sorry for the

last time when I shouted to you and pushed you out. We unraveled, discon-
nected; I cut your connection off. We're too late to fall into love since we both
can't be as pure as the first love. There's no union since then.

You, an arrogant unicorn, wrote this memoir. I wish that you'd do a simple
remembrance. To be honest, Leo was what I desired. It was a bittersweet moment in my life when Leo and I broke up, and I met you. Now he and I belong
to two different worlds. But he can't let me go. I was powerless to being drawn
by him. That's why I had been refusing you.

The time is on your side. I wrote this playlist message to let you know my
little history. The first time we met was in that hotel where you and I looked
but couldn't express ourselves three years ago. I want to commit to you for ten
years like the song "Reykjavik" described. Though you, a monkey king, have
the manhood of "Canon in D Minor," you can still score a victory in our family life. I can make out with you in "flying a pigeon" style whenever you need
it before we get married.

I hate I'm in love with you. I did "talk the talk" but never "walked the
walk." I was kind of guilty on the charge. If you break up with me, I don't
want to be remembered by you. Life is like a dream; I had enough broken
songs.

Whom do I want to see most when all this is settled down? It's you, a
lovely fox. We just need to meet, to make out, to do it. I want, want, and want
to see you. Do you know that? But March is not the right time to make the
decision to come forward to you. This is your answer.

Would you be overjoyed to cry when we meet again? Are you going to be
a new man growing from a "withered tree in the spring"? Somehow, I can't
escape from your love. I want to die for this but dare to do so. Is there still any
love left for you to love me?

I still have a lot of things I want to talk to you about.

This's not an ideal situation. But the next meet would be 8/31 when I
come to you, setting off a chain reaction. I'd arrive at night to have a good time
started. Hmm…how about three o'clock in early morning?

Tauri felt surprised about her openness. She must feel vulnerable! How I wish I
could hug her, he told himself.

Well, does she care about my size as far as I can score? I sure would be. He laughed
out.

Is she going to do a hand job before we get married? What a sweet lover she is. Tauri
immediately got horny.

Tauri looked at the long-stemmed red roses in the vase and felt only pure love for her. Tauri thought about this and wrote a text message to her.

Libi/Bae, my lady, my honey bunny,
The Valentine's roses I bought for you are still blossoming!
> Only hear your playlist like steps rattling.
> Can't wait to see your beauty unveiled,
> My whisper of love is to you exhaled.
> The songs "24. Arrogant," "25. Unicorn," "26. The Memoir"
> I got it.
> Are you willing to be my coauthor?
> The songs "18. Love You," "19. Ours," "20. Unravel," "21. Love Too late," "22. To Be Good," neither you nor I can participate in our past. How can I grow old before you arrive?
> I had been on a wild ride of the mysterious and exciting life since I met you. We're wasting every day in vain since we're not in each other's arms. I thought about this many times and concluded that you're my fate. No complaints and no regrets!
> The songs "71. Final: 831 Chorus," "72. I Want Lost You," "73. Chain Reaction," "74. The Evening Stars," "75. Wonderful Time Arrival," "76. Three O'clock at Early Morning."
> When your body, mind, heart are in the same place, you'd be happy to enjoy your first night.

Oh, you'd be relieved of a breakthrough.
Oh, you get a wish fulfilled for your grown-up run.
Oh, I'd get lost for our touch and play for the fun.
Oh, I'd cherish the opportunity to be your *one*.

Fell in love to let us to try;
looking forward to make us fly.
So precious, no regret, no complaint;
the excitement turns my face tainted.

I'd be devoted to your love even more,
because this moment makes our bond soar.
as long as you're with me,
This finally set us free.

I miss you!
Good night!
Tauri

⊹⊷≡◉⊜≡⊶⊹

Libi continued to update her playlist. She maintained her top ten songs to show her steady commitment for her plan.

Look! Libi had a reunion plan. Tauri gasped when he read a few more times to reassure himself.

"Does she just want to experience her first night?" Tauri opened his mouth wide. He kept thinking about the last section of her playlist.

He suspected Libi used the name of song to compose her message. If that was the case, it'd be translated as "Final plan happens at 8:31 p.m. in evening; the beauty will be until 3:00 a.m."

Libi even mentioned the place she potentially stayed in the song "It Is Only Six Inches Away from Your Teardrop." This gave him a reason to believe that she may live under his eyesight or in the next house.

Did I see two out-of-state car license plates recently? he recalled.

Yeah, Libi will come to see me tomorrow at 8:31 p.m. and leave at 3:00 a.m." Tauri got excited.

His excitement energy was picked by tarot readings. The tarot channel "Getlife333" published a video on February 18, 2020, titled "Taurus: Last Week of Feb. Sudden Clarity to What's Needed to Achieve Your Goals!"

Another tarot channel "Thick and Spiritual528" published a video on February 22, 2020, titled "Taurus: A Beautiful Miracle Is About to Occur in This Relationship!"

⊹⊷≡◉⊜≡⊶⊹

It was a sunshiny Sunday. The grass in his yard was turning baby green under a fifty-degree temperature.

Hmm…an early spring is here! Tauri smiled to himself. He had waited for this moment for a long time.

He went to take a nap after a three-mile run at the gym and turned his phone to speaker mode to be alerted when Libi's text or phone call came.

Oh! The divine is in action! He exclaimed as he noticed that clock showed 3:33 p.m.

He knew this book had been cocreated with Libi and guided by the divine, which would show the people's benefit by an interaction with the higher power.

He looped through the tarot readings to get sense of the trends for Taurus and Libra. At least two tarot readers suggested that Taurus should try a different approach.

In the evening, he noticed she still kept the last section of the playlist: "71. Final: 831 Chorus. 72. I May Lose You. 73. Chain Reaction. 74. The Evening Stars. 75. Wonderful Time Arrival. 76. Three O'clock at Early Morning."

He reconfirmed his understanding on her playlist. He ran through in his head what would unfold for this magic night.

He sent a text message to her.

Libi,
I'm waiting for you tonight!
Love.
Tauri

"I'm ready, I'm ready!" Tauri sang and smiled to himself. He had prepared for this night for the last three weeks. He looked around at what he had gotten in recent days: the different types of red candles, both big and small, to light the rooms; a few dozen roses to make the flowerbed; the pure white bedsheets for her first girl night; and most important of all, the playlist with the songs they shared with each other since they connected.

The sixty red candles lit up in a heart-shaped ring to greet her when she came in. Would she be surprised? Tauri couldn't wait to see her smile. Oh! This is like the story of Cupid and Psyche in the Greek myth. Ms. Psyche was carried to make love with Mr. Cupid at the evening and carried away when the morning comes, he uttered.

Tauri had been sitting quietly on sofa and looking out through half-open blinds in his window since 8:31 p.m. No one showed up after six hours.

He reaffirmed himself that she'd come at three o'clock in the early morning after the evening was almost gone.

At 2:43 a.m., Libi still hadn't changed her playlist.

"Will she come as she said in the playlist?" he exclaimed.

At 2:45 a.m., he worked on the final touch for his preparations. At the same time, he ran through what would unfold in the next ten minutes.

Here comes Libi in a hoodie! She is approaching my door. But I already saw her through my window. I will open my door before she knocks and let her in and lead her toward the living room.

There's a heart-shaped red candle ring twinkling. Those tiny lights spark in her eyes. She saw the rose petals scattered along the way leading to the stairs. She looked at me for a moment as I nodded without saying a word.

The candles were lit on every corner of the wall and each step of the stairs where the red, pink, yellow, and white colors formed a floral pathway leading upstairs. The faint lights in the bedroom from the candles highlight a king-size bed, which occupied most of the space. The glittering white silky bedcover made her feel as pure as if an angel touched; dark-red rose petals formed a heart shape in the center of the bedsheets.

She smiles toward me in a mystery way as she touches on the edge of the bed. She...

Tauri was pulled back from his daydream by the alert ringing on his phone he had set up for five minutes before three o'clock.

At 2:55 a.m., everything seemed ready. He put on his favorite white shirt to make himself look cool and handsome.

At 3:00 a.m., he stood next to his door and waited for her step to come...

Chapter 23

The Commitment: Chenlu

Tauri had been prepared for this day for a long time.

Would Libi come as she said in the playlist?

Is today the day? He can't hide his excitement.

At 2:45 a.m., he started to disable all the smoke detectors and lit the sixty candles making up the heart ring.

At 3:00 a.m., he stood at the front door and waited for her to show up.

The street was dark and quiet. Under the faint streetlights and the sconce at his porch, he could easily see if Libi was approaching.

At 3:00 a.m., there was no one on the street.

At 3:05 a.m., there was no one walking.

At 3:15 a.m., there was no one nearby.

Tauri sent a text message with a candle picture to her: "Libi, I am waiting."

At 3:25 a.m., Tauri decided to step out and look around.

"This is a sleepy street on this early morning!" Tauri murmured.

At 3:30 a.m., he realized Libi wouldn't come at all.

He closed the door and put out the flames on the candles.

Go to bed as quick as possible to catch up on my sleep. Tauri had only one idea in his mind. He didn't feel mad or sad; he only felt drained.

He knew a busy Monday was waiting for him.

The next morning, he looped through new tarot readings during his breakfast coffee time. The tarot topics he paid attention to were changed from "the commitment" to "pulling back."

The tarot channel "HiddenTruthTarot Tana" published a video on February 23, 2020, and offered the advice titled "Taurus Weekly Feb 24–1 March 2020: Taurus, You Got This!"

Financial gain? Closed one cycle of my life? I guess Tana was right. This reading is my writing block, which will bring financial gain. Tauri got it.

Another tarot channel, "Sunny Forest Tarot," published a video on February 24, 2020, for her advice titled "Taurus: February 24–March 1. Realizing Why You Pulled Back, but All Roads Lead Back to You!"

"I chose those tarot reading titles falling inline my expectation, intuition, but never pay attention to other information." He nodded to himself to make sense out of it. Tauri talked to himself when he listened to those readings.

He drafted the message and sent a text to her.

Libi/bae, my lady,
It'd have been the most romantic moment in our life last night. You did your part; I followed. Unfortunately, we didn't carry through it. It'd be a Mr. Cupid and Ms. Psyche story in modern times.

When I think about what we have done for the last two months and realized how far we have come to the "now" moment, we reconnected and recommitted in this virtual space. You fought for your happiness by disagreeing with your mom and friends; you showed the greatest courage to plan this magical moment. You'd take a huge risk to go to another person's house at 3:00 a.m. Is it?

Yes, we didn't carry through it. I was not mad; I was a little disappointed. See, I have only one rose for you. The rest are rose petals now.

We set the goal too high to be able to achieve. It's a leap of faith to trust your intuition and trust me, the man you love.

If we did carry through it, I'd have treated you as you wished; I'd not go beyond what you don't want to do. Think of me as a better person you're in love with. If I am not, you'd find a reason to leave me. Fair enough?

We may try one more time. Maybe we're just regular "people in love." I'm not that old and ugly; I don't care what other people say. When you come to my place, nobody knows who you are. We can cook dinner, grab the ice cream in town, or have "that possible night" to listen to our playlist.

The next day, Libi updated the last section of her playlist.

46. "Mr. Northbound"
47. "At Last, I Want to Go to Your Place Possibly"

48. "It's Always the Little Things"
49. "At Evening"
50. "Three O'clock at Early Morning"

"Oops, she did that again!" Tauri seemed to see her left open mouthed as she realized what just happened last night.

Tauri wrote a message and texted it to her.

Dear Libi,

I wanted to write something to you on the bed and fell into sleep at three o'clock this morning.

The songs "45. Mr. Northbound, 46. At Last, I Want to Go to Your Place Possibly, 48. It's Always the Little Things, 49. At Evening, 50. Three O'clock at Early Morning."

Do you want to ask me about my feelings if you carry through on that? I respected you deeply since I knew your past. In fact, you told me you still keep your girl's first night. This shows your moral integrity and honesty in a love relationship. What you had planned to do was in your imagination and creativity. This would make our daily life richer, more exciting, more attractive. By learning your playlist, I was able to learn enough dialects to understand your current and previous messages. This just proved you're a kindhearted girl; you dared to pursue your own happiness. This makes me love you more.

Our love is fated. No matter how many twists and turns we're experiencing, we'd eventually come back together. According to tarot readers, this "sharing" has made our relationship level up. It unstuck our situation, made us have a sense of belonging, a commitment.

We're unique. Our relationship is special. This gives you and me a chance to understand what ordinary lovers can do for months or even years.

Of course, our Chinese heritage is still to keep our feeling as pure as the jade if you did come. We have our trust on each other as a lifetime partner. Our story would be the "Cupid and Psyche" Greek myth happening in modern times. Premarital sex may be able to free people from postmarital issues like character conflict, sexual life discord, etc. We've been in love for more than three years. If we fulfill our wish, I'm happy and excited. By the way, I'm horny when I think about this. If you decide to leave the best to the most beautiful time, I respect and support you.

In considering the girl's first night, the woman didn't enjoy physically based on the statistics. We need to plan for a longer time to let us relax together.

We'd start to get to know each other's body, then relax our minds by taking a bath together, have a foreplay like the song "Shark." Those presex actions would allow the woman to be fully relaxed to accept her partner's entry. This would leave the girl's first night the best pleasant experience and avoid any psychological shadow in the long term.

Your body, you decide.

I'm in love with you.

Love.

⊷━◉ ◉━◈

The following morning, he woke up with one idea in his mind.

"No matter what I do, I cannot convince her to have direct contact with me," he uttered.

He decided to hold off on that date idea for a while.

As usual, he drove on the narrow highway to his office. He suddenly burst out a song with his full lungs.

He heard himself sing "O Sole Mio: You Are My Sun," by Luciano Pavarotti. His emotion was flowing out from his mind and heart. That was his genuine feeling toward her. Finally, he felt he had gotten his energy back from the drained last few days.

Some tarot readers suggested Taurus pull energy back to improve this relationship. Tauri actually was in the mood to hold back his message to her.

Before he went to bed, he texted her his voice recording of a tiny version of the song "O Sole Mio."

Dear Libi,

I decided to remove you from my mind when I got up this morning. I burst out in song during my drive to work. Later I realized it's a song singing to you, my bae.

You're my sun!

Love you and good night!

⊷━◉ ◉━◈

It was a busy Friday morning. Tauri was pulled into nonstop office work for a whole day. He found Libi had left a message once he had a chance to check Libi's playlist.

Chenlu, a Chinese word for promise. Does she offer an oath? Tauri yelled it out.

Oh! She did miss me! Does she comfort me by telling me her boob size? Double C! Huh! Tauri laughed.

1. "The Sky You Can't See"
2. "It's Not Good to Make a Decision on March"
3. "Many Times"
4. "U-Turn: Lil Dee"
5. "The Blue Sky and White Cloud: No Party"
6. "Unicorn"
7. "Memoir"
8. "Wednesday"
9. "Simple Remembered"
10. "I Will Definitely Love You"
11. "Bullshit Youth"
12. "As If Look Like a Youth"
13. "2.14: Double C"
14. "I Wanna (Everlasting Truth Remix)"
15. "A Fresh Feeling"
16. "Harmony Candy Wind"
17. "Even If It's Your Happiness"
18. "Raindrops Echo"
19. "You: Good Luck"
20. "Those Heart-Pulling Jokes and Long Daydreams"
21. "West Lake: Pain"
22. "Nonstop"
23. "Heartbroken"
24. "Forever"
25. "Walking Horse"
26. "Awaken"
27. "I Hate I Love You"
28. "Myself"
29. "Missing You Is Like a Sickness"
30. "It's Married Song"
31. "Face Mask"
32. "Who Do You Want to See Most When This Is Ended?"
33. "Puzzle"
34. "You Told Me"
35. "Wish You and Me"

36. "Fox"
37. "Lend Me 2020"
38. "There's No Reason"
39. "Only Six Centimeters Away from Your Teardrops"
40. "She's Not"
41. "Cough, Poor, and Love"
42. "Never Been Barcelona"
43. "After School: PRC Naked"
44. "Life Is Short"
45. "I'm Possibly About to Lose You"
46. "Like a Fish"
47. "A Commitment: Chenlu"
48. "This's It"
49. "Modern Anxiety"
50. "Think about Your Days and Nights"
51. "My Desire"
52. "Think about You! Want You to Think about Me"

Tauri was overjoyed after he fully understood what Libi had tried to say. He felt her golden heart.

Their energy was picked up by the tarot channel "Deep Thoughts with Dana." She published a video on February 28, 2020, to offer advice titled "Taurus: Things Have Changed."

Another tarot channel, "Consciousness Evolution Journey," published a video on February 27, 2020, to describe this event titled "Taurus: Shifting Relationship Cycles, Love Story, March 2020."

"OMG, our story is written in the stars, described via zodiac sign energy interaction by tarot readers," Tauri uttered.

"A date coming?" Tauri couldn't hold off his smile and burst into loud laughter again. He imagined her doing a boob-shaking Zumba dance.

Tauri spent the rest of the evening patiently installing two new curtains in his bedroom. He wanted to make his room secure, safe, and ready for Libi to come.

He sent a text message to her.

Libi, my sweetheart,
I just installed two curtains in my bedroom. I'm very happy about that.
For the song "19. Person In My Dream at My Youth Age," is your person in your dream always a pure, romantic person?
I'm a love idealist. I don't care about enduring the pain, suffering more

hardship as long as what I lost could be recreated, recovered, rebuilt, as long as I can have your heart, make you happy!

I'm also an optimist. My passion is to make bitterness into sweetness. My creativity is to bring the light into the darkness. My inspiration is to turn a pessimistic situation into an optimistic future. I'm the part cocreator of my own universe with a higher power.

My personality is resolute with the zodiac sign Taurus. I have strengths as a reliable, patient, practical, devoted, responsible, well-grounded person. I'm also stubborn, complicated sometimes. I like cooking food, listening to music, enjoying romance, living a luxurious lifestyle. I would focus more on the things that can be touched, watched, heard, and smelled in the physical sense. I rarely do sudden changes; I would plan any big changes at very early stages, with each step building up until I reach the goal. I don't like complications and would be willing to spend time to simplify it with clear logic. I want to have everything under control. Fortunately, I am learning a great deal to surrender myself to the things I can't control since I met you.

My zodiac sign, Taurus, is an earth sign, along with two other signs: Virgo and Capricorn. I can see things from a grounded, practical, and realistic perspective. I find it easy to make money. I can stay on the same projects for years. My stubbornness can be interpreted as commitment. It's my ability to complete tasks, whatever it takes. This makes me a great lover, so I'd always be there for you.

My love ruler is Venus, the goddess of love in Greek myths. It represents attraction, beauty, satisfaction, creativity, and gratitude. This makes me an excellent chef, lover, and artist...well, it's too early to say I am a writer yet. I like to learn established things and find ways to improve and make them better. I don't like to criticize or to be criticized. No matter what the challenge is, I can bring a practical solution to a chaotic situation.

If you define purity and innocence as being curious about the world, this is who I am. I do the planning in the medium to long term and am focused on the short term, the "now" moment. Sometimes I may improvise things to do. For example, I booked a hotel in the morning, purchased a ski ticket at noon, and drove four hours to Vermont in the afternoon last month.

If innocence means no experience or no knowledge in the love relationship, I am not innocent. I can't change my past. Can you?

I wrote a little poem, "Kiss You Everywhere":

Kiss your cheeks,
kiss your ear drops,
kiss your hair,
feel the love in the air.

Kiss your wide forehead,
kiss your pretty eyebrows,
kiss your big, round eyes,
kiss you till my throat dried.

Kiss your sweet dimple,
touch your trembling lips,
stir at your tongue,
felt the earth turning hung.

Climb up your "mountain,"
trek down your deep valley,
feel the sweet Hami Melon,
can't wait for that moment.

Tauri went to bed and couldn't fall to sleep. He thought about how long he and Libi had come to this point. He had been looking forward to the day to meet Libi for so long that he didn't even believe this day would come.

The next day at his lunch break, he scanned through tarot reading titles on an online video-sharing site. A few tarot readers talked about Taurus's upcoming meeting with the love interest.

The tarot channel "San Tarot" picked up this energy and published a video on March 3, 2020, for advice titled "Taurus: Their Presence Throws You Off."

Libi responded with an updated playlist.

"Ugh! She's upset about this book. It's good for her to talk about her concern." Tauri nodded to himself.

"Oh! Her desire was put off. What do I do to comfort her?" Tauri sighed. "Does she entice me to give up this story with her youthful beauty?" Tauri laughed about her silly idea.

1.   "The Story of the Songs"
2.   "Remote Desert"

3. "It's Not Good to Make a Decision on March"
4. "Snow at Summer and Flower at Winter"
5. "Meet"
6. "Wonderful Youth"
7. "Memory"

Tauri felt her agony toward the book. He felt really sorry for Libi.

By writing this book, I was able to cleanse the painful experiences and bring this greatest love story into this world. I truly believed it. Whenever I thought about this, my pain, loneliness went away, Tauri thought.

His energy was picked up by a tarot channel, "Holistic Fashionista," which published a video on March 11, 2020, to offer the advice titled "Taurus March 2020: The Soul Contract You Made Before You Came Here."

"Even though I made the disclaimer this book is not a memoir, it'd still hurt her and other people. Should I give up this book?" Tauri uttered.

Yeah! I got this spiritual gift to be strong enough to be an amateur writer at the rock bottom of my life. I'd never dreamed about being an author a few years ago. Would I give up?

Libi had been wishy-washy in the relationship in this virtual world. This book is the only thing I can hold physically in my hands. Can I give up?

This book is guided by the divine, written on the stars, and described via tarot readings. Is it too important to give up?

Tauri thought about all those questions.

Libi or book? His heart was torn.

CHAPTER 24

Shelter in Place

AN EMAIL FROM his CEO asked all employees to work from home starting Monday, March 9, 2020, immediately.

Tauri was ready. He had prepared for this for a few days. He went to buy frozen protein like frozen seafood, beef, and chicken, canned meals, and other essential items like tissue paper and bathroom rolls to prepare for the lockdown.

I can stay at home for one month at least. I also can shelter Libi to come to stay with me. He thought about Libi.

"Tauri, one of your coworkers was diagnosed as coronavirus positive," one of his team members wrote to him.

Gosh! This virus is near us now! Am I going to survive this pandemic? Is Libi going to be OK? Am I going to see Libi again? He felt pessimistic about this unknown future.

If the spirits want Libi and me to carry on this divine mission, we'll come out stronger! He gradually developed his confidence in surviving this pandemic.

The depressing news flew into his phone, computer, and TV every day. The only joyful moment for him was to go through her playlist.

Her playlist was like a baby talking. Let me build up her song vocabulary. As he was making progress, he could even see her playful, smiling face.

"Would this be the first time her playlist used my appearance to make me look smaller, insignificant on my self-esteem?" Tauri uttered.

1. "Stranger under My Skin"
2. "We Are Different When We Meet Again"
3. "The Blue Sky and White Cloud"
4. "Don't Ask Who I Am"
5. "Anonymous"

6. "Fish at Deep Sea"
7. "Last Party"
8. "I Don't Wanna See U Anymore: NINEONE"
9. "You Are One of My Stupidest Romances"
10. "Been Forever"
11. "The Shape of You"
12. "Think about You"
13. "I Am Sorry! Thank You!"
14. "Your Appearance"
15. "To Be Content"
16. "Girl"
17. "Sad Love"
18. "Do It Before Sleep"
19. "No Desire"
20. "Amazing Beauty"
21. "Even If Let You Kiss"
22. "Come to Have Hot Pot"
23. "The Heart-to-Heart Conversation"
24. "Ceremony for Love Affair Stealthily"
25. "I Am Not Happy in This City"
26. "Want the Freedom"

She does care about my health and wants to have an affair with me secretly after all that offensive language. He sighed.

I am very proud of myself. I can't change my past, my appearance, my shape. But what I can do is to keep a positive attitude. The only one beating me down is me, myself.

Tauri raised his head up when he thought about her insult.

Tauri began his first week of working from home since the coronavirus started to spread across the United States. The mayor of New York announced shutdowns of the restaurants, Broadway shows, and health clubs.

That was her city. She was right in the eye of the pandemic epicenter. Her last known address to me was in New York. Her new company address is in Manhattan, New York City.

Tauri texted a message to her on his luncheon break.

Libi, my dear,

This is the first week I do "work from home." Suddenly, I thought about the lyric "It felt like a jade if you belong to a family."

Bae, you are the home of my soul. Am I the home of yours?

I want to drop face masks and immune support gummies like vitamin C and elderberry to you.

Love you!

The tarot channel "Mermaid Scales Tarot" picked up their interaction energy. She published a video on March 16, 2020, to offer advice. It was titled "Taurus: Once You United, Nothing Will Stop the Power of This Union! Mid-March General Love Reading."

Another tarot channel, "Empath Butterflies Tarot," published a video on March 15, 2020, to offer her insight. It was titled "Taurus, March 2020: They Want to Show You a Love of the Lifetime."

"Did this reader refer to my energy interaction with Libi?" he uttered.

Tauri decided to text her directly about his mind.

Libi, my lady,

There'll be less chance to contract the virus in the countryside. In fact, the coronavirus will spread heavily in New York City in the next two weeks.

Do you want come to my place?

The song "24. I Am Not Happy at This City, 25. Want to Be in Freedom," Libi, I really don't want you to live the fearful life during this pandemic. If we know in our hearts that we'll eventually be together, you'll be comfortable to move in with me. You don't need to prove your independence; you can be yourself instead of being fearful of the gossip. Who cares? This's a fruition of four years of yearning for each other, the destiny of our fate.

Bae, I want to marry you. The age gap between a couple is ordinary in this society. If we're really a twin flame, we'll eventually be in union together. I don't want to wait to marry you when I'm ninety-two years old. We should seize the moment now to tie the knot.

Love!

Libi seemed to have a good mood after she went over Tauri's message. It gave her a picture of what it would look like for thirty-year age gap when they got married.

She added a new song, "Ing Ing," to her playlist. Its lyrics were so flirty that he wanted to reach out and kiss her. She removed the song "To Be Content." She seemed to have overcome the obstacles of the age gap and appearance that had been hanging over her mind for a long time.

Leave it to the divine, to the higher power. The solution would present itself! he uttered as if he were whispering to her.

⊶▬◉▭◦⊷

Tauri went out for a run at a local high school during his lunchtime. A few people were there to exercise. People kept their distance from each other due to fear of the virus. He liked to jog at the track and field since he could count the three miles as the twelve cycles. He'd start track 1 to track 6 and then follow track 6 again and back to track 1. This way, he could be sure he finished the full three miles.

An idea came into his mind during his run. He wrote a short poem and texted it to her.

Libi, my bae,
Whom do I want to see most when this lockdown is over?
Want to hug you, to be with you on the bed without covers.
I don't care what I am saying is too wordy.
It's my fire burning inside and not too dirty.
Do you know I really miss you?
Remove your face mask and be kissed all over by your boo.
No matter what I do,
I just want to see you.

⊶▬◉▭◦⊷

She made her playlist into a full flirtation letter he had never experienced.

Wow, she is flirting with me again after she wanted to break up two weeks ago. What a V-shaped emotional roller-coaster ride. He gasped. Tarot energy predicted this! He yelled it out.

Does she come back with the song "I Really Love You So-So Much?" Look! She is on the playful lighthearted energy with a song: "I Don't Miss You a Bit."

He laughed aloud. He can picture her as she does a girlish rolling eye and lips out face.

1. "Ing Ing"
2. "Who Do You Want to See Most When Everything Is Ended?"
3. "Sleepless Fly: Have a Kiss, Take a Shot to Make Out"
4. "Grease and Tasteless"
5. "When I?"
6. "Shape of You"
7. "Don't Want to be Friends with You"
8. "She Is Not: Gold Digger"
9. "Sleepless"
10. "I Really Love You So Very Much"
11. "Ceremony for a Secret Love Affair"
12. "Fish at the Deep Sea"
13. "I Don't Miss You a Bit"
14. "Don't Think about Him"

Tauri was pumped up. He grew his daily ritual to handle his daily work in the early morning and then text her a love message during lunchtime.

Libi, my love,

The Whisper of Love (I)
Your voice is the music in my ear; make me enchanted with your playlist hardwired.
Your cold stream breath is icy; let me be the warmer to make your heart unfrozen.
Your weight is reduced by two pounds; let me put it on top of my heart.
You must like to drink soda; you made the bubble from my chest go up and up.

Oh, my lady! Do you want to say "I don't like you"? Was it a cover to be a thief?
Oh, my beautiful girl! Do you have closed eyes that can't see my heart on sleeve?
Hold on, hold on, let me get something before it's getting dark,
Stay put, stay put, let me hurry up to come to give you a hug.

I want to get your approval to have a day off,
I'd wait for you on the city hall at the front entry step.
You'd be in front of the clerk's desk,
You can't escape from the happiness or misfortune by being my wife.

Tauri seemed to be finding his creative juices when he thought about Libi. The rhymes of the poems came up one after another like spring water.

After he finished his work, he texted her another poem.

The Whisper of Love (II)
Is it time to finish your work?
You've been sharing the playlist as my perk.
Are you tired today?
You've been running the whole day in my mind.

Do you ask me what do I want to eat tonight?
I whisper to you I want to eat you out for a while!
Do you ask if I lie?
I did lie. Lie. Like you as a butterfly!

Hey, girl, you said I am too greasy,
I just want to make our conversation a little spicy.
Hey, girl, watch out the dirty coming out from your mouth,
I only have a thought to kiss your lips and touch your south.

Tauri took a day off to work on his book. He continued to write a poem to her.

Hey, "The Fish at Deep Sea."
A Sip, by Tauri

My heart is pumping harder at this moment since I'm a stranger under your skin,
Don't know if I've heart disease or I'm constantly praying.
I started to write a book just to study your hobby,
Tried to mark some imprints even I'm sloppy.

I see you at my dream,
Your face looks as red as the strawberry in the rain.
I can't help to reach out my lips
Want to have only a few sips.

This isolation was not easy. Tauri worked at home alone. He had to cook three meals a day, take vitamin C, and eat enough proteins, vegetables, and fruits to improve his immune system. He felt all he did every day was eat, eat, eat. The only joy he had was to write something to her.

At lunchtime, he sent her a daily message for his frustration.

> Libi, my lady. Thinking about you made me feel horny. You had to make up the time we lost in our journey.

> Another day to wait,
> Another week to wait,
> Another month to wait,
> Another quarter to wait.

> The autumn foliage already covered the park trails,
> The fresh snow hung a silver coat on the pine fir tree with white gale,
> The spring breeze melts the icy ice into a gurgling brook,
> The early summer affection makes the cherry blossom blush your look.

> Another half year to wait,
> Another year to wait,
> Another world to wait,
> Perhaps forever to wait.

> Bae, I am determined to wait,
> I have so much time in my life to spend,
> It's not too long compared to a few hundred years.
> Willing to wait till I say, "I love you" in your ear.

The following day, she responded with a new playlist with the number one song "Lake."

Whoa! She is telling me her side of love story. He felt her warm heart.

What? Did she want me to masturbate to take care of my desire now and have a big sleep with her at a reunion? He yelled out.

Did she call herself a firing temper as a kid in Mars? Yes, she did have a bad temper. Tauri sighed.

Did she clarify the boy at the online dating site with her on that night was fake? He wondered why she brought it up.

She called herself not ugly but elegant. He laughed it out. He knew she was pretty and was his dream girl.

1. "Lake: I Will Find You"
2. "Ing! Ing!: Flirting"
3. "Sold Out: Hawk Nelson"
4. "Who Do You Want to See Most When Everything Is Ended?"
5. "Sleepless: Lil Chaos"
6. "Whatcha Reckon: Josh Turner"
7. "Oh, You Nah"
8. "Have to Love"
9. "Mr. Amnesia"
10. "Grease and Tasteless"
11. "Dictionary and Bible"
12. "City under Siege"
13. "Sleepless: Lil Chaos"
14. "Sleepless Fly"
15. "Why We Here"
16. "No Balance between Mountain and Sea"
17. "When It Is Gone?"
18. "Think You, Want You to Think about Me"
19. "Back to That Day"
20. "Lover Boy 88"
21. "Lonesome, That Is It"
22. "Crying in the Party"
23. "Iron Arm Astro Boy: GHK"
24. "Solace"
25. "Sadness to Aurora"
26. "Loves You"
27. "Love Me, Don't Leave Me"
28. "Fairy Tale and the Whisper of the Love"
29. "Silence"
30. "You Decided to Leave Me"
31. "Focus"

32. "Good Night: Lil Ghost"
33. "Unravel"
34. "Refrain: Aimer"
35. "Cheek"
36. "Talk, Think, Want, Love"
37. "You Are One of My Stupidest Romances"
38. "Deserted Island"
39. "7538 (Me U-Remix): KT"
40. "When I"
41. "Ease and Justified"
42. "Still Want to Break up"
43. "Get Old Sincerely"
44. "The Sky at Silent Night"
45. "Story of Mercury"
46. "Psycho (Pt. 2): Russ"
47. "Team Work: Jony J/UZ"
48. "Every Step in Slowly"
49. "Ga-Er-Gu-La: Look back"
50. "When She Is Gone"
51. "If the Surrender Is Needed"
52. "Youth Rebellion Manual"
53. "Best Singer"
54. "Road-North-South Highway"
55. "If I Am Mr."
56. "Devil from the Heaven"
57. "The Tour Song: Quark"
58. "You Can't See"
59. "All Yours"
60. "Take It before Bedtime"
61. "Stars Filled in the Sky"
62. "Stillness"
63. "Sorrow of the Love"
64. "Mr. Busy Man"
65. "Alchemy"
66. "Girl with Firing Temper"
67. "Who Understand the Wondering Heart"
68. "Crazy to Think about You"
69. "Movement under Comforter"

70. "The Love Story: First Episode"
71. "Start to Understand"
72. "One of the Slow Song"
73. "Powerless"
74. "Let This Song"
75. "Anonymous"
76. "Can't Say Goodbye"
77. "Coolest Kid"
78. "Double Hand Sword"
79. "Pass the Time"
80. "Spread the Love over the World"
81. "Write to Whom"
82. "The Answer to the Puzzle"
83. "Still Meet You at This Big World"
84. "Big Sleep"
85. "Courage"
86. "Psychiatrist"
87. "Muttering"
88. "Sparrow"
89. "Boy"
90. "Your Answer"
91. "Conversation with a Kid on Mars"
92. "Hibernation"
93. "Fake"
94. "Da Tian Boy"
95. "That Girl Talked to Me"
96. "I Suspected You Had Come"
97. "Raise a Cat before Dating"
98. "Baby, I Am Not Ugly"
99. "Elegance"
100. "Hold You"

My gosh, she cared about my sexual and mental health. Tauri seemed to get her approval for masturbating. It'd feel normal and whole when he is with her physically.

Should I pour my energy to write this book to divert my desire away?

This energy was picked up by tarot channel "Angel Love 333." She published a video on March 25, 2020, to offer her advice. It was titled "Taurus Weekly: You Will Receive a Kind Message! March 25–31 Tarot Reading."

Tauri was amazed how the tarot reading was resolute with their love relationship. He's a Taurus zodiac sign; Libi's a Libra. He looked back at the roller-coaster emotion ride for the last few weeks.

She had been using the song "Lake" to express her determination to come to this reunion, like the water at lake evaporating itself to embrace the cloud. If she put her words on her foot, are we already together? Are we going to survive this pandemic to finally be in reunion?

He had many questions in his mind.

CHAPTER 25

The Quarantine Separation

THE COVID-19 PANDEMIC took a toll on people's lives. There were over seven thousand lives lost to this virus in New York City alone at this point. He could feel the air with the siren from the ambulance echoing on the street.

Stay home! Stay in. It is good to be alive.

No matter how hard he tried to convince Libi to move into the countryside where few people were infected, she'd not budge. The only way to give her the comfort was to write more text messages to her.

The next morning, Tauri got up and hopped on his computer to look at her playlist.

Oh! She put a "stop" on our date! She wanted to wait for the "big bang." He yelled it out. The empty room echoed his voice.

1. "The Love Story between the Wind and the Songs"
2. "STOP"
3. "Under Mount Fuji"
4. "Why: AY/2-DO?"
5. "Baby! Baby! BIGBANG"
6. "Fall Out of Love: Ashleigh Ashton"
7. "I Really Love You So Very Much"
8. "Ing! Ing!"
9. "At Double Happiness Invitation Street"
10. "GOOD NIGHT: Lil Ghost"

He wrote a text message to her.

Libi, my morning sunshine,
Ing! Ing! Kiss cheeks.
I got why you stop our date. The reopening is going to happen soon.
Are you going to get married? To whom? I also want to…to marry you!
You're my love. I'm exuberantly excited when I think about the moment to marry you.
I wrote a poem, "A Daydream Moment":

You're the sweetheart at my dream,
You're my inspiration steam.
You're the pursue of my ideal,
You're my genuine desire can't conceal.

Your long hair is as pretty as the silky falls,
It grows in my heart as if something sprawls.
Your pure eye is as clear as the water in Lake Tahoe,
I gaze at your pupil as if I'm drawn into a black hole.

Your aromatic breath as fresh as the spring wind flow,
It makes my desire to be near you to grow.
Your smile as bright as a cherry blossom bloom in May,
It makes my mood sadly or joyfully sway.

The morning is always in the sunshine when I have you on my side,
The evening is always on a date when I take you for a ride.
There'd always be a little bunny wife when we're married,
Every moment is in the honeymoon guaranteed.

You're my partner in enjoying happiness,
You're my teammate to conquer the world ambitiously.
You're my past-life love and this life affection,
You're my destiny, which sounds like an addiction.

In response, Libi updated her top ten songs to confirm her "stop."

1. "STOP"
2. "Under Mount Fuji"

3. "Why: AY/2-DO"
4. "Baby! Baby! BIGBANG"
5. "Appointment"
6. "Mr. Loneliness"
7. "Fall Out of Love: Ashleigh Ashton"
8. "Just Kiss a Moonlight and Go Sleep"
9. "I Love You So Very Much"
10. "Bring You to Take a Rocket to Fly to the Beach of the Blue Planet"

In the evening, Tauri sent a text message to her for more song comments.

Libi, my bae,

Ing! Ing! Playing, playing!

I'm not afraid of getting the coronavirus at all. If my immune system cannot handle this virus, I'm not eligible to tie the knot with you. If I failed, I lived my best life up to now. What's the best way to end my life while I was still in love with my dream girl? Tactically, I'm cautious to protect myself and be safe to stay inside my apartment. In addition to this, I keep in touch with nature just kept my mind in sanity. In fact, I drive along the seashore for an hour every day to feel alive.

I thought I had the coronavirus already. Remember three months ago when I told you that I need to go to bed earlier? I had a low fever on that day. I went to have a hot shower and slept over ten hours instead of six hours on my regular night. I coughed slightly then. After I did my stretching exercise for a few days, I returned to normal. I wish I went to get a test to confirm it.

I ate the best protein, fruit, veggies, and vitamin C. I drink like no tomorrow will come. I do work out every single day. I felt excellent about myself. How about you?

I truly missed you! It is only a one-hour drive from my place to Manhattan since there's no traffic. I can easily pick you up in the morning and send you back in the evening.

Do you know why it's a challenging for us to breathe normally? We have been depressed ourselves, missed each other, thirsted for our love for such a long time.

I'll blow a kiss to moonlight and go to sleep now!

Tauri's motive to get up in the morning was to check Libi's playlist. This shielded him from watching the news of how bad this virus enraged this world and kept an upbeat mood.

She kept updating her playlist before he got up in the morning every day.

Is Libi an early morning person? Tauri asked himself. Sometimes, he stayed up until 1:00 a.m. to check Libi's playlist and found no changes. To his surprise, there was something new the following day.

The situation in New York City was dire. There wasn't enough medical personal protection gear in the hospital. One picture even showed a nurse using a garbage bag as a protection cloth.

Tauri worried about Libi. He texted her a message.

Libi, my princess.
I wrote a poem, "Never Forget."

I can't forget your hug,
have the courage to walk on the street with your luck.
I can't forget your smile,
The messages writing to you made me worthwhile.

Why are there so many obstacles between the people who're in love?
Why are they so far away between mountain and sea cut one core into halves?
Why is there isolation among us?
Would it be a divine way to delay this genuine love to combust?

I'd rather wait for you for many years,
I want to better myself instead of being in tears.
After I earn your passion and enter into your life,
we still date as if we meet the first time in foggy.

I don't want to forget that past contract, let me say, at 1874.
Even though there are more than one hundred years to explore.
It took me more than a lifetime to find you,
How can I dare to waste the karma to pursue?

I'll never forget the oath done as the milk spilled on the ground,
I'll never forget the excitement as the puzzle resolved with joy like a crown.
I'll never forget the sleepless night thinking about you,
I'll never forget the love red wired at the deep of the soul.

I'd never forget the divine mission,
The calling to be a bridge between humanity and the high power to have a fusion.
It's the destiny we must have,
To be happy and blessed on the divine behalf.

＊━◯ ◯━＊

Tauri and Libi's energy exchange was picked up by the tarot channel "The Tarot Diviner." She published a video on April 8, 2020, to offer advice. It was titled "Taurus May 2020. True Love Comes after Facing Your Fears about Love: Single Taurus Tarot May 2020."

Tauri felt this reading was so resolute with his situation. He applied what he learned from tarot readings as the divine guidance to pursue his true love, passion, and dream girl. His experience would give people know-how to interact with the divine world and gain guidance to pursue their happiness.

I'm determined to publish this book by recording my experience to pursue a union with Libi. She also wants the same. We're each other's wish fulfillment.

＊━◯ ◯━＊

Tauri got up this sunny morning and felt energized for the upcoming Easter religious holiday. His company was in the fourth week of the lockdown. Like other businesses in his state, they were waiting for the government to give them the green light to reopen the office.

It was a somber day in US history yesterday. Two thousand people lost to COVID-19 in a single day. A warning was issued from the White House that the pandemic would reach its peak in the next two weeks.

He went to the local grocery store to pick up another two weeks' worth of supplies. He was ready for the long game.

I wish Libi were with me! We'd definitely have so much fun together for lockdown. He laughed while he watched videos of funny stories about the lockdown.

"Taurus, you need to use your time wisely. You'll need to share your knowledge from your experience." Tarot readers reminded him. He felt the urgency to get the book done.

How about leaving clues at the end of each chapter for the next chapter? He was excited for this idea and arranged the events to try out.

He read Libi's playlist a few times. He better understood what was in her mind every time he read.

Did she keep marriage in her mind? Tauri felt happy in his mind, like a glimpse of the light breaking out from the cloud during this pandemic time.

⊷➾ ☞⊶

It was Good Friday, a religious holiday for the resurrection. The virus forced everyone to stay at home. The only thing that made his day bright was the hope for the new life after this pandemic was over.

He texted a message to Libi.

Libi, my lady,
The songs "4. Baby! Baby! BIGBANG, 5. Appointment, 6. Mr. Loneliness, 7. Fall Out of Love: Ashleigh Ashton, 8. Just Kiss a Moonlight and Go Sleep":
We're two adults genuinely in love with each other. I don't care what others say a bit. I don't have any contact with my neighbors; no one cares about who is my girlfriend. I'm a legal bachelor with a court certificate. The least fear in the United States is the gossip. The people wouldn't talk each other if they don't get along. They'd have their own niche friend circle.

I want to see you, touch your hair, kiss your lips, let you know how much I love you. You're my true love. Don't overthink. In fact, if you accept my invitation to come to stay a week, it'd be an extraordinary romantic life unfolding under this extreme pandemic circumstance. If we die due to the virus, we'd not be in any regret.

I wrote a poem, "Amazing," for you:

Since we're roommates,
let's cook a nice dinner together.
Since we're fresh lovers,
let our hearts be healed and recovered.

Since we're in deep love,
Let us touch to have emotion evolved.
Since we're each other's beloved,
let taste our honey juice to make us unstuck.

Since we're a couple,
let's combine our heart, soul, and body into one to cuddle.
Please release those self-limitations;
we can make this life journey extraordinary.

Tauri felt crazy sending all those text messages to her, one following another. That is what people do with no tomorrow. He smiled to himself.

Their energy was picked up by a tarot channel, "Ace of Pentacles Tarot," which published a video on April 13, 2020, with a title of "Taurus Mid-April: Love Is Here! This Is Deeper Than Passion! Take Things Slowly."

Another tarot channel, "The Tower Cup Girl," offered a reading on April 12, 2020, for her advice. It was titled "Taurus, If You Knew What Was Coming, You'd Relax!"

"Gosh, would this be the power of the manifestation that tarot readers have been talking about all the time?" Tauri always wondered why his energy had been reflected in those tarot readings.

⊷═◐◖═⊷

An optimistic message comes from the news media.

"The worst is over in the US for COVID-19." He read it at his sunny breakfast coffee table. He really enjoyed this bright spring morning and wondered what would come next in his life if COVID-19 were over. I wanted to have Libi as my wife.

"Hey, it's the pandemic time; the world might end tomorrow. Who can blame my bold action for asking for her hand?" Tauri talked to himself and laughed it out.

He sent a morning text message to her.

Libi, my sunshine.
My love, can you be my wife?
Love you!
Tauri

Libi responded to him by updating the top ten songs on her playlist.

1. "Wait for You"
2. "Commitment"
3. "In Love with You Deeply"
4. "Wait"
5. "Delay Execution"
6. "Appointment"
7. "Wait"
8. "Double Happy Invitation Street"
9. "Mr. Lonely"
10. "Standstill"

Tauri sent her a text message about his feelings on this beautiful morning.

Libi, my little lover.
Ing! Ing! Kiss, kiss!
I wrote a poem, "A Kiss of the Love" while I listened to the song "Just Kiss a
    Moonlight and Go Sleep."

This kiss is the most treasurable moment in my life,
I've been waiting for such a long time to thrive.
I dreamed about this moment many times,
I woke up in the early morning with smiles.

I toasted with my red dinner wine,
I do daily workouts to make my body top-line.
I place my lips gently on your forehead,
expressing my admiration and giving my comfort.

I lean forward to rub against your nose,
express affection like Eskimo to make my pose.
Lean my face with eyelashes to bat with your eyes,
a fluttering sensation like a butterfly arises.

Placed hands on your shoulder, peck on your cheek to have a kiss,
an emotional feeling pouring out with an abundance of bliss.
Put my kiss on the back side of your palm,
admired my sunshine for keeping my action calm.

Clue my lips to align my eyelids with yours just below the browbone.
A gesture of sincere love and care arises from this angel kiss grown.
Gently nibbling your eardrops on the earlobes,
the most erogenous and romantic kisses draw us into black holes.

Wonder between your upper and lower lips,
An intimate yet subtle single-lip kiss keeps us aroused.
Gently bite you on your neck and keep sucking,
The erotic mark kiss stirs up a fire of desires to make us drunken.

Bite your open mouth to make your tongue elusive,

An intimate and seductive kiss to win your heart is intrinsic.

Place my tongue to touch softer yours and let them make up the missing days,

Here come the most erotic, expressive, and arousing romance from my french
kiss.

Placed my tongue strokes against your tongue rapidly,

express nothing less than intense passion as if a lizard is cruising.

Delicate bites and nibbles on your nose, cheeks, chin, and eventually planted on
your neck.

A profoundly sensual kiss spontaneously as we calm down from intimate sunset.

My moon,

My boo,

My sleepover,

with you!

⟶▦◯◖▦⟵

Their energy with thirsting for this love was picked up by the tarot channel "Dane
Hart Tarot." She offered a reading on April 13, 2020, titled "Taurus, Stunning! This Is
Powerful || Psychic Empath Tarot Reading."

"Oh! Ms. Dane Hart's story about formation of pearls soothes my mind! That was
such an encouragement! I am so thankful for her to offer this reading at this moment."
He talked to himself.

⟶▦◯◖▦⟵

Tauri's birthday was coming in. The zodiac sign Taurus was for birthdays between April
20 and May 20.

Does she have a plan to celebrate my birthday? Tauri asked himself since Libi
had been posting a song called "Cake: Difficulty Mountain." He had joked about
the "mountain" part. Now he felt she might have this song to express the different
meaning.

His guess was right. Libi updated her playlist to mention the "cake" again.
He had renewed hope his birthday would be a reason for her to celebrate this
connection.

The tarot world was predicting this reunion; Libi was also planning the event via her playlist. Her state was about to reopen from the pandemic shutdown. Things seemed to fall into place.

Could this be it?

Tauri asked himself and the universe...

CHAPTER 26

My Heart Will Move On

OVER FIFTY THOUSAND people in the United States were lost to COVID-19, reported on the news this morning. This was not even at the end of the stay-at-home order yet. But a downward trend was also reported in COVID-19 cases, hospitalizations, and deaths in New York State and City. The optimistic mood was returning. The mayor of New York City even talked about a parade to celebrate the victory when the pandemic was over.

In Tauri's mind, he hoped New York City could lift the stay-at-home order so he and Libi could have an opportunity to meet again. He got a sense Libi wouldn't be willing to date him since she worried about his safety.

Tauri had been working on his book. He always had trouble telling the story from Libi's playlist in a creative way. He tried the different ways and felt happy about his idea evolving as this story progressed. At the end of each day, he drove out to the beach and just gave himself a glimpse of nature so he could switch his mind from this painful reality into his imagination for his writing. In his spare time, he listened to the tarot readings, which brought him very optimistic stories about the zodiac signs Taurus and Libra.

He developed a habit of texting messages to her at lunchtime and checking the responding messages from her playlist. Those messages had been part of his lifeline, keeping him going under this lockdown. He imagined Libi staying at the empty apartment building in Manhattan surrounded by the deserted streets with a noisy siren in her ear moment by moment.

A little bit of a love message would light her day up.

The tarot channel "Sacred Phoenix" picked up their energy and published a video on April 24, 2020, to offer advice. It was titled "Twin Flames: Taurus—You Two Will Commit to Each Other. A Key to Magical Gateway."

OMG, does someone already know what Libi and I are working on?

I only told my daughter Lara. No one else knew what I was doing. Tauri was amazed at what the tarot readers could do.

⊶▦⊙▦⊶

At the end of his working hours, Tauri found her new playlist for her idea to celebrate his birthdate.

1. "Empty"
2. "Fly"
3. "Circle"
4. "Cake"
5. "It Is My Sea"
6. "Best Location"
7. "Could We?"
8. "Drive to Tea House"
9. "Windy Season: Be Solo"
10. "At the Bottom of Mount Fuji"
11. "Felt"
12. "Sadness to the Aurora"
13. "GOOD NIGHT: Lil Ghost"
14. "New Things"
15. "Innocence Years"
16. "Life's a Struggle"
17. "Youthful"
18. "Intro"
19. "Journey to Mercury"
20. "Open the Door to the World"
21. "E-r-Gu-Na"
22. "Love as If"
23. "You Can't See: Rainbow Plan"
24. "All Yours: Rainbow Plan"
25. "King and Beggar"
26. "STOP"
27. "Ideal"
28. "We Become Friends Finally"
29. "Sorry, I Don't Understand Your Pain, but I Understand What You Mean"
30. "Nothing on You"

31. "Sleepless Night: Little Chaos"
32. "Never in Love Before"
33. "Enchanted Dangers"
34. "Meet"
35. "Ruins on the Love Space"
36. "24: Like an Eel"
37. "Why Can't You Rescue Me When I Can't Get into Sleep?"
38. "The Color of Wind"
39. "Missing Words at Evening"
40. "Honesty"
41. "I Missed You a Little Bit: Treasure Boy"
42. "Escapes"
43. "You Are the Sky in April: Princess Worries Reliever"
44. "Those Sleepless Nights and Unforgettable Things"
45. "Bloodshot Freestyle"
46. "Out from Isolation"
47. "When You"
48. "R"

Oh! She wanted me to meet her alone. Where? "Bottom of Mount Fuji"? That must be Downtown Wall Street; "Fu" is "rich" in Chinese.

She is still in her "innocence years," a virgin. Did she want to "open the door to the world"? Did she worry about our relationship as elusive as "24: Like an Eel"? Ha ha.

"Bloodshot freestyle"? That sounds like "sugar high" to me!

OMG, did she want to "R" once "out from isolation"? Are we going to do "R" grade actions?

⭤

The next day was a windy and cloudy Sunday. Tauri read through the news about the coronavirus in New York City and felt that Libi might have peace of mind since the virus infection rate had fallen to the lowest level since April 1, 2020.

Tauri checked Libi's playlist. He found no changes. He read the playlist through many times to double check his understanding of her birthday plan.

If Libi wants to date me without contacting me, the only way to do it is to use known information to plan it.

Tea house? How can I figure out where it is? But I knew that it's about the time to open up to each other. He nodded to himself.

His energy was picked up by the tarot channel "Deep Thought with Dana." She published a video on April 26, 2020, to offer advice for the zodiac sign Taurus. It was titled "Taurus: Love April Bonus."

Tauri felt that this was totally resolute with their situation. They had a thirty-year age gap. Tauri was more accomplished in his career and life.

Yes, it's time now! If it's not now, then when? He questioned himself in his mind.

Libi was open to breaking the "king and beggar" relationship cycle. Could we be regular friends, an equal give-and-take love connection in this new beginning?

⊷⇒ ⇐⊷

Tauri noticed that Libi had updated her playlist in responding to his text message.

I got it. She used a letter "last" as a meaning of "next." He smiled and was happy to accumulate her dialogues day by day.

Did she postpone the birthday cake gathering till summer? He covered his face to blind himself for a moment.

1. "Fly"
2. "Last Dance"
3. "Empty"
4. "Circle"
5. "Cake: Difficult Mountain"
6. "Last Dance"
7. "Summer Night"
8. "Windy Season: Soler"
9. "Honesty"
10. "Sadness to the Aurora"
11. "Can We?"
12. "Open the Door to the World"
13. "All Yours: Rainbow Plan"
14. "King and Beggar"
15. "Summer Night"
16. "Drive to Tea House"
17. "We Become Friends Finally"
18. "Nothing on You"
19. "Summer Night"
20. "Sleepless Night: Little Chaos"
21. "Enchanted Dangers"

22. "24: Eel"
23. "The Color of Wind"
24. "Escapes"
25. "Those Sleepless Nights and Unforgettable Things"
26. "Bloodshot Freestyle"
27. "Out from Isolation"
28. "When You"
29. "R"

Tauri sent a text Libi to express his disappointment.

Libi,
It makes me feel empty every minute when I think about you.

The tarot channel "Amethyst Angel Light" picked up this energy and published a video on April 26, 2020, to offer advice. It was titled "Taurus: Time to Take In on All Your Good Karma—April 27–May 3."

"Oh! This tarot reader did predict the repeat cycle and prelude my changes." Tauri talked to himself.

He texted Libi one word, "Empty," along with a few photos he took while he drove on the seashore. He had high expectations for this date since she actually put her thoughts on this.

It sounds like a moving target for a date she planned. Tauri was especially tired of writing the same story repeatedly. He needed to wrap up this book and move on to his new life.

Since the tarot reader predicted Taurus would encounter a "trickster energy" and be resolved by itself, he felt relieved.

I would be tricked if she doesn't show up at the dance club! Yeah! I am in a higher view under the guidance of the spirits.

He went to his bed and fell into sleep right away. When he woke up, it was a beautiful sunny Saturday morning.

"Who would go with me since we had such an age gap?" Libi asked at her playlist.

Not a problem! He jumped out from the bed. He felt very confident about joining physical activities with her.

Yeah! I'd be easy to lie down with her on the bed or on the lawn at Central Park for a day like this. Tauri smiled to himself.

Am I going to the dance floor with her?

He went to have a three-mile run for his weekly activity as he usually thought through some issues. I have so many hobbies to go with Libi on our social life!

He drafted a message and texted it to her.

Libi, my windy Saturday sunshine,
In responding to your songs "Bring Me to Find Night Life" and "Dan Bălan: Lendo Calendo," I want to bring you to the nightlife. We'd be like Lendo and Calendo, an attractive dance couple. The dance move is straightforward to me. Give me five minutes, I'd make you an expert. That's something I planned if we did that song "Possible Night" date.

We can start with a country dance. I'd play the music of "Alabama," by Dixieland Delight, and start with three-step moves: You start with right feet back, then left feet back, and then right feet forward, OK?

We'd make a "sweetheart" move. I'd hold your hands, step back from one another, and then push your waist backward. You're now in a spooning position. "One-two, one-two."

Next, we'd do a "behind the back." I'd grab your hands from behind your back and lead you around behind me; you'd hold my hands from behind my back and then swing back in front. "One and two, one and two."

And then, we'd make a "pretzel and mirror." First, we'd swing around behind the other side to glaze each other on the left side, then turn around behind the other side to glaze each other on the right side.

Followed then, we'd make a "spin-out." I'd launch you into two outward spins. We then release your hands to spin you 360 degrees and then bring your back around.

Finally, we'd make a "basic dip." First, I'd place my hands on your waist and move into a square position, and then I'd spin you counterclockwise and dip you over my knee.

After we enjoy the American country dance, we'd then do ballroom dance. I'm good at the waltz. Let us turn on "On the Beautiful Blue Danube: A Der Schönen Blauen Donau," by Johann Strauss II.

I'd hold your right hand with my left hand and stretch my right arm to hold your waist with your left arm on my shoulder to keep my body and head straight; turn my head to stare at my left palm.
One-two-three, one-two-three,
One-two-three, set us free!
You step back, I step forward, it may begin to look awkward.
You step forward, I step back, you're on the right track.
I stand in still, you would turn; your energy would burn.
You stand still, I would turn; our credits had been earned.

Turn with the flow! Turn with the flow!

Turn with the flow! Your move is glowing!

Are you tired of ballroom dance? Then, we'd do the tango. Tango is easy. Chinese artists Zhao Lirong and Kong Hanling already have the essence of it. I'll play the music "La Cumparsita." Can you follow me?

Tan-go, tan-go is just for a walk;

Hold your chest, tight your belly, and tangle your legs.

Three steps forward; just remember the words.

Fourth step closed; your move is posed.

Fifth step twist your waist; start to get a taste.

Sixth step wave your hands; joy came into your mind!

Is it easy to remember, right?

Then we would do a freestyle dance. I will play "Lendo Calendo" by DJ AJIN. Please remember to do each step four times, OK?

We start with the "still hip shake." Just shake your hips on the spot: one and two, one and two, one and two, one and two.

Next, we do the "four steps side snake wider": left move one, two, three, four; then right move one, two, three, four.

And then we make the "throw pizza" move. Think about using your hand to hold a pizza and throw it to someone else, OK? Throw a pizza left side; then throw a pizza right side.

Following by the "shove the snow," just like using a shovel to clean the snow, OK? Shove the snow left side, shove the snow left side; then shove the snow right side, shove the snow right side.

Next, we do a "ride a horse" to reach the pinnacle of our dance party. Think about riding rodeo and raise one hand to whip it, and turn 360 degrees around. One, two, three 90-degree turn; one, two, three, 180-degree turn; one, two, three, 270-degree turn; one, two, three, 360-degree turn.

Finally, we make the "jump" routine. Jump up and wave your both hands in the air at the same time. One two three, one two three. One two three. One two three.

Let's end with a breakdance finale. Jump to turn 360 degrees to the original spot. One, two, three, jump 360 turns; one, two, three, jump 360 turns; one, two, three, jump 360 turns; one, two, three, jump 360 turns.

Are you tired now? Let's do the slow dance. I'll play the music of "Unforgettable," by Nat King Cole. You'd place both your hands on my shoulders as I hold you your waist tight. We sway slowly with the music: "Unforgettable, unforgettable…"

"Libi, I...I...I am in love with...I am in love with this music, no, with you!" A wispier voice echoing in your ear.

Love you!

Tauri felt good about what he sent. *I would write anything to make her smile at this dire pandemic situation,* he uttered.

⊷═◉═◼═⊷

Tauri returned to his regular office work after he took a week off for his birthday break. He was buried by his piling up tasks waiting for him.

Libi updated her playlist in the afternoon to make an astonishing proposal to lay out what she called the "right path."

Wow! This'd be a breakup situation.

50. "What You Can't See: Rainbow"
51. "The Tree at the Spring"
52. "Thirty Years Apart"
53. "At Far Place"
54. "Hometown"
55. "Stop Work"
56. "Mr. Busy Man"
57. "Believe"
58. "The Summer Night: Hush"
59. "Sorry, No One Wants to Depend on Each Other"
60. "To Live Forever"
61. "Soft Light"
62. "Radioactive"
63. "My Heart Will Go On"
64. "Brother and Sister"
65. "The Right Path"

What? Did she mention people at my age already "stop work"? She doesn't want to depend on each other to live forever. Oh! She wants to move it on, only in a "brother and sister" relationship.

Tauri felt speechless. He didn't know how to answer Libi.

I've already told her I'll find my true love to carry on the divine mission. Play the role as the bridge between humankind and high power. I'll live with my moral standard; I'll not have my family and be in love with someone else at the same time.

Is Libi too low on a moral standard? Do I spend my energy in the wrong place?

What's my happiness if she's not with me? He took a deep thought to reflect himself.

My happiness is to finish this book. I'm sure I'd find someone who'll be in love with me, to build a family with me. Maybe it's time for me to move away from Libi's playlist! His mind ran crazy but quickly calmed down peacefully.

Well, I did what I could do to fulfill this divine mission. If it's meant to be, it's meant to be!

This'd be the first time Libi brought out a breakup in this virtual realm. She didn't want to break up, even when she shouted to him and ask him to never contact her again but still posted the song "Lake: I Will Find You" on her playlist.

Our final breakup time might just come!

He looked at her playlist and draft of his book…

CHAPTER 27

Unlock the Hearts

LIBI PROPOSED TO change their relationship after they meet this upcoming summer one more time.

Yes, Libi did open up. She did reveal her true intention at this point. But she was looking for balance between love and life, Tauri uttered.

This would be the first time she brought out to break up, even though she politely called them "brother and sister." His heart was heavy. He had no idea how to reply to her message. He went to the tarot world to find the answer.

Trickster energy coming in this week for Taurus?

The tarot channel "Baba Jolie Guided Message" had already predicted on May 11, 2020, titled "Libra: Nothing but the Truth! But Do You Believe It? Bonus May Message 2020."

Another tarot channel, "Katy Tarot," published a video on May 10, 2020, offering advice. It was titled "Taurus: This Upheaval Will Be Worth It! May 11–17."

Oh! Will Libi and I work out? How? I knew I could write this as part of the book, which would be a "gift." But could she change her mind?

The tarot channel "Stay Wild Star Child" released a video on May 11, 2020, even pointing out the similar reading for Taurus and Libra. It was titled "Taurus, Wow! Must Watch! Important Confirmation! Don't Run from This! Love Tarot Reading, May 2020."

Tauri realized Libi spoke her truth. It's amazing this sudden breakup energy was already predicted by the tarot world, and even more magically, the spirit had already offered this guidance to calm him down.

"The spirit is right. I'd be gentle for myself. Most of all, I'd forgive the hurt from her 'right path' proposal. In my opinion, this's a betrayal of our love. In the future, this'd also be a betrayal for her new family, my family. Since she is for her best interest, I'd forgive her with no hard feelings." Tauri talked it out.

I want to be away from her playlist. I am tired of it. I have enough materials to finish this book. I'd be in peace, no matter what happened, Tauri told himself.

Once he set up his mind, he made peace with himself and looked forward to getting ready for a new phase of his long-stuck love life.

After a good night's sleep, he woke up with Libi on his mind.

I need to keep positive and explain my position. When I think about the negative aspect, I manifest negative things in my life. When I think about positive things, I can manifest positive things in my life. He remembered that was the tarot readers' advice.

Tauri noticed that Libi continued to maintain this same set of playlists. Looks like Libi intended to stick to her position.

1. "Dan Bălan: Lendo Calendo"
2. "Bring Me to Find Night Life"
3. "The Blind Love Meets with a Deep Love"
4. "Fly"
5. "Mr. Amnesia"
6. "All Falls Down: Alan Walker"
7. "It's Always the Little Things"
8. "Asphyxia"
9. "Sold Out: Hawk Nelson"
10. "Hometown: Mama"
11. "Go Time"
12. "Dan Bălan: Lendo Calendo"
13. "Empty"
14. "We Are Different When We Meet Again"
15. "At Silent Night"
16. "Wait a Moment, Wait for Me Longer"
17. "Intro: The Dawn—Dream Tale"
18. "Breath and Life: Audio Machine"
19. "Memory"
20. "You Are Only Passersby"
21. "Lendo Calendo"
22. "Baby Don't Know Why: Ms. OOJA"
23. "Señorita: Shawn Mendes"
24. "You Are My Everything"
25. "It Became Dark Suddenly"
26. "Wanan"
27. "No Intention for Competition"
28. "22"
29. "Dan Bălan: Lendo Calendo"

30. "It Cannot Be Balanced between Mountain and Sea"
31. "Dream Mirror"
32. "Perfect Love Letter"
33. "Adagio for Summer Wind"
34. "Nothing Ever Happened"
35. "Sleepless Night: Little Chaos"
36. "Numb"
37. "Loveless"
38. "Asphyxia"
39. "Book about the Fish"
40. "Sunflower Feelings"
41. "Exuberated"
42. "Mountain"
43. "Girl! How Can I Let You Suffer?"
44. "You Are My Love at Youth Age"
45. "At Tower"
46. "Eightieth-Year Style"
47. "Live a Nonpurposive Life"
48. "It Is the Wasteland Everywhere under the Eyesight"
49. "Can't Grow Up"
50. "E-r-Gu-Na"
51. "Astronomia"
52. "We Connect Secretly"
53. "Liu Chuan Fu and Sola Aoi"
54. "The Tree in the Spring"
55. "Thirty Years Apart"
56. "Far Away"
57. "Still"
58. "Mr. Busy Man"
59. "The Summer Night: Hush"
60. "I Am Sorry, No One Wants to Be Codependent on Each Other"
61. "Live Forever"
62. "Soft Light"
63. "Radioactive"
64. "My Heart Will Go On"
65. "Brother and Sister"
66. "The Right Path"
67. "How Can't You Say I Don't Love You"

68. "Escaped under the Darkness"
69. "Last Dance"
70. "Got It"
71. "Pain"
72. "The Truth That You Leave"
73. "Never Had Love"
74. "The Fish at the Deep Sea"
75. "I Don't Like Living in This City"
76. "Love the Career; Love Beauty More"
77. "Beauty"
78. "24/7: Aspirin"
79. "Lost Word at Night"
80. "Heart as Quiet as the Calm Water"
81. "The Loved One Is Apart Between Mountain and Sea"
82. "You Are the Sky in April: Princess Worries Reliever"
83. "Light and Shadow"
84. "Can You Send Me the Message?"
85. "Sunset/Sunrise"
86. "How Can I Hold You?"
87. "A Several Yours"

"Oh! Libi still believed our right path to be a 'brother and sister' relationship."

"I need to chill down." Tauri talked aloud. He felt no incentive to reply to her message. By the evening, he had gotten even more depressed. He started to think about what he'd do if she wanted a sudden breakup. To him, this was an order from Libi.

"Hey, I am afraid you will find a younger girl than me in the future. We'll meet one more time and be like 'brother and sister.' After that, I'll move on from you." Tauri read a few times to make sure he didn't get it wrong. His confidence in her love was diminishing little by little.

The tarot world must have a lot of videos talking about this. He found out that some of readings were almost made specifically for him.

My gosh, is it my energy dominating the Taurus community? he wondered.

The overall readings for Taurus in recent days were very upbeat. The tarot channel "BE. ByHER" released a video on May 10, 2020, titled "Taurus, Let's Talk. I Feel Powerless Because I Have a Lot on My Plate. May 10–17." She called it a "misunderstanding" for Taurus. She advised a need to communicate to clear it out.

Libi was not happy when she found out the "blue bus" girl gave me a six-month deadline to respond to her love expression to me. Does she want to me to prove I didn't flirt with the blue bus girl? Tauri asked himself. He drafted the message and texted her.

Libi, my love,
My thoughts for the songs "26. Wanan," "27. No Intention for Competition," "28. 22," "29. Dan Bălan: Lendo Calendo," "30. It Can't be Balanced between Mountain and Sea" are that I have traveled a thousand miles trying to hold your hands. I'm not interested in anyone else. You're my true love. Our love is written in the stars, which you'll find in the tarot reading on Taurus or Libra. I have no contact with her, the blue bus girl, anymore.

The songs "52. We Connect Secretly, 53. Liu Chuan Fu and Sola Aoi."

Are you with someone? I don't have anyone. You are my only one, the *one*.

The song "84. Can You Give Me the Social Message (Original Copy)" and "85. Sunset/Sunrise." If you unblock my WeChat access, I might find a way to set the permission for you to see my posts again.

The songs "60. I Am Sorry, No One Wants to Be Codependent on Each Other, 61. Live Forever, 62. Soft Light, 63. Radioactive, 64. My Heart Will Go On, 65. Brother and Sister, 66. The Right Path." Are you going to change our relationship from "lovers" into "brother and sister" simply because the lovers will depend on each other? What's the love for? We'll make our name in history by our creative project and enjoy our life together since we align with the divine and higher power purposes.

The songs "86. How Can I Hold You?" "87. A Several Yours."

Dear, I am all for a colorful dating life.

How about we jump from the sky to hear our screaming at Tandem Skydiving, Long Island?

How about we join relay teams to swim across the sound just to listen to your yelling from the jellyfish bit?

How about we hop on the ice-skating field to let me grab your hands before you fall down at Rockefeller Center?

How about we ride a bike to have a race to win the three-mile trail in Central Park?

How about we go whitewater rafting to laugh at your curve on your wet T-shirt?

How about we run the Boston half marathon to let you watch me pass over you?

How about we step on the Wave Canyon in Coyote Buttes, Utah, to feel the wonder of the nature?

How about we hike a beehive trail at Acadia National Park to see who is the winner of that day?

How about we do a "hide and seek" in the field of "purple lavender by the bay" in Long Island to have summer fun?

How about we sing karaoke on Sunday night to see who can get a higher score?

How about we spend a whole afternoon at the American Museum of Natural History to find the whereabouts from the song "That Old Paint"?

How about I have Broadway night with *The Phantom of the Opera*?

How about we walk along Fifth Avenue from Chinatown to Central Park to enjoy Christmas lights?

How about we have "That Possible Night" at your apartment to dance the "Lendo Calendo" till midnight?

How about we sit on your sofa to watch the movie *Fifty Shades of Grey* to enjoy our fantasy intimacy just right?

How about I nib your eardrop and whisper to you…love?

Tauri went to the tarot world to get the answer. He was shocked to find that their love was be read via the tarot cards from the zodiac signs for Taurus and Libra.

It's really written on the stars. It's destined. It's determined before they even get into this world. It's the contracted in previous life or 5-D world. It's determined by the higher power realm. Tauri exclaimed and wondered what it meant for Libi and him.

The tarot channel "Consciousness Evolution Journey" released a video on May 13, 2020, to offer her guidance. It was titled "Libra + Taurus Love Story: Written in the Stars."

"My gosh, this is like a private reading for Libi and me." Tauri gasped.

"OMG, this is divinity's hand boosting us when we're at our lowest moment of this love connection," he yelled.

Am I the star seeds far, far away from this galaxy? Tauri laughed as if he were in the Star Wars movies. But he happened to see their energy interpreted through the tarot cards.

Will this connection ultimately find its way to come together? He had this question in his mind.

A few days later, Libi updated her playlist to leave a message for him.

1. "Bring Me to Find Night Life"
2. "Fly"
3. "It's Always the Little Things"
4. "The Blind Love Meets with a Deep Love"
5. "It Became Dark Suddenly"
6. "Dan Bălan: Lendo Calendo"
7. "Asphyxia"
8. "Can't Grow Up"
9. "Wait a Moment, Wait for Me Longer"
10. "Remember"
11. "You Are Only Passerby"
12. "Go Time: Mark Petrie"
13. "Lendo Calendo: Dan Bălan"
14. "Empty"
15. "Old Story (New Edition)"
16. "We Are Different When We Meet Again"
17. "Perfect Love Letter: Old Wolf"
18. "Nothing Ever Happened"
19. "Let It Out"
20. "Amnesia: Lil Chaos"
21. "NUMB: XXXTENTACION"
22. "Asphyxia (Piano Ver.)"
23. "Book about the Fish"
24. "Sunflower Feelings: Kuzu Mellow/Korou"
25. "Exuberated (Swang Remix)"
26. "Return of Prodigal"
27. "Mountain: Difficulty"
28. "The Summer Night"
29. "Old Love"
30. "Girl! How Can I Let You Suffer?"
31. "We Are Still Separated: It Was My Fault"
32. "At Silent Night"
33. "You Are My Love at Youth Age"
34. "Asphyxia"
35. "At Tower"

36. "Floating"
37. "The Love Song 1990"
38. "Live a Nonpurposive Life"
39. "It Is the Wasteland Everywhere under the Eyesight"
40. "E-r-Gu-Na"
41. "We Connect Secretly"
42. "Intro: The Dawn—Dreamtale"
43. "It Is My Sea"
44. "Liu Chuan Fu and Sola Aoi"
45. "Lendo Calendo (DJ AJIN Remix): DJ AJIN"
46. "You Are at North"
47. "Far Away"
48. "Mr. Busy Man"
49. "Summer Night: Hush"
50. "Sold Out: Hawk Nelson"
51. "I Live in the High-Rise Building"
52. "I Am Sorry, No One Wants to Be Codependent on Each Other"
53. "Thirty Years Old"
54. "Ideal"
55. "Happy Ever After"
56. "Absolutely Loyal to Each Other, Relatively Freedom"
57. "The First Episode of My Love Story"
58. "I Can Only Take Care of Myself. You Will Need to Take Care of Yourself."
59. "We Are Regular People; We Will Separate When the Time Comes"
60. "When the Love Is in the Past"
61. "My Heart Will Go On"
62. "I Heard That the Love Came Back"
63. "Baby Don't Know Why: Ms. OOJA"
64. "Brother and Sister"
65. "The Silence Is Gold"
66. "Breathe Normal"
67. "You Got It?"
68. "Last Dance"
69. "There Is Rain in Beijing"
70. "Señorita: Shawn Mendes/Camila Cabello"
71. "I Was Never in Love"
72. "Wanan"

73. "The Fish at the Deep Sea"
74. "No Intention for Competition"
75. "I Don't Like Living in This City"
76. "Love the Career; Love Beauty More"
77. "NINEONE#"
78. "Beauty"
79. "24/7: Aspirin"
80. "Lost Word at Night"
81. "Heart as Quiet as the Calm Water"
82. "You Are the Sky in April: Princess Worries Reliever"
83. "All Falls Down: Alan Walker/Noah Cyrus/Digital Farm Animals/Juliander"
84. "I Know You Know I Love You"
85. "Sunset/Sunrise"
86. "Dream Mirrors"
87. "How Can I Hold You?"
88. "Several Yours: Joyful Boy"

Oh! Did she call me a "señorita"? Am I that old? Did Libi come back to this love now? Tauri read a few times to make sure that he got her coded message.

"Yep, she is a 'return of the prodigal,'" he yelled out! He jumped as if he were doing a stretch.

Did she say she love me? Wow, she described our love age gap as "sunset/sunrise" and our relationship as dream mirrors. OMG, what an emotional roller coaster!

Tauri knew Libi would always be in love with him. But he was not sure if she would live with him in this physical world. Yeah! She admired the spiritual love relationship from her old WeChat posts, a kind of platonic love without having sex. But Tauri is a Taurus zodiac sign, an earth sign being satisfied via four basic human senses: see, smell, touch, hear. He'd feel his need to be met when he saw her beautiful body, smelled her aurora, touched her creamy face, heard her soft voice. He wrote a message and texted her.

Libi, my love,
My thoughts on the song "57. The First Episode of My Love Story."
Don't forget other things: I want two babies, one girl and one boy, one cat, one dog.
The song "84. I Know, You Know, I Love You."
Truly? I know "you love me" from the bottom of my heart. I can feel it

from all the hints. But I want to hear from you in person. Who would make all my suffering go away? My journey worth it?

I would smile in my dream now.

Kiss & love

⊷⊨◉ ◉⊨⊷

The tarot channel "Sincere Tarot" published a video on May 16, 2020, offering advice on the book project. It was titled "This Relationship Will Never Be the Same! Taurus Mid-May 2020. Tarot Forecast."

Another tarot channel, "Goddess Intuition," published a video on May 16, 2020, to offer advice on twin flame energy. It was titled "Taurus, May 16–31, This Is Destiny Fulfilled!"

"Is it my ultimate dream coming true?" Tauri uttered.

The New York State governor announced the extension for the stay-at-home order.

Does it mean that I can't see Libi for another month? Tauri uttered. He received an email from his town that local beaches and parks were already opened.

The memorial date was over as the official summer kicked in.

Will Libi keep her promise to meet with me on a summer night?

Tauri looked at the sunny blue sky and threw his question to the universe!

CHAPTER 28

The Love Matters

TAURI GOT UP this regular summer morning. He found his social media feed was flooded with a video showed an African American man pinned to the ground by kneeling for eight minutes.

"I can't breathe, I can't breathe," he murmured. He died in front of the camera. Tauri's heart was sunken. He heard so many horrible stories and remembered there were massive protests in New York City years ago where Libi stayed. A tsunami of a social injustice protection movement was about to engulf the whole nation in the middle of a once-in-a-century pandemic.

He sent Libi a text as usual.

Libi, my love,
My tulips grow from a flowerpot that longed for the light. It grew extremely big and outward to the window to greet the sun. My heart is yearning for your love.
Did you hear that I missed you so very much?

The tarot channel "Pure Guidance" published a video on May 21, 2020, titled "Taurus June 2020: You Are in for a Ride of a Lifetime || Tarot & Astrology Reading by Pure Guidance."

She advised, "Taurus, you're the king; you're the divine; you're given all the tools to achieve the life you always desire to."

Another tarot channel, "Tarot Victorian," published a video on May 23, 2020, to offer guidance. It was titled "Taurus June 2020: Pay Attention to the Date, Major Changes."

My gosh! This reading described my relationship with Libi; we have the true love. Oh my gosh! She described my relationship with Ms. Aquri. She's sure to try to control every aspect of my love. This'll never with me. Tauri gasped.

Tauri felt the same way. It'd be the ride of a lifetime if he and Libi could have a the reunion and get married. He was also happy to be read by tarot readers that he and Libi were a power couple. He felt relief for himself and his ex. They were fated to be the way they were now.

⊷═◉ ◉═⊷

The news continued to flow in about the hundreds of demonstrators marching in the streets in Minneapolis to protest social injustice. The protests spread to other cities like wildfire. The slogan "I can't breathe" was adopted quickly to express the emotions under this extreme pandemic and social environment.

Tauri wrote a message and texted her.

Libi, my love,
Dear "fish at deep sea," I'm a hungry wolf. Give me your address. I'll come today to eat you.
My Thoughts about the song "Ing! Ing!"
I want to see you have a silly smile toward the mirror,
your joyful feeling from inside out made you dearer.
I want to kiss your cheeks to see them blushed,
Your invisible emotional wall got crushed.
I want to hear your heartbeat thump, jump, pump,
Your solid and round mountains standing up, up, up.

⊷═◉ ◉═⊷

The tarot channel "Real Housewives of Tarot" picked up this energy and published a video on May 28, 2020, to offer guidance. It was titled "Taurus: Heaven Sent Connection Taurus!"

Tauri felt content. Though he watched the protest events evolving with a worried eye, his mind was immersed in Libi's love. But Libi's refusal to come out to connect with him directly made him feel resolute with the slogan.

"I can't breathe with this love!" Tauri told him in silence. "I can't send her social media messages. I got no response from my text information. I got no face-to-face contact for almost two years. I got no information about her whereabouts. I'm at the total mercy of her love. She could walk away at any time or evaporate at any moment, for any reason. I wouldn't know what happened to her!" he told himself. "This is totally unfair and unjustified!" Tauri thought about the reasons why he was resolute with this slogan. "I am suffocating with her treatment!" He thought about this.

"Tauri, as a zodiac sign Taurus, you have a unique divine gift; you have a divine connection. The spirit is with you. You're a magician with everything available at your hands to achieve your happiness. Please continue to work on what you had been working on. Everything would fall into place." The tarot reader's voice echoed in his mind.

In the evening, the news showed the horrible scene outside the White House. The tear gas was deployed to clear out the road to the church.

"Oh my gosh! The coronavirus caused an almost 20 percent unemployment rate, and then came with nationwide unrest for social justice," he uttered. He felt depressed.

"I don't know where she stays in New York City. I'm totally in the dark," Tauri told himself every day when he woke up in the morning.

This energy was picked up by the tarot channel "Awakening to Spirit." She published a video on June 2, 2020, to offer advice. It was titled "Taurus: When You Realize That You Are the Light at the End of the Tunnel."

Another tarot channel, "Staller Wilde," published a video on June 1, 2020, to offer guidance. It was titled "Taurus: Justice, Victory, Wished—June 2020 Psychic Tarot."

Hmm, I didn't see Libi for almost two years. He thought a moment and nodded to himself.

"This cocreation book project is the lantern that will bring healing power into this world. That will be the light in the tunnel!" he exclaimed.

New York City announced it would implement a curfew after 8:00 p.m. to reduce the infection rate for COVID-19. There was a memorial service held for the victim of this social injustice movement a few days later.

That was horrible. No one deserves to die in this way. Life is so valuable, fragile. Once it is lost, it can never come back. It's only love, love for life, that prevents tragedy from happening. So life matters, love matters, Tauri told himself.

Tauri didn't go to the gathering at his town for those events. He wanted to go. His nonprofit organization actually donated to the local police department for COVID-19 protection gear.

"Hope Libi is safe!" he uttered and went to check Libi's playlist.

Oh! She felt the same with me for the fragile life. Once it is lost, it never gets back. Tauri raised his eyebrow.

"Poor girl! Did this trigger her emotion to think about her own life?" Tauri sighed.

"She seems to have lots of ideas for the book. Did she actually write them down?" he murmured.

1. "Dan Bălan: Lendo Calendo"
2. "Love Me Like You Do"
3. "Prays for You!"
4. "Don't Have It anymore"
5. "Why Would I Ever"
6. "Radioactive in the Dark"
7. "Centuries"
8. "The Phoenix"
9. "We Are One: Kelly Sweet"
10. "Want to Be Your Cat"
11. "Sleepless Night: Lil Chaos"
12. "Yearn for You"
13. "We Are Different When We Meet Again"
14. "Disqualification"
15. "Sleepless Night: Little Chaos"
16. "No Reason"
17. "There for You: Martin Garrix/Troye Sivan"
18. "River: Charlie Puth"
19. "Send It: Austin Mahone/Rich Homie Quan"
20. "She Is My Sin: Nightwish"
21. "Numb: Linkin Park"
22. "Love Yourself (Natio Remix): Natio/Justin Bieber/Conor Maynard"
23. "Man in the Moon"
24. "Irresistible: Fall Out Boy/Demi Lovato"
25. "Sold Out: Hawk Nelson"
26. "Myself"
27. "Thirty Years Old"
28. "Price Tag"
29. "In the End"
30. "DAY LOVE NIGHT"
31. "So: Lo—Kate Havnevik"
32. "Soldier"
33. "At Bottle World of the Teapot"
34. "The Mighty Fall"

35. "I Am Not Your Oriental Fish"
36. "I Want My Tears Back: Nightwish"
37. "Folklore of Hungry Wolf"
38. "The Silence Is Gold"
39. "Mistletoe: Justin Bieber"
40. "Insomnia: Craig David"
41. "Get Closer: Big Year"
42. "Fly"
43. "Sleepless Fly: Have a Kiss, Take a Shot"
44. "Rescue Me"
45. "The Poem Written by Wondering Cat"
46. "It Is a Joyful Thing to Do by Skipping Breakfast"
47. "Lover Boy 88"
48. "Garbage"
49. "Lover Boy 88"
50. "Exposed"
51. "Rumor"
52. "The Man at the Moon"
53. "Wait"
54. "Worry Reliever"
55. "Love Me, Don't Go"
56. "GOOD NIGHT: Lil Ghost"
57. "Stay: BIGBANG"
58. "Lost Love"
59. "The Herald of Autumn"
60. "The Last of the Real Ones: Fall Out Boy"
61. "Green Lemon"
62. "Almost Home"
63. "Havana: Camila Cabello/Young Thug"
64. "Summer Night: Todd Li"
65. "Love Song 1990"
66. "7(Me U-Remix): KT/Chiu Chiu"
67. "Cake: Difficult Mountain"
68. "When I: Fi9"
69. "Like Chun Jiao"
70. "We Are Still Separated: It Was My Fault"
71. "Don't Wanna Know/We Don't Talk Anymore: Sam Tsui/Alex Blue"
72. "Psycho"

73. "Team Work"
74. "Still Waiting For"
75. "Troubled Youth: Bones"
76. "Closer"
77. "Bye, Bye, Bye"
78. "LOSER"
79. "Justin Bieber Medley: Anthem Lights"
80. "I Hate Myself for Loving You"
81. "Joyful Place"
82. "Hand Clap"
83. "Faded: Alan Walker"
84. "Reykjavik"
85. "Take a Bow: Rihanna"
86. "Like It"
87. "Victory"
88. "Wild Kid"
89. "The Sky Filled with Stars"
90. "Double Happiness Invitation Street"
91. "Immortals"
92. "Warriors"
93. "Thoughtful Person"
94. "I Am You"
95. "Fire"
96. "Turnin'"
97. "Lendo Calendo: Dan Bălan"
98. "Feeling U"
99. "To Whom"
100. "Here with You"

Tauri translated her playlist into the message.

My "Lendo Calendo,"
Please love me like you do. I prayed for your safety. Life is valuable and fragile. Once it is lost, it will never get back. Why would I participate in the evening gathering under the dark? There's a once-a-century pandemic raging and riots with fire on the street in the late evening. Remember that we are the ones, a mirror to each other. I want to go with you as your lover cat.
There's little chaos surrounding my streets, which caused the sleepless nights. This

caused me to yearn for you even more. Though we will be different when we meet again, I am more mature and independent with a job. What happened on the street is still well beyond what I can handle.

I also had sleepless nights thinking about you, our relationship. There's no reason why I can't be there for you when the time comes. My love is flowing to you like river, now and at this moment.

That old me was my sin. You're my wish. After we linked it up again and separated, you loved yourself and become a better version of you to be like a man in the moon, shining, unreachable. You're irresistible to me. In my heart, you belong to me and sold out.

When I turn thirty years old, my value will reach in highest point and decrease as my age grows. We're "senior love youth" like "day love night." I'd go with my lonely journey quietly and stay at the lowest level of society until I die. That would be my mighty fall.

I'm not your oriental fish to just be with you to make you feel good; I want my tears back and to enjoy my happiness. I knew you're like a hungry wolf pursuing prey like a pretty girl like me. But the silence is the gold. If you only want to have a kiss under mistletoe to commit and have sex, that'll cause additional sleepless night for us. As we're getting closer to our big year, marriage, we can do a "fly." I mean we can spend a sleepless night together to have a kiss and take a shot. That will rescue me from my heart-pulling yearning for you.

This's my thought about our next step from your wondering cat. We can get into the next stage of our relationship without dating, like skipping breakfast to go to lunch directly. You're my lover boy with me everywhere, like the garbage I'd never get rid of. When I saw you again, you'd authentically reveal you to me. I would see if your six fingers' rumor is true. You're like a man at the moon waiting for my love. You're my worry reliever. Just love me. Don't go.

My little ghost, have a good night. Please stay with me for that big bang. I know we are losing time for the lovemaking. Your sex drive is cooling down like the herald of autumn, but the overall relationship is still at an early stage, like a green lemon. We are almost home. I told you that we can get together to have that summer night to play the song like "Havana," I mean "Banana," and sing the love song "1990" like a regular couple. We will commit to each other as "7538," to celebrate our success to overcome those obstacles.

Dear, after I took off to pursue my independence from you like Chun Jiao in a Hong Kong movie, we're still separated. That was my fault.

It's a kind of teamwork for our cocreation book project with spirits. That's what I don't want to talk to you directly. I am still waiting for you to finish it. You seem to have trouble reaching the finish line, but you're getting closer and closer.

My idea is to start the book with a "bye, bye, bye" scene after our last dinner, and then get into that bittersweet moment of my life with Leo. After that, I'd write those heart-pulling moments like the mirror scene described in the song "Let Me Love You," by Justin Bieber, followed by unfolding the events when I took off to my new life since I hate "I love you" and highlighting my joyful moment of clapping hands when I finally reconnect with you again. I'd transition to the event I shouted to you and push you out from my life, then turn into the story of competing my love with the young handsome guy described by the song "Reykjavik." Finally, I'd conclude with the event of "Cupid strikes an arrow" as we take a bow to connect again. I like the happy ending in the last chapter as we finally meet at the street where you twice gave me a happy feeling under stars filling the night sky. This will make our love immortal and be remembered forever as the warrior.

My thoughtful person, I am yours. There's a fire, a wheel of fortune turning, that makes this story magical and exciting.

My "Lendo Calendo," I felt you and will always be with you.

He replied to Libi with a text message.

Dear Libi,

I'm sure you will be safe both from the virus and riots at night. If you ever want to be safer, come to stay with me. You can work from my place. I can pick you up in the daytime to avoid the curfew. We'd be together to get over this period of difficult time. My heart is with you.

Our love is the magic, the legacy, a mark on human history.

With our love, you brought out my curiosity of everything about you, your life, your safety, because I am convinced you are part of my life, my life purpose, and my life mission!

With our love, you brought out my desire to turn the silly things into the good, amusing aspects of life! You made me truly happy. You uplifted my spirit. Sometimes I don't feel possible; you even made me think the worst situation can seem to be fun!

With our love, you brought me hope, which made me believe our relationship would stand the test of time. There's goodness in this world.

With our love, you brought me serenity. When I have your love and you have mine, as if we're wrapped in the arms of each other, it brings us a sense of peace, calm, safety. In the opposite, our life will fall apart into chaos.

With our love, I felt gratitude and appreciation for what we have; I am grateful for the cocreation project with spirits we have been working on.

With our love, I felt the swell of pride, which is something extraordinary in our life. It's pretty awesome and overwhelming.

With our love, it brought us the inspiration for my life, the world, the spirits. You had been genuinely inspiring me, motivating me to achieve greatness, the excellence to become something I never even imagined a few years ago.

With our love, it brought us the word "awe." It let me realize how awesome you are! How delightful you are! How crazy you are.

My babe, I want to hold you as if you're my pet cat now. You must be very delicious with your "early tree in the spring" aurora. I want to taste your tender lips, see your blushing face, touch your joyful tears, smell your body fragrance.

I want, I want, I want you.

Love.

"If everyone loved life, would the tragedy in social injustice be preventable?" Tauri uttered.

⤛══◯ ◯══⤜

The writing work was so tedious. Tauri had to collect the material first, do the research to make a story, modify sentences considering the grammar to make it readable, and make sense from the last paragraph to the next story.

When he looked back on what he had done so far, he congratulated himself for something he couldn't believe was one year ago. He recalled he had been writing, writing, writing since last September. He got better and better in constructing the story line. He developed his passion for writing in his middle school language arts class in his teenage years. He didn't learn English until he was in high school. He'd had the wildest dream to write a book. This was his first realistic endeavor to write something he truly loves and cherishes.

I was lucky. I followed the step-by-step guidance from spirit, Tauri told himself when a tarot reader explained exactly what happened at his situation. He had high respect for the tarot readers, whom he called "tarotists." They should be highly respected since they have to understand the tarot cards, which is a professional job; they have to understand numerology, which is the mathematician's job; they have to apply logic and rationale to the different scenarios trained by the higher education. Most of all, they have to show positivity, compassion, and empathy to apply psychology knowledge with a passion for those readings. He was convinced that those energy forecasts were brought into human society on a personal level, which was like moving the Mass from church into the home, where people can interact with the divine at their fingertips.

He counted day by day for their reunion as he listened to tarot readings to monitor all his life perspectives, like watching live broadcasts for energy related to Libi's feelings. Then, those energy readings would be confirmed by Libi's playlist. Though he didn't have any direct contact with Libi, he knew the reunion would happen, since it was destined to happen.

This energy was picked up by the tarot channel "Consciousness Evolution Journey." She released a video on June 8, 2020, to offer advice. It was titled "Taurus: You're an Earth Angel! Angels' Messages & Guidance."

Even Tauri expressed "humble" love to Libi. He knew he was powerful, unique. He will bring healing energy to mankind. He deserved Libi's love.

He raised his head when he thought about this.

Even though the tarot reading picked up my energy at the specific moment of the time, the energy from my thought or her thought could change, Tauri reasoned.

"Would she really be there to meet with me on this upcoming anniversary day?" he uttered.

Tauri would rather believe than disbelieve.

CHAPTER 29

Anniversary

"PLEASE DON'T CRY and be angry about what happened!" Libi reminded him in her playlist.

She had a plan to meet at their third anniversary.

Tauri was in a good mood. He looked at the petals from tulips falling down in his vase and felt the divine's gentle reminder for fresh flowers, like roses for this love.

The red is for the love; the white is for the innocence; the deep pink is for the appreciation; the light pink is for the admiration; the coral is for the desire; the yellow is for the friendship; the orange is for the fascination; the lavender is for the enchantment; the red-and-white mix is for the happiness. He went back to his picture collections to see what kinds of roses he was in the mood for.

"Libi deserves all the roses," Tauri uttered. "But I want happiness at this point."

He worried that Libi might not show up at their last dinner place at the same time.

A tarot channel, "BohemianAirGoddess," picked up his energy and published a video on June 9, 2020, to offer advice. It was titled "Taurus, Your Worry Is Unnecessary. Have Faith in Outcome."

Tauri wrote the message and texted it to her during his lunchtime.

Libi, my sweetheart,

Haru-Haru. Why is my clock running so slow?

It's still five hours, thirty-seven minutes, and fifty-three seconds away for us to meet. I had the belief that a promise is "a promise." There's ancient Chinese folklore of a boy, Weishen, who promised to meet a girl under the bridge at a specific time. He held on to a pile to await the girl. When the flood came, unfortunately, he refused to leave and didn't survive.

"Rather than break faith, you declared you'd die."

"Who knew I'd live alone in a tower high?" Chinese poet Li Bai in the

Tang Dynasty wrote in his poem "Chang-Kan Life Journey." When people loved each other, they kept their promises.

I am so looking forward to meeting with you. Let's see who's wilder, who's sexier tonight.

Is today the "date" to meet after two years of isolation from each other? He was happy that he'd finally move his life into next phase.

⊷➡◉◉⬅⊶

Tauri finished his work earlier than usual. He pulled out all the clothes he had bought since he became single and picked up a thin blue silk T-shirt. He had worn it last year when a photo was taken and shared it on social media.

She must notice it and will recognize it when I show up. He nodded.

Tauri shaved his beard and washed his face. Then he hopped into his Mercedes and drove out at 5:00 p.m. so he had enough time to catch up for a meetup at 6:30 p.m. when they'd met last time two years ago.

Should I put some cologne on? He reminded himself of one thing he always wanted to do before he went out with her. He pulled a U-turn and drove back to his home.

This is a date, right? He smiled at himself. He put a handful of cologne under his arms. He felt like going for a first date as a boy.

He decided to drive along the street next to his office complex to see if the building was still there.

It seems ages since I came to this place last time! He had missed his workplace for almost three months already. Unfortunately, no time line was set for the office to be reopened due to the fear of the second wave of the coronavirus.

Libi would like to see my car clean! He noticed a carwash and swerved his car to get the service.

"The restaurant only offered pickup and street drip. Street drip?" Tauri read a notice on the wall. There were ten tables with sun umbrellas in the courtyard. A water spring was still there. A little traffic was passing this quiet street next to the train station.

"Can I order the drip? Table for two!" he asked the waitress. He looked around and didn't find Libi.

"Sure, go to find the table." The waitress pointed the tables in courtyard.

Tauri sat at the small table on the far side of the courtyard where he could see anyone coming from the street. The waitress brought him the menu for the "drip."

"Do you need a drink or anything?" she asked.

"I want to wait a little bit," Tauri told the waitress. The train came and went; the street was empty and still.

"Sir, do you need a drink or to order anything?" the waitress reminded him again.

"How about a beer?" Tauri didn't actually like the beer. He'd enjoy a cup of red wine to avoid the extra calories taken in, but he felt boyish to drink beer on a summer night alone.

A half hour later, Tauri's beer was almost gone.

"Do you need to order now?" Tauri heard the waitress's voice again. He started to think that Libi might not come.

"Sure. Please give me the four-course drips." Tauri ordered his favorite choices from the menu: a warm cheese dip with vegetables, cubes of bread, apples; a plate of green salad; a kabob of shrimp, beef, tuna fish. What he liked most was the signature dessert of melted chocolate with marshmallow, fruit mix, and a cake cube.

He worked on his meal course by course as he went through Libi's playlist to group the songs into sections to make sense out of them.

In her top ten songs, there are two sections. The first section is about "Don't Cry"; the second section is about "Good Night: Want, Think, Make, Love." There's nowhere she mentioned dinner. Tauri was shocked to conclude this.

She did mention in the song "Good Night." Does it mean she'd come to my place directly? Tauri felt it was a possibility. He recalled Libi shared a song "Sold Out" ranked after "Jim Restaurant."

Could the song "Sold Out" means "canceled" or "no go"? He questioned himself. He checked an online dictionary that the term "sold out" means "planned and firmed."

Tauri quickly paid the bill and drove back to his place. He found no one waiting at his doorstep. He rushed upstairs to read Libi's playlist again. Three new songs had been added to the top ten songs since the last time he checked.

"6. Your Girl, 7. Salute, 8. Talking Boy, Talking Girl."

Tauri finally realized what Libi told him was indeed "sold out," "no go." Tauri felt extremely tired. He went to his bed and fell into sleep with the tarot reading recordings on and on.

Tauri felt refreshed from all the burdens with good sleep from the previous night. He went through nonstop dreams floating somewhere. When he woke up at almost 10:00 a.m. on Saturday, he decided to go on a late-morning three-mile run.

It's a perfect sunny morning, seventy degrees Fahrenheit in crispy air. He gradually got his strength back at the end of his run.

Something in my life has to be changed. No matter what I try, Libi will not come forward to meet me. What do I do? If it's a twin flame, it should be in reunion finally.

He felt free from his worries. At one moment, he even wanted to remove any URL links to Libi's playlist.

I can and could be free from her playlist. Can't I? Tauri thought about this. That would be the last communication channel for him to get into her soul in this physical world.

Tauri read through her playlist again. He realized a song, "Good Night," seemed to ask him to be relaxed; another song, "Coming Home," appeared to have some special meaning.

Coming home? Is she moving into my state, since she mentioned in the song "I Don't Like This City"? Or am I her home, as she is my home for our souls to rest upon? Tauri thought the questions as he stared at the blue sky. Tauri didn't have a desire to text Libi; at the same time, she didn't update her playlist throughout the day. They were entering a new phase of the relationship. Either they wanted to step up or fade away from the last available communication channel.

The tarot channel "Water Star Vibes" picked up this energy and published a video on June 13, 2020, to offer advice. It was titled "Taurus! You are About to See Them in a Totally Different Way! Tarot Reading."

"One stone to kill two birds? I guess she must refer to the cocreation book project and fruition of this love." Tauri seemed to hear this guidance.

⤜⟐⟐⤛

One day had passed since they failed to celebrate their third anniversary.

Something needs to be changed. This connection had to be restarted by either face-by-face meeting or direct communication. Tauri constantly kept this idea in his mind.

"Your word is so powerful. You could create a most beautiful dream, or you can destroy everything. You need to avoid arguments. This could only create beauty, love, heaven on earth," tarot reader "Jennifer Walker Zen" reminded her audience at her reading for the zodiac sign Taurus.

In this virtual world, everything for Tauri and Libi looked like it was moving in a positive direction. "Maybe I misunderstood Libi's message!" Tauri heard the spirit call.

Well, she didn't say that she'd come! She didn't want to see me cry. He continued to go to the tarot world to find out what Libi's intention was.

The tarot channel "San Tarot" picked up this energy and released a video on June 8, 2020, to offer her advice. It was titled "Taurus: You're Really Going through It."

"Yes, I'd give up an idea to actively pursue a date with her at a specific time and place. I'll let it happen naturally! I guess she is waiting for me to finish the final two chapters," he uttered. He sent a text message to her about this thought.

Libi, my dear love,
I bought a white-and-red rose bundle that represented happiness and hoped you were there to accept it. It's my fault I didn't think thoroughly from your shoes.

You have to walk through the fire, a pandemic, and riots in the current circumstances. So it wasn't safe to travel.

I enjoyed a summer night out myself, even though I missed you dearly. I wish you were with me.

In thinking about the songs "17. A Summer Night," "18. Wilder Than You, Sexier Than You," "19. Don't Guess," I ran out of ideas to get a date with you. It'd be upon you to let me know when, where, how we can meet again. Please contact me directly and clearly without any confusion. Sometimes, the miscommunication could lead to life-and-death situations.

Your boyfriend is waiting for you to start this new beginning of our life. I'm available on Sunday, weekdays from Tuesday to Thursday. Time is not an issue. I can always make myself available on Friday or Saturday. I even want to take some time off for a vacation with you.

I had an idea of what we can do when we meet. We may take some time off to drive to places like Yellowstone National Park, Niagara Falls, or Arcadia National Park. There are so many things we can explore together.

Bae, I want to build memories with you.
Stay safe.
Kiss from my heart.

⊷═◑ ◐═⊶

Tauri continued to scan through the most recent tarot readings throughout the day. Two tarot channels acknowledged their heavy energy.

The tarot channel "NicLoves" published a video on June 11, 2020, to offer her advice. It was titled "Taurus: I Got Your Back, My Love, June 15 to 21 Weekly Love."

The tarot channel "Bon Without Boundaries Tarot" published a video on June 11, 2020, to offer her guidance. It was titled "Taurus: What Have They Done for You Lately?"

"Yes, I put my heart in this cocreation project with Libi and Spirit," he yelled. "Libi created the playlist; the spirits provide the writing blocks from tarot readings to guide this connection. OMG, I am totally in sync with the spirit!" Tauri uttered. But he lost the direction to convince her to meet again.

From her playlist, he seemed to get the idea she wanted to meet up after the book project was done.

That was not possible since she and I are cocreators on this project. Tauri wanted to close this chapter and this book so they could move on to the next life stage.

In Tauri's mind, his relationship with Libi was like two neutron stars in each other's gravity field. They'd circle each other slowly and finally pull the part of the mass to the center. Their stars would be stretched out, shredded; their high-energy particles would be ejected at the speed of light to reach the universe. Some of their characters that didn't belong to their future life would fall beyond their horizon. The rest of their core would collapse into each other to create a black hole for their love.

Tauri gasped when he thought about this analogy.

Well, the good news would be once we're in our own black hole, time will be frozen forever. Our gravity will become infinite at the singularity. He murmured.

It's as over ten suns' mass packed into a sphere sized similarly to New York City. The gravity was so huge that there was no light escaping. Tauri thought further about this.

Another good thing would be the high-energy jets that would be the basic ingredients to form the new star. His optimistic view returned.

Ultimately, it would not be a bad thing to be a black hole. For example, a galaxy system might be formed in the center of the black hole, such as the Milky Way galaxy. Tauri laughed out.

"Can she really mean what she said?" he asked himself.

After a few days' silence, Libi updated her playlist to leave a new message to him.

1. "Ant"
2. "Aspirin"
3. "Two of Us"
4. "My Heart Is as Quiet as the Calm Water"
5. "Support Each Other for Our Life Journey"
6. "The Rumors"
7. "No Man Land"
8. "The Girl as Pretty as I Am Is Not Easy to Find"
9. "There Is No Reason"

10. "By the Campfire"
11. "There for You"
12. "Astronomia: Vicetone"
13. "Thankful"
14. "Easy Come, Easy Go"
15. "I Will Accompany You Wherever You Want to Go"
16. "Burning at My Heart"
17. "It Creates Sparks among Us"
18. "Is What I Want"

Tauri translated her playlist into the message.

Dear, I'm like an ant crawling slowly to reach you; you're like the aspirin healing me. Those are the pictures for the two of us.

My heart is as quiet as the calm water. We support each other in our life journey. For me, there seemed to be a rumor no one can compare to you touching my life as you do. For you, you can't easily find a girl as young, as pretty as me. We're each other's wish fulfillment.

There is no reason to delay our reunion at the last place we met. I'd be there for you when divine timing is here. I'm very thankful for those tarot readings, which guided me for this love. I'd take it easy to come and leave for our date. I'd go with you wherever you want to go. This desire is burning in my heart. It creates a spark among us, which is what I want.

Tauri ran through a few possibilities and scenarios. He was so looking forward to this memorable summer night she promised.

CHAPTER 30

The Ideal Thirty

IT WAS JULY Fourth weekend, a US national holiday. Tauri usually watched the thirty-minute firework show at the town's beach. His favorite spot was the sandy edge of the water so he could almost feel the fireworks shooting into the sky right in front of him even one mile away offshore from a boat. Tauri didn't expect any public firework display this year due to the pandemic.

He had high hopes he and Libi would use this time to get together. They hadn't seen eye to eye for two years.

It'd be great to ask for a full-scale date to end this suffering. Tauri felt funny to think about the term "full scale."

He found that Libi moved one new song, "The Ideal Thirty," into the number one position in responding to his love expression.

If it is meant to be, it is meant to be, Tauri told himself. By the end of the day, Libi had reduced the number of the songs in her playlist from nineteen to fourteen to present a more concise message.

1. "The Ideal Thirty"
2. "Ants"
3. "For Us"
4. "We Are Together to Support Each Other for Our Life Journey"
5. "Rumors"
6. "No Man Land"
7. "There Is No Reason"
8. "Astronomia"
9. "Thankful"
10. "Easy Come, Easy Go"
11. "I Will Go with You to Wherever You Want to Go"
12. "Aspirin"

H. L. Howard

13. "What I Want"
14. "My Heart Is as Quiet as the Calm Water"

⊷⊜⊷

This Independence Day came and went quietly, just as he expected. The small fireworks boomed in his neighborhood here and there. He still felt that something should happen between him and Libi. But no change was on Libi's playlist.

He decided to venture out to Flushing, New York, a little Chinatown outside of Manhattan, to do his grocery shopping.

There was little traffic along the road; only a few people walked on the street. He remembered people walking shoulder by shoulder on the pedestrian walkway only three months ago.

It's still in the pandemic. People were scared to come out. He talked to himself. He drove back home without a one-minute stay after he got his stuff.

After dinner at his home, Tauri went to the local beach for a walk. It was a low tide with a wide strip of sandy ground exposed. Tauri walked with his bare feet to touch the water and tiny sand grains. He felt energized.

How I wish that I could walk with Libi at this moment.

I have done whatever I can do to move this relationship forward. It's like moving three steps forward and two steps back. There's still one step forward at the end. Tauri smiled to himself.

"Libi and I didn't meet on the second anniversary since the last dinner; she even missed our fifth anniversary since we met the first time. I don't understand why?" Tauri kept asking himself again and again.

The tarot channel "San Tarot" picked up this energy and published a video on June 5, 2020, to tell a good story. It was titled "Taurus: Cosmic Lovers."

"Yes, I did turn inward to conclude that I did all I can to have Libi meet with me. What I can do at this point is to surrender this to the universe. If Libi doesn't step up to move this relationship, there will be no relationship," he uttered.

There are a few significant tasks at hand. She seems to want me to finish the rest of the remaining chapters of this book before we can meet. He nodded to himself.

⊷⊜⊷

"New York City is reopening now." Tauri was happy as he read the news. The people in the city can enjoy more services, including personal care services. The restaurants have been open for outdoor seating since June 22.

260

Would Libi be willing to come out to have dinner with me? he wondered. Libi revised her playlist to tell her plan.

1. "Ideal Thirty"
2. "Easy Come Easy Go"
3. "Ant"
4. "What I Want"

Tauri felt encouraged to see her stepping up. But there was no action item.

Does it mean that I'd have to wait three more years to see her face again? He gasped. He had been out of his previous relationship for over two years now. He'd had a few opportunities to start a new life with other girls. In his mind, Libi was what he wanted.

He felt unsure about his future.

→►═◑ ◐═◄←

Tauri felt cold on the bed but a little hot on his forehead when he got up for the new day.

OMG, am I getting sick? He was alerted. It'd be big trouble to get sick at this pandemic moment. He finally realized he had a low fever. He went to have a hot shower and went to bed in the early evening.

Hope I didn't get coronavirus. He popped up this thought, which scared him to hell.

"If I caught the virus and recovered, Libi would be proud for me having a strong body." He talked aloud and turned the worry into joy, as if he were a kid showing a school scorecard to his parent.

The following day, he got up and felt fresh.

"That was the virus. I got it. I beat it." He had only one idea in his mind. He felt tightness in his upper body.

During his lunch break, he decided to have a three-mile run. He could barely catch his breath during the run.

I need to continue to keep my routine, he told himself. After he finished his regular half-hour body stretch at end of his office hour, all the symptoms had disappeared.

"I survived this virus. This is the magic." He yelled it out as he realized it. "OMG, this is really more magic." Tauri noticed only one song left on her playlist.

1. "Ideal Thirty"

Tauri got her memo.

This love is crude and painful. It had been imprinting her every move into my heart. Tauri came up with this thought before he went to bed.

I guess that I can't have a romantic dinner with her at the city. What about the summer night? he questioned when he woke up the following day.

Libi's energy was picked up by the tarot channel "San Tarot." Ms. San was a great storyteller who always used metaphors to explain the situation. She published a video on July 11, 2020, to offer advice. It was titled "Libra Overwhelm Causing Cold Feet."

"I totally got it. The summer night is the date calendar San was talking about. Libi must freak out about this date," he uttered.

She and I have dreamed of this for the last half year during the most challenging time in our life. As Ms. San said, if it were six months ago, she'd be meant to meet with me. It's not a connection issue; it's in Libi's mind to be self-limited. He sighed.

"Libi, take a step back as an observer. Just go easy with the 'summer night,' have fun, go with the flow." Tauri talked silently, as if he spoke to her.

The news had just reported zero confirmed infection cases in New York City since the pandemic had hit for the first time, the epicenter of the nation's coronavirus outbreak. It marked the end of a four-month period since the city reported its first COVID-19 fatality on March 11, 2019. The city kicked off its phase-three reopening on Monday. The nail salons and tanning studios were allowed to open. Indoor dining in the city had been postponed indefinitely, as in other states.

The summer months came. Tauri's company gave everyone a Friday off to release the stress of working from home.

It had been difficult for him since the layoffs happened in his company. On a personal front, Libi had not been active in using her playlist to express her feelings.

She didn't want me to find her. Tauri thought about that.

Even though I have her information, I don't know if Libi will pull down her face and shout me away just like last fall. Tauri sighed.

Tauri's heart was heavy before he got into bed. He fell into sleep with the tarot readings video on. As he got into the early morning, he was half awake and half asleep.

He felt that he was kissing someone. There were two objects with yin and yang in the Taiji diagram flying around. They circled and turned clockwise. He reached out to grab the shadow half of the circle and returned with an empty hand.

"Ha ha! You're silly. That's just light elution, is it?" Tauri heard someone lying on the bed next to him laugh like a morning ring bell. He reached out his hand slowly to the bright half of the circle and followed the movement. He suddenly closed five fingers.

"I did it." Tauri held this half of the circle.

The light emitted and penetrated his hand and lit over their foreheads.

"Let me try it." He heard a low, soft-pitched voice. He realized it was Libi next to him. He saw her stand up. She was in his white shirt with two buttons on. Half of her front shoulder was opened. She had on lacy hip-hugger panties on with long legs up to the thigh. Her two firm, round tits made his shirt full in the front.

He recalled that Libi had come here for "that possible night." They cooked, danced, took a bath together. When they turned the light off, she allowed him to hold her until they fell asleep. He remembered she slapped his hand when he moved to touch her private garden and told him to stay away, to leave that best for the last.

"I can get you. Here I come." She ran around the bed and jumped over his legs.

"I caught it; I got it." Libi held another half of the circle.

They both held a half circle, glowing brighter and brighter. Its edge was emitting a soft vibration sound to notice each other's existence.

Tauri noticed the force pulling his half toward her.

"They are pulling; they belong to each other," Tauri uttered and whispered to her.

As each half circle slowly moved together, the light glowed brighter. They finally united together into one circle with a huge light coming out from the edge of the half. Then, it started to circle again and faded away in front of Tauri's and Libi's eyes.

"They belong together to reach balance." She looked at him with a dreaming eye wave.

He seemed to understand her excitement.

"Come here," she whispered in his ear.

He found Libi lying down at the bed naked, with two legs close to each other. She formed a small triangle space below her private garden. His manhood was in full motion; he found her guiding his rod toward the leg space. He's surprised she adjusted her leg to have him against her soft skin without entering her.

He moved up and down with her rhythm. She twisted her face as his moan grew louder. He pointed his hot banana to find her entry. Finally, he felt that he was right at her doorstep.

"Stop!" Libi yelled. "Stop!" Libi pushed him away forcefully.

He woke up from this early morning dream. His boxers were wet with some sticky stuff.

"It was just 5:30 a.m. Did this yin-and-yang energy mean Libi and I would merge it together, like making love?" Tauri asked himself. He went back to bed and fell into sleep again.

"Did my dream imply Libi would take some actions to meet with me and eventually agree with our marriage?" he murmured.

He had doubted the accuracy of the readings.

The tarot prediction of energy was pretty accurate. It reflected past and current energy and even future energy. But the outcome of the energy would depend on results from interacting with other energy. The tarot reader predicted "creative and inspiring power" for Taurus this week. Tauri had trouble focusing on writing last week. As time went by, he regained focus and wrote a few good pieces.

When tarot readings mention the "gift," it means the creative idea coming in on that time, Tauri summarized. Again and again, what he experienced proved the tarot's magic power.

The tarot channel "Angel Love 333" picked up this energy and published a video on July 12, 2020, to offer advice. It was titled "The Message You Have Been Waiting For! July 13–19 Tarot Reading."

Yes, I am waiting to date Libi after two years of separation.

Yes, I'll be in training at my company this week.

Yes, Libi's moon sign is the Cancer zodiac sign. He nodded and nodded.

Other news made Tauri happy. New York City had reached a significant milestone in its COVID-19 fight. Most businesses reopened with appropriate social distancing measures: the gyms, cultural institutions. The indoor dining areas were the exception.

It was midsummer already. Tauri expected Libi to tell him the timing of "that special summer night." Another weekend was over with no change on her playlist. After Tauri finished his work on his busy Monday, he found out Libi had removed her playlist totally.

What? Speechless again?

Did I do something wrong? Tauri questioned. His heart was heavy. He remembered only twice that she'd left empty space on her playlist. The first time, Libi expressed she was "speechless" since he misunderstood her playlist. The second time, she had removed her playlist after they broke up and pursued individual love lives.

"Libi agreed to have the date at July 30 or in August, as this tarot reader mentioned! Did she want to cut off the only connection with me?" Tauri asked himself. This was first time he felt their relationship was easy to fall apart like the "stardust."

CHAPTER 31

Always in Love

TAURI CLICKED THE URL for Libi's playlist at the "current week" and found an empty web page.

"Oh! Did she remove her playlist completely?" he exclaimed. When he clicked "all time" playlist, one hundred songs showed up.

Hmm! Does this mean anything? There is no reason for her to delete her playlist. No breakup! No big changes! He was perplexed.

He stared at her "all time" playlist screen for hours.

Unless she wants to express something. Would she use this playlist to tell her story? Tauri realized this might be her response for plan for the "summer night."

1. "Nothing Ever Happened"
2. "The Lie and the Love Song"
3. "Rashomon"
4. "The Tree in Early Spring"
5. "#Lov3 #Ngẫu Hứng: Hoaprox"
6. "The Love Song about the Wind"
7. "It Is Dark Suddenly"
8. "Sexier Than You, Wilder Than You"
9. "Take It Slow"
10. "Lake"
11. "Life: Tobu"
12. "Fly"
13. "Live in Your Ears"
14. "Don't Guess"
15. "Fade: Alan Walker"
16. "Bring Me to Find Nightlife"
17. "Wait for You"

18. "On the Way"
19. "Good Body Shape"
20. "How Do You Feel?"
21. "Never Have It Again"
22. "Shape of You: Ed Sheeran"
23. "Dan Bălan: Lendo Calendo"
24. "My City"
25. "Aspirin"
26. "To Be My Cat"
27. "Lifeline"
28. "The Mountain and Sea"
29. "All Is Yours"
30. "There Is No Love to Love"
31. "Want to Keep You Here"
32. "Need to Keep Secret for the Whisper of the Love"
33. "Take It Slow"
34. "Lovesick: BINGBIAN"
35. "Slave"
36. "Terminal Illness"
37. "Open the Door to See the Mountain"
38. "The Innocent Years"
39. "The Old Paper before Bedtime"
40. "I Want You to Know: Zedd/Selena Gomez"
41. "This City Is Not a Pleasant Place to Stay"
42. "Fade Again"
43. "The First Half of July"
44. "Journey to Mercury"
45. "This Age"
46. "The General"
47. "Almost Home"
48. "Okay"
49. "GOING GO"
50. "Easy Come, Easy Go"
51. "Only Three Years Apart"
52. "Focus"
53. "Come to Have Hotpot Tomorrow"
54. "T: Ty"
55. "Ideal Thirty"

56. "I Don't Know"
57. "There Is No Party"
58. "Ambition"
59. "Empty"
60. "Little Careless Seller"
61. "Mr. Suspicious Person"
62. "Mr. Amnesia"
63. "Lover Boy 88"
64. "On the Way"
65. "The Beautiful Place to Stay"
66. "Love9"
67. "FALL IN LOVE"
68. "Do You See It"
69. "Red Rose"
70. "There Is Absolutely No Opponent"
71. "The New Love and the Old Love"
72. "You Are Just a Passerby"
73. "Green Lemon"
74. "Strategy of the Empty City"
75. "Old Lover"
76. "PDD"
77. "Sweet Grape, Red Eye"
78. "The Belief"
79. "The Announcement Balloon"
80. "When You Are Gone"
81. "GOOD NIGHT: Lil Ghost"
82. "Sleepless Night: Lil Chaos"
83. "Waiting For"
84. "We Are Still Separated"
85. "Eightieth-Year Style"
86. "Forget It"
87. "The Love Came Too Late"
88. "Help Yourself"
89. "You Are Far Away"
90. "The Magic Time Thief"
91. "Ing! Ing!"
92. "The Love Story: Episode One"
93. "Go with You on This Life Journey"

94. "Only Want You to Know"
95. "Coming Home"
96. "Make Mistakes Repeatably"
97. "Is What I Want"
98. "Mountain"
99. "The Martian Came"
100. "Sleepless Night: Lil Chaos"

He was familiar with most of the songs. Wow! This is her story. He was excited to translate her playlist into the message.

There has been nothing ever happening described in your story, an imaginable story line. I didn't commit to Leo and have a plot to marry you for ten years and go back to him. I'm still in innocent year at my love life. That story line was a hoax.

I fell in love with you unexpectedly and out of my control. It's like the wind came suddenly on that peaceful night when I stayed at your hotel with my friend. I told myself I was younger, sexier, wilder than you; I'd come to look for you and take time to move toward you without your notice.

As the time went by, it'd be a good idea to share my playlist with you as if I lived in your ears to be with you. With this playlist, I imagined the dating life with you like having dinner, walking in the park, dancing in the club. No one would guess we're in love since I faded away from you.

Please wait for me. Our love is on the way to fruition. I did a model photo shot for an online dating company and looked very pretty and attractive. You found out and felt the same way. Right? I didn't pose or model since then. In contrast, you have a so-so body like an ordinary guy at my city.

You're my aspirin. Please be my cat, my loved one, my lifeline. Though we're apart between the mountain and sea, I'm yours with my mind, my soul, and my body. All is yours. I don't feel any love left for my past relationship with Leo. Hope you feel the same with your ex. I want to keep you as my loved one; I'll need to keep you as the platonic love via the whisper of love. Let's take this relationship slow.

I had your lovebug infestation until it reached the point I can't bear it anymore. I made myself your love slave and felt like having a terminal illness. I want to open my heart to express it to you. Can you feel what I felt?

I kept my innocent heart, mind, and body for you. I read your text message before I went to bed. I want to let you know I don't like to stay in the city away from you.

I went to fade away from you after that dinner in that July two years ago. We had been in two separate life tracks without any interactions, like Mercury and Earth. You're almost at your senior year, as old as a "general." We're almost home with each other. I'm OK with this age gap.

Let's keep going and going for the time being. If our love is easy to get, it'd be easy to be gone since we have the thirty-year age gap. Please focus on working on the book.

I don't know if we could come together to have a dinner like a hot pot and make out since I want to get married at age thirty. It's going to be three years away. So, there's no party, no reunion for us now.

For your ambition of this book project, even if it's going to be a success, I still felt empty for our future foundation. I'd be like the song "A Careless Seller" described; once I got married, I'd take care of you for the rest of your life.

Mr. Suspicious Person, a memory-loss lover boy at an age like eighty-eight, our love is on the way. Once I figure out our future home to stay in, I'd come forward to you and be in reunion with you. Do you see that? It's my love as deep as a red rose. I'm absolutely so brilliant with a high IQ that I don't think that I have any competitor for your love. You're my old love and new lover at the same time. But you'd be a passerby person in my whole life since I'm still a green lemon to be matured.

My "empty city" strategy was to cut off our connection in order to conquer your heart. It's inspired by the ancient Chinese novel *Three Kingdoms Evolution*. This resulted in exactly what I expected, which is outstanding. Since you're my old lover, it's my dream coming true to get your hands. That strategy finally led to the fruition of my bittersweet love. I had faith in you, in myself, in our love.

This is my confession, my oath to you. I'd stay with you until you rest in peace. I've had numerous sleepless nights to think about this and make this decision.

I am still waiting for when you are done with your part. It's my fault we're still in separation. I'm yearning for our ordinary family life together like cooking, watching a movie, raising kids...

Hmm! Forget about my rambling. I talk too much. You wouldn't understand why I'm doing this. Our love came too late. You need to take care of yourself since you're far away from me. The time is like a thief taking your youth, your energy, your look away from me, curving the wrinkles at your face.

Ing! Ing! Flirting from me. Your book is just our episode one of our love stories. I'm determined to go with you on this life journey.

Just want you to know I intentionally missed our dates a few times. That's what I want to see my power of love. I had to travel across a distance to see you every time you ask for a date. I was agitated myself for not being able to come. I had a big temper like a Martian. I had sleepless nights for regretting doing that.

⊷▰◌▰⊶

Tauri couldn't believe how deeply Libi was in love with him. He went to the tarot world to act as a cross-watcher to listen to Libra's reading, the video for Libi's zodiac sign.

The tarot channel "Secret Tarot" published a video on July 27, 2020, to describe their love story like a biography. It was titled "Libra August 2020: I Watch Your Life Play Out in Pictures from Afar."

"That was resolute with our situation. I read her playlist to know that she is OK," he uttered.

Libi and I met only a few times, with the figure counted on one hand. He smiled.

Yep! I was inspired by Libi's love and went to pursue my independence from my previous marriage. I did overcome all the obstacles in order to pursue her love. He stared at the sky outside of his window to think about this.

That's not the point. This love never took off the ground. He recalled a few times they interacted with each other.

Is Libi going to empty everything first and start fresh with me? Tauri wondered about her empty playlist.

⊷▰◌▰⊶

Tauri's life had been as busy as a mad dog in recent days. By the end of the week, he finally felt his workload lighten up.

He didn't expect Libi to post the new playlist. But to his surprise, she'd left a brand-new playlist for him.

1. "Young and Promising Youth"
2. "On the Way"
3. "Pray for You"
4. "Unicorn"
5. "Almost Home"
6. "Sexier Than You, Wilder Than You"
7. "Thankful"
8. "123: Fusion"

9. "Who Will Go with Me for This Life Journey: Beyond"
10. "On the Way"
11. "Grey Track: Beyond"
12. "Flaws"
13. "Night Shine on the Night"
14. "The Sinner"
15. "Silence Is Gold"
16. "To Mr. Anonymous"
17. "Big Ants"
18. "Understand"
19. "Lightly Mature Woman: 27"
20. "How Are You Now?"

I am very thankful she is honest with me. Tauri thought about it.

Did she have more "gray track" to come clean for this new beginning? Tauri questioned. Would this be related to the online dating site history? He always wondered about the role she played. She mentioned to him she worked as a bookkeeper.

Did she actually work as a lead girl who accepted the dating requests?

Does it matter to me? Why should I be that person to judge her? one voice inside Tauri questioned.

Well, I am curious to know the story, another voice in Tauri insisted. He always imagined what happened on that night when he bumped into her at her house.

You told her you'd love you unconditionally. Would that be "no matter what"? Tauri asked himself.

"Why don't you focus on what you are doing?" He gathered his thoughts back to what he needed to do to move this book project forward.

The tarot channel "San Tarot" released a video on July 30, 2020, to offer advice. It was titled "Taurus: You Feel It but Can't See It."

"Oh! Spirit is asking me to take a trip to get into the next phase of my journey?" Tauri gasped.

"Would that be the summer retreat with Libi?" Tauri yelled it out. He thought about this for quite a while already.

"A gift from spirit during the trip? That sounds very attractive," Tauri said.

He slept on this idea for a few days and decided to go somewhere to see what would happen. After his lunch, he took a nap on the couch to think about where to go.

This place would have something related to a new beginning. It would be reachable by car. Tauri thought about this.

New York? New Haven? That was the place I went all the time.

New Orleans, Louisiana? New Albany, Indiana? New Berlin, Wisconsin? New Braunfels, Texas? That is too far away.

New Bedford, Massachusetts? New Britain, Connecticut? New Brunswick, New Jersey? New City, New York? New Rochelle, New York? He went through those cities starting with "New." He almost ran out of ideas. He continued to search the word "new" online, and more cities showed up.

"Newark, Ohio? Newark, California? Newnan, Georgia? Newport Beach, California? Newport, Virginia? Newport, Rhode Island?" Tauri read through one after the other.

"Wait a minute! Newport in Rhode Island sounds familiar. Would that city be the place where my former boss bought the rental house and stayed there in the summertime? Yeah! Is Newport a very nice ocean coastline where one of my friends went for a six-mile walk?" he uttered. It was about a two-and-a-half-hour drive.

"Newport? Something related to 'new'? Only three hours away. Let me drive there to enjoy the sunset."

He jumped out from the couch and took his car keys and sunglasses. After five minutes, he found himself in front of the driving wheel of his Mercedes.

As he drove north along the I-95, he put random tarot recordings on his speakers. A tarot channel, "Kayleigh Jean," published a video talking about the creativities titled "Taurus: August 2020, Thriving throughout the Complexity! It Is All Working Out for You."

He thought about his book project. It started with his love relationship with Libi and bumped into the spirit world via tarot world.

There had been three dimensions in this book: my life, Libi's playlist, writing block from tarot reading, a cocreation with spirit. How can I add additional dimensions to make this book more attractive?

Could Libi add her life story as one dimension? What about my experience from a humble start into leadership at a nonprofit organization? How about my start-up failure? Could I add my spirit knowledge level-up from a beginner to expert as like a knight starting as a new soldier but moving to the top? It would be the story like Luke Skywalker in *Star Wars* or Guo Jin in *The Legend of the Condor Heroes*.

Tauri felt excited about those new ideas.

Would those dimensions dilute the essence of this great love story? Tauri debated in his mind.

After a one-hour drive, his mind turned to Libi's playlist. At one time, she used the songs "7538" and "East and West" to express her commitment. He texted her about his plan about kids. He always wanted one son like him and one baby girl like her.

Would I want this boy to be another Taurus? Yes, a Taurus can take a leadership role and live a comfortable life. He smiled to himself.

Would I want this girl to be another Libra? Libi is pretty. Be in a good relationship with other people. Libra is only the zodiac sign symbol with no animal connection in all the twelve zodiac signs.

Tauri laughed out loud. This had been an inside joke he and Lara played all the time. Whenever Lara's not happy, he brought out this "no-heart" joke to break her tears into laughter. They'd push and bump each other to laugh their heads off.

There is no heart in the Libra sign. That was really strange.

Tauri started to recall all the zodiac signs to see if it were actually true.

Well, there are twelve signs in the zodiac calendar and four groups of signs in the four seasons.

It starts with Capricorn season, with dates ranging between December 22 and January 20. The Capricorn is an animal, sea goat or mountain goat with a half goat body and half fishtail. It's an earth sign; one of my nonprofit organization leaders is in this sign. Tauri thought through his interaction with him.

And then it enters the Aquarius season, with dates ranging between January 21 and February 18. Aquarius is a water bearer. It's an air sign, which is Libi's sign group; yeah, my ex is in this sign. His mind went through all the struggles in the past to see how far he had come to this point now.

Then it gets into the Pisces season, with dates ranging between February 19 and March 20. Pisces's symbol is two fish tied together yet jumping in opposite directions. It belongs to the water sign. My elder daughter Pisci is in this sign; she is loyal to her friends. She can definitely keep the secrets within herself and compartmentalize life. Tauri thought about her. He was very proud of her; she was very independent. Even though they barely talked, she had inherited a lot of good traits from him.

It was followed by the Aries season, with dates ranging between March 21 and April 20; an animal: ram with face and horns. It belongs to the fire sign group. Tauri can't relate to anyone with this sign. He called it a sign for the spring session.

After Aries was the Taurus season, with dates ranging between April 21 and May 20. Taurus symbolizes a bull with a face and horns. It belongs to the earth sign group. It's my sign. Tauri knew three Tauruses who worked in leadership positions at his nonprofit organization.

Now it got into the Gemini season. It's in early summer, with dates ranging between May 21 and June 21. Gemini is a twin person as a companion. It's part of the air sign group, which Libi's sign is in. He knew the name from one of the databases someone named.

It was followed by the Cancer season in summertime, with dates ranging between June 22 and July 22. Cancer is a crab that uses one arm to grab the material and another arm to reach the spiritual world. It belongs to the water sign group. It's the moon sign for Libi, which relates to emotion and feelings. Tauri can see his story with Libi in the tarot reading for Cancer.

In the deep summer, it gets into Leo's season, with dates ranging between July 23 and August 22. Leo is a lion who has an amazing attraction to people, with spirit emboldened. This sign belongs to the fire sign group with initiative and passion. Tauri suspected his moon sign related to Leo. He asked his dad about his birth information; his dad couldn't recall his birth time at the age of eighty-nine.

When it gets into early fall, it's Virgo season, with dates ranging between August 23 and September 22. Virgo belongs to the earth sign group. Tauri thought about the perfect marriage season in the fall.

In the deep autumn, it comes into Libra season, with dates ranging between September 23 and October 22. Libra is a symbol of a scale. It belongs to the air sign group. This sign is ruled by Venus, the goddess of love. Taurus and Libra are on opposite sides of the equation. Tauri thought about this. He was aware that Libra people had enormous impacts on his life. He went to Beijing to visit his cousin, a Libra, to understand Libras. His daughter Lara, another Libra, was his joy and stress; Libi, a Libra, was his love with a "love and hate" relationship.

If I don't taste bitterness, how do I know the sweetness? He smiled to himself.

Then, in deep autumn, it comes into Scorpio season, with dates ranging between October 23 and November 22. A scorpion is ready to use its stinger to do some work. It belongs to a water sign—good at sex! Tauri laughed it out when he thought about this.

In winter, it gets into Sagittarius season, with dates ranging between November 23 and December 21. Sagittarius is an archer who is ready to shoot the arrow into spiritual realms. It belongs to the fire sign group. In ancient times, Sagittarius was a powerful fighter to be admired. He nodded to himself.

Libra is a nonanimal sign. Its scales can be used to balance and maintain life. Libra people must be good at the profession of a judge, or something like that. Tauri finally pulled his thoughts back to Libra again.

Would it be great to tell a parent when it's the right time to get pregnant if they want to choose the profession for their kids? Tauri got excited for this idea.

In addition to this, the parents can find out if they are compatible with their kids.

"OMG, would those ideas be the gifts referred to by Ms. San's reading?" Tauri exclaimed.

He felt very happy. Even though he hadn't reached the destination yet, he had already fulfilled what he came for.

There couldn't be any better gift than this. He smiled to himself. Tauri was so touched. He felt the romance and joyful happiness right in the air for him to grab.

Life is beautiful! He smiled and smiled, like a silly boy.

CHAPTER 32

A Retreat to Acadia

TAURI HAD A road trip alone to Newport, Rhode Island. He realized that the "gift" the tarot reader had referred to came from his meditation, his own ideas.

Yeah! Though the ideas came out during the trip, the tarot reader described it via a card reading in the virtual realm. Would there be a visible universe actually happening? He thought about it.

After he came back home, he immediately checked her playlist for their retreat plan.

1. "Don't Guess"
2. "Floating to North"
3. "Remember the Songs Since the Last Decade"
4. "Pray for You"
5. "Slave"
6. "Double Happiness囍 (Chinese Wedding)"
7. "Everyone Will Travel the Same Direction"
8. "Trip Song"
9. "The Midway"
10. "With You All the Way"

Tauri scanned through tarot reading videos. He found a lot of messages reflecting his situation and things that were about to happen on the ground. Tauri read through the titles to get a sense of it.

⊷▅▆◉ ◉▆▅⊶

The tarot channel "Secret Shaman Oracles" published a video on August 8, 2020, titled "Taurus: Persevere for Positive Change & Big Dreams—There's a Sexual Union of True Bliss."

The tarot channel "Empress of Love Tarot" published a video on August 6, 2020, titled "Taurus Manifestations Coming to Fruition. Just Hold On!"

The tarot channel "Ganesha Tarot, Dr. Soni" published a video on August 8, 2020, titled "Taurus: Entry of Your Soul Mate—August 2020 Monthly Tarot Reading."

The tarot channel "Tarot Victoria" published a video on August 7, 2020, titled "Libra Weekly August 8–15: The One You Love."

Oh! Every sign is pointing to our reunion at this retreat! Libi agreed via her playlist. OMG, she even wants to have her girl first night with me in Chinese wedding style!

Tauri felt happy. Libi didn't update her playlist to opt out from this trip. In fact, she asked him to wait at home. He wrote her a message and texted her directly.

Sweetheart, I am humbled and honored to be your first man to make you a true woman. Tauri talked in his heart.

Bae, I'm also a new boy; I did my homework to learn how to make a girl's first night a joyful memory.

Bae, I don't want you to miss your work. It is going to be around eight hours' drive. We can take it off around 10:00 p.m. from my place on Tuesday evening and take a two-hour nap between 3:00 a.m. and 5:00 a.m. at the "Rest Area" along the highway. We should be able to get there around 9:00 a.m. You can still join your morning meeting on time. Either way, if you don't want to change the plan, I will wait for you at my place until 11:00 a.m. on Wednesday morning.

His heart filled with a warm feeling he had missed for such a long time.

⊷▭◉ ◉▭⊶

Tauri heard a knock on the door. A young lady with a vast pink reflection in sunglasses stood in front of his door. It was Libi. Tauri didn't show any emotion, as if he greeted a stranger.

"Come in, please." Tauri took over her suitcase. He felt he had just spoken to her yesterday.

Tauri hugged Libi gently, just like they did three years ago, once she stepped inside and made sure the door was closed.

Libi looked around this small living room in this alien environment. She felt so familiar with his text messages and photos: a small lover set sofa, an empty space displaying the heart-shaped candles, the coffee machine showing the divine number, the vase with roses.

"Wash your hands?" He led her to the kitchen and flipped on the faucet to adjust the water temperature at the sink. He knew this was a most critical step followed by everyone to fend the virus away recommended by the government.

Tauri held her hands and spread the antibacterial foam over and started to rub. Libi withdrew a little bit and gave up to let him hold.

"One Mississippi, two Mississippi, three Mississippi, four Mississippi…"

Tauri smiled as he counted the time for twenty Mississippis. Their fingers twisted against each other.

He finally held her hands. He thought about so many ways to initialize physical contact with her and didn't expect it to be this easy.

It just happened and took place naturally. A thought flashed in his mind.

"How are you? Libi." Tauri twinkled his eye as he used the paper towel to dry her hands. She smiled and smiled and stuttered without a single word. The reunion was not like what they thought of crying and laughing. It looked like two long-lost friends getting together again.

"Why don't you refresh yourself so we can head out?" he asked. "Would you like to drink anything? You would choose the soda." He turned on the phone with a speaker to play the song "Sexier Than You, Wilder Than You." They stared at each other with a smile. They didn't need to say anything; everything was already echoed in their mind.

"Well, since you are here, I don't have to deliver to your place again. Here is the German chocolate I brought for you. I still kept it in my refrigerator. Let's open it to see why it's special." Tauri brought up the topic of the last breakup.

"Tauri…" Libi still wasn't used to saying his name. "I…" She opened her mouth but stopped.

"S-h-u-u-u…" He placed one finger on his mouth. "There is a long drive ahead of us. Let's pack up and head out. We have ten hours in the car to talk." Tauri loaded Libi's stuff in his Mercedes.

"Ooh, let me get your safety belt on." Tauri opened the side door and seated her in the front passenger side; he remembered a unique name for that seat, called "navigator" or "shotgun."

"You don't need to navigate or use the shotgun to protect me. You just need to be relaxed." He tweaked his eyes a few times.

He leaned forward gently to give her a cheek kiss as he checked her safety belt.

"So glad you made it." Tauri smiled with a shivering voice.

He got into the driver's seat, adjusted the mirror and seat, started the engine, and set up the GPS location.

"Are you ready?" Tauri asked. He noticed that Libi's legroom was not enough for her. He grabbed her head cushion and used the left hand to reach her seat-adjusting panel to move the seat backward. Suddenly, he lost his balance and collapsed over her body. They both laughed out at each other when he regained his balance. Though they'd just met twenty minutes ago, Tauri and Libi seemed to never have been separated in the last three years.

Tauri started to drive along I-95 northbound. He had a chance to glance at her face under the bright sunlight. She still had a swan-egg-shaped face, with big eyes behind her sunglasses. Her eyebrows seemed to be carefully highlighted as an attractive natural shape like a willow leaf; her skin looked tender, reddish coming out from her brownish pale skin. Libi noticed his gaze; she turned her head away to stare out her side window.

A silence seeped in. They could only hear the hoarse sound from the tires grinding on the road. Neither of them tried to break the air. There're so many questions and puzzles they wanted to straighten out. After a few minutes, he found Libi had fallen asleep. Tauri drove at a steady speed to let her feel comfortable.

"After one mile, keep left." The GPS navigation voice took over the empty space in the car. At the two-hour mark, he pulled the car into a rest area to have his bio break.

"Are you OK?" Tauri asked.

"I was so tired. I barely slept last night." She replied without opening her eyes.

Tauri continued to drive steadily to let her sleep. They finally arrived in the small town of Bar Harbor, Maine, in the late evening after nine hours' drive.

"You can have the bed next to the window. I'm going to take the bed inside." He rolled his back and jumped on the bed. He bumped it up and down.

"Freedom!" he yelled. "Vacation!" He held both hands up.

"Taurus, you'd be a beginner at the love." The tarot reader's voice echoed in his dream.

→➡◎ ◎⬅←

"When do you want to go to sleep?" Tauri asked Libi.

"You can go to bed first," Libi replied and didn't raise her head as she pulled her computer out to check her email.

"Come on. It is early morning now. You'd never get everything done," Tauri proposed. Libi thought a moment and nodded. He turned off the lamps except for the night light at the door entry.

"Go to another bed, please." Libi smiled at him as he tried to squeeze into her bed.

"I just want to come over to have a night talk, like in the dorm." Tauri squeezed his eyebrows and rolled his eyeballs. Libi blew a kiss to him and pointed him to another bed.

"OK, you've a lot of questions. I'll give you an answer if it's only related to myself." She started to set the rules of engagement.

"Same to me." Tauri felt safe talking in the dark.

"You can ask the first question." Libi broke the silence.

"Sure, let me see what I want to know most." Tauri thought for a moment. "Are you the owner of the playlist? Yes or no with a straight answer." This was the most important question he wanted to get confirmation with her directly.

"Yes, I am. Those playlists connected us together, which I told you via the song 'Living in Your Ear.' Now we're at the same hotel room. Do you still have this question?" She felt offended.

"Fair enough. Was Monicana's photo with a white-and-dark-blue patterned skirt on the online dating site yours?" Tauri felt the necessity to clarify this. Libi told him that she didn't wear skirts at their last dinner. Tauri was convinced that the girl definitely looked like her and got hurt, which led him to make his effort to rescue her when he saw a scar on her shoulder. Libi did give him a hint in a song called "Body Shape."

"Yes, that's mine. The scars on my shoulder were caused by a car accident." She stopped. Tauri sensed that she didn't want to talk about the dating-for-cash scheme. She acknowledged the dating site in a song called "Talent Company"; she then described the danger in the song "Chasing by Hungary Wolves."

"Is your bra size a cup C?" Tauri felt it safe to ask a flirting question.

"This's not fair. You asked two questions already." Libi avoided this question by attacking back.

"It's my turn." Libi took it over.

"Are you broke?" Libi didn't really know his financial situation after his divorce. She knew he lost his big house and moved into a small rental apartment.

"Hmm. I have a few rental properties, some stocks, and some cash in the bank. I am definitely able to cover a moderate wedding expense without going shirtless," he joked. Though he had to fulfill his financial obligations, he was confident of taking care of himself.

"Great! What do you do if you don't have a girlfriend with you?" Tauri heard the muffled sound coming under the blanket. She must be hiding her face under the cover. She wanted to reconfirm the question in the song "Take Care of Yourself" and proposed her idea in the song "Movement under Comforter."

"Do you mean masturbating?" Tauri didn't directly answer the question.

"What about you?" He pushed the ball to her. He sent a text message to ask her to do it remotely with him. She responded with a song "Nothing Ever Happened."

Tauri felt they were starting to be honest with each other.

"Aspirin, come over," Libi said. Aspirin was the nickname she gave to him recently. She leaned forward to give him a lip kiss.

Tauri's body was frozen. He wanted to kiss back with passion, but he couldn't make a move.

Oh my gosh! What just happened? Tauri's mind went into a whirlwind. He finally felt nothing about all the misunderstandings, mistreatments, the sense of abandonment. His eyes were wet, like the feeling of kid misunderstood by their parents. He made peace with her for all the mind games she did via the playlist to train him, trick him.

Thank Libi! The last three years of no contact made me stronger in the spiritual sense, Tauri told himself silently.

How I wish that she could reach peace with herself. She went through all her heartbreak, family feud, her disappointment in the age gap with me. This caused uncertainty in her future. Tauri kept this thought in his mind before he fell into sleep on this peaceful night.

⊷⊫◯◉⊨⊷

When Tauri woke up the following morning, he opened the curtain from their room; the morning sunlight flew in. A deep blue sea was displayed as a picture on their wide window.

"Good morning, sleepyhead! Good morning, sunshine!" he uttered. Tauri had a chance to look at Libi, who was still asleep. She was in her nightgown with two white stripes on her naked shoulders; she looked really pretty.

"How was your sleep?" Tauri asked.

"I was half asleep and half-awake until early morning," she replied without opening an eye.

"Did I snore loud?" Tauri knew he'd snore when he was too tired.

"Yep, sort of. I don't get to be in the same room alone with another man." Libi grinned. She wanted to say that she was not a girl who easily stayed a night with another guy.

"Did we sleep together three years ago?" Tauri made a silly face.

"Nasty boy! We were at the same hotel room; we did not sleep together, OK?" Libi jumped up from the bed and came to tickle him. Tauri rolled to another side of the bed to avoid her. Their laugher filled the room.

Tauri and Libi settled their breakfast and sat in the car to begin the first day of vacation. They were in silence for a moment to understand what happened yesterday.

"Bae, what do you want to do next?" Tauri called her "bae," as he always did in his text message. She replied with a song called "Short Hair" to indicate that long-haired girl named "Bae." A Libra person would plan the event ahead of time carefully. As a Taurus, he could be very stubborn and improvise at the same time.

"Well, I came to this trip without any plan. Go with the flow. Shall we?" she replied. "We can do whatever you want to do." Libi looked at a map on her phone screen with a smile.

"I didn't spend time to figure out the route. How about we drive around at Acadia National Park first, and then we settle our plan?" Tauri suggested.

Tauri finally parked his car on the top of the mountains, on Cadillac Mountain. A grand 360-degree view over Bar Harbor showed up in front of them. He found a flat place to sit. Libi followed him to sit and lean on his shoulder.

"Bae, I got a fascinating idea." Tauri broke the silence.

"What? Bring it all out!" Libi grinned. She was still immersed with this magnificent view.

"How about we come back in the evening to make out under the stars?" Tauri whispered into her ear.

"Wild boy, is that the only thing you're thinking at any moment?" They laughed out loud. Tauri felt their flirtation heating up.

As he drove the car down the mountain, he saw a sign: "Sandy Beach, One Way Only" on a turn. He pulled his car on that road.

"Yeah! We are going to Sandy Beach," Tauri announced.

He and Libi walked separately to avoid the attention of the onlookers after they got out of the car.

⊶⋙◐ ◑⋘⊷

A beautiful crescent shape of the beach with a cliff on the back appeared in front of them as they walked down. The waves were pushing white water over the edge of the beach from the far blue sea, the white-yellowish, powdered sand in the center, black pebbles and rocks on each side of the crescent. This makes this sandy beach special.

"How about a spare foot walk?" Tauri smiled at her and turned his face toward the beach.

"No." She looked around and then looked at her white sneakers.

"Sunbathe? See, some girls are doing it," Tauri said. He knew Libi wouldn't want to do it.

"Do you want the red spots showing up on my face?" Libi asked back. She had posted a photo to show her sunburn face on a July Fourth week a few years ago.

"All right! Let walk to the rocky place to take a break." He tweaked as he saw a few couples kissing each other on the back of the cliff. "I knew you'd say 'Nasty Boy' again. I'm joking. Let's walk around." Tauri smiled.

Tauri led Libi toward the rocky side of the beach. He noticed Libi had trouble maintaining her balance while she walked on the rocks. He lent his hand to hold her; then, they naturally held each other's hands to slowly walk around. Tauri picked out one piece of stone and threw it over the water. The rock slid over the water and jumped a few spots.

"Hey, let's do the stone skipping! It's a sport," Tauri suggested.

"Like what you did? How did you do it?" She saw some kids playing.

"See, it looks easy. It's an art of throwing." He picked up a stone and threw it on the surface of the water again. It bounced three times and left three sets of the circles.

"That's easy. Let me try it!" Libi picked up a stone and threw it on the water. It went directly into the water without even sliding.

"What? Let me try it again!" Libi felt magic. She picked out another stone and used her force to throw it a little farther away. It dived into the water again.

"What's your secret? How did you do that?" Libi got curious now.

"See, I picked up a flat stone as round as possible, as thin as possible. This's the basis for a successful throw." Tauri handed one to her. She took it and threw it out. It dived into the water straight.

"Secondly, you need to stand near the water to have the right posture, like this," Tauri explained. He held her hand to match his arm; his body was on the back of hers. Their cheeks were next to each other.

"Let's lower the body. Turn ninety degrees to sway three times. One, two, three, throw," Tauri shouted out. The stone flew out and landed on the water surface to bounce over from landing spot into another dot and fall into the water.

"I did it, I did it." Libi's face turned red. He saw a fresh high school girl's pink face.

"Let me try it again." She got one bounce.

"Can we try it together?" Libi leaned back to him to practice a few times. As their bodies stuck to each other, Libi felt something stand up against her hip. She turned back and saw his malformed pants like a tent projected up. Her face turned from pink to red.

"Does a man also behave like that?" She whispered to him and had him on her back to hide from the rest of the people.

"Man does that for his girl," Tauri whispered back.

Libi slowly gained the skill after intense exercise. She got more than two bounces now.

"See, I can compete!" Libi exclaimed.

"Well, there're two kinds of competition. The stone skipping and the stone skimming." He raised his head.

"What we did was the stone skipping. The current world record was eighty-eight bounces. My best record was like ten bounces." Tauri smiled.

"The stone skimming measured the distance between the first skipping point to the last bounce point. The current record is 121.8 meters. You have to have at least two bounces to be qualified." Tauri talked continuously. Libi listened and listened. Suddenly, she realized this man she had been in her mind was just a playful boy, not a playboy. He's the boy she wanted to have a joyful life with.

"Honey, what else do you do to have fun that I don't know about?" Libi took another look at him.

"Like paddle boarding or kayaking?" Paddle boarding was something he always wanted to do with her. "Do you know how to swim?" Tauri looked at her. They looked at each other and felt they could have so many things to do together.

⊷═◉ ◉═⊶

"Bae, what's your plan? It looks like perfect weather in the afternoon: seventy degrees Fahrenheit and sunny. How about going hiking on the Beehive Trail?" Tauri asked after lunch. The Beehive Trail was the most challenging hike at Acadia National Park.

"Do you see if I can climb that mountain?" Libi uttered. She had read some posts he texted to her. Hiking Beehive Trail was like doing rock climbing.

"Sure, you can. I guess you can't if you don't try it." Tauri brought out the point that breaking their self-limitation prevented them from connecting with each other since the last breakup.

"What do you think of my shoes?" Libi asked as she started to pack. Tauri noticed her putting a white sneaker on.

"I'm sure it'd be OK; better than sandals. Are you OK if your shoes become gray ones after the hike?" Tauri reminded her.

"Can I stay in the car?" Libi murmured.

"For a shoe? Come on! Don't ever worry," Tauri assured her.

"My T-shirt? Too hot or too cold?" Libi raised her voice. Tauri moved away from his computer to look at her. She wore a brand name T-shirt popular in the city.

"Looks great walking on Fifth Avenue." He smiled. "You'd want outdoor sport attire for weather like windy, cold, hot, rain," Tauri suggested. "Can I lend mine to you?" Tauri handed over his blue T-shirt to her. Libi turned her back toward him to put on. When she turned around, Tauri's eyes brightened up. Her girl's mountains pulled her T-shirt up and exposed her flat belly.

Libi turned twice and stopped to be in front of him with her head high. She avoided her eye touching with his gazing look.

"You lo-o-o-ok really sexy!" Tauri lost his words.

"My hair?" Libi continued.

Tauri was able to look at her hair at close range now. She had long black hair trimmed neatly over the shoulder that reached her mid waist. He still had the silky-smooth feeling even though he'd stroked it three years ago.

"Would it be a good idea to tie it up?" Tauri took back his thoughts and focused on the practicality of these activities.

"A bunch or bun?" Libi showed him a few styles. Her eyes turned bright when she faced him.

"I love either of them. It'd be better if you put a hat on to prevent the dust or bug falling," he added. Libi put her white baseball hat on.

"How about this?" Libi posed as she did in the photo for the online dating site.

"I like it." Tauri reached out and flipped hat backward.

"The gusty wind would blow it away." Tauri softened his voice as he combed her hair. She leaned her head on his shoulder and enjoyed this quiet moment. Tauri kissed her cheek as she kept herself there and moved her face away after a while.

"Honey, be sure to put on the ultralight protectant cream to avoid sunburn on your pretty face." Tauri reached out his palm to touch Libi's face gently.

"I forgot to bring it myself. This is good, actually great." Libi reached out to give him a cheek kiss. Tauri enjoyed this kind of flirtation physically. He sensed their desires for each other were building up via more and more occasional touches.

After he parked his car at the service center, Tauri put on his hiking backpack and led the way toward the entry point of the trail.

"Are you ready?" Tauri smiled at her. Libi looked to top of the mountain and held her hat from dropping off.

"I'm not sure. I'm not good at hiking, especially rock climbing." Libi hesitated.

"Can you trust me? We're going to make it; you'll make it." Tauri talked as they looked at the road made of the different sizes of boulders. Tauri took a deep breath and stepped on the first stone. In his mind, he didn't even know if he could make it.

It took them twenty minutes to reach the bottom of the cliff.

"Let's take a break before the cliff climbing," Tauri suggested. He opened his backpack to look for the drinks.

"Soda or sparkling strawberry water?" Tauri gave her two options.

"Sparkling strawberry water." Libi took over a small can of water. Tauri looked at her. Their smiles met in the air. That smile came from her song "Sexier Than You, Wilder Than You." It described a scene of a pretty woman drinking soda and playing with a fifty-year-old man. Libi used this song to tell him it was Tauri whom she used the playlist to talk to.

"Let's roll," he announced as he tightly his strapped on his backpack and followed her.

There was a cliff slope ahead. They couldn't see the top of the mountain. The path led to the zigzag roads with a few turns visible to them. A group of teenage girls passed them and went to be in front of them.

"One step at a time." Tauri talked and kept an arm's distance to guard her. At this point, they had to use one hand to hold the safety iron bar on the edge of the rock to maintain their body balance. The group ascended slowly. After a few zigzag turns, they stopped in the middle of the cliff. The traffic slowed down to wait for the people in front to climb over the challenging part.

"Look, this view is so beautiful. The harbor is right under our feet," Libi yelled out. She leaned her body on the rock to rest herself. There was no safety rope to prevent anyone from falling out.

"Ye-e-e-e." Tauri looked back.

It was a picture-perfect view: the mountain stretched out toward the deep blue ocean; a few islands were dotted across the harbor.

The traffic moved again. Tauri and Libi followed the group to reach one stop. Then everyone had to use both hands to grab the safety iron bar to pull their body up. It was Libi's turn. She tried a few times and failed.

"Bae, do you want me to push you?" Tauri felt that she needed help.

"Sure." Libi looked back at him. Tauri fixed himself with one hand on the safety iron bar and another hand to push Libi's hip. She moved one leg up across the rock to land on the platform. After a few tries, she moved up.

"Do you want me to pull you up?" Libi asked.

"Hmm," Tauri replied. Libi held one of his hands to give him a boost. He leveled himself up finally. They both raised their hands for a high five.

"Lib, when we support each other, we can climb the mountains. We'd better do it together." Tauri smiled.

"E...m...m." Libi nodded.

They followed the group of girls to get into the last cliff. The climbers were in a complete stop in front of a pass carved out from the rock. The hiker had to lower the girl to crawl over it slowly. One of the girls in front of them was stuck in the middle of the pass and hesitant to move over.

"Don't look around." The team leader looked at the edge of the cliff and shouted. "Only focus on what is in front of you." She softened her voice. "You're going to be OK." She encouraged the girl, who finally walked over that narrow path.

"Bae, don't worry. Just do what they did. Focus on one step at a time; don't look around. You're going to have to take care of yourself." Tauri lowered his voice. "Do you want me to go first?" Tauri asked.

"Yes. Are you sure you can do it?" Libi asked in doubt.

"Do we have any choice?" Tauri looked back at the long line of people waiting.

Tauri took a deep breath. He held the rock edge on the left to keep his balance. He walked slowly as he lowered his body to avoid the rock over his head, to keep it steady.

"Look straight; don't look at the cliff side on the right," he uttered. "One step, two steps, three steps." He counted as if he walked in his crawl space basement at his apartment. He finally made it to the other side.

"Come on, honey! Lower your body and walk slow. You're going to be fine," Tauri shouted out to Libi. She tiptoed to inch forward and stopped in the starting point of that narrow path.

"You'll be fine. Just lower your body and keep moving. Look at me, look at what's in front of you; take it easy, easy, e-e-e-a-sy." Tauri slowed down his normal talk. He extended his hand to grab her when she finally reached the end of that path.

"Yeah, we made it." She hugged him at the edge of the cliff. Once they climbed a few more steps, they found themselves on the top of the summit. A wood plate was imprinted with "Beehive Summit. ELEV 520 FT 160 M."

"I made it; you made it. We made it," Tauri whispered to Libi as they sit next to the plate to take a selfie.

"How do you feel, hon?" Tauri handed over a soda to her.

"Wow, that's quite the experience. Sometimes we need to support each other; sometimes we need to walk on our own path." Libi bubbled out a few words as she drank up the whole bottle.

"Yeah, that'd be our life." Tauri looked at her as she rested her head on his shoulder.

They enjoyed this moment after a long, difficult individual journey.

"Can we go to Cadillac Mountain?" he proposed as they sat in the car after the hiking.

"In this pitch-black night?" she asked.

"Will you trust me? We're going to be fine," he assured her. "We're divinely protected. Right?" He smiled. Tauri had been staying alone since he moved into his rental apartment one and a half years ago. He had been writing, writing, writing, accompanied by her playlist and the tarot readings. When he played the tarot reading, he didn't feel alone at all. He had a team of tarot readers with him.

He drove the car to climb this zigzag road. Libi opened the side window. She reached her head outside to feel the evening wind.

"Look, there's a car coming toward us," Libi yelled out. Tauri immediately applied the brake to slow down while he was about to make a 180-degree turn onto a zigzag road. A car slid over the left edge of the vehicle. Tauri almost felt there to be a direct hit. When he finished his turn, he was happy to have a "navigator" on his side.

Libi actually held her breath to watch his drive. No matter how carefully he drove, he watched himself driving on the edge of the cliff.

"We made it again," Tauri exclaimed.

There were over ten cars already there. Some were RVs; some were cars, like his. All those cars had their headlights off. It was very quiet and dark with the faint parking lights on. Tauri turned off the engine and stepped out. The bright night sky showed up; the Milky Way galaxy shone across the dome and made the surroundings visible.

"Look, how beautiful the sky is!" Libi uttered.

Tauri held Libi's hand to walk her on the flat rock away from the parking lot. He unfolded the blanket and put it on the ground. They lay down to stare at the sky.

"Look, that's the Big Dipper." He pointed to the sky.

"What's the dipper?" Libi asked.

"A dipper is a spoon like big tool in the kitchen. It's made of two parts: a round part to hold soup and a long stem held by hand." He smiled. "Just kidding," he joked. "Look at the shape of the star system. That was the Big Dipper, 'Bei Dou Seven Stars' in Chinese astrology." He explained further.

"See, there are four stars in a square shape making up the base of the dipper, three more stars as a long stem. If you extend the long stem line farther, you can find a brighter one called the North Star." He saw Libi's eyes sparkling. "The North Star has been used for ancient sailors to navigate the open sea," Tauri added. "Do you know the bright star on the north side of the sky?" He turned his hand to point to that star.

"That bright star? What is the star called?" she asked.

"That's Venus, ruler of love; it's actually the ruler of zodiac sign Libra and Taurus, our planet," Tauri explained.

"Where is Libra? How does Libra look?" Libi was eager to know her star constellations.

"Look at the southern part of the sky." Tauri brought up a compass on his phone to fix the direction. "There's a quadrangle forming a scale. Look at the balance beam made up of Alpha and Beta Librae. They are the weighing pans made up of Gamma and Sigma Librae." Tauri checked the web to read it out.

"Do you know that Libra is a Latin word represented as the scales held by the Greek goddess of justice? Am I going to be treated fairly?" Tauri smiled at her.

"How?" Libi was puzzled.

"When you kiss the left cheek, you need also kiss the right cheek." Tauri gave a hint.

"Wild boy!" Libi leaned forward to bump his right cheek first and left cheek with a blipping sound. "Are you happy now? Anything else you can make up to do 'nage nage' with me?" Libi asked. She used a song called "Nage, Nage, Nage" to hint at intimacy.

"Don't be mad at me. Libra is the only zodiac constellation representing an object,

287

not an animal. In other words, there is no heart within Libra." Tauri expected a punch from her.

"Nonsense. Do I have no heart?" Libi questioned.

"Let me hear it to make sure it's coming from your heart." Tauri leaned his head onto her tilt and extended hand to cover another one.

"Go away!" Libi pushed Tauri away a little.

"Did I asked to be treated fairly? I also need to treat you in a balanced way." He talked in a smiling voice.

"Well, show me the Taurus constellation to see if there's a heart," Libi demanded. Tauri turned on his cell phone to search for the constellation Taurus.

"That's not fair. Don't you know your own constellation?" Libi demanded.

"I just studied Libra. I want to know you inside out." Tauri joked. Libi looked at him. She tightened her clothes to wrap them up, as if his eye could see through her body.

"OK, Taurus is one of the recognizable constellations in the sky. There's a V-shaped horn in a bull. When bulls get angry, they launch an attack like this." Tauri lowered his head and slid from her round base into the top of her half ball.

"Stop! Lover boy 88." Libi held Tauri's head and fixed it on the top of her front.

"Taurus is enchanted in love with Europa, a princess, the daughter of Agenor, the king of Phoenicia in Greek mythology. One day, the beautiful Europa saw a white bull grazing near her dad's herds. She was curious and climbed on to take a ride. The bull walked smoothly and carried her to a place called Crete. There, the bull was transformed into a human called Zeus. They fell in love with each other and got married to live a happily-ever-after life." Tauri read some articles from his phone.

"So, Zeus was disguised as a bull to get near beautiful Europa?" Libi reasoned.

"No, the white bull was disguised inside by Zeus. When he was eating grass around, the white bull is a living thing." Tauri highlighted "living thing."

"It's easy to find the Taurus constellation, even in an urban area. See, there are three bright stars: the Aldebaran, Elnath, and Alcyone. The Aldebaran is the thirteenth brightest star in the sky. It's just sixty-five light-years away." Tauri's eye brightened. "I came from there. I wish, some days, I could go there, my home." Tauri looked at the sky to imagine what it would look like to arrive at this orange gas star system, the nebular cloud photographed by the Hubble Space Telescope.

"Did you come from the Aldebaran, Elnath, or Alcyone system?" Libi further questioned his joke.

"Well, my system was destroyed by the Devil Goddess-Caprica Star system. My folks and bull guards were evacuated here." Tauri talked as if the story he told were real, not coming from *Star Wars*.

"We had been hiding our identity for generations to wait for the divine awakening. The awakened prince would lead us to go back to restore our kingdom," Tauri imagined.

"Who would be that person?" Libi asked.

"I don't know yet. But there had been folklore in the Taurus community. That's why I found you and fell in love with you. Maybe there's a bigger purpose for me, for us. We're in past-life love. Right?" Tauri asked her.

"Can I go with you for the journey?" she asked.

"You're definitely in the picture. You see similarities: Europa and Zeus in a bull, you and me with the huge age gap. You're destined to wake my power up." Tauri looked at the sky. He raised his arm as if he had a sword to point to the Caprica star system.

⊷═◉ ◉═⊷

"Are you OK?" Libi touched his forehead to check his temperature. He took off her hand and kissed it as if he were bowing to a princess to start a romantic dance.

"Where I can find it?" Libi demanded.

"We can't see it until the winter and the early spring in the northern hemisphere." Tauri felt disappointed.

"Tauri, did you fall in love with me at first sight?" Libi pulled Tauri back from the sky into the memory that happened four years ago.

"I felt fresh air coming in when I saw you. I felt different." Tauri recalled that energy.

"That's not true. Tell me," Libi demanded.

"Well, I felt an electric flow while we accidentally touched. You electrified me." Tauri tried to find the right words.

"You launched the electrified magnet attached to me. You fell into love with me first. Did you?" Libi smiled. Libi's eyes were sparkling; her voice was soft. The warm emotion flowed out from Tauri's mind.

"Li...bi, I want to tell you that I was and am in madly love with you." Tauri's voice was slow and steady. He felt that his throat was shivering and vibrating. His hands were shivering; his teeth chattered.

"Bae, I want to say. I-love-you. I-e-i-Loo-vee-y-o-o-o-u." He felt relief that he finally talked it out.

Libi got up and lowered her face to place her lips on him. Their lips glued together. Tauri felt warm and wet lips on top of his. He moved up and down and then left and right for gentle touch with her. A strong desire drove him to start to nibble her, seal off her mouth and make it like a vacuum space. As time went by, all his motion flow out to suck it tight until they both felt asphyxia.

Tauri felt unconscious, floating into the air. He pulled out before he passed out. He heard Libi collapse down to the blanket and breathe heavily.

"You're hurting me." Libi had never experienced this strong emotion. Her heart was beating wildly; her teeth were clattering.

"Are you cold?" Tauri could feel her shivering. He took off his blue jacket and covered it on her naked shoulders.

"E...m...m." Libi closed her eye.

Tauri was so excited that they had a passionate kiss, the ultimate kiss for this commitment, a kiss for a lifetime. He didn't know how to express his excitement for this love.

He stood up and shouted out aloud into the night sky.

"Libi, I love you." The high-pitched voice spread out far away. There was no echo since they were at the top of the mountain. "Libi, I love you! Libi, I love you! Libi, I love you!" Tauri shouted aloud three times. He had thought about how to announce his love for a long time; he finally did that. He felt a perfect moment for his confession. He stopped and tried to hear the echo coming back from the universe.

After a few moments of silence, the sounds echoed back from all directions.

"Karen, I love you!" A young man's voice came from their left side.

"John, I love you." A woman's voice came from their right side.

"Olivia, I love you." A girl's voice came from the cliffside.

"Isabella and Paul are in love." One guy changed the lyric.

"Charlotte and Zach loved each other for fifteen years." They seemed to be in love with public expression. Whenever someone shouted out, laughter also followed. The voices became a chorus that lasted from the moment and moments.

Tauri and Libi hugged tightly in silence to listen to this love symphony. They knew why those cars were parked there now.

Tauri tweaked to Libi.

"See how easy you could be to be the light for others. We're going to be a lighthouse for humanity."

"E...m...m." Libi still didn't answer directly.

"Bae, I want to make love with you here," he whispered in her ear.

"E...m...m." Libi was half asleep and half awake.

"E...m...m. E...m...m. E...m...m. No!" Libi raised her voice as she felt his hand move from her waist gradually toward her top. "Let's go home." Libi stood up.

He wondered if Libi wanted to go back to the hotel to sleep or make love with him. When he took another glance to the night sky before he got into his car, a shooting star went across the sky. He felt the magic brewing in the air.

CHAPTER 33

The Dreamy Land

TAURI AND LIBI left their minds in the magic moment in the night sky.

"Bae, can we drink a cup of wine to warm up?" Tauri felt like he might catch cold. "You said we'd get drunk one day. Is today the day?" Tauri looked at Libi like a high schooler getting permission from the grown-up.

"I got drunk with a sip of wine. How about we play a game? The loser drinks." She grinned.

"Play a game?" Tauri got excited.

"Play the hand guessing game: rock, scissors, paper, shoot." Libi figured she played with her friend often to determine who would wash dishes; she'd have the advantage over him.

"Let me refresh myself. Is it winning on the scissors cutting the paper, the paper wrapping the stone, the stone breaking the scissors?" Tauri had not played for many years. Libi nodded.

"Rock, scissors, paper, shoot! You have the stone," Tauri yelled out. He looked at his two fingers. He lost the first try. He filled the small tea cup with the red wine and drank up.

"OK, second round." Tauri could feel that Libi would change the hand with the paper.

"Rock, scissors, paper, shoot! Libi, you have the stone again." He put out two fingers; he lost again. He drank another cup of wine and scrutinized her winning smile to think about her next move.

"Rock, scissors, paper, shoot! Paper. You have stone. I have paper. I won." Tauri was proud to announce it. He knew that Libi was a stubborn person. She'd do the stone again.

"Hey, you're too slow. That's cheating," Libi protested.

"I got it right. I won, you lost," Tauri insisted. He felt he already lost two rounds. Libi had a reason to drink at least once.

"This is not a total loss. To be fair, it is only a half loss." Libi declared her victory. Her Libra scale was brought up.

"OK. I'll drink half; you do another half. This is called cross-cupped wine." Tauri teased her. In Chinese tradition, cross-cupped wine is the starting step for the newly wedded couple before they can get into first marriage night.

"Go away! Let's drink." Libi was angry with a smile. Her face turned pink.

After a few rounds, Tauri lost most of the games, even though he had high hopes of beating her. Libi was so smart in this game. I need to change the game to overtake her. Tauri came up with an idea.

"Libi, this game is boring. There are only nine possibilities. You're an expert on statistics. No fair." Tauri reminded himself he had the best chance to convince her by bringing up fairness. The Libra person operated at balance.

"What else do you want to play? Do you know Chenyun, the word game like the idiom relaying game?" Libi asked.

"No, I'm not good at that." Tauri refused. He still remembered his experience with the total loss with the "blue bus" girls.

"How about a finger guessing game—a drinking game at feasts in China?" Libi's bubbled out.

"Do you know the finger guessing game?" Tauri raised his eyebrow.

He analyzed the situation. She might have a fresh memory about this game. But it's played at the dinner table by guys. The girls are usually not good at it since they don't drink liquor. He hadn't played for years and had a better chance of losing.

Libi was really opening up and showed no distance at all. As a matter of fact, they both had the strong desire to expect something bold to happen.

"Libi, to be fair, when I lose, I drink wine, no problem. What about you?" Tauri asked. She hesitated. There were 720 combinations of one hand from her and another hand from him. She was not sure she could guess.

"I'm not good at drinking," Libi insisted. She crossed her arms to show her wall. The game was stopped. A moment of silence seeped in.

"How about I drink wine? But you have to do something." Tauri made a face.

"What's that?" She knew he could come up with some wimpy scheme.

"Let's play a 'taking off clothes' game," Tauri suggested.

"What? How?" Libi yelled out.

"We take one item off from the body if someone loses," Tauri explained.

"Besides this, when I lose, I'll drink a cup of wine." Tauri offered an additional incentive. Libi was shy as she expressed in the songs "Innocent Year," "Tree at Early Spring." Her face turned brown-red from the pink. She'd heard about this game before. She wouldn't play with anyone in a thousand years. But Tauri was her true love. She had daydreamed about making out with him.

"Sure. Let's turn down the lights," she demanded. "With one rule: you don't come over to touch me. OK?" Libi was afraid this game would get out of control.

"I assure you." Tauri would do anything to play with her.

"I want to exercise a few rounds," Libi exclaimed.

To play this game, each side presented a few fingers from one hand at the same time; the winner was called when the total number of the fingers matched with what the winner shouted out.

"Libi, we can use the following term with a single hand." Tauri proposed. "For zero finger, we can call it 'hand off.' For total count as one finger, we can call it 'unicorn.' Two, call it 'twin flames.' Three, call it 'three cups.' Four, call it 'four seasons.' Five, call it 'five hands.' Six, call it 'six lucky.' Seven, call it 'seven wonders.' Eight, call it 'eight horses.' Nine, call it 'nine cycles.' Ten, call it 'happy family.' OK? For example, if I present two fingers and call out 'Four seasons,' I'd expect you to show two fingers so I can win. Two plus two equals four." Tauri showed his fingers and took her hand to arrange two fingers out.

"There are three scenarios from your side. If you present two fingers and call 'Four seasons,' we both win, or no winner is called for this round." Tauri looked at her puzzled face. "If you present fingers other than two and call the number equal to the total count of both fingers, you'd win. See, you present five fingers and call, 'Seven wonders.' The result is two plus five equals to seven. You're the winner." He held her hand to play with her fingers.

"If the total of fingers added doesn't match with what we called out, no one wins. We continue to play until one of us wins." Tauri stopped and gave some time for her to digest those scenarios.

After a few rounds of the exercise, Libi was ready for the game.

"Let's begin. One, two, three. Four seasons." Tauri shouted out and presented three fingers with his right hand. He saw Libi's three fingers and heard her "Seven wonders."

"I won; I won. Four plus three equals seven," Libi shouted out.

"OMG!" Tauri drank one cup of wine.

"Are you sure we play the 'take clothes off' game?" Tauri looked at Libi to see if she was still on. She nodded with a smile. He knew he couldn't get away from it. He pulled his T-shirt up and took it off from his head.

"What do you think?" Tauri stared at her. Tauri was proud of his body, especially the upper side. He kept the routine to do full-body exercise every day. His muscles were built up on his chest and arms. His flat belly looked like a six-muscle-pack shape if he stood up with a straight pose but not as flat as a bodybuilder's. He felt good about himself.

Libi's face was pink. Tauri didn't know if she was shy or drunk with the wine. He evaluated the situation. There were three items on his body: a T-shirt, shorts, boxers.

One piece was gone; two articles left. He smiled to himself. He had to win in order to stay in the game. He scanned Libi. She seemed to have at least four pieces on: a T-shirt, a bra, jeans, panties.

"My gosh, look at what I got myself into," Tauri uttered.

"Let's play a second round." Libi showed her confidence to win this game.

"One, two, three." Libi called out, "Eight horses" with her five fingers; she expected him to have three fingers. Tauri called it "Five hands" with two fingers.

"No one won," Libi shouted out.

"Seven wonders." Libi shouted out with five fingers again. She guessed that Tauri would present two fingers again. What she heard was "Eight horses" with his three fingers.

"I won! I won! I won!" Tauri jumped out and raised both hands and danced around. Libi verified the result and kept it silent.

"I won, I won. It's your turn to take one article off," Tauri demanded. Libi thought a moment and turned her back to take off her T-shirt. She lowered her face to avoid his eye touch.

Tauri stared at her sitting at another end of the bed. She was with her blue jeans and a white lacy sports yoga bra with thin shoulder straps. He could see her tits half covered. Libi did tell him in a song, "So. Far. So. Good," for her body shape; she later confirmed in a song, "2.14: Double C" for her bra size. Tauri admired her perfect size with her artistic posture. He couldn't wait to win more rounds to see her bare chest he had dreamed to touch.

"Round three. Let's do it." Tauri pumped up. His face was red; his voice was hoarse.

"Happy family." Tauri shouted out with a full hand out. He heard her call, "Nine cycles" with her three fingers. After five seconds of hesitation, they realized there was no winner and continued to play.

"Seven wonders," Tauri shouted out with a full hand out again. He heard Libi call "Nine cycles" again with three fingers.

"Five hands." Tauri changed his strategy to present two fingers. He heard Libi call "Seven..." with five fingers. She barely caught the rhythm as she didn't even speak out a full term as "Seven wonders."

"I won." Libi jumped out. "I won! I won! I won!" She sang with the tune from the song "Wilder Than You, Sexier Than You."

"Here you go, sir. Drink the wine, please!" She sat on the bed with a dance move.

"And take your item off. Yeah! Yeah! It's your turn!" She drew a half circle in the air to pose a "please" gesture.

Tauri drank up the wine and took his shorts off and left his boxers on. He looked down and found his boxers like a malformed small tent. He felt embarrassed. She shifted her eyes away from his body.

I need another win to finish this game and be safe. She smiled to herself. Tauri evaluated the situation. He didn't really want to admit to being defeated in front of his lover.

An equal chance she'll lose her bra or I'd be defeated totally. I have no choice except winning, but my reward will be huge.

"Let's continue to play." He felt he had nothing to lose. He had one item left. If he lost the only remaining item, he could stay in the game by drinking the wine.

"One, two, three, eight horses." Tauri presented five fingers. Libi stretched out three fingers and called out, "Five hands."

"I won! Five plus three equals eight." Tauri felt lucky. "I won." Tauri laughed it out. "My lady, please take one thing off." Tauri made a gesture as if he tipped his gentleman's hat off and bowed to her. She took her jeans off before he raised his head from his bow.

Tauri looked at Libi again. She was in a white bra and pink panties. Her shoulder was naked with a white bra strap; her legs were long with silky skin. Her panties covered a small part of her hip. He felt his blood pouring up in his head.

"You, Libi, bae, you have a gorgeous body." Tauri lost his words. Libi stood up in front of him to show off her body shape and long legs. She jumped to show her deadly female attraction as her half ball was waving up and down.

"You, stay in your place, please." Libi sensed him wanting to lean forward. She continued to jump as if on a trampoline instead of showing her sexy body in front of her lover.

"Are we done, or do we stop right here?" Libi demanded.

"I'd want to take my chance." Tauri hesitated for a moment. He analyzed the stats. Libi presented three fingers at the first round, five fingers on the second round, three fingers on the third round, three fingers on the fourth round; he noticed that pattern. Libi would present three fingers at most times and then five fingers. He expected she would have better odds to show five fingers in the next round. He needed to avoid presenting either one finger or three fingers to avoid Libi's result guessing.

"Let's do it," Tauri demanded.

"One, two, three. All hands on deck." Tauri presented five fingers and called out a result of ten. Libi stretched out five fingers and called out, "Eight horse."

"I won!" Tauri shouted out after a five-second delay. "I won! My five plus your five equals ten," Tauri exclaimed.

"'All hands on deck' would be total of twenty." Libi shouted out to argue.

"We already agreed to have one hand to play before we started," Tauri insisted. "I won." Tauri felt on top of the world. "I won." Tauri grinned.

"Can I drink wine? I don't want to do what you wanted me to do?" Libi talked with a little voice.

"Is a rule a rule?" Tauri brought out his stubborn side.

Libi turned back and untied her bra. When she turned back to face him, he found her half balls covered by her hands. She looked down at the ground or looked into the air as if she didn't know where her eyes would rest.

"No fair. You use hands as an article," Tauri uttered with a smile. "Let's play the next round." Tauri had a strategy in his mind.

"One, two, three, five hands." Libi presented her five fingers. Her half ball bounced out like a rabbit. Two round tender mountains displayed in full.

"One, two, three…" Tauri stuttered as he stared at her bare chest. He forgot what he was supposed to do. He bit his lips to remind himself he was not in the museum. He saw her treasures he dreamed to touch. Libi noticed his eye invasion. She pulled back her hands to cover them up again.

"I don't want to play anymore. I want to go sleep now," Libi bubbled. She put back her bra and slid herself into the bedcover entirely. Tauri could only see her hair exposed outside.

"Good game! Good game!" He uttered and went to bed with his boxer tent on.

⊷▭◉ ◉▭⊷

Tauri and Libi got up the next morning as if nothing had happened last night. He continued to work on his book project; she caught up with her office tasks.

Tauri opened the curtains and found the blue sea turned into gray water. It was a drizzling day. He decided to have lunch at the park.

After he drove to pass through a densely foggy road, he stopped his car at a roadside spot to overlook the Atlantic Ocean.

Libi brought out the lobster roll they had ordered last night.

"It's delicious. Did you notice the real lobster meat? You can save the dirty steps to pull the shell from the steamed lobster." Tauri showed this to Libi.

"Why does a lobster turn red after it takes the warm bath? Because she is shy when she is naked," Libi teased with his old joke.

Tauri and Libi talked about random topics. Sometimes they didn't want to talk; the silence was a talk. Sometimes they talked a lot as if they never ran out of topics.

"Lib, do you want to walk to Jordan Pond?" Tauri still didn't get used to calling her what he did in his texts, like "bae," "my love," "honey."

From the park brochure, Tauri learned the trail at Jordan Pond was a rocky road circling the pond. The water was so pure that the naked eye could see through up to 150 feet deep in the lake. He decided to hike to Jordan Pond even though it was raining; he figured the rain would be over when they reached there.

"I'll skip. Do you mind?" Libi looked at the dark clouds and heavy rain.

"You stay in the car and wait for me back." Tauri nodded. "Can I have a hug?" Tauri smiled. He hugged her and gave her a cheek kiss. They had stayed together since this trip started. He got used to having her everywhere. Now he was about to walk alone again. He scanned the map and chose the largest route to explore.

It was raining and windy. No one else was on the road. Tauri stopped and took a picture at the entry of the pond. He stepped on a graveled stone paved road, which was wide enough to have a horse carriage pass through.

After a five-minute walk, he noticed a direction sign: "Jordan Pond House" pointed back. "Mountain Circle" pointed straight.

Why was there no sign for Jordan Pond Trail? Tauri puzzled. He decided to go straight along this road to find the entrance to the pond with a trail over three miles long. He'd spend two and half hours walking through his local state park. This's not a big deal for him since he walked four to five miles almost every Sunday.

The rain became a downpour; the wind blew momentarily. The fog took over the road. He barely saw ten feet away. All his thinking was to keep his cell phone and wallet dry. Though he placed all the items in a plastic bag to seal them off, he found water seeping through his small umbrella and dropping into his pants, backpack, sneakers. He felt no end in sight, one turn after another.

"How I wish that I had some things like tarot readings to guide me for this trip right now." He thought about a personal drone flying ahead of him to send back the real-time image to let him explore. He found a place to take a break.

One hour had passed. No sign to the Jordan Pond Trail.

He continued to walk, and finally he reached the direction signs.

"Directions to Gorge Lake, Mountain Circle, Bar Harbor. No sign to Jordan Pond?" Tauri read the signs. He convinced himself he had been on the road circling the lake since he could see the water.

I must turn back right now or get lost in this mountain. It will get dark in about two hours. Tauri alerted himself. He immediately made a U-turn to walk quickly to where he had come from. He felt lucky there was only one way to go back.

It's beautiful to see the forest, the fog, the drizzle, the sound of the stream. Tauri calmed his mind to enjoy the scenery as he walked at the fastest pace he could.

Tauri had time to think though his relationship with Libi. He was thrilled when he was with her at this "now" moment.

The key to having a successful relationship with her is love, only true, unconditional love. Their zodiac signs were ruled by Venus, the goddess of love, the planet of sexual pleasure, the ruler of the sign of Libra and Taurus, and the two opposites of Venus. They had totally different personalities and characteristics.

Well, Venus's sensual side was imprinted within Taurus, an earth sign in astrology; Libra, an air sign, embeds Venus's romance and harmony-loving side. Tauri thought about this.

Someone put a nickname as "peasant girl, the Taurus" versus "city girl, the Libra." He smiled at this analogy.

We can build a happy relationship only if we embrace what we don't want to deal with in our inner ego. It felt good. Focus on the tender love, he uttered.

If we can align with the "now" moment, we'll have a successful relationship. He recalled some of the advice he learned from the tarot readings.

At last, he arrived at the starting point of this walk. He looked around and found a small wood plate: "Jordan Pond This Way!"

"OMG, I missed the sign. It took me two hours to come back. What a detour! But that was a good detour, a divine detour!" he uttered.

"Northshore: 1.5 miles." Tauri read the direction. He walked a few minutes. He started to like it.

"Guidance! Guidance! It could save that detour. In my life journey, I'll avoid a similar situation if I follow the guidance from spirits and the divine." Tauri talked it out.

It was a trail built three feet away from the lake and constructed with two half-tree widths, which would only allow one person to pass. The wood path was lifted by a wooden foundation above the rest of the rock and dirt.

He enjoyed it. He even met with a few hikers there.

"You came back finally. I worried about you." Libi yelled it out when she saw him. She handed over a paper towel to dry his face.

"I made it to the Northshore side." Tauri skipped the detour story due to missing the sign.

"So glad that you're safe and back in one piece." Libi showed a worried face.

Someone did keep me in her heart. Tauri talked silently; his heart felt warm.

"I need a hot bath right now." He sneezed.

"Thank you, Acadia. A big life lesson just like the major arcana in the tarot world." He thought about this as he drove off the park with every inch of his body wet.

As long as I have Libi sitting right next to me, I am happy. Tauri smiled.

⤜⬤ ⬤⤛

Once they got into the hotel room, Tauri immediately went to the bathroom. He took off all his wet clothes from head to toe, filled the bathtub with hot water, and jumped in to lie down. He kept the hot water flowing in until his body gradually warmed up.

"Libi, can you help to hand over some dry clothes?" Tauri asked.

"Boxers, T-shirt, shorts, anything else?" Libi asked.

"That's good enough," Tauri replied. He dried and covered his body with a towel. Tauri saw Libi come in; his blood immediately boiled up. He pulled Libi in and gave her a lip kiss; he felt her respond back passionately and clued with her to get really emotional. He fumbled to unbutton her shirt and untied her bra.

"Hold on. Let me take a bath." Her face turned red as she burst out.

"Take a shower; call me in when you are ready," Tauri whispered.

"Hem ahh. Wait until I call you, OK?" Libi knew he wanted to take a bath together, which was good to let her relax. She walked into the bathtub with a bra and panties on. Her naked shoulder made him hard.

Tauri closed the bathroom door for her. He immediately worked on the surprise he had been preparing for this moment. He removed everything from his bed, opened a box with eighteen red glass candles painted by him with a permanent red marker, added two AAA batteries, and arranged those candle lights in a heart shape. He then pulled the petals off from the red rose bundle he had brought from home and spread them into a heart shape. As soon as the lights in the room were turned off, a red heart-shaped candlelight ring showed up.

Tauri was pleased with what he saw. He knew the smoke alert wouldn't be triggered.

"I am ready." Libi called him in. Her naked back faced him. "Can you help to clean my back?" Libi asked.

"I would love to," Tauri replied; he stepped into the bathtub.

"Can you hand over the body wash?" Libi's eyes were closed since she was washing her hair. Tauri found the body wash liquid, poured it into his palm, and put it over her neck and the rest of back to give her a body massage. He grabbed a handheld jet spray to clean her as she stood still to enjoy his work. Tauri dried her up carefully as if he were cleaning the *Venus de Milo* statue, the goddess of love from Aphrodite sculpture.

"Close your eyes. Let me show you something," he whispered to her and held her hand to walk out.

"One, two, three, ta-da." Tauri counted. A red heart shape shone in front of her with inner rose petals and outer glass lights.

"This's beautiful, amazing." Libi opened her mouth wide. "How did you do that?" Libi uttered as her eye sparkled in the faint light. "I love it. I love it. I love you." Libi gave Tauri a passionate lip kiss.

"Bae." His eyes were wet. He couldn't believe what he'd heard. "Do you really love me?" He whispered to her as he pinched his hand to feel him in this physical world.

"How can you say this? You have been with me for almost all my wonderful youth years." Libi yelled out. Tauri knew they had been in each other's lives since her early twenties. Now she's in her late twenties. "Every day, you're with me. I can't have a good smile without thinking about you," she murmured. "Even if I am with other boys, I can't grow my relations with them with you in my mind." She felt the burden release as she talked it out. "I fought for you with my mom; she refused to talk to me since then." She wept. "None of my friends understood me. You are only thing I have." Her voice trembled as she grabbed a tissue to clean her face. Tauri was shocked to see how deeply she was in love with him.

"See, you said that we don't do 'Sweet Grape, Red Eye.' Now you have a red eye," Tauri joked. He didn't know how to calm her down.

"Do you know how tough it is for me to pursue this love?" Libi held him tight and rested her head on his shoulder. "I can't talk to anyone about my love, my pain, my joy, my loneliness." She whispered in his ear with clacking her teeth. "We have a thirty-year age gap. What do I do when you're in your senior years?" Libi's emotion flew it out like the flood came out from the gate. "You are broke. I wanted to have our living place ready before I came forward to you." Libi continued to dry her tears. "You didn't date other girls, did you?" She looked at his eye straight. "I'm here with you; all you can't see now is yours," she uttered to him. She used the song to give him the green light to do what they had been planning to do. Tauri didn't know what to say. He just held her steadily.

Was it the time for me to take her as my girl, my lady; was it the right moment for me to combine the two into one, to make our love as a whole? Tauri's mind was booming on this idea.

Tauri swept the lights scattered in the corner of the room; he led Libi onto the bed and laid her down.

"Libi, honey, do you trust me to take the lead?" Tauri smiled. She nodded. They gazed with each other and felt the growing inner fire. They were about to begin the "Chinese Wedding," a ceremony to let him to "open the bud," her hymen.

The room was lit up with little red dotted candle lights scattered across the room.

"Dear, I am going to sing the song 'Kiss Everywhere,'" Tauri whispered in Libi's ear. She knew what he meant wasn't to sing a song, to make her fully ready for her first night. They kissed and kissed and felt time stop in another world.

"Hon, I'll sing a song, 'Cheeks,' now," Tauri whispered.

"E…m…m…" They both know Libi used this song to let Tauri know he can kiss her face. Tauri was pleasantly surprised that what he learned from her playlist fully applied now; he didn't need to talk. Everything was written in her playlist.

"The answer is within yourself!" Tarot readers always provided the best advice.

"Remember the scale! Keep balance, take care of both sides," Tauri told himself. He had prepared for this day and learned three techniques to kiss air, lips, and tongue from the online video.

"I will sing a song 'The Cake: Difficult Mountain,' OK?" Tauri mumbled.

"Eh!" She didn't open her eyes. Tauri was confused about what this song meant; he initially thought she meant her tits. After his research, he found out people use the jargon "Cake" to refer to girl's private hairy triangle. But the second part of the name, "Difficult Mountain," reconfirmed his guess. She hinted he can climb a difficult "mountain," the "hills," and the "slippery slope." The room was silent. Tauri could just hear their heavy breath. They genuinely felt each other in their mind, heart, and physical body.

"Can I sing a song, 'Come to Have Hot Pot Tonight'?" Tauri whispered.

"Emm!" Libi jiggled. She had a unique way to express the meaning of the song; she used the name as the expression sometimes. She added the lyrics as part of her expression in other times; she also used the singer's name as part of her expression. The song "Come to Have Hot Pot Tonight" was an invitation to have a hot pot dinner in a literary term, a self-cooking event served at a boiling pot at the top of a portable gas burner on the dinner table. People dipped the food to cook and eat. It was very popular in Asia, especially in China. Under the love affair situation, this song came with the meaning like "Come to eat me out!"

The time seemed frozen.

"Can I sing a song, 'Chinese Wedding,' 'Open the Door to the World'?" Tauri asked in a hoarse voice. "Bae, are you ready?" Tauri murmured.

"E...m...m," she whispered in a tiny voice too faint to be heard.

"Do you want to hold it to lead the way?" Tauri asked.

Libi giggled. She used a song "Canon in D Minor" to describe his manhood. She wanted to know if his size was as small as a D-cannon on the scale of A, B, C, D. He laughed at that moment.

"How do you boys hide it if it's always this large and this long?" She touched it and was curious about this. Tauri didn't have time to explain. "Can you put the raincoat on?" Libi reminded him. Tauri would rather enjoy the nature-blessed way from the dawn of humanity.

"Eh, I'll put a condom on; I chose the ultrathin lubricated brand. We're going feel the same," Tauri uttered.

"Want to help me out?" He smiled at her. She hesitated for a moment. She opened the wrapper and carefully placed it onto it; she then slowly rolled down to the end of his manhood.

"It's definitely not a D minor. Can I really take it in?" she uttered.

"Bae, whenever you want to stop, please yield it out or push your hand to stop me. OK?" Tauri whispered. She nodded.

They both breathed heavily.

Tauri seemed to run his three miles with Libi. He sensed he was about to fully erupt; he sped up as if they got into the final one hundred meters. He saw the finish line that he can be free and released. He seemed to have his chest touching the string of the "finish line ribbon." His thrust engine was fired off.

It came so quietly. His uncontrollable shivering pushed their souls out like a rocket launching to the sky.

They found themselves sitting on the floating Ariba, the seventh heaven. There seemed to be a place having an eternal peace. People were free to run, laugh, kiss, hug, free from the worry of race, gender, age difference.

They looked down to see everything unfolding on the earthly ground like a stage show.

"Look, there's a ritual performing. A cord was cut in half and imprinted into two different beings, a boy and girl. The master spread holy water to send them off for a divine mission." Tauri and Libi both yelled it out. They looked each other and smiled with a knowing.

"Watch this! The grown-up man and woman in the marriage ceremony at ancient time. They exchanged wedding vows and kissed for a happy forever life. Are they Adam and Eve to play as a bridge between humanity and divine world?" Tauri pointed to another episode unfolding. They felt something related to them.

"My gosh! The war, the suffering, the separation? That couple were searching for each other. Was that time in 1874?" Libi uttered. They stared to each other to recall the past life in the generations. "See, that man is thirty years older than the girl. How would they match in this life?" Libi uttered.

"Oh! That's the electric magnet attraction when the man touched that girl. Then they slept in a peaceful night like a baby." Tauri whispered to Libi. He noticed the gray hair in that man's beard.

"Huh? That girl moved into the boy's ear to stay? Look! The love seeds are planting in each other's hearts as the music flows." Tauri yelled to another show as Libi giggled.

"Uh? They were in isolation with the pain, suffering, heartbreak, and sorrow." Libi gasped to watch another episode.

"Yee! Look! The soothing energy from the tarot team flowing in to guide them into the right path." Tauri pointed to another one to show her.

"Wow! That's our family with a son, a daughter, a dream house," Libi exclaimed with joy.

"Look, that's our Chinese wedding. What? The cheering, crying with tears, and blessing from a team of tarot readers, angels, spirits!" They watched and realized that's their story.

"This journey ended with a baby, our book. That's our cocreation with divine."

Tauri and Libi hugged tightly together. They looked at each other and realized they were actually one entity.

One of Tauri's favorite tarot channels, "Dane Hart Tarot," picked up their energy and blessings. A video was released on August 11, 2020, to offer advice. It was titled "Taurus, Be Ready! This Is Deep."

⊹⊱∘═◉═∘⊰⊹

The next morning, they found themselves waking up in each other's arms.

As he opened the window, the sunlight immediately filled the room. The air was crispy; the sky was water-washed sky blue. The sea was deep blue.

Tauri stopped his car along a small trail on the cliff, a few steps away from the Atlantic Ocean. A bell was ringing from the sea. This made them feel like walking toward a temple.

"Dong, dong, dong." They stopped and listened to the sounds silently. A feeling of purity was in the air. After last night, they were finally in a sacred union. It was a dream come true for both of them.

"Bae, are you regretting falling in love with me?" Tauri looked at Libi with deep love in his eyes.

"Yes, oh, no, not a moment. Are you?" Libi stared back and leaned her head on his shoulder. They both looked at the place where the sound of a bell was coming from. There, there was an open, deep blue sea waiting for them to explore without limitation...

Acknowledgments

First of all, thank you, dear reader, for reading my writing. I'm honored and humbled to have your eyeballs and thoughts going along with this book.

I always felt an invisible hand that nudged me to go through the start to the finish line. I'm so thankful for the inspiration from YouTube tarot reading channels referred to in the Tarot Reading References at the end of this book.

Thanks for my family, my extended family, which inspired me in one way and another. Chelsea, Claire, you guys are the treasures in my life; my late mom, who taught me the resilience of life; my dad, who has the goal to live over one hundred years easily; my brothers and sister who helped me grow; my uncle and aunt-in-law, who offered the opportunity to change my life; my counselor at my high school, who taught me the discipline and persistence to achieve the goal; the colleagues at my first high school teaching jobs who spent countless nights together to read the legendary author Jin Young's series "Hero Born," published by MacLehose Press; my mentors, who encourage me to pursue my professional goals.

Special thanks for my incredible editing team: Sarah, Jordan, Jenna, Lydia, Brandon, Heather. You guys are awesome, and you've all surprised me with how supportive you've been and how professional you are.

Thank you.

Tarot Reading References

This is a reference page for all tarot readings mentioned in this book. I recognize their creative work and ownership of this content. The videos of the Tarot readings are from www.youtube.com. The inspiration for playlists is from music.163.com.

About the Author

H. L. Howard is interested in a variety of subjects, including science, software engineering, tarot reading, and zodiac-based emotional intelligence. He has had a long career in business Analysis. His writing career fulfills his childhood dreams and remains a craft he feels is inspired by a higher power, which is also a big theme in his works.

Howard likes to cook at home and eat at fine restaurants. He also enjoys road trips to national parks and skiing with his daughter. He currently lives in Connecticut.

Learn more about Howard and his books at his website, www.themelvilleverse.com; YouTube, @melvilleverse; Twitter, @melvilleverse; and Instagram, @themelvilleverse.

www.ingramcontent.com/pod-product-compliance
Lightning Source LLC
Chambersburg PA
CBHW031335020726
47499CB00005B/1275

* 9 7 9 8 9 8 7 0 9 7 6 3 2 *